10837173

SPEEDSUIT POWERS

THE REVELATION

BOOK 3

Speedsuit Powers
The Revelation Book Three

This book is a work of fiction. Any references to historical events, real people, or real locales are used fictitiously. Other names, characters, places and incidents are the product of the author's imagination, and any resemblance to actual events or locales or persons, living or dead, is entirely coincidental.

The poem, "What About Your Dreams" was written by Allen Paul Weaver III and is from the book, Transition: Breaking Through the Barriers. It is also used in the previous Speedsuit Powers novels.

Conceptual designs for cover art and illustrations created by:
Allen Paul Weaver III / Radiant City Studios, LLC

Cover image designed by:
Shawn Alleyne, Allen Paul Weaver III

Cover Layout designed by:
Robert Giorgio, Jeff Tyler & Allen Paul Weaver III

Interior Design:
Allen Paul Weaver III

Illustrations drawn by:
Allen Paul Weaver III

Published by: Radiant City Studios, LLC
Books may be ordered by contacting:
Allen Paul Weaver III at: www.SpeedsuitPowers.com /
www.AllenPaulWeaver3.com

ISBN: 978-0-9961045-5-5 (pbk)
Printed in the United States of America

This book is dedicated to the memory of
Sheree Williams

July 15, 1975- July 21, 2015

You started this journey with me as one of the editors for Book 1. More than an excellent editor, you were my friend.Your sudden death shook me to my core. Honestly, when you died, I didn't want to write this story anymore. The pain was too great and your memory was too strong. But, after several weeks, I was reminded of how much you believed in this story and I knew the last thing you would want me to do is stop trying to impact others through my writing. So, eventually... I "picked my pen back up."

This book is written in honor of you.Thank you for your example of what it means to be a genuine, loving, humble, fun, laughing, impacting, thoughtful, creative, God-honoring human being. Let us see where this all will lead.This is not goodbye... Just see you later.

[]

And to our youth who are struggling to hold onto their dreams... Keep pressing forward! Your dream will not create itself. So, get to work and make this world better than when you found it. And always remember: the greatest bully you encounter in life is not the one outside, but your own negative self talk. Conquer that bully and nothing will be impossible for you.

CONTENTS

CHAPTER ONE

DON'T START NONE—WON'T BE NONE

TEN MINUTES AGO CURTIS WAS ALMOST two blocks from his home, talking to Kelly and Treyshawn on the phone. Then four men jumped out of a black sedan and abducted him. It's Monday, August 12, 2013. 7:10pm.

Darkness. No sense of time or space. Slowly, the void gives way to a back-and-forth swaying, as a low, vibrating sound steadily builds. Wafts of fumes register the smell of… gasoline. The surrounding textures feel… damp.

Curtis' eyelids flutter as he regains consciousness—the back of his head throbbing. Darkness surrounds him, but a quick movement of his arms reveals his wrists are strapped together by something—possibly duct tape. A shake of his legs reveals his ankles are not restrained.

Where am I? he thinks. *What happened?* Images of his abduction rise to the forefront of his mind. His heart beats forcefully in his chest as he kicks and screams.

"Somebody help me! Let me out of here! I don't like the dark!"

But the sounds of music and a car's engine drowns him out. Panic sets in as he gasps for air. He presses upward, presumably against a trunk door. But it doesn't budge. *I can't breathe!* Curtis shuts his eyes tightly and tries to regulate his breathing using the techniques Kevin and Kelvin had taught him. It's been a while since he's had an asthma attack, but without his inhaler, this is all he can do. Soon, a memory of one of his father's journal letters rises from his subconscious.

Curtis,

Light shines brightest in the dark. There will be moments in life when your surroundings will grow extremely dim. There will be times when you will encounter opposition because you want to do what's right. No matter what you do, no matter how hard you try to shine your light, there will be times when it seems like darkness just scoops you up against your will and carries you away to an unknown place. In these moments you will be most tempted to give up. But don't you do it.

Most of us fear the dark because we don't believe we possess enough light. We let bad situations and terrible people go unchecked because we are afraid their darkness will smother us. But again, light shines brightest in the dark. A single match set aflame can illuminate a room. And the brilliance from a lighthouse can pierce through the thickest fog. Both are enough for others to see their way out. Christ calls you light. So, don't let the darkness extinguish the light that you are. Keep doing good. Keep pressing forward. Keep reaching. Keep fighting for the life Christ died to give you.

Run, Son. Run your dreams! Light shines brightest in the darkness. But at some point, the light will break through the dark veil and burst forth like a thousand suns. I love you.

Your Father.
Malcolm Powers

As Curtis recalls his father's words, another memory surfaces in his mind.

[]

2002. Powers New Jersey residence.

An eight-year-old Curtis lies on the bathroom floor with the lights off—whispering. The door is locked. His mother stands on the other side, in the hallway, ironing clothes for the next day.

"Curtis! You've been in there a mighty long time! What are you doing?"

"I'm praying to God!"

"Praying to God? About what?"

"I want to run faster than everybody in the world. Like a superhero!"

"God's *not* going to do that," Miranda squawks back.

"Why not?" Curtis yells through the door.

"What you're asking is impossible. Now open this door right now!"

A moment later, the lock disengages as a sulking Curtis exits with his head down and his shoulders slouched. Miranda looks at her young son, kneels down and softly grasps his face in her hands.

"Curtis," she says while looking deeply into his eyes, "I don't want you to think God doesn't *do* the impossible. He does. But it's often not in the way we expect. He's given you a *beautiful* mind. And if you want to run in life—in whatever you decide to pursue—you will have to use it."

[]

The Present… 7:30pm.

Curtis' opening eyes are once again greeted by darkness. But his breathing is now calm.

"I was asking God to do something for me," he whispers. "Maybe God wants to do something *through* me. Maybe… he wants me to use my mind to figure this out."

[]

"What do you mean Curtis was taken?" Miranda yells into her phone as Kelly cries on the other end.

"Treyshawn and I were on the phone with him when some men drove up and took him!"

"Where was he?" Miranda asks.

"About a block from your house!" Treyshawn replies.

Miranda drops her phone and runs for the door.

"Ma!" Omar shouts. "What happened to Curtis?"

"He's been kidnapped! Call the police!" Miranda storms out the front door of her house, exits through the gate to her front yard and breaks into a full run.

"LORD, please don't let anything bad happen to my baby! Please! I can't take this!" She stops in front of some skid marks on the pavement. Looking around, she notices a phone sitting under a nearby car. As she picks it up, she screams at the top of her lungs. It belongs to Curtis.

[]

A black sedan speeds down the highway with Curtis locked in the trunk. He thinks about the memory and how he opened the bathroom door in the dark because he knew where the doorknob was.

"What do I know about my abduction?" He says to himself. "I got a glimpse of the car before I was knocked out. It seemed new." He sniffs and can still discern that 'new car smell' intermingling with the aroma of gasoline. He thinks to himself, *Most new cars have an emergency release lever inside the trunk so that no one gets locked in by accident.* Curtis' hands fumble around until they find what he believes to be the access lever.

"The car is still moving. I need to wait until it stops." Minutes pass like hours as the car continues its speedy trip. "We must be on a highway," Curtis surmises. "Who are these guys? Where are they taking me?"

Music fills the car's inside cabin as four men focus intently on the road.

"This job is gonna make us a lot of money!" one kidnapper shouts while the other three sit quietly.

"You *keep* saying that," another replies. "We know already. That's why we took this job."

"Sorry. I'm just excited."

"Well, shut up and focus," a third kidnapper interjects. "We don't get paid until the package gets delivered."

"This is as good as done," the first kidnapper retorts. "We got the kid and we're close to the spot!"

"Just keep your eyes peeled," the fourth kidnapper snaps as he taps his gun against the car door. "Ain't nothin' done until it's done." He turns towards the back seat, "This is why I don't like newbies. You don't know anything!"

"I knew enough to get this job!"

"We're just doing your old man a favor. Now, don't get cocky!"

The car decelerates as Curtis' body slides towards the rear of the trunk, just behind the back seats of the car.

"We're going downhill," he mumbles. "Maybe we're on an off ramp."

The car turns left.

"Gotta get ready."

A minute or two passes as the car slows to a halt. Curtis hesitates as the engine idles. He slowly counts to five and then pulls down on the release hatch, just as the car's engine revs and begins to pull away. The trunk pops open and Curtis jumps out, hitting his head on the hood! He grimaces at the stinging pain, glances down several streets, and runs off towards the setting sun.

"What the—!" The driver slams on the brakes as he notices the open trunk in the rearview mirror! The four men jump out the car, turning just in time to see Curtis banking down a side street a block and-a-half away.

"How'd he get out of the trunk?"

"And how is he moving so fast?"

The lead kidnapper examines the trunk's emergency release lever. "You had one job!" he yells in a deep Italian accent.

"I-I forgot!" the newbie stutters.

"I told you to disable the release a week ago!"

"Doesn't matter!" the second kidnapper yells. "We're all toast if that kid gets away!"

"He's cut," the lead kidnapper declares while looking at the trunk's latch. "Look for blood!"

Two kidnappers give chase as the other two jump back in the car. The engine roars and the tires squeal amidst clouds of smoke as the car speeds ahead and then spins around to aid in the pursuit.

Curtis' legs pound the pavement with every ounce of strength he can muster! He streaks past brownstone-after-brownstone as he looks for a safe place to hide. Good thing they didn't check my shoes, he thinks to himself while wiping blood and sweat from his face. Beneath the cuffs of his jeans is a pair of modified, high-top sneakers: each one outfitted with a kinetic leveraging system. These Kinetic Redistribution Sneakers have a smaller lever system than his boots. And instead of a spring-loaded structure, these sneakers work using specialized, industrial–strength rubber bands configured in a parallel formation. While the high-tops are not as powerful as the KRBs, they still give an increased spring-to-step ratio. They have a considerably leaner, more streamlined profile than the boots—making them easily concealable under almost any style of pants.

Curtis barrels around a blind corner and collides with a black man walking with several bags. They both tumble to the ground—hard.

"Are you crazy?" the man yells.

"I'm sorry!" Curtis replies.

As they both scramble to their feet, Curtis notices that the man is wearing a black and silver workout outfit and is in incredibly great shape. The man looks at him.

"Wait. Aren't you Curtis Powers?" He looks down at the duct tape around Curtis' wrists.

"Yes! Please help me!" Curtis exclaims. "Some guys tried to kidnap me! And they're right behind me!"

"Quick! Follow me!"

The man grabs Curtis and his bags. They run five houses down, spring up the stairs and quickly enter the home. The man slams the door shut and engages three different heavy-duty locks. He sits Curtis down on a couch in the living room and gets a hand towel and medical kit from the kitchen.

"You've got a gash on your head. Let me bandage it up. By the way, my name is Eric."

Curtis scans the room while Eric tends to his wound. Battle dress accouterments from different cultures adorn the walls, along with several educational degrees and certifications. Two photos of Eric with another man in a police uniform rest on the fireplace mantel. In one they look serious. In the other, they are laughing hysterically. Next to the picture frames are four competition trophies. On the coffee table in front of him, sits several sports magazines, some mail and a bible.

Eric finishes the bandages and pulls out a switchblade. Curtis throws his hands up while jumping back. But Eric smiles as he grabs Curtis' wrists and quickly slices through the duct tape.

"Sorry. Didn't mean to scare you."

"Yeah? Well you did."

"Seriously, I didn't mean to. But tell me… what happened?"

[]

The street lights begin to activate as two kidnappers huff and puff at a corner a half block away. Their car screeches to a halt beside them. "Anything?" the lead kidnapper yells.

"It's no use. We've got nothin'."

"You'll *be* nothin' if you don't find him!" the second kidnapper roars.

"It's getting dark and we've checked every driveway and backyard on this street," the third kidnapper yells. "He's not here!"

"Well, he didn't just disappear into thin air!" the lead kidnapper snaps.

The fourth kidnapper bends over to catch his breath and sees something, "There," he points.

The two men get out of the car and the four converge on a small trail of blood. They follow it for a few feet and come to a place where a number of drops of blood are pooled together.

"He stopped here."

They continue to follow the trail for half a block until it leads to the stoop in front of a cream colored house. The four men look at each other as their leader silently motions his directives. Two of them head to the back of the house as the first two cautiously ascend the steps to the front door.

DING DONG.

Curtis and Eric stare warily at the door. "Over here!" Eric grabs Curtis and pushes him into a closet on the other side of the room.

DING DONG. DING DONG.

"Don't move," Eric commands as he closes the closet door, grabs the bandages from his medical kit, wraps his forearm and heads for the front door. Curtis opens the closet door just enough to see the majority of the living room—including the front entrance.

DING DONG. DING DONG. DING DONG.

Eric takes a breath and quickly opens the door while talking… "Sorry I took so long! Was in the bathroom… wait, you're not the Chinese delivery guy."

The two kidnappers look at each other and then back at him. "Do we *look* Chinese to you?"

"No, of course not," Eric laughs—trying to hide his nervousness. "Can I help you with something?"

"Yeah. We're looking for a guy who may have stopped here. Black. Kinda tall. Wearing glasses."

"Black like me?" Eric chuckles. "You just described half the people in the neighborhood. Do you have any *other* specifics?"

The second kidnapper looks past Eric and motions for his partner's attention. "Can I be more specific? Sure. This kid was bleeding. Left a trail of blood from half a block away that leads right to your doorstep and to those bandages on your table."

"Oh, those are *my* bandages." Eric says in a huff. "Just as I was coming home about 15 minutes ago, some stupid kid came running around the corner and knocked me down. I cut my arm on the pavement," Eric moans as he rubs the bandages on his forearm. "Was going to come out and clean it once the Chinese food got here. You know, that kid *does* fit your description. He yelled 'sorry' to me as he ran up the block. Are you guys cops? What did he do?"

"Are you sure he ran up the block?"

"Pretty sure."

"Ok. Thanks for your time. If you see him again, call the local precinct." The two kidnappers turn to leave as Eric starts to close the door.

"Whew," Curtis exhales from the closet. "Glad that's over."

Just then, the lead kidnapper snaps around, grabs Eric's arm and rips off the bandages.

"Hey!" Eric shouts.

"Well what do ya know!" the second kidnapper chuckles as both look at Eric's forearm.

"You must heal *real* quick," the lead kidnapper observes. "Not a scratch on ya!"

Eric presses hard on the door as the men push their way in, causing Eric to stumble back while throwing up his hands in surrender. "I don't want any trouble!" Eric cowers as he steps back into the center of the living room.

"Tell us where the kid is and there won't be none."

The lead kidnapper reaches into his jacket for his gun. The second kidnapper scans the room and notices the cultural battle dress on the walls and the trophies—with the martial arts championship figurines on top. "Wait!" he yells… but it's too late.

Eric's fearful expression changes to a sly smile as he rushes both kidnappers. The first barely gets his gun out as Eric parries it away, locks the man's arm at the elbow and shoulder joints and spins a kick into the second man's abdomen, while flipping the first man over on his back— dislocating his arm.

"Arghhh!" the first kidnapper yells as he drops his gun and grabs his shoulder. Eric kicks the gun away as the second kidnapper rips his firearm from his hip holster and aims it at Eric's head. The man fires twice, but Eric dodges each round—based on his assessment of the man's stance and the positioning of his arm as he pulls the trigger. Eric snakes around the kidnapper's arm, breaks the man's wrist, and slams him to the floor. He grabs the gun, stands—and with a fluid motion of his hands releases the clip from the firearm and ejects the loaded round from the chamber.

"Curtis!" Eric yells. "Let's go!"

Curtis bursts from the closet, as both men squirm on the floor in pain, and follows Eric out the back door and down the stairs to a shed in the backyard. Eric disengages the lock on the shed, flings the door open and retrieves his motorcycle. "Get on!"

Curtis grabs the helmet and turns to mount the vehicle. "Look out!"

Eric instinctively turns with his helmet in hand and knocks the gun away from the third kidnapper—following the strike with a spinning back kick to the side of the man's jaw. The kidnapper crashes into the metal trashcans a few feet away, as the fourth kidnapper attacks with a flurry of punches. Eric dodges and blocks each blow and easily redirects the attacker's momentum—using it against him. The fourth kidnapper lands on top of the third as Eric jumps on his bike, fires up the engine, throws his helmet on and takes off with Curtis.

The motorcycle leaps from the narrow driveway to the street and takes off down the block. A moment later, the four kidnappers stumble from the house to their car and give chase.

"Who was that guy?

"He broke my wrist!"

"He's gonna be dead when I get my hands on him!"

"I'm gonna keep my distance!"

"Just shut up and drive!"

Eric and Curtis zoom through the streets. "Where are we going?"

"To the police station!" Eric slams on the brakes as they discover that the most direct route is blocked due to construction work. He spins the bike around and takes off down a side street. They blast past people, places and things—dodging as much as they can. The black sedan barrels through the same streets, closing in with every second, demolishing anything that gets in its path.

A mother with her baby enters the walkway, unaware of the oncoming vehicles. She screams and jumps back onto the curb and Eric swerves to miss her and the child. He loses control of the motorcycle and both he and Curtis are catapulted off of the vehicle as it slams into a parked car. They both land with a hard tumble, flip-flop numerous times and skid to an abrupt stop. The sedan screeches to a halt next to them as the four kidnappers jump out, restrain them and throw Curtis into the backseat and Eric into the trunk. Then, in a plume of smoke, while onlookers gape, the car roars off into the distance and hangs a hard-right down a side street.

[]

New York City. One World Trade Center. 9:00pm

The sun has dropped beyond the horizon as Chasm and Erica ascend in one of the tower's elevators. They rise above the 100th floor and can see most of the city.

"The view is spectacular," Erica whispers.

"That it is," Chasm replies. "All of the dazzling lights make things seem almost... magical."

"It's hard to believe we're going to have offices here."

"We need a New York presence. Sure, I could keep our NY offices in their current location on the Upper West Side. But the world needs to know that America doesn't back down to terroristic threats. Having businesses occupy the very place where such a tremendous tragedy happened helps to send that message. And my company needs to be a part of *that* movement."

RING. RING. RING. RING.

Erica looks at the caller ID on her digital tablet and turns to Chasm. "It's Miranda Powers."

He looks slightly surprised. "Transfer the call."

With the press of a button, Erica transfers the call to Chasm's phone. He presses the side of his custom-made earpiece and smiles widely. "Well hello, Miranda! To what do I owe the honor of your call?" His smile immediately vanishes as his tone turns serious. "What time did this happen?"

Erica looks concerned.

"You have my *every* resource at your disposal. Have you called the police? Good. Erica and I just happen to be here in New York for several meetings. I will clear my calendar and handle this immediately."

Erica begins clearing all scheduled meetings.

"You are very welcome. Remain calm. We will call you as soon as we have additional information." Chasm hangs up the call, "Curtis has been kidnapped."

"What?" she yells as he stops the elevator and presses the 'down' button.

"Call my head of security and then call the police. Someone has made a very *big* mistake."

[]

An undisclosed warehouse near the Brooklyn Navy Yard.

Two hooded men sit, strapped to their chairs in the middle of an open space. A spotlight shines on them, but the rest of the building is dark. The four kidnappers hunch over a desk in a corner—the lead abductor on his phone.

"Again, I'm sorry for the delay. Yes, Sir. We have 'em. Yes, there are two. The kid was with some guy who put up a real fight. Understood. Thank you, Sir." He hangs up the phone as his fellow cohorts look at him anxiously.

"What did he say?"

"Keep the kid. Kill the other guy and get rid of the car. Pickup is in one hour." He stands to his feet and turns towards the newbie. "You get to kill the other guy."

"B-But I've never killed... anyone before!" the newbie exclaims.

"First time for everything," the second kidnapper replies with a slight smile. "You can use my gun."

"D-Don't one of you guys want to do it?" the newbie counters.

"Any one of us can do this," the third kidnapper quips.

"But you were the one talkin' like a 'Big Man' earlier," the lead abductor adds, "so you get to do it... *Big Man*."

The second kidnapper takes out his gun, cocks it and hands it to the newbie. "Go ahead. We'll watch from here."

The newbie turns towards the center of the room. "W-Which one is the *other* guy?"

The three others groan. "Pull their hoods off so you'll know. And put your mask on first!"

The four of them put their ski-masks on as the newbie sluggishly walks over to the captives. He removes the hoods from Curtis and Eric, who squint as their eyes adjust to the bright light.

"Where are we?" Curtis asks.

"I-I'm sorry," the newbie mumbles as he shakily raises the gun in front of Eric.

"Whoa," Eric says calmly. "You don't have to do this."

"Y-Yes I do. I'm sorry."

"Don't be sorry," Eric desperately looks the newbie in his eyes, "be good. You *know* what's right."

"Yeah," Curtis agrees. "You know what is right."

"I-I thought this was just going to be a bag-and-drop… I didn't think—"

"Go ahead and do this already!" the lead kidnapper shouts from the darkness. The newbie flinches at the sound of the command.

"You *don't* have to do this," Curtis says firmly.

The newbie looks at both of them nervously. "They said I have to kill you. If I don't, they'll probably kill me!"

"Do it already!" the command comes again.

The newbie's finger tightens around the gun's trigger. "I-I'm so sorry!"

"FREEZE!!!"

Doors burst open as police swarm into the warehouse with their guns drawn.

"NYPD! NOBODY MOVE!!!" In seconds, officers adorned in tactical gear surround the kidnappers. "NYPD! DROP YOUR WEAPONS AND GET ON THE GROUND! DO IT NOW!!!"

Dogs from the K-9 unit bark wildly as a police helicopter hovers overhead with its spotlight shining through the windows. The abductors drop their weapons and fall to the ground as they are subdued and taken into custody. Four officers approach

Curtis and Eric and cut away their restraints. "All clear!" The officers yell to the leading commander.

"Alright. Let them in."

Miranda, Kelly, Treyshawn, Jim and Omar rush in and practically run Curtis over with hugs!

"Mom! Guys!" Curtis yells in jubilation.

"Curtis!" Miranda exclaims through her tears as she sees the bandages on his head. "Did they hurt you?"

Eric looks on with a smile.

"I'm fine, Mom! How did you find us?"

"That would be *my* doing," Chasm says as he, Erica and several federal agents approach the group.

"Mr. Montgomery!" Curtis breaks from the group and gives him a hearty hug. Chasm laughs as he warmly embraces his protégé. "How did you find me?"

"You have my business card somewhere on your person!"

"That's right!" Curtis shouts as he steps back, pulls out his wallet and retrieves the card. "So you can track the card, too?"

"That would prove apparent," Chasm states in a rhetorical tone. "I am glad we arrived here in time."

"Yeah! Another couple of seconds..." Curtis turns and runs over to Eric. "Everyone. This is Eric. If it wasn't for him, you might never have found me."

"Well Eric," Chasm says, "we are completely in your debt."

"And *I'm* in your debt, Sir. Another few seconds and I would have been dead!"

Miranda hugs Eric, "Thank you for helping to keep my son safe. One day soon, dinner's on me."

"And she can really cook!" Curtis adds. The group laughs as Miranda faces Chasm and gives him a long embrace.

"Mr. Montgomery," she says through her tears. "Thank you... you saved my son. And I will *always* be in your debt for that. We couldn't have gotten him back without you."

"I'm glad to be of service, Miranda. And please... call me Chasm."

[]

An Undisclosed Location. Several hours later.

A well dressed man sits comfortably in his plush leather chair— surrounded by shadows. The light from television and computer screens bathes him in an eerie glow. His elbows rest on the arms of his chair, as his fingertips are pressed together in front of his chin. The 11 o'clock news, on *several* channels, relay the unfolding events as reporters stand in front of the warehouse where Curtis Powers was held captive. Currently, the man's focus is on Caitlin Connors as she gives her report.

"As you can see, the warehouse behind me is swarming with police officers and federal agents as they attempt to ascertain the reason behind the abduction of Curtis Powers and another individual. Thankfully, with the help of billionaire, philanthropist Chasm Montgomery—who happened to be in our city for meetings, law enforcement officials arrived just in time to stop an apparent execution. I mention Mr.Montgomery— who left with Curtis and his family some time ago—because he is an alumnus of the same university that Curtis attends and has become one of Curtis' mentors. Let me say that I have had the opportunity to interview Curtis on several occasions, as well as research his life story. All I can say is that he is one of the nicest, most inspirational young men you will ever meet. Unfortunately, this incident illustrates that being famous also makes an individual a target for nefarious characters. Fortunately, the criminals were not able to carry out their intentions. Hopefully, law enforcement will be able to get to the bottom of this incident."

The phone on the man's desk begins to glow—as does the custom-made earpiece in his ear. He taps on the side of his ear and speaks.

"Yes. No. I am not surprised. We knew there was a high probability that things would turn out as they did. Young Mr.

Powers is *very* resourceful and that other man who tried to help him proved to be a thorn in our side. No. This is not a failure, but merely a learning experience. A plan is only as good as those who carry it out, and the four kidnappers were not as good as they purported to be.

"What's the latest update on the Powersuit? Good. I want to see the working prototype within the next two weeks. It will soon be time to initiate the next phase."

[]

Powers Residence. Tuesday, August 13, 2013. 3:00am.

Curtis sits on the couch, talking on his phone. "Thanks again for everything."

"No problem. Glad I could help," Eric replies. "When I woke up yesterday morning, I didn't think I'd be playing bodyguard for the famous Curtis Powers."

"Neither did I!" Curtis laughs. "I've never seen anyone move like you did—except for my friend Gavin. He knows Jiu Jitsu."

"So do I," Eric admits, "I've also studied Krav Maga and a few other martial arts styles."

"Wow!"

"But, it's cool your mentor was able to track you down. That business card must have some serious tech built into it."

"Yeah," Curtis replies, "it does."

"Well, Mr. Powers, if you ever need me. Just call."

"You got it. Thanks Eric! You know… I never did get your last name."

"Peterson. My name is Eric Peterson. Have a great night."

They both end the call as Curtis sits quietly on the couch. His phone buzzes with numerous texts from Gavin. He texts back—letting Gavin know he is fine and will talk later.

"I am so glad you are home," Miranda announces as she walks into the living room with a cup of milk and a plate of warm cookies."

"Mmmm. You make the *best* homemade cookies, Mom," Curtis smiles as he eagerly takes a few bites. "Especially at 3am."

"Omar rolls in from the kitchen. "We need to talk about security. Any idea why those men abducted you? Did they say anything?"

"No. But I could faintly hear them talking to someone on the phone. He said something about someone coming to pick me up."

"What do you think this person wants?" Miranda asks. "A ransom?"

"Don't think so," Omar muses. "We didn't get a call from them with any demands. They had Curtis long enough to do that if that's what they wanted. Maybe they wanted Curtis for the Powersuits."

"You mean like they wanted me to build something for them?"

"I know. Sounds crazy right. Like something right out of the movies."

"Who knows what they wanted," Miranda huffs. "Chasm said he'd work with the authorities to get to the bottom of everything. I'm just glad you're home. All of us are."

"And I'm glad to be home," Curtis agrees.

"But there is one more thing," Omar says as he holds up Chasm's business card. "Did you know Mr.Montgomery could track you with this?"

"...No," Curtis hesitates.

Omar looks intently at his brother and his mother, "I wonder what else he hasn't told us."

"Are you saying that he had something to do with my kidnapping?"

"I don't know what I'm saying. It's just odd, he didn't tell you or us about everything this card can do."

"He probably didn't tell me because it's proprietary technology that's not even on the market yet!" Curtis replies in a frustrated tone.

"That's a valid reason," Miranda interjects.

"Besides," Curtis continues, "Mr. Montgomery has gone out of his way to help us."

"I'm just making an observation," Omar counters.

"Well, let's not jump to any conclusions," Miranda asserts in a calming-but-stern voice. "Mr. Montgomery has been extremely helpful to us. And we will continue our relationship with him in goodwill until we are given a reason not to."

CHAPTER TWO

SAVING FACE

TUESDAY AUGUST 13, 2013. RIKERS ISLAND Prison. 2:27pm. Many of the prison's inmates are outside in the yard. Some are exercising; others are playing sports on the field. Still others just sit around and talk, some about their past regrets and future hopes; others about their heinous plans. Treyshawn Sr. exercises alone. His reputation among the inmates looms just as big as his hulking frame. He is *not* one to be messed with. In addition to his obvious size, he is also known to be a ruthless fighter.

The top part of his orange prison jumper hangs tied around his waist as he sweats profusely. He's just finished his third set of 100 pull-ups. As he wipes the sweat from his face, several other inmates approach.

"Hey T. Rock! Word is that yo' kid broke you."

"*Nobody* breaks me, Tyrone."

"Yeah, well, that's what I *heard*."

Treyshawn Sr. turns around and faces his five fellow inmates. "You can go back to whoever told you and let them know if they want to keep their tongue, they best shut up."

Tyrone and the other inmates look at each other warily. "Well… just don't let your boy disrupt our plans."

Treyshawn Sr. cracks a smile. "Ain't nobody disrupting our plans. We gonna get up outta here real soon."

[]

Sunday, August 18, 2013. Rikers Island Prison.

Treyshawn sits at the cold round table, wondering if his father will make an appearance. He looks around at the other prisoners meeting with their families and friends.

BUZZZZ.

The gate opens as two guards escort Treyshawn Sr. to the table. They remove his handcuffs as he sits down right in front of his son.

"Thanks for coming," Treyshawn utters while clearing his throat.

Silence.

"Why did you agree to see me if you're not going to talk to me?"

Treyshawn Sr. scans the room, counting all of his fellow inmates and taking notice of who is sitting closest to him.

"This was a mistake," he says abruptly while standing up.

"Dad. Wait!" Treyshawn stammers. "Don't leave yet. If you want to sit in silence… then that's fine with me."

Treyshawn Sr. looks down at his son's desperate expression and slowly sits back down. Moments of silence pass by as they stare at each other. Treyshawn smiles slightly at his father. His father glares back with a blank expression and then leans towards his son.

"I… read the journal you left me," Treyshawn Sr. half-whispers.

"Really? Did you like it?"

Treyshawn Sr. hesitates. "I want you to know what *kind* of man I am."

Treyshawn sits in silence, waiting for his father to continue.

"I've *killed* people: literally and figuratively. I've used people for my own benefit. I've manipulated and coerced situations to get what I've wanted. And anyone who got in my way; anyone who wouldn't back down—got eliminated." Treyshawn Sr. looks deeply into his son's eyes.

"I am not a good man, Trey. When you leave here today, don't *ever* look back. If you are trying to be a *good* man, then I am not the one to show you how. It seems like your friend who gave you the journal is better suited for the task."

"But you're *still* my father," Treyshawn replies softly.

Treyshawn Sr. motions to the guard, who walks over and hands him the journal. He slides the book across the table to his son.

"It's yours, Dad," Treyshawn smiles. "Keep it. I go back to college tomorrow. But I'll come back to visit you."

The two guards come back over. "Time's up."

Treyshawn Sr. leans across the table and smacks his son across the face—knocking him off the bench. "I don't care what you say!" he bellows through the entire visitors' center, while standing to his feet! "I still don't want to see you!" He holds out his hands as the guards handcuff him and pick up the journal.

Treyshawn rubs the side of his face as he scrambles to his feet.

"Fine!" he yells. "Be that way!"

Both father and son glare at each other as they retreat to their separate exits.

[]

The Bronx. Shakira's house.

The front door opens and slams shut as Treyshawn storms into the living room. Shakira turns abruptly from her television show to face him.

"Trey! Why you slamming my front door like that?"

"Cause my dad is crazy! That's why!"

Shakira gets up from the couch. "Baby, what happened?"

"I don't know, Ma!" Treyshawn answers while pacing the room. "It seemed like we were making progress! At first he didn't want to talk to me, but then he started sharing about what kind of man he is. We had a moment, Ma… a *real* moment. At least I thought we did! Then the guards came over to take him back to his cell and he smacked me across the face so hard I went flying off the bench!"

Shakira looks at her son in apparent shock, and then laughs.

"What's so funny, Ma?" Treyshawn yells. "That's not funny!"

Shakira raises her hands in a calming fashion as she reins in her laughter. "I'm sorry, Trey. I know this isn't funny."

"Then why you laughin'?" Treyshawn protests.

"He was saving face."

"What? What you mean?"

"Trey… *think* about it. How many people were in the room?"

"The place was packed!"

"So, there were a lot of other prisoners there?"

"Yeah! So?"

"Your daddy is known as the person you don't mess with. Hard. Cold. Calculating. And he's in a place where weakness is showing anything *other* than anger. I know your daddy. It takes a whole lot to get him to 'have a moment.' Just a few days ago, you forced him to confront himself. Then today, he opened up to you even more. So, your connection was real. But after you leave, he still has to stay in prison."

"So, he almost knocked my teeth outta my skull to make a point?"

"The next time you see him, you ask him."

CHAPTER THREE

MAKING PLANS

MONDAY AUGUST 19TH. THE MONTGOMERY GROUP headquarters is located just outside Atlanta, Georgia. Chasm sits in his private penthouse office on the 17th floor. For most of the morning, he's been in back-to-back meetings with potential partners. For the bulk of the afternoon, he's been stuck at his desk reviewing contracts and other immensely detailed documents. He stops for a moment to breathe and rub his eyes as his phone rings. He looks at the caller ID and smiles as he quickly picks the receiver up.

"Miranda, it is so good to hear your voice again," Chasm beams as he reclines in his office chair.

"Thank you, Chasm. You are always so cheerful," Miranda replies from her kitchen. "I wanted to again thank you for your help with Curtis."

"Miranda, you have thanked me enough. I'm glad to help."

"I know. I know. It's just that you single-handedly averted every mother's worst nightmare."

"Well, when you put it that way… You are most welcome. But that's not the *only* reason you called."

"No. It's not. I wanted to know if you would have an opportunity to check on Curtis once he's back on campus. He told me before he left that he was fine. But, after such a serious ordeal, I just want to be sure."

"When does he return?"

"This Friday."

"Good. His classes start next Monday, so I will make a point to talk with him on Sunday.

"Thank you."

"May I also make a request of you?"

"Sure thing."

"Since you are indebted to me," Chasm smiles, "I would like to invite you to come down for a tour of my facilities. Then you can also visit Curtis and see his workspace."

"That… sounds like a wonderful idea."

"Of course, I will take care of all the travel and hotel arrangements and associated costs."

"You are very kind Chasm, but I am capable—"

"I *know* you are capable, Miranda, but this is my invitation… so I will foot the bill."

"You are very kind. Very well then. I will send you some dates."

"And I will talk with Erica as soon as we end this phone call."

"Thanks again. I look forward to seeing you in a few weeks."

"As do I."

"You mean you look forward to seeing yourself too?" Miranda quips.

Chasm laughs heartily, "I have always enjoyed your quick wit and sense of humor. I look forward to seeing you in a few weeks. Enjoy the rest of your day."

Miranda laughs, "Enjoy your day, as well."

Chasm gets off the phone and calls Erica to his office. She takes her usual seat.

"Did she agree to the trip?" Erica inquires.

"She did. Start working on the details. I want to 'wow' her from the time she arrives in Atlanta until the time she arrives back in New York.

"Spare no expense," Erica mimics in her best 'Chasm' voice."

Chasm smiles at her. "You almost have it down. Still needs some work. On another note: with everything going on, I want you to step up your efforts. We need to *own* Curtis."

[]

Wednesday, August 21, 2013. The Powers' Residence. Bronx, New York.

Curtis, Omar, Miranda and Jim sit and listen as Roger "Chase" Maxwell, from the X-Games Athletic Creation Group in Denver Colorado, prepares to deliver his presentation. His assistant has finished setting up all of the equipment. Before them sits a table, with a computer laptop and 40-inch flatscreen display screen. On the left side of the table stands a 7 foot tall pull-up banner which reads: 'Welcome to the Compressor-X Games!' On the right of the table stands a large display board with full-color illustrations to explain the concept.

"Thank you for coming to visit, Mr. Maxwell," Miranda smiles.

"Please, everybody calls me 'Chase.' And thank you for agreeing to meet with me to hear my proposal. When I saw the video footage of your Windsuit demonstration, I knew instantly that your idea could be the next great X-game!"

"We researched your company," Omar admits.

"Great. So, you know my company's mission is to demonstrate what is possible when the limits of human strength, creativity and innovation are pushed. I desire to show people that anything is possible. If you can think it, you can do it. And your story—as Team Speedsuit Powers— surely demonstrates this reality."

"OK," Miranda says. "Let's see what you have."

Chase smiles broadly as he crouches slightly and raises his hands up in anticipation. He inhales deeply… and like a tennis ball being hit by a racket, he begins.

"Imagine a stadium full of people watching two teams battle for points while wearing suits that give them localized control over the wind! To be able to use a compressed air system to block and redirect thrown objects is completely unique! What you're about to see is an upscale version of your demonstration, with the added players and point structure. The objective of round 1 is to gain points by reaching various checkpoints, as they make it to the goal at the end of the course for the big score. The objective of round 2 is the gain points by knocking out your opponents. In many respects, the Compressor-X Games is like playing Dodge Ball on wind-infused steroids!"

Roger presses 'play' on the computer and the animated video begins. High-impact-bass-infused music blares as an aerial view of a stadium with a rectangle court swoops onto the screen. The stadium is full of cheering fans as eight players in Compressor-X Powersuits step to the side of the field. Three flank both sides while two take their place at the edge of the starting line. Ball stations line the entire length of the court.

ROUND ONE: A whistle sounds as the two players power-up and rush onto the field, in an attempt to successfully reach several checkpoints. The six players on the sides of the court pick up the balls and throw them at the moving targets. The two players use their Compressor-X suits, in conjunction with teamwork to block, and redirect the balls away from them—without being hit. The game progresses as each team-of-two scores points by reaching checkpoints and the goal post. The opposing team of six gain points by hitting their opponents with the balls.

ROUND TWO: Teams of four take to both halves of the court. Each side has its own ball stations. Various elements of the court rise so that the interaction between players becomes more three-dimensional. The whistle blows as each player powers-up their suit and engages in an all-out assault to knock out the opposing team members. In this *new* configuration, players can use certain parts of the court for height elevation, protection, as well as runways that provide designated access to the opposing team's side of the court.

The video stops similarly to how it began—in the midst of the thunderous applause of fans.

"So, what do you think?" Roger asks.

Miranda turns to Curtis. "You created the Compressor-X suit. What do you think?"

"I like it!" Curtis shouts. "Mr.Maxwell, you took my idea and gave it a real upgrade!"

"Do you really think this type of game could catch on with the public?" Omar asks.

"Are you kidding me?" Roger replies. "You would be giving people the opportunity to put the wind in the palm of their hands—to manipulate objects without having to touch them! That's the closest thing to telekinesis! Besides, do you think I would have flown all the way here from Colorado if I didn't think this idea had merit?"

"And we really do appreciate you taking the time to come and make your presentation," Miranda replies. "So, if we *were* interested in pursuing this opportunity, what would you need?"

"Well," Roger replies, "you all control the patents for the suit. So, we would need you to either build the suits or give us the licenses to build them ourselves. Then of course, we would need you all to train the players on how to use the suits, test the court and help design the balls and other equipment. Of course, you would get a fee for all of this work, as well as get a percentage of ticket sales, merchandise, etc..."

"So," Jim interjects, "how would you roll out the game?"

"First, we would build everything at our test facility in Colorado and make sure every aspect of the game is perfected. Then we would secure a stadium location that is surrounded by a large demographic who would attend this type of extreme event. And if the responses you received from your tour is any indication... people are going to eat-this-up!"

"Mom," Curtis asks. "What do you think?"

Miranda looks at her sons, then at Jim and smiles. She gazes at all of the concept illustrations and the banner. She then focuses her attention on Roger 'Chase' Maxwell. "Mr. Maxwell. If we can work out all of the logistics and you can guarantee that Curtis' story is shared in some type of multimedia format at each game so people can be *further* inspired, motivated and educated, then we have a deal."

Mr. Maxwell and his assistant smile as he extends his hand to Miranda. "That sounds perfectly reasonable to me."

Miranda shakes his hand, as does everyone else. "Team Speedsuit Powers looks forward to working with you."

[]

Sunday, August 25, 2013. The 49th floor of The Commerce Club.

Chasm and Curtis enjoy the high-class experience of the dining area as they wait for their food to arrive. Classical music fills the room, accentuating an atmosphere already permeated by the aroma of exquisite cuisine.

"Curtis," Chasm smiles as he puts down his glass of wine, "your mother wanted me to see how you were doing."

"So, now you're keeping tabs on me for her?"

"I am merely speaking on behalf of someone who loves and cares deeply about you."

"I'm... fine."

"Are you?" Chasm leans in Curtis' direction. "This is *me* you're talking with. I already know you are *not* one hundred percent alright."

"How do you do that?"

"I am an observer. Part natural talent, part developed skill. So, tell me. What's on your mind?"

Curtis looks down at his glass. "Things are getting *serious*, now. I mean, things have always been serious in my life... but now—I could have died."

"We *all* could have died on any given day."

Curtis looks up at his mentor.

"That's the lesson," Chasm continues. "No day is promised to us. Not tomorrow. Not even this afternoon. All we have is right now— this very second."

"But you don't know how I felt! Being abducted and locked in the trunk of a car. Being chased through the streets. Being held at gunpoint! It was terrifying!"

"More than when you confronted Justin and Amanda in Colorado?"

"Yes. *Way* more!"

"Why?"

Curtis gathers his thoughts. "In Colorado, I knew I had an advantage. Justin and Amanda were like me. I understood what it felt like to be bullied. So, while I was still scared, and knew I could possibly be injured… or be killed, I felt like the odds were in my favor and that we all could walk out alive. But I didn't know *anything* when I was kidnapped!"

Chasm takes a sip of his wine as he looks at his young protégé with deep concern. "Only a *very small* number of people know what I am about to share with you."

Curtis sits up straight in his chair—at full attention.

"I told you my adoptive parents had me educated at some of the best schools in the world."

"Yes, you did," Curtis agrees.

"On one particular day, I was kidnapped."

"What happened?" Curtis blurts out in a half-whisper.

The waiter arrives with their food and places each plate on the table.

"Let's eat first," Chasm says, "and then I will continue with the story."

"Are you kidding," Curtis protests. "I'll eat the food cold! Keep going with the story!"

Chasm chuckles as he concedes and continues his tale.

[]

1976. International High School. Europe.

An 18 year old Chasm exits the building—wearing his green and brown school uniform. He is surrounded by fellow classmates, friends from all over the world, as they engage in intense, jovial conversation. They part ways as each is met by their driver and enters their private car. Chasm is the last to reach his driver, Martin Franklin, who is also his personal bodyguard. Martin steps out of his car—a black BMW sedan with tinted windows and diplomatic plates—and scans the area as his young ward approaches.

"Hello Chasm," Martin says as they both shake hands. "How was school today?"

"You ask me the same thing everyday, Martin," Chasm replies as the rear door is opened for him to enter.

"And you give me the *same* answer," Martin utters with a smile. A moment later, they are driving away, having just passed the school's security checkpoint. "Seriously. How was school?"

"It's getting better."

"You came in the middle of the semester and it's been three months."

"You know my adoptive parents, Martin. They believe in throwing you in the pool even if you don't know how to swim."

"It's been two years since they adopted you. When are you going to call them your parents without any pre-cursor handles?"

"When I feel completely comfortable as a black male with adoptive white parents."

"We've talked about this before."

"I know, Martin. I know."

"They're not going to give you back. They love you... even if sometimes their love is tough. I've been working for them for fifteen years. Trust me. They would not be shelling out this kind of money on you if they didn't care about you." Movement catches Martin's eye as he looks in his rearview mirror. "I need you to buckle up."

"Why?"

"There's a car behind us. It's been with us since we left school and it's been making all of the same turns that we have made. It may not be anything, but I'm not waiting to find out."

Chasm buckles his seatbelt as another car approaches in front of them and turns into their lane. Martin swerves just in time to avoid a collision, putting them on a side street, which leads to a dead end brick wall. Martin picks up his car radio and calls for help as three cars pull up behind them.

"What's happening?" Chasm yells.

"I need you to stay calm," Martin orders as several men with assault rifles exit their vehicles. "Listen. No one is getting in this car—not with its ballistic and explosive paneling."

The masked men raise their guns and let loose with a hail of bullets! Each round sounds like mini explosions as they ricochet off the car. Chasm screams as the car rattles back and forth. Martin throws the car into reverse and slams his foot on the gas pedal. The men jump out of the way as the BMW barrels through their makeshift blockade. The BMW almost makes it off of the side street and onto the main road before Martin yells.

"Get down!"

One of the assailants pull the trigger on a rocket launcher and the projectile streaks directly towards the car. On impact, the car erupts in flames and is thrown several feet into the air… landing on its side. The interior cabin begins to slowly fill with smoke.

"Martin!" Chasm yells in the midst of violent coughs. "Martin! Are you OK?"

Martin almost coughs up a lung as he turns to Chasm and forces a wary smile.

"I'm still here. Listen, we're in trouble. Are you hurt?"

"I don't think so!"

"Good. I need you to climb out through the trunk and run as fast as you can!"

"But what about you? I'm not leaving you!"

"If you stay, then we both might be dead!" Martin pulls out his semiautomatic weapons. "Go! I'll cover you!"

Chasm reluctantly climbs into the trunk.

"Don't stop running until you get to the compound!" Martin pops the trunk as he opens his door.

"Good thing these doors have hydraulic assist." He stands up, propping his feet on the dashboard and his chair and brings his guns to bear on the assailants. Chasm jumps from the trunk and breaks into his fastest run! Martin opens fire, causing the assailants to duck for cover.

Chasm runs down the street, with the sound of gunfire fading behind him. Tears and blood blur his vision, but he doesn't stop running. Soon the gunfire stops, but he doesn't stop running. As he cries profusely, the only thing he can focus on is making it to his parents. He can see their compound in the distance—about four blocks away. The gates open as a squadron of security vehicles rush towards his position. His fear and grief give way to jubilation.

But a dark colored van roars upon him from behind. The side door slides open and two masked men snatch him from the pavement.

"Nooooooo!" Chasm screams as the door closes shut and the van swerves left down a side street. And then… black… as one of the men throws a hood over his head.

[]

The Present.

"What happened next?" Curtis half-whispers at the top of his lungs, with a bug-eyed expression. "You can't just stop a story in the middle of the action like that!"

"Sure I can," Chasm smiles. "It is my story to tell."

Curtis slumps back into his chair in a huff, "Why did you stop?"

"Because the rest of the story is for another time." Chasm calls the waiter over to their table. "Sergei, please have them re-heat our food. I'm afraid my young protégé and I were engaged in a lively discussion."

"Yes, Sir." Sergei immediately removes their plates with a smile.

"I want you to know that I *do* understand what you've been through."

Curtis sits quietly, looking down at his hands.

"What's on your mind?"

"The business card…" He pulls it out of his pocket. "Why didn't you tell me that you could track it?"

"I didn't know I *had* to tell you."

"You don't. It's *your* technology."

"I deal with people on a need-to-know basis."

"And I didn't need to know."

"Honestly? No. If you did, I would have told you. Although, I thought you might have surmised the possibility given everything I *did* share with you about it."

"It never crossed my mind."

"Even though I can track you at any moment with the card, I don't spend my time or anyone else's following your every move. As important as you are… you are not *that* important."

Curtis looks at Chasm as they both laugh.

"If I can be frank with you," Chasm continues, "no one tells anyone *everything* all at once. People couldn't handle that."

"True… So, where do we go from here?"

"Well, you will start your classes tomorrow and I will go to work. In a few weeks, we'll meet here again and I will introduce you to my mentor, Dr. Edmond Randolph Winters."

CHAPTER FOUR

YOU NEED TO KNOW…

SATURDAY, AUGUST 31, 2013. THE MONTGOMERY group facilities. Atlanta. It is the end of the first week of school. Curtis and Erica have spent the past few hours working on some preliminary logistics for several upcoming projects. Now, they sit in her office—about to eat a meal they just brought down from the staff cafeteria.

"That took longer than I thought," Erica laughs.

"Yeah," Curtis concurs as he takes a bite of his hamburger.

"So, how'd your first week of classes go?" Erica asks as she eats some of her french fries.

"Brutal! But I'm holding. This year is just as hard as last year!"

"That's because the work is harder," Erica replies.

A few moments pass as they both eat and drink in silence.

"So, tell me," Curtis inquires, "how did you start working for Chasm?"

"That is a *long* story," Erica replies.

"We've got time."

"OK…" Erica concedes. "When do you think Chasm and I first met?"

"Mmmm," Curtis purses his lips as he pushes the bridge of his glasses securely on his nose, "while you were in high school?"

"Good guess. But I actually met Chasm while in middle school."

[]

February 23, 2002. Indianapolis, Indiana. Middle School.

A 7th grade Erica Cosway sits, staring out of the window in the principal's office. Her parents stand—both engaged in a heated argument with the principal and her science teacher.

"You know this is wrong!" Jerome Cosway Sr. objects. "My daughter should have won *first* place!"

"Now, Jerome," Principal Smalls states, "I'm sorry, but you know these competitions can be complicated."

"Complicated?" Jerome scoffs in amazement. "Compared to my daughter, the boy who you gave the award to has a science project that looks like a kindergarten student did it!"

"I don't think that's fair," Travis, the science teacher, chimes in.

"*Now* you want to talk about fair?" Erica's mother replies.

"Now Emelyn," the principal warns. "Let's not go there."

"Why not?" Emelyn crosses her arms. "Travis just brought it up! Erica has passed every aptitude test you have thrown at her! Her I.Q. is off the charts! Yet, you *still* give her mediocre grades."

"She zones out during class!" Travis interjects.

"She zones out," Jerome interrupts, "because she grasps the lesson faster than anybody else in the class."

"We keep saying she should be skipped to a higher grade, but the district keeps holding her back!"

"I've read the records," Principal Smalls interjects. "You want to talk about fair? Let's talk about it. Who's helping her? There's no way your daughter is doing all of this without help. Seriously, doing two hours worth of homework in 30-40 minutes? That's impossible! Jerome, you're a factory worker. And your wife here is a paralegal. Both of you are average and so are the rest of your kids. And I'm supposed to believe that Erica here is some kind of child prodigy? I am going to propose an in-depth investigation into this issue. When I find out how she's cheating, she will be expelled!"

KNOCK. KNOCK. KNOCK.

"The door is closed for a reason!" Principle Smalls yells as it quickly opens, revealing a tall black man standing in its threshold.

"Who are you? Can't you see my door is closed?"

"I'm Chasm Montgomery," the man says while stepping into the room confidently.

"Ah, Dr. Montgomery!" the principal concedes. "I'm sorry, can you give us a minute?"

"My apologies for the interruption. Your secretary was not at her desk. I heard the commotion and decided to knock. My plane was late due to a last minute meeting in Florida. I know I was scheduled to be the guest judge for the science fair. Even though it ended a short while ago, I took it upon myself to examine each entry. I came here to tell you that there has been a mistake."

"Mistake?" Principal Smalls asks. "What kind of mistake?"

"The young man who won first place—Tyler Richmond."

Erica turns around from the window and makes eye contact with the stranger. Mr. Montgomery smiles warmly at her.

"What about him?" the science teacher asks.

"His science project was not as thorough as the young woman who won second place."

Erica and her parents begin smiling.

"I'm not sure what criterion was used to determine the winners, but Erica Cosway's project is clearly more advanced than *all* the rest. I would like to meet her."

[]

The Present.

"Whoah!" Curtis marvels. "That's wild!"

"I know, right?" Erica laughs as she moves one seat closer to Curtis. "You should have seen how the principal and science teacher turned all *kinds* of shades of red!"

They both laugh hard.

"Little did I know that Chasm had already been reviewing the files of every student who showed any type of scientific aptitude. He became my family's advocate and—as he likes to say—spared no expense to transfer me into the best schools where I could truly be challenged. I was the valedictorian of my high school. Chasm brought me to Georgia Tech and I graduated undergrad with a dual science degree by the time I was 21. And here I am, getting my masters in Biomimetics and working for the *great* Chasm Montgomery."

Erica and Curtis share a long stare and a warm smile. Curtis grows nervous and leans away from her.

"Erica—"

She quickly closes the distance between them and kisses Curtis passionately… and he does not immediately stop her.

"What are you doing?" He stammers as he slowly breaks away from her embrace. "You know… I'm *with* Kelly."

"You may be with her," Erica counters, "but I *know* you think about me. I think about you, too."

"That's not the point." Curtis stands up and takes several steps away from her.

Erica stands as well, but doesn't move from her position. She looks at Curtis warmly.

"Kelly's a wonderful girl. But you know we have so much more in common. Imagine all the things we could do together!"

"That's what I'm trying not to do!" Curtis shuts his eyes and shakes his head as he paces the room. "Oh, man. I can't believe this is happening!"

"I'm sorry to do this to you." Erica takes a few steps towards him. "I really am. And I'm not trying to cause trouble for you and Kelly. It's just that this is the second time I almost lost you and I can't imagine going one more day without you knowing how I feel. I've never met anyone like you. Just know that you have *options*. I won't push the boundaries again. I won't even mention that this happened. But if you decide you want to be with me… I will be here... waiting."

CHAPTER FIVE

WIDE OPEN

COLLEGE IS IN FULL SWING AS the second week of classes commences. September has begun and everyone's back in their routines. Treyshawn and Johnny are now roommates in California. Kelly and Clamille continue to grow in their friendship. Gavin has returned, however, he is temporarily bound to a wheelchair while he goes through physical therapy to aid his recovery from being shot in the back.

Georgia Tech University. Dorm room.

"Hey CP, I was thinking. If your Conduit suit *accidentally* stopped bullets, what would happen if you actually *designed* it to stop bullets?"

"Gavin, we've been through this before."

"I know. It was just a question, bro."

"A better question is: how can we mechanize your wheelchair until you can get back on your feet?"

"Way ahead of you, bro!" Gavin pulls a folded sheet of paper from a pouch on his wheelchair and opens it up."

"Nice..." Curtis says as he looks at the diagram.

"And I put together a parts list. My dad's going to pick them up next week. Want to help me put this together?"

"Definitely!"

"We can do it right here in the room."

"You got it!"

"I've also been working on designs for a remote controlled robot vehicle. I call it, The Ant. I've already started building it at my dad's house."

"Wow! You've been keeping busy."

"When you're stuck in a wheelchair, you've got time to think."

"When can I see the robot?"

"I'll let you know when it's done. You're going to love it!"

[]

Spelman College Campus.

"Girl," Clamille says to Kelly as they walk across campus, "I am SO GLAD to be free of Tyreese!"

"Me too," Kelly agrees as they both laugh.

"I didn't realize how he was slowly choking the life out of me until he was gone."

"I'm glad you get a second chance to have a better life," Kelly replies softly. "Not every girl is so lucky."

"Luck didn't have anything to do with it," Clamille declares. "You did."

The two walk for a moment without speaking as they replay the memories of the Intervention in their mind.

"So," Kelly asks, "what did you do for August?"

"After I got back from our tour, my mom took me on a 'mother daughter' trip to the Bahamas!"

"Now, that sounds wonderful!"

"Oh, it was!" Clamille laughs. "We had a wonderful time and it was great to get a chance to bond again. All the drama with Tyreese gave us a lot to talk about."

A girl and guy, approaching from the other direction with their hands full accidentally collide with Kelly and Clamille. Books and papers drop in every direction as they apologize to each other.

"Sorry!" Kelly and Clamille say, while trying to hold their things.

"No, I'm sorry I didn't see you," the other girl replies as she tries to catch her papers.

In the melee, Kelly reaches to pick up some books and the young man's hand accidentally touches hers. She instinctively pulls it back.

"I'm sorry," he says with a warm smile—gazing intently at her face.

"No problem," Kelly stutters while looking away, trying not to notice how handsome he is.

The four stand up—finally having secured all papers and books.

"Clamille?" the girl says in a surprised tone.

"Lizzy?" Clamille utters—surprised as well.

Both girls hug and quickly exchange small talk for a few seconds before making their introductions.

"Kelly," Clamille smiles, "This is Lizzy. We had two classes together last semester."

"Yeah," Lizzy adds. "I wouldn't have made it through one of them if Clamille didn't help me study!" Lizzy motions towards the young man. "This is my cousin, Carlos."

"How are you ladies doing?" Carlos says with a broad smile as he shakes their hands.

"Hey Carlos," Kelly and Clamille say in unison.

"Are you just visiting?" Clamille asks.

"I attend Morehouse. So, I'm not that far away."

"Oh, a Morehouse Man," Clamille answers in a flirtatious tone.

Carlos continues to smile, but his eyes are focused on Kelly.

"Well, Carlos was just helping me bring some books over to study hall. I'm meeting with my tutor in ten minutes!"

"OK," Clamille says. "Don't let us stop you. We should catch up later. I wanna hear all about your summer vacation."

"You got it," Lizzy agrees.

"Hey," Carlos interjects, "can I come?"

"Girls only," Kelly quips.

"Maybe next time then," Carlos laughs warmly without breaking his gaze. "Hopefully, there *will* be a next time."

Kelly blushes as she looks away.

"Cousin? Why are you flirting with Kelly?" Lizzy asks.

"Besides," Clamille adds, "she's got a boyfriend!"

"You do?" Carlos asks.

"Yes," Kelly states firmly, "I do. And he's great."

"Well," Carlos counters, "if things don't work out with your man, I *am* available."

[]

University of California, Berkeley. Dorm room.

"First week down. How's it going?" Johnny asks as he sits on his bed.

"Pretty good," Treyshawn answers while looking through one of his notebooks at his desk. "It was tough tryin' to get used to things last year, but I feel better about everything now."

"One year down," Johnny smiles, "Three more to go!"

"Listen," Treyshawn says while turning around in his chair. "I'm glad you agreed to be roommates."

"We may have started off on the wrong foot," Johnny replies, "but the sky is the limit! Not only can we work together on our assignments, but we can also have some great parties too!"

"Parties?"

"You're from New York. You don't party?

"Oh, I used to," Treyshawn declares confidently. "Back in the day, I loved parties! But now that I'm tryin' to do something different with my life, too much partying can be a distraction."

"OK. So the key word then is 'moderation.' We won't party too much. Just enough to have a good time."

Treyshawn turns back towards his desk and mumbles under his breath. "What am I getting myself into?"

□

Atlanta. Church. Evening time.

It's Wednesday night and Curtis finds himself walking to the same small church not far from his college campus. A mid-week prayer service is in session. Curtis quietly enters and sits in the back of the sanctuary. He leans forward and rests his head in his hands.

"God?" he breathes heavily. "Please help me. This whole situation with Erica is… it's unacceptable." He leans back against the pew and looks up at the ceiling. "So what, the girl is drop-dead gorgeous!" he half-whispers. "And we have so much in common." He brings his hands up over his face. "She kissed me… and man can she kiss!" He takes another deep breath. "I am in *so* much trouble." Curtis hears approaching pitter-patter of feet and opens his eyes to find Javier standing next to him.

"Hey Curtis!"

"Hey Javier!" Curtis sits up—trying to muster a happy mood. "How are you?"

"I'm good! I see you took my advice and made the new suits!"

"Yep!"

"I've got more!" Javier proclaims excitedly. "How about a suit that shoots fire? Or one that can climb up walls? Did you work on the super strength one yet? Or what about a suit that creates force fields?"

"You do have a lot of ideas," Curtis laughs as he throws his hands up. "And I am working on a design for an augmented strength exoskeleton."

"Augmented? What does that mean?"

"When you augment something, you make it greater by adding something else to it. So, in this case, the exoskeleton will hopefully give the wearer more strength to lift heavier objects."

"That is so cool!" Javier shouts, causing his mother and others—up front—to turn around disapprovingly. Javier ducks while Curtis waves.

"Didn't this happen *last* time I was here?"

"Sorry," Javier whispers, "I get too excited sometimes and forget to use my 'inside voice.' Can I get up now?"

"Sure," Curtis chuckles. "The coast is clear."

Javier stands up, waves bye and makes his way back over to his friends. Curtis sits for a few more minutes before leaving the church to head back to his dormitory.

[]

Curtis arrives back at his dorm to find Kelly waiting in the lobby.

"Curtis!" she shouts as she runs to him. They both exchange a long embrace. Kelly tries to kiss him, but Curtis turns his head slightly and meets her lips with his cheek. She looks at him strangely. "What's wrong?"

"Sorry." Curtis does his best impression of a cough while clearing his throat. "My throat feels scratchy. I don't want you to catch whatever I'm coming down with."

"Aww..." she smiles. "You are always looking out for me."

You have no idea, he thinks to himself as he forces a smile.

"So, we finally get a chance to see each other since getting back to Atlanta," Kelly smiles. "It's been a real busy week!"

"Who you telling!" Curtis exclaims. "It's like the professors have been itching for classes to start so they can dish out more homework!"

"You ain't never lied!"

"What's cool though, is I'm meeting Chasm's mentor on Saturday!"

"Wow. That's great. I wonder what he's like?"

"I'll let you know."

They both leave the dorm to get a bite to eat.

[]

Saturday, September 14, 2013. The Commerce Club. 49th Floor.

Sergei leads Chasm and Curtis through the dining area as a well-dressed man, sitting at their table, rises from his chair with a smile.

"Chasm!" The well-dressed man, advanced in years, exchanges a strong handshake.

"It is great to see you again." Chasm smiles.

"And you must be Curtis!" the man places both of his hands firmly on Curtis' shoulders. "I've heard so much about you."

"Curtis," Chasm smiles broadly as he clears his throat, "This is my mentor, Dr. Edmond Randolph Winters."

"It's a pleasure to finally meet you, Sir," Curtis remarks while shaking his hand.

"Please sit down," Dr. Winters invites. "I want to hear more about you and your exploits!"

Later, after their meal…

"And that's how I got here." Curtis smiles.

"To hear you tell your story is simply… fascinating," Dr. Winters replies. "What a marvelous conclusion. Thank you Curtis."

"I'm glad you liked the story."

"Liked it? I loved it!" Dr. Winters sips his wine. "One of the great lessons I've learned in life is that when one season ends, it's as if you've come to the end of a chapter. And when you turn the page, a new chapter—a new *adventure* is ready to begin!"

"Wow. I've never thought about it quite like that before."

Dr. Winters smiles knowingly, "So now, my boy, what will you do in this new chapter you've just begun? What kind of legendary tale are you writing?"

"Well, I've never thought of my life as being 'legendary.'"

"Oh, but it is," Dr. Winters urges, while Chasm watches the entire exchange with a grin. "You will be 20 years old next year and you have already done more in the last six years of your life than most people have done in a lifetime. To me, *that* is the definition of 'legendary.'"

"So… what do you think I should do?" Curtis replies as he looks down at his plate, contemplating his past and future.

"I can't tell you how to run your dreams, Curtis. No one can. You have to determine that for yourself. But Chasm and I can most certainly encourage you to run—and we can assist you in navigating the environment, while providing much needed resources to help ensure your success. That is the beauty of having a mentor. A mentor doesn't tell you how to live your life, but rather we help you see how you *could* live your life. We help you see options… choices and the potential consequences that can ensue from the decisions you make with your life. Now if you ask us about a specific direction you want to take, then we can give you a specific course of action based on our learned experience. Otherwise… just think of us as… facilitators." Dr. Winters turns towards his protégé. "Isn't that correct, Chasm?"

Chasm sits forward in his chair with an obvious grin. "Everything that is required to run your dream is already in you, Curtis. You just need help to bring it all out. Your family and friends have helped to get you to this point. Dr. Winters and I can open up opportunities that will take you the rest of the way —as far as you want to go."

"Chasm, you were right," Dr. Winters states with an excitement in his voice, "Curtis *is* something special. With the right help, he can definitely go extremely far in life." Dr. Winters faces Curtis and gazes at him intently. "Whatever you want to do; wherever you want to go; whoever you want to meet; we want to help facilitate your success."

"But why?" Curtis asks. "Why me?"

"It's called 'paying it forward.' I'm sure Chasm mentioned that when I discovered him, he was at a very low point in his life."

"Yes. Yes he did."

"He had just lost his adoptive parents in a horrific crash. He had to leave a prestigious college in Europe to prepare for their funeral. When I saw him afterwards, at the repast, he was sitting alone in a corner. No one was talking to him. Quite frankly, if I can be honest, no one knew quite what to say. He was the heir to a vast inheritance, yet he had lost his direction *and* the two people who had transformed his life."

"What Dr. Winters didn't know at the time," Chasm shares, "was that I had planned to end my life that night, after everyone had gone. I didn't care about the money. What good was it when my parents were dead? But he wouldn't leave. He insisted on staying the night and we continued talking until dawn.

"I paid forward the blessings from my life and he pays forward his blessings. Together, we have helped to discover a long roster of individuals who have gone on to use their gifts, talents and skills to change the world. We *want* a better world, Curtis. And we believe you can play a pivotal role in making the world better for everyone. Will you let us help you?"

Curtis thinks about the proposition for a moment. "You've already provided the scholarship for me to go to school. I might as well see where this adventure leads."

"Great!" Dr. Winters exclaims. "You have made an excellent decision. Here's what I want to do for you. After we leave here, I want to take you to our tailors. They will gather your measurements and create a completely customized wardrobe just for you. No more buying off the rack, Curtis... Not unless you *want* to. What do you think about that?"

"Wow! I-I don't know what to say!"

"You can start," Chasm smiles, "with thank you."

"Thank you! Thank you so much!"

"You're welcome, Curtis." Dr. Winters laughs. "It's time to get you ready for the *next* level!"

CHAPTER SIX

MEETING PLACES

MIRANDA ARRIVES BY TAXI TO THE Niagara-on-the-Lake restaurant in Canada. The date is Saturday September14, 2013. Once again she makes her way through the restaurant to the back patio area, which overlooks the river. Marge sits at the same table as their last visit, this time joined by a gentleman. They both stand as Miranda nears the table.

"Miranda," Marge welcomes with open arms, "it is good to see you!" Both women share a long hug. Marge then pulls away and motions to the gentleman. "This is Emmanuel Harte. The greatest accountant to ever live!"

"Well, I don't know about that," Emmanuel laughs.

"To me, you *are* the greatest!" Marge counters.

"Well, it's nice to meet you," Miranda adds with a handshake. "Marge speaks very highly of you."

"No one can follow a money trail like Emmanuel Harte!" Marge proclaims proudly.

"I do what I can," he replies modestly as they take their seats.

"I can tell by your accent that you are from somewhere in West Africa," Miranda declares.

"Ah. Have you traveled to West Africa before?"

"My husband and I have visited Ghana and Nigeria several times."

"That is marvelous!" Emmanuel chuckles. "What do you think of West Africa?"

"I love it! The people are so warm, friendly and hospitable."

"Now, I see why Marge speaks so very highly of you, as well. You have been to my beloved homeland, Ghana!"

All three of them laugh.

"My wife is from Brooklyn. Our firstborn is Matthew. Our second born is our daughter, Nana. You know, my son wrote a letter to your son last year."

"Really?" Miranda asks with great interest.

"Yes," Emmanuel continues. "He was very excited about your son's Speedsuit invention."

"Well, we get so much fan mail. I'll ask my sons if they came across Matthew's letter."

"Thank you so much!" Emmanuel smiles before getting serious.

"Now, I have reviewed all of Marge's documents."

"And what do you think?" Miranda eagerly asks.

"Now, please wait a minute," Marge interjects. "Both of you know how I like to approach important business."

"With tea," Emmanuel and Miranda utter in unison.

"Yes," Marge smiles warmly, "With tea." She calls over the waiter and places an order for them all. For the next thirty minutes, in between spots of tea, they catch up on family and other interesting events.

"Now," Marge declares with an air of diplomacy, "let's get to the business at hand."

Miranda and Emmanuel glance at each other with a smile.

"I have reviewed all of the documents," Emmanuel states. "These are definitely incriminating for the Firm. On the surface, things seem legitimate, but if you dig deeper and follow the money, certain aspects of their building projects just don't add up."

"In what way?" Miranda queries.

"A number of the Firm's substantial building projects seemed to have been acquired for far less than what seems reasonable. I crosschecked the amounts in these documents with various city files and there is an obvious discrepancy."

"In other words," Marge adds, "someone has fudged the numbers."

"Correct," Emmanuel continues. "But there's more. As Attorney Phillips and I researched these projects, in many instances previous residents left their homes under questionable circumstances."

"You mean they were forced out," Miranda notes.

"Yes," Emmanuel agrees. "Those who weren't bought out, were forced out through other means... violent coercion, questionable fires, sudden deaths, etc..."

"My God," Miranda utters while covering her mouth. "Are you saying that the architect firm my husband worked for was responsible for displacing families?"

"Yes," Emmanuel responds. "The Firm has been directly and indirectly responsible for the displacement of lower and middle income families; those who paid taxes, as well as the homeless, and at least one school and group home. Also, some of the police cases were never solved. I think, at some level, the police and members of the judicial system were paid off."

"We haven't found *all* of the pieces yet," Marge adds, "but once we do, we'll have enough to go to the authorities and hopefully get some kind of justice."

Unbeknownst to the group, an individual, approximately 200 feet away, is taking numerous photographs of their meeting.

"What about Malcolm's life insurance policy?" Miranda inquires.

"We looked into that too," Emmanuel replies. "Someone went to great lengths to make it look like your husband canceled the policy on his own. But an associate of mine has recovered some deleted emails from one of the Firm's network servers. According to them, John Whaley gave the order for one of his subordinates to 'handle' the situation."

"You actually have that in writing?" Miranda exclaims.

"Yes. I gave the actual email to Marge for safe keeping with all of her other documents."

"Then we've got him!" Miranda half-whispers. "We have proof!"

"We have proof," Marge says with a cautioned satisfaction. "But Miranda, we also have a situation on our hands that is much larger than we could have imagined. I knew the Firm took part in some unethical projects, but Emmanuel revealed to what extent the Firm participated. And it's much more than I expected. In several situations, they even spearheaded the efforts. For a company like this, run by men like John Whaley—to do what they've done—we're not sure how far this stretches. There's a very real chance that at some level, even city government leaders and politicians might be involved."

"So what do you suggest we do?" Miranda asks.

"We may be sitting on a ticking time bomb," Emmanuel replies. "Let us pray it never explodes."

"What we do," Marge strongly suggests, "at least for the time being—is wait."

After several minutes of additional conversation, the meeting ends and the three head in their separate directions. Miranda contemplates the last two hours as she walks from the restaurant, passes through a large crowd of tourists in the front quad and steps into her waiting taxi. The car pulls away from the curbside and heads for the train station.

[]

Monday, September 16, 2013. Rikers Island Prison. Visitors center.

Shakira sits at the cold round table, staring at the father of her son. Treyshawn Sr. stares at her without blinking.

"So, how have you been?"

Silence.

"Are you gonna talk to me at all?"

Treyshawn Sr. sits on the bench like a rock. "What you want 'Kira?"

"You haven't said anything since you sat down." Shakira replies. "That was five minutes ago."

"Maybe I don't have anything to say to you," he scoffs matter-of-factly.

"You don't have to put up this charade with me, Trey. Our son told me everything: about why you don't want to be a father, about the journal, and that you read it."

He crosses his arms. "Did you put him up to this?"

"No. I wish I had. Guess that says something about the kind of mother I've been. Always letting my anger at you be my anger at him. But, no. *This* is all your son."

"Well he's hard-headed."

"And who do you think he got that from?" Shakira smirks.

Treyshawn Sr. raises his eyebrow, "From both of us, apparently."

Shakira shakes her head and smirks, "He also told me you almost punched his teeth out the last time he was here."

"He told you that, huh?" Treyshawn Sr. cracks a smile as both of them break into laughter for a brief moment.

"So, what'd you tell him?" Treyshawn Sr. inquires.

"I told him why you did it."

"And why did I do it?"

"We both know why you did it."

"Yeah…" Treyshawn Sr. concedes, "but don't think this makes things good between you and me."

"I didn't come here for us," Shakira responds calmly, "I came here for our son. He wants to know you… and honestly, I'm not sure I want him to. But that's not my decision to make. Whether you want to accept it or not, you *are* his father. I just ask… that you be honest with him. That's the least you can do."

[]

Friday, September 20, 2013. The Montgomery Group facilities. Atlanta.

"Wow! This place is amazing!" Jim exclaims.

"Mr. G," Curtis laughs, "you look like a kid in a candy store!" Curtis just finished giving Jim Grabowski a basic tour of the facilities. Now, they have entered Curtis' workstation office with a couple of smoothies from the cafeteria.

Jim scans the room, "With all my prior visits to Atlanta over the last year, I can't believe this is the first time I'm seeing this place. And you have your own lab?"

"Yep. It's crazy, I know. I had a workspace on campus, but since that got compromised, Chasm—Mr. Montgomery—gave me a workstation that is usually reserved for his interns."

"This intern workstation makes my workshop at home look like a kiddie factory!"

KNOCK. KNOCK.

Jim and Curtis turn towards the door as Erica enters.

"Erica," Curtis utters, trying to hide his sudden nervousness.

"Hello Curtis." Erica beams with her beautiful smile. "How are you Mr. Grabowski?"

"Hello Erica," Jim smiles. "It's good to see you again."

"You as well," she smiles warmly. "I heard you both were in the building and wanted to stop by and see if you needed anything."

Jim looks at Curtis as he averts his eyes.

"No, thanks. We're good," Curtis says nonchalantly.

"Okay," Erica replies in a chipper tone while trying not to seem too eager. "I'm down the hall if you need me."

With that, she's gone.

"It must be great working with her and having such a close connection to Mr. Montgomery," Jim muses.

"Yeah," Curtis hesitates.

"What's the matter with you," Jim inquires. "All of a sudden it's like the wind got knocked out of your sails."

"Nothing," Curtis huffs. "Are you ready to go now?"

"Go?" Jim looks at Curtis strangely. "We just finished the tour! And I thought we were going to work on planning the next round of exhibition runs."

"We can do that somewhere else."

"It would be great if we could do that here, like we planned. Being in this environment might help stimulate some new ideas."

"Mr. G! Let's just go!" Curtis yells.

A silence that had never existed between these two fills the room.

"I—I don't think you have ever raised your voice at me before," Jim declares with an air of disappointment.

"I'm—" Curtis takes a deep breath as he looks down at the floor. "I'm sorry, Mr. G. It's just that... there's a lot going on right now."

"Apparently," Jim agrees. "Where's the bathroom?"

"Huh?" Curtis looks up.

"I have to use the bathroom. Then I'll go back to the hotel and we can finish things up tomorrow."

"OK." Curtis replies flatly while still looking down at the floor. "Make a right and go to the end of the hall. Men's bathroom is on the left."

Jim silently exits the room as Curtis starts pacing the floor.

"I can't believe I did that!" he grumbles to himself. "This is crazy. I gotta tell him—but I can't tell him! What if he tells Kelly?" Curtis groans in frustration and plops down in his chair. A few minutes later, Mr. Grabowski returns.

"OK. I'm ready to go."

"Mr. G. Wait." Curtis jumps up from his chair and approaches his mentor. "I am so sorry," he whispers while hesitating. "There's...something I've got to tell you."

Jim looks Curtis directly in his eyes, "You and Erica kissed."

Curtis stumbles back as his bug-eyed expression registers his tremendous shock. "How—how did you know that?"

"Son," Jim says softly, "I'm old enough to know the signs when I see them. How you got nervous when Erica entered. The way you both looked at each other. Her overly chipper tone. Your sudden desire to leave. Then you raised your voice at me. It doesn't take a rocket scientist to know that something happened." Jim leans against a nearby desk. "I get it. She's very attractive. You both have a lot in common. That combination makes for a *difficult* situation."

"So—so what do I do?"

"I'm surprised you even have to ask," Jim says with a mix of annoyance and frustration.

"Why are you upset?" Curtis asks in a defensive tone.

"Because you and Kelly have been through so much together. She's been there to support you since 9th grade. She has always been in your corner. She has stood up for you. She has traveled with you across the country and around the world. She loves you. And you have to ask, 'what should you do?' You *tell* her what happened. That's what you do. You don't keep this a secret from her. And then you take whatever anger she dishes out and hope she forgives you."

"It's not… that easy," Curtis turns away.

"It. Is. That. Easy." Jim counters. "You're just too afraid to do it. I know this is tough to hear but—"

"Maybe," Curtis cuts him off. "Maybe you should go."

Jim's face changes several shades of red. "Listen, Son—"

"I'm not your son," Curtis says with a mix of defiance and shame. "I never was."

Jim shakes his head as he picks up his bag, pulls a letter out of the side pocket and places it on the table. "I know you're *not* my son. I'll find my way back to the hotel." Jim exits the room and makes his way to the elevator.

Curtis sits in his chair and reluctantly wipes tears from his eyes. After a few moments, he walks to the table and opens the envelope. Inside is a letter from a Children's hospital, inviting Team Speedsuit to visit in an effort to bring hope and joy to their cancer-stricken patients.

CHAPTER SEVEN

LEVEL ZERO

CHASM AND ERICA DESCEND IN ONE of his eight private elevators. With the insert of Erica's card key, the elevator continues past the lobby, the basement, the lower basement and into the expansive "off-the-books" underground testing facility. The digital display on the elevator panel reads: Tuesday, September 24, 2013.

"Level Zero," the elevator's female artificial intelligence voice declares as the doors prepare to open. "Chasm Montgomery and Erica Cosway are cleared for entry."

The elevator doors open as Chasm and Erica exit onto a long corridor, guarded by numerous security personnel. At the end of the hallway is a set of large blast doors. Two security guards acknowledge their arrival and open the secured entrance. The heavy doorway rises up to reveal a huge, multi-leveled, compartmentalized testing facility.

"Each time we walk through these doors," Erica comments, "I feel like we've entered another world."

"We have," Chasm replies with noticeable amusement.

"This never gets old," Erica smirks.

"The world down here—" Chasm continues.

"I know," Erica interrupts, "The world down *here* will change the world above."

They walk past experiment-after-experiment: some dealing with military-grade weaponry, others pertaining to new forms of ground, air and sea transportation, energy generation, robotics and a host of other undertakings. They finally arrive at one of the testing stations and enter. Inside, the engineers are working at a feverish pace.

"I am here," Chasm addresses all in the room. "Now, show me what I want to see."

The engineers take a few steps back from the tubular casing which houses an upgraded version of the Mach-1 Speedsuit. Then, Dr. Hitachi, the lead engineer, steps forward.

"Mr. Montgomery," Dr. Hitachi says, "the suit is ready. As you know, we put the initial design specs together, based on the known performance parameters of Curtis' Mach-1 Speedsuit. Then, based on your orders, we upgraded the suit with considerable enhancements."

A second engineer continues the report, "Lets start with the bodysuit: It's a twelve-layered design. The outer shell is made out of multi-layered composite polymer foam. It is soft to the touch, but absorbs and dissipates 92% of the kinetic force it may encounter through impact trauma. Unfortunately, a side effect of the energy dissipation is increased heat. So the next few layers of the suit work to keep it cool for the wearer. Underneath that are the insulated electrical layers. There are several battery compartments built into the suit itself. It also uses electromagnetic resonance to generate electricity from the installed 'movement plates.' So, the more the wearer moves, the more electricity is generated, which keeps the batteries charged and supplies extra power to the rest of the sub-systems."

"Good," Chasm smiles. "Tell me more."

A third engineer speaks up, "The final inner layer of the bodysuit is for wearer comfort. The suit interfaces with a powered exoskeleton, which is designed to take the increasing stress loads of the various components and the actual running *off* of the wearer. The exoskeleton and suit interfaces with the Electromagnetic Kinetic Redistribution Boots— EKRB's for short. We surmised that Curtis' Kinetic Redistribution Boots have to be preset based on the number and type of springs that are used. So, they are customizable, but they only have one operating level at a time.

"Our EKRB's—in theory—will allow the wearer to instantly 'dial in' the exact amount of repulsive force needed to surmount greater and lesser distances and heights."

"Theory?" Chasm responds.

"We've never done this before," the engineer replies. "We developed these boots from the incomplete design specs you provided. So, in that sense, all of this is still a theory."

"Understood," Chasm nods, "continue with the presentation."

"The soles of the boots have also been outfitted with the latest in positive traction rubberized treading. This will give your wearer an increased ability to stop or turn on a dime."

A fourth engineer approaches and taps the backpack housing. "This is my favorite part," he grins. "This vortex pack uses similar technology to what Curtis has designed, but as you can see the configuration is *very* different. Instead of one turbine which produces a single column air-flow, we have opted for a one-to-two configuration: a smaller, more efficient single turbine connected to two propulsion nozzles. This design should produce more thrust and provide increased maneuverability for directional changes.

"Also," a fifth engineer adds, "we upgraded the communications system with an integrated heads-up-display. As far as we know, Curtis' suit has a basic array with limited heads-up-functionality which projects his speed and battery power onto his visor. He can also hear his team's radio frequency as well as a number of police emergency channels. Our system, allows the wearer to hear additional communication frequencies, view all pertinent speed/suit/vitals information on the visor and see with night vision and infrared/thermal imaging."

"Basically," the first engineer concludes, "this Powersuit should run circles around Curtis' Mach-1. We anticipate—when fully powered— the wearer of this suit will be able to run at speeds in excess of 150mph. Perhaps even 200mph. The Mach-1 currently caps just under 100mph."

"Excellent," Chasm says, clapping gleefully. "I want to see a demonstration as soon as possible. Thank you everyone."

Chasm and Erica exit the room and continue surveying other projects which are housed in that section.

"When we finally reveal this upgraded Speedsuit to Curtis, he will know the benefit of being able to work with an unlimited budget. Then he'll understand that having access to our resources will open up opportunities for him that are completely beyond his expectations."

"That will make a great present," Erica adds. "He probably won't know what to do with himself. I'm sure he'll be ecstatic."

"Yes. Hopefully, happy enough to remain with us for a *long* time."

"Do you have a name for the new suit?"

"It's the Mach-2. No need to reinvent the wheel."

The pair stop to survey their latest, mechanized, Wearable Armament Response suit. As they watch it lift several heavy objects and blast a number of targets, Chasm turns to face his protégée.

"Erica."

"Yes, Chasm?"

"It's time you receive a promotion."

"A promotion?" she exclaims.

"Yes. You have not only been loyal to me and my vision for all of these years, but you have also proved to be invaluable to this organization."

"Thank you, Sir."

"Since when do you call me, Sir?" Chasm smiles.

"Well, you just gave me a promotion and you *still* sign my paychecks."

Chasm laughs. "Well, I guess that does qualify me as a 'Sir!" And since we are on the subject, this is not a lateral promotion. Your compensation will increase as well."

"So, what is my new position?"

"One day—not today—but one day I can see you running this company. What do you think about that?"

Erica stands silent before her boss… unable to adequately put her words together.

"I—I thought… I *thought* that you were… hoping to groom Curtis for that responsibility."

Chasm gazes at Erica's expression.

"There it is."

"What?"

"That expression you displayed when we first met. When you turned around and looked at me in your principal's office: a mix of wonder, excitement and a bit of hesitation."

"That was a long time ago."

"And look how far you've come. I know you have parents, but in some sense, you've been like a daughter to me."

Erica smiles, "You truly changed my life. And I've always wanted to make you proud."

"I *am* proud of you," Chasm smiles warmly. "I have *other* plans for Curtis. But starting tomorrow—you will be my new Director of Operations."

"Director of Operations!" Erica gasps. "That's a *big* promotion!"

"You are already involved in almost every aspect of this company. This is the next natural step. Being my Director of Operations will give you a greater understanding of the other side of running a business of this magnitude. And since you are graduating soon, I think this will work out just fine. My current D.O.O. wants to transfer to a new oversees division early next year. You can train with him several days a week so you can take over when he does."

"I… thank you… But I don't know. This is a big responsibility."

"Don't start second-guessing yourself now," Chasm smiles. "I have been told that I am an impeccable judge of character. Do you concur?"

"Yes, I do. You are."

"Then if I believe you can do a job, know that you can do it."

[]

Friday, September 27, 2013. Atlanta International Airport.

Miranda arrives in 'baggage claim' to find a well dressed man standing nearby, holding a sign which reads: "M. Powers." She greets him and he retrieves her bags and escorts her to the waiting navy blue Rolls Royce at the curbside outside.

"Oh, my," she chuckles to the driver, "I've never ridden in a Rolls Royce before!"

He smiles and nods, as he opens the rear door, "There is a first time for everything, madam."

"Oh!" she gasps as she enters the vehicle. "I didn't expect to see anyone *else* in here."

"Well, it is *my* car," Chasm smiles warmly, "As my valued guest, I wanted to surprise you and make sure you received stellar treatment and accommodations."

They shake hands as he gently pulls her hand up to his lips. "Having you here is a… delight."

Miranda blushes and slowly pulls her hand away, with a smile gracing her lips, "I will admit, you are *very* charming."

"I have arranged for us to have dinner now, followed by a tour of my headquarters so you can see where your son works. Then I will drop you off at your hotel. Tomorrow, you can surprise Curtis."

"Sounds like a nice plan to me."

"I'm glad you agree. Off we go!" The car's engine quietly purrs to life as the automobile speeds off from the curb and heads downtown towards the restaurant.

[]

Powers Residence. New York.

"What do you mean she's not here?" Jim asks, as he and Omar stand at the open door talking to each other.

"She flew down to Atlanta," Omar replies. "You're more than welcome to come in and hang out, if you want." Omar steps back as Jim enters.

"So, she went to visit Curtis?" he asks, while plopping on the couch.

"She's gonna surprise him tomorrow. But actually, she went down at the invitation of Mr. Montgomery."

"Really?" he exclaims, while jumping up from his seat. "Is that wise? Why didn't she tell me?"

"I don't know, but she's trying to get more information about what may really be going on with the life insurance policy. Apparently, Curtis saw a picture of Mr. Montgomery with John Whaley in his office. That's enough to spark some curiosity about the connection."

"So, she went by herself?"

"She didn't want to cause any suspicion. Believe me, I'm not happy about it either, but you know how my mom can get."

"Yeah," Jim hesitates. "Listen, there's something you need to know."

"What is it?"

"Your brother and I… we got into a spat the other day."

"Arguments happen," Omar shrugs. "That's a part of life."

"True," Jim concedes. "But that was the first time your brother *ever* raised his voice at me."

"What? Curtis? You're kidding right?"

"I couldn't believe it either. But it happened."

"So, what caused it?"

"I should let him tell you. Maybe you can talk some sense into him."

"Mr. G. What happened?"

"He and Chasm's assistant—Erica," Jim takes a deep breath while shaking his head, "they… kissed."

"Oh, man," Omar exclaims! "*That's* not good! Not good at all!"

"I think it only happened once, but that's really one time too many!"

"Kelly is going to kill him."

"That's if he tells her."

[]

Upscale Restaurant. Atlanta.

Miranda and Chasm arrive and enter the classy establishment only to discover that all the tables are empty and shrouded in shadows, except one in the center of the room. A soft spotlight illuminates it from above, while three round candles float in a bowl of water in the middle of the table. Seven waiters stand at the ready in their red and black uniforms, while a quartet sits in a nearby alcove playing soft music on their stringed instruments.

"Are we the only ones here?" Miranda asks surprised. "Where are all of the people?"

Chasm's smile lingers as he holds the moment of anticipation, "I figured it would be nice if we had an evening together alone. So, I bought out the restaurant."

Some time later… as an eclectic mix of Jazz and Classical music plays softly in the distance.

"Chasm, this is one of the best meals I have had in a very long time! Thank you."

"You are very welcome. Do you mind if I ask you a question?"

"Sure."

"Please forgive my intrusion, but I've been wondering why a wonderful woman like you has not remarried."

Miranda sits quietly as she contemplates her answer.

"I'm sorry," Chasm recants, "You don't have to answer that."

"No, I'm fine," she exhales. "I guess… well, I really haven't had time to pursue any romantic relationships. But honestly, after being married to a man like Malcolm, he was *so* kind and caring and fun-loving. He always saw the best in our boys and me. Really, any other man would be hard-pressed to measure up."

"What about you and Jim Grabowski?"

Miranda looks at Chasm with a mix of disbelief and humor. "Oh, *now* you have intruded!" she laughs."

"Alright," Chasm declares, smiling and holding his hands up in surrender, " I'm backing up now. Strike that from the record!"

"Too late!" Miranda yells as they both laugh. "Jim is a wonderful man. We get along very well and he is good to my boys. Right now, he's the closest thing to a plausible romantic relationship that I have—even though our relationship is not romantic."

"I see…"

"But what about you?" Miranda challenges. "Are you in a romantic relationship?"

"I am married to my work," Chasm states firmly. "I don't have time to be in a non-platonic relationship."

Miranda smiles faintly. "That's too bad."

Chasm raises his eyebrows somewhat. "Well, if I met the *right* woman, it is possible that I could make some time."

[]

Atlanta. Spelman Campus.

Curtis and Kelly get out of a taxi and walk to her dormitory.

"You've been on edge all night," Kelly presses.

"You think so?" Curtis asks.

"Yes. We played put-put golf. We went to the movies. And we ate. You were there with me, but it's like part of your mind was somewhere else."

"I'm sorry. It's just that... a lot is going on right now. I'm under a lot of pressure."

"I'm sure," Kelly agrees. She takes a hold of Curtis' hand and pulls his arm around her shoulders as they walk. "Harder classes. Omar getting better. Speedsuit runs. Gavin getting shot. Your... kidnapping. I know you're dealing with a lot. But I'm here to help. It seems like you've been holding things together up until a week or two ago. What happened that made things so much more difficult?"

They both walk in silence as she waits for an answer that never comes. Kelly stops walking and pulls away from him—searching his eyes. "Is—is it us?" Kelly asks, the tears in her eyes ready to overflow.

"No..." Curtis hesitates.

"It *is* us." Kelly utters.

"No, it's not," Curtis counters.

"You don't love me anymore?"

"Of course I love you, Kelly."

"Then what is it?" she whispers. "*Who* is it? Is there someone else?"

"The problem is *not* us," Curtis admits. "The problem is me."

"What does that even mean?" she asks, her hands flailing.

"I wish I could explain—"

"Then go ahead and explain! I thought we didn't keep secrets from each other!"

"I'm... sorry." Curtis' eyes begin swelling with tears.

"Well," Kelly declares with a mix of pain and resolve, "when you are ready to tell me what's going on—you know where to find me. But if you wait too long, I may not be here when you come to your senses." She abruptly walks to her dorm, leaving Curtis alone on the pathway to contemplate his next decision.

[]

The Montgomery Group headquarters.

Chasm gives Miranda a tour of his empire.

"So, this is your headquarters," Miranda says. "I'm very impressed."

"Thank you," Chasm replies. "These facilities consist of nine aboveground buildings sitting on 12 acres of land. And I have several offices in New York and a number of divisions overseas."

"So," Miranda queries, "how does it feel to have all of this?"

"How does it feel? This allows me to make an impact on the world."

"No," Miranda counters, "*how* do you feel? I mean, you were abandoned by your biological parents, were placed in foster care, weren't adopted until you were 16 and now you run a multi-national company that's worth billions of dollars! You are the perfect example of a quintessential 'rags to riches story.' How does that make you *feel*?"

Chasm smiles as they both walk to one of his private elevators. The door opens as the female voice speaks: "Welcome Dr. Montgomery."

"Wow," Miranda laughs. "The elevator talks!"

"They all do," Chasm chuckles, "But only my private elevators are programmed to say my name whenever I enter them for the first time each day."

"It's a nice touch." Miranda nods as they enter and Chasm puts his hand on the palm scanner before pressing the penthouse button. The elevator doors close and a slight acceleration is felt as it begins to rise.

"Back to your original question. I feel... fortunate. Yes, this *does* excite me. But I can honestly say sometimes the excitement is smothered by the sheer weight of what is required to oversee my company. Early in my career, I could get my hands dirty trying to build whatever my mind could conceive. I love inventing and innovation! Now, I still have ideas swirling around in my head, but I have to delegate them to my team—a *very talented* team, but a team nonetheless. I receive reports on progress while having to be increasingly focused on the bigger picture. The tremendous mental energy it takes to manage all of the moving parts of an organization… It can be exhausting at times."

"Private Penthouse Level," the female elevator voice declares. The doors open and they step out into a short corridor. The lights blink to life as Miranda is taken by what she sees and hears.

"Oh, my," she says while covering her gaping mouth with her hands. "This is… beautiful."

Before her is an entire open-level apartment, the floors and walls adorned with the latest and most exquisite materials and interior designs. Six-foot high windows outline its perimeter.

"*This* area makes it easier for me to cope with my isolation."

"I can see how this would be helpful!" Miranda agrees. "So, this is where you live?"

"This is the main place where I live," Chasm replies. I do have a house across town and several vacation homes around the world, but I spend most of my time working out of this building. So, it's helpful to have this space. I have all of the accoutrements of a luxury apartment, including a private office and workspace."

"So, you hold your meetings here in your private office?"

"Some of them. The rest are held in my company offices on this building's executive level."

"So, when you had the science competition and Curtis was a guest judge, which office was he in?"

"The one on this level. Why do you ask?"

"Oh, he told me how nice your office was—along with every other inch of this facility," she laughs.

"Well then," Chasm leads the way, "let me show it to you." A moment later, Miranda finds herself standing in front of a wall full of photographs from all over the world. Chasm checks his messages while she scans the wall. *Here it is. The photo Curtis told me about.*

"Wow," she whispers.

"What is it?" Chasm inquires.

"Do you believe in six degrees of separation?"

"Yes. I do believe if a person looks closely enough, they will find that they are six people away from someone they want to meet. In some cases, even less. Why do you ask?"

"Because, in this picture you are standing with one of the founding partners of the firm where my husband used to work before he died."

"Really?" Chasm asks while approaching to look for himself.

"Yes," Miranda confirms. "You are standing next to John Whaley. That is an amazing coincidence."

"It is. Sometimes the world is smaller than we think."

"So, how do you know him?"

"Well," Chasm smiles while pointing at the photo. "That's me —when I was much younger. And this distinguished gentleman to the right of me is my adopted father, James. On the other side stands John Whaley. My father and Mr. Whaley had known each other for years and collaborated on numerous business ventures. And he was one of the first investors for the firm."

"How often do you see Mr. Whaley?" Miranda queries.

"Not much, since my adoptive parents died when I was in college. We talk from time-to-time, perhaps two to three times a year for birthdays, Thanksgiving, Hanukkah and Christmas."

This does sound like a plausible story, Miranda ponders. *But what if there's more to his story than what he is telling me?* "Well, again, you have a wonderful office and headquarters," Miranda smiles broadly. "I can see why Curtis likes working with you."

"Thank you, Miranda," Chasm smiles. "And speaking of your son, I would like for you to encourage him to take full advantage of his college opportunities. As you know, good things work—when you work them."

"Yes, they do," Miranda utters, as an unexpected yawns escapes.

"It's late. I should get you to your hotel."

"Thank you, Chasm. I *am* a bit tired."

"It's been a long day and you need your rest. Tomorrow you get to surprise your son."

"I am looking forward to it."

With that, Chasm leads Miranda to his car and arranges for his driver to take her to her hotel.

[]

The next day…

Curtis arrives at his workstation and walks into his office.

"Surprise!!!" Miranda yells, rising from Curtis' chair.

"Mom!" he jumps back while grabbing his chest. "You scared me!"

"You should have seen the look on your face!" Miranda laughs as she gives her son a big hug. Curtis laughingly shakes his head as they sit down.

"What are you doing here?"

"I was in town for some business and wanted to surprise you!"

"Well, you sure did!"

"So, how are you doing?"

The office door opens.

"Curtis—" Erica says as she abruptly walks into his office, "—Oh, hello Ms. Powers. I didn't realize you were here." Erica glances at Curtis.

"Hello Erica," Miranda beams. "I was in town and wanted to make a surprise visit. How are you?"

"I'm fine, thank you for asking," Erica smiles. "How are you?"

"I am well, thank you," Miranda nods. "I don't want to keep you two from your work."

"Oh, no," Curtis interjects, "you're fine, Mom."

"Yes, Ms. Powers," Erica adds. "Spend time with your son. I can come back later." Erica smiles and quickly leaves, closing the door behind her.

"She seems like a nice young lady," Miranda states matter-of-factly.

"Yeah," Curtis utters while trying not to sound nervous. "She is."

Miranda turns towards her son. "So, how are you and Kelly doing?"

"We're… not doing too well," Curtis admits.

"Oh, no. What's the problem?"

"We got into a fight—well more like a disagreement."

"About what?"

"Mom, I don't want to talk about it," Curtis shrugs.

"Curtis, I'm your mother. What could be so bad that you can't tell me? It's not like you're cheating on her," Miranda laughs.

Curtis glares at his mother. "Mr. G told you?" he shouts.

"Told me what?" Miranda replies. "And don't raise your voice at me like that!"

"He didn't tell you?" Curtis asks, in a more controlled fashion.

"I haven't spoken to Jim, so I have no idea what… you… are…"

Miranda gasps. "Wait. You—you and Erica?"

"Is it *that* obvious?" Curtis groans.

"You are cheating on Kelly with Erica? Why?"

"I'm not *cheating* on Kelly, Mom!" Curtis half whispers as he glances at the door and back. "Erica kissed me."

"And what did you do?" Miranda probes.

"I… I stopped her," Curtis hesitates, "eventually."

"So, she kissed you and you didn't stop her right away," Miranda states flatly.

Curtis nods his head.

"And what did Kelly say about this?" Curtis looks away. "You haven't told her?" Miranda concludes.

"No…"

"So, you two got into a fight because she knows something is up, but doesn't know what exactly?" Curtis nods his head. "Ok," Miranda gives her son a big hug. "Listen baby. You need to tell Kelly what happened."

"No," Curtis pulls away. "I don't have to tell her."

"Curtis, your father and I didn't raise you like this. A girl kissed you. It's not your fault. But if you don't tell Kelly, then it *becomes* your fault."

"I don't want to talk about this anymore."

"You like Erica, don't you?" Curtis sits quietly. "I get it. She's an older woman who is amazingly attractive. And, from what I gather, she is just as smart as you, if not smarter. I can see why you would be interested in her."

"Mom, I said I don't want to talk about it," Curtis states in an increasingly forceful tone.

"Fine," Miranda snaps back. "*I'll* talk and *you* listen! There will always be women who are more attractive than Kelly. And there will *always* be men who are more attractive to Kelly than you. That's a given. What matters is that you and Kelly have made a *commitment* to each other and that you have been through so much together."

"You don't think I know that, Mom?" Curtis shouts.

"Curtis!"

"No, Mom! Please. Just stop! You don't think I know how hard this is? You don't think I know how much Kelly has been there in my life and how much she loves me? I do! And you and Mr. G beating me over the head isn't helping me!"

"I'm not *beating* you over the head, Son! And I'm sure Jim isn't either. It's just sometimes, we need to be *reminded* about the good things we already have."

"I don't need to be reminded. I love Kelly."

Miranda looks at her son as she picks up her bag and jacket. "I know you are frustrated. But I don't appreciate your attitude." She walks to the door and opens it. "Curtis," she speaks resolutely, "if you really love Kelly... then you will tell her the truth." With that, Miranda walks out of the room and leaves Curtis to his thoughts.

CHAPTER EIGHT

BREAKING UP IS HARD TO DO

CURTIS SITS AT HIS DESK IN his dorm room, caught in the throes of his homework. He growls, yet again, as he crumbles up another sheet of paper and throws it into the growing pile in his garbage can. His cell phone rings. He picks it up and looks at the caller ID. He puts it back down and rubs his tired eyes. After the fifth ring—just before the phone's voicemail kicks in—he answers it.

"Hey Omar," Curtis utters.

"What's up, Bro? How you doing?"

"I'm trying to do my homework. It's Sunday afternoon and I'm still not done," he grunts.

"Sounds like you're frustrated," Omar replies.

"I am!" Curtis snaps.

"Maybe," Omar says, with a bit more force, "you're problem *isn't* your homework."

"So, what's my problem, then?" Curtis retorts.

"You know what? If I was there right now, I'd knock that attitude of yours right out your mouth."

"Sorry..." Curtis huffs.

"Don't be sorry," Omar replies. "Just fix your attitude."

"Easy for you to say."

"Look. This is gonna keep eating away at you until you tell Kelly about Erica."

"Does the *whole* world know about this now?" Curtis huffs. "Who told you? Mom?"

"No. Mr. G told me. And by the way, mom made it back safely this morning. Thanks for your consideration."

"Sorry. I've been busy. Glad she made it back."

"And she *did* tell me you two had an argument."

"Yeah."

"Curtis, this is not like you. Yelling at mom and Mr. G is not cool and keeping this situation from Kelly is definitely not cool. You owe mom and Mr. G an apology. And you need to talk to Kelly."

"If I tell her, she'll kill me!"

"If you don't—and she finds out—her killing you will be the least of your problems. Which do you prefer?"

"The part where she doesn't kill me."

"Be a man, Curtis. Tell Kelly what happened and let the chips fall where they may."

[]

A few hours later…

Curtis and Kelly walk through the quad on the campus of her school. They see an empty bench and decide to sit.

"Thanks for agreeing to meet me," he nervously makes eye contact.

Kelly nods without breaking her stare. "Why wouldn't I meet you? What is going on that's got you so nervous?" Curtis rubs his sweaty hands shakily over his jeans a few times as he takes a deep breath.

"What I have to tell you is not easy."

"I already know that," Kelly replies firmly. "That's why you've waited weeks to get to this point. So, just tell me already!"

"Erica and I—she kissed me."

"You kissed her?"

"No, she kissed me!"

"Did you stop her?"

"Not… immediately."

"So you kissed her back!"

"I did not!"

"But, you didn't stop her." Kelly's eyes reveal her disappointment.

"She caught me off guard!" Curtis mutters. "Can't we work this out?"

"Maybe," Kelly hesitates, "maybe we should take a break for a while."

"Don't do this," Curtis whispers.

"No," Kelly counters. "I need time to think. *You* need time to think."

"There's nothing to think about. You are the one I want."

"If that were true, you would have told me right after it happened."

"I thought," Curtis struggles to find his words, "I thought you'd kill me. I was afraid."

"That may be true," Kelly admits. "But did you ever stop to think that *my* hurt would be more important to deal with than your fear?"

"…No." Curtis stares at the ground.

Kelly glares into the distance as she stands to her feet, "Was it crazy for us to think we could make it this far?"

Curtis stands up behind her, "Don't do this." He takes her hand in his. "I'm sorry."

"I know," she says as she pulls away from him. She then faces him, forces a smile and kisses him on his cheek. "Erica seems to be everything you want. She's absolutely gorgeous… And she's a prodigy like you. And me? I'm just a dancer. I can't compete with her."

"Kelly, don't—" Curtis tries to hold her hand.

"No!" she commands while pulling away from him, "One of us has to be strong enough to admit that maybe this is as far as we go." With tears in her eyes she hugs him. For what seems like forever, with eyes full of tears, he hugs her back.

"Goodbye Curtis." Kelly lets go and pushes away from the young man she's loved for the last four years. Curtis silently watches as she runs down the walkway, back to her dormitory.

CHAPTER NINE

FLYING HIGH!

A STRING OF BLUE MEDICAL BENCHES line one side of the room. Various pieces of exercise equipment rests on the other. A skeletal sculpture hangs from a rack, right next to human anatomy posters on the wall. Omar puts his shirt back on and hops off one of the medical benches as months of grueling physical therapy have now ended.

"Omar," the physical therapist states while checking off boxes on her clipboard, "This is your last session. Your doctor and specialist have cleared you. You have officially made a full recovery!"

"That is great news!" Omar smiles widely. "Thanks so much, Laura. If it weren't for you... You gave me my life back."

"I'm glad I could help. Just make sure you keep doing your exercises so you can keep your back strong. That will also aid with your alignment."

"You got it!" He exclaims while giving Laura a big bear hug.

Omar leaves the therapy office and takes the narrow elevator down to the first floor. As he exits the building and walks up 72nd Street, he retrieves his cell phone from his pocket and makes a call.

"What up, O?" A voice shouts from the other end.

"Quade!" Omar replies. "How have you been?"

"Good, man. Giving everybody a run for their money!"

"You better behave! Those hospital nurses are no joke!"

Both men laugh.

"I appreciate you, man?" Quade admits. "You call every week: same day, same time."

"Someone has to make sure you stay outta trouble," Omar chuckles.

"So, you're good?" Quade inquires.

"Yep!" Omar smiles. "Just got a clean bill of health!"

"That's awesome! I just had my last skin graft over the weekend. Been cooped up in this hospital for months, can't believe I'm finally going to be going home soon."

"I'm happy for you, bro."

"Omar?"

"Don't say it, Quade. You say it every time."

"And I'm going to keep saying it. If it wasn't for you, I would be dead. I owe you my life. Any time. Any place. You call me and I'm there."

"Thanks bro. Same here. You know that."

"I should have listened to you. Then we both wouldn't be in this mess."

"What's done is done. You have to let the regrets go; otherwise you won't be able to move forward with your life."

Quade sits quietly, "My discharge papers are comin' soon."

Omar arrives at the top of the subway stairs, "Mine too. Listen, I'm about to go underground. Will talk with you later?"

"Hopefully, when you call next week, they'll tell you I'm not here."

[]

University of California, Berkeley…

Treyshawn's art class has just ended. He's staying behind to continue working on his drawings. His phone rings—but the number comes up PRIVATE.

"Hello?" Treyshawn utters hesitantly.

"Hey Trey," a familiar voice replies.

"Dad?"

"Yeah, it's me."

"Wow," Treyshawn places his drawing pencil down, "I didn't expect you to call me."

"Yeah. I just wanted—I wanted to say—when you come home, it would be great if you could... visit."

"So you could punch me again?"

"Sorry about that," Treyshawn Sr. chuckles. "This... is all new to me."

"Mom said you did that to save face."

"She's right. I did."

"Do you have to 'save face' every time I come? Cause if you do—I won't be coming that much."

Treyshawn Sr. laughs. "No. Just that one time."

"Good," Treyshawn chuckles, "then I guess I'll come by for a visit."

"Great... Enjoy your day little man."

"You too, Dad."

[]

A few days later...

A private jet streaks across the morning sky. Chasm and Curtis head out to the Midwest again. Very little conversation takes place as Chasm is engrossed in virtual meetings and Curtis is engrossed in homework. Once they arrive in Colorado, Chasm gets into one car and Curtis gets into another. Both drive off to their separate destinations.

[]

Curtis sits at the cold table as Justin and Amanda are brought from their cells.

"Hey, Curtis!" Justin and Amanda exclaim. "How are you?"

"Hey guys," Curtis smiles warmly as they sit and shake hands. "It's good to see you two!"

"It's great to see you," Justin states. "How's life on the outside?"

"Yeah," Amanda inquires, "especially since the kidnapping."

"Life is… OK," Curtis states flatly. "But I didn't come here to talk about me. I wanted to see how you both were doing."

"We are holding it together," Amanda responds.

"Yeah," Justin agrees. "It's still tough, but we just take things one day at a time."

"Our case was moved up," Amanda shares. "We are going to trial sooner than we expected."

"Good," Curtis says. "It means you'll get to tell your story while these issues are still at the forefront of everybody's mind."

"You know who came by to see us?" Justin grins.

Curtis shakes his head, "Who?"

"Chad."

"Really?" Curtis exclaims.

"Yes. Really." Justin replies. "His dad and his attorney told him not to do it. But he came anyway."

"He actually apologized to us," Amanda smiles. "He actually said he was *sorry* for everything he did."

"What about his girlfriend?" Curtis asks.

"They're not together anymore," Justin replies.

"I know what *that* feels like," Curtis mutters under his breath.

"What'd you say?"

"Nothing. Nothing worth repeating."

"You know, there's a lot of people who are against us," Justin says, "but I feel like now there's also a lot of people who are *for* us."

"Yeah," Amanda adds. "We keep getting mail from all over the country. Even around the world!"

"Mostly from people who've been bullied for years and survived. They're hoping our situation will raise awareness and lead to real change."

"That is the hope," Curtis smiles. "*Real* change."

[]

Chasm's private jet streaks across the evening sky. The golden-red sun sits partially on the horizon as its rays glisten across the ocean waves—creating the illusion of a moving walkway on the water.

Curtis stares out the window, "We've never gone over the ocean."

Chasm smiles, "We've taken a slightly different flight path because I have a surprise for you."

"What is it?"

"Buckle your seatbelt."

"Oh, no. Not maneuver 66?" Curtis says while putting on his seatbelt.

"No, my boy!" Chasm laughs. "Something much better!" Chasm presses the intercom and speaks. "Pilot. Prepare for LEO maneuver."

"Yes, Sir," the pilot replies. "Sixty seconds until LEO maneuver."

"LEO?" Curtis questions.

"Remember I told you this jet had several modifications?"

"Yes."

"And remember I told you I've been in Low Earth Orbit?"

Curtis' eyes open wide at the realization, "Low Earth Orbit... L.E.O."

Chasm nods his head in delight as he motions towards the window. Curtis looks out just in time to see the wings sweep back into a Delta configuration. He hears a rumbling underneath his seat—coming from the belly of the plane.

"What's that noise?"

"Those are the RAM jets deploying," Chasm shouts as the turbo jets scream.

Curtis is forced into his seat as the plane's acceleration increases tremendously in an upward arc trajectory. The jet rockets into the sky at an almost 90-degree angle. Curtis screams as the aircraft spins before leveling off at a 45-degree angle. The RAM jets engage—propelling the jet even faster! Several sonic booms explode as the g-forces pulling on everyone's body intensify! Curtis strains to look out the window, his eyes squinting from the sunlight. Just then he notices the slight curvature of the earth's surface. Suddenly, the g-forces diminish.

"Whoa," Curtis mutters, "This *feels* strange!"

Chasm smiles as he reaches into his pocket and pulls out a pen. He holds it up for Curtis to see and then lets it go. To Curtis' amazement, the pen doesn't fall to the desk, but rather it floats effortlessly in front of them, spinning slowly around its axis.

"No, way…" Curtis whispers with tremendous excitement.

"You can take your seatbelt off now." Chasm releases his restraints and begins to float as Curtis cautiously disengages his belt buckle. He slowly rises out of his seat and begins to float around the airplane's cabin with Chasm and the two flight attendants.

"Look at me!" Curtis yells as he takes a classic 'superhero-flying pose.' "I'm flying!"

"Technically you're not," Chasm laughs as he floats on his back with his arms behind his head. "But this sure does *feel* like flying!"

Curtis stares out the window again and can clearly see the curvature of the earth, as well as the stars with such naked clarity. "The stars… the moon… they all look so clear," Curtis says in an awed tone.

"We're above the atmosphere," Chasm replies. "There's nothing to obstruct your view."

"Wow…" Curtis floats in front of the window. It's then that he notices the wings and other parts of the plane's fuselage. Small bursts emanate from several nozzles—seeming to control the direction and rotation of the plane. "Are you serious?" Curtis yells.

"You saw the thrust nozzles," Chasm chuckles. "We are so high up, there is not enough air for aerodynamic control of our aircraft. So, we have to use directional thrusters, similar to what the space shuttle or the space station uses. And just in case you're wondering, we are able to breathe, because the entire cabin has its own pressurized air supply."

"People are paying thousands of dollars for the chance to get into low earth orbit," Curtis replies. "And you're already doing it!"

Chasm smiles at Curtis' comment. "I am happy to say the technology my company is developing is at minimum—ten years —ahead of anything other similar companies are doing. We are leading the way into a new and bright future."

Several minutes pass as they float around the cabin, trying a variety of acrobatic maneuvers before the time comes for them to restrain themselves in their chairs again. The pilot begins his decent, as the pen floats in front of Curtis' face. Suddenly, it drops to the desk and rolls across the surface.

"There's a lesson in that," Chasm shares as he grabs the pen with two of his fingers, "…in this entire experience."

"What is it?"

"The higher you go in life, the more clearly you can see. The more you can do. *Down there…* gravity says when you let the pen go, it falls. *Down there* says, when you try to look around, the haze clouds your vision. But *up here* you can see everything. *Up here* you can fly. *Up here*, when you let the pen go… it floats."

Curtis nods his head in agreement.

"It takes a lot of energy to get up here," Chasm continues. "You have to pull away from everything that's trying to keep you down and hold you back. Some things are good and helpful when you are on that lower level. But when you finally get up here these things no longer matter. And it also takes less energy to stay up here. The question is Curtis, 'where do you want to be?'"

CHAPTER TEN

LIFE-CHANGE

OCTOBER 2013. CLAMILLE RUSHES ACROSS CAMPUS to get to her next class. Her face wrinkles as she struggles to carry her book bag—filled to the brim—and her class project—a model made out of cardboard. In her haste, one of her sandals slip off—causing her to trip and fall. Her books and project crash to the ground as a group of students move about in front of her, but no one stops long enough to help her up. As she scrambles to her feet and the crowd parts, she sees him—standing thirty feet in front of her. Clamille stumbles backwards as Tyreese slowly approaches her.

"You're not supposed to be here," Clamille yells. "How did you get past security?"

"I guess security isn't as secure as you think," Tyreese quips as he stands still. "I came to say 'hey' is all. Just wanted you to know that I was back and that I'm thinking about you."

"Well, I'm *not* thinking about you!" Clamille replies forcefully. "You need to leave—now."

Tyreese throws his hands up in surrender as he slowly backs away. "Whatever you want, baby. Whatever you want."

"I'm not your baby!"

"Alright. But I still love you. See you, Clamille."

"If I see you again, I'm callin' the cops!"

Tyreese saunters away, leaving Clamille shaken and afraid.

[]

Bronx. Rikers Island Prison.

Treyshawn Sr. and two inmates sit around a table in the prison yard. Three others guard them as the rest of the inmate population are engaged in other activities.

"So, we still movin' on this, T-Rock?" Tyrone asks in his gruff voice.

"Put too much into this plan to punk out."

"Months of planning. Sneaking supplies. Gaining people's trust. You betta not back out."

"What makes you think I'mma back out?" Treyshawn Sr. growls. "Don't forget who you talkin' to."

"I ain't forgot. I just know your son been around a lot lately. Wouldn't want him to change your mind."

"Don't you worry about my son. You just make sure you got your stuff together. Ten more months and we'll be free."

"Still don't know why we got to wait so long."

"I keep telling you, Tyrone. Strategy. This ain't no sprint. This ain't even a marathon. This right here... is a triathlon. We gotta take our time with this and wait for the right moment to execute."

[]

University of California, Berkeley.

Students pack up their sketchpads and drawing utensils as class ends. Professor Melody shuffles through the studio, handing out envelopes.

"As you all know," Prof. Melody advises, "the Art and Design department is putting on its annual student art gallery. All of you will have the opportunity to present one-to-two pieces. This year's theme for the gallery is: Life-Change."

The class breaks into lively chatter as she continues speaking.

"Myself and the other professors," she yells, "have determined where each student's work will be placed. Some of you show much promise, and as a result you have been given a more prominent space to showcase 3 pieces of your art."

The class conversation increases exponentially.

"These letters will give you all of the pertinent details."

Envelopes are ripped open as each student looks for their presentation spot. Treyshawn feels a double tap on his shoulder and turns to find Angel smirking at him as he holds up his envelope's contents.

"Sorry you won't be showcasing three pieces as I will be."

Treyshawn smiles widely as he holds up his paper: "Priority Display Section. Three pieces."

"Prof. Melody must be blind if she let you in," Angel scoffs.

"Blind or not, I'm in," Treyshawn counters. "But you surely must have been a mistake. I should go talk to her right now."

Angel pushes Treyshawn away.

"Don't get mad," Treyshawn laughs. "You started!"

"Whatever," he huffs—with a slight smile—as he walks away.

Treyshawn shakes his head, packs his bag and heads for the door as the other students exit the room. He strolls slowly down the hallway. *This is one of the biggest opportunities I've ever had,* he thinks to himself. I don't even know where to start. As he exits the building and walks into bright sunlight, he stops and gazes at his long shadow. *I got it,* he thinks to himself, *I will create three pieces that represent my life journey.*

CHAPTER ELEVEN

CAPITALIZING

MIRANDA CLOSES THE MAILBOX AND WALKS back inside her house with a large stack of envelopes. She flips through each at the living room table and sorts them into four piles: one for her, for Omar, for Curtis and for the trash. Omar comes down the stairs in jeans and his usual tank top, while drying his face with a towel.

"Do you feel fresh?" Miranda asks.

"Yeah. Glad I finished mowing the yard. Even more glad to shower!"

"Here," Miranda chuckles as she hands Omar his pile. "I'm glad too. Your aroma was very strong."

"Hey!" Omar laughs as he checks the envelopes.

"An envelope from the navy came in."

"Yeah," Omar agrees as he just gets to the certified mail.

"What is it?"

Omar opens the packet and reads the cover letter.

"These are my discharge papers."

"Your discharge papers?"

"Because of the accident, the length of my recovery, and the time I've already invested, they are giving me an honorable discharge."

"My baby is home for good?" Miranda asks as tears fill her eyes.

"Looks that way," Omar smiles broadly. "Still some final things to wrap up, but yeah—looks like I'm home for good!"

Miranda hugs her firstborn son.

Atlanta. The Montgomery Group facilities.

"What do you mean there is a problem?" Chasm grimaces.

"Well," Dr. Hitachi stutters. "Yesterday the preliminary results on the Mach-2 operational system came back favorable. But today, for some reason, the suit won't power up and the power cells keep overheating."

Erica watches quietly, while holding her tablet.

"I suggest you figure out the reason for the issue and get it working," Chasm replies. "If there was a problem, you should have notified me *before* I came all the way down here. Time is money. And your money is about to be docked for wasting my time."

"U-understood Sir," Dr. Hitachi mutters as the others work feverishly to figure out the problem. "Perhaps its just a loose connection or a circuit board that shorted out."

"We will return in five minutes, in case it is a simple problem to fix." Chasm turns abruptly and walks out as Erica tries to catch up with him.

"We have created Warsuit exoskeletons without so much as a hiccup," Chasm vents, "but now we try to replicate and enhance Curtis' Speedsuit and there is a problem? If my plan is to succeed, this suit has to work!"

"I'm sure the engineers will figure it out," Erica attempts to comfort her boss. "You know, it's easy to make mistakes when you're tired. I checked the engineers' time sheets. It's been a while since any of them have had a vacation. They could just be overdue for some R&R."

"You know," Chasm says as he stops and turns towards Erica, "you could be right. Fire them."

"Chasm!" Erica shouts.

"I'm just kidding," he laughs. "After they get the suit working and everything checks out, give them a two-week vacation. I want them at their peak efficiency. Come, let's go back inside."

Chasm and Erica enter the lab again.

"Is it working?" Chasm asks.

"I'm s-sorry, Sir. We still haven't figured out the issue."

"Fine. Erica will examine the suit. Everyone else, leave your equipment right where it is and take an immediate two-week vacation."

The engineers all look at each other warily.

"No. This is not a joke," Chasm responds, "and you are not being fired. Take the next two weeks to rejuvenate yourselves and we will come back to this with a fresh slate. Erica will lock up after you've left."

[]

Chasm enters his private elevator as his cell phone rings and announces the name of the caller in his earpiece. He smiles as he accepts the call.

"Curtis!"

"Hi Chasm!"

"How are you doing today?"

"Good!"

"Hold on one second."

The elevator stops as it announces, "Top floor. Penthouse Suite." Chasm enters his apartment, while removing his suit jacket.

"Now, to what do I owe this call?"

"It's been days and I'm still dreaming about the LEO flight!"

Chasm laughs heartily, "That's my boy! I'm glad you liked it!"

"Liked it?" Curtis exclaims. "I loved it! That was the most amazing thing I've ever done! The feeling of freedom… it was awesome."

"So, you called to share that with me?"

"Uh, yeah. And just to say hello. I got out of class a little while ago and just came from the cafeteria. Sorry if I interrupted anything."

"No need to be sorry," Chasm replies. "If you *had* interrupted something, I would have told you."

"So, anything exciting going on today?"

"Not at the moment. I had hoped to see the unveiling of a new project, but my engineers ran into some technical difficulties."

"Do you want me to take a look?"

"No. Not yet. I have Erica going over everything with a fine-tooth comb. But when it's ready, I definitely want you to see it."

"What's the project?"

"Sorry. You'll have to wait. But, how's your young lady friend doing?"

"Kelly?"

"Yes. Kelly."

"Well," Curtis hesitates, "we're taking a break for a while."

"I'm sorry to hear that. Did something happen?"

"We just don't see eye to eye on some things."

"Well, if there's anything I can do, do not hesitate to let me know. And if Erica can help you in any way, feel free to call her."

"Uh, thank you. I'll keep that in mind."

"Good. Anything else going on in your life that I should know about?"

"I did get a letter from a Children's Research Hospital. They invited me to visit their kids as Jetstream."

"That's wonderful!"

"I still have to work out the particulars to determine the event date."

"Excellent. Let me know as soon as you have one. I will make sure the media is present to capture everything."

"That's cool, but I don't care if the media is present. What matters are the kids."

"That's all well and good, Curtis. But you should care about both."

"But I'm not doing this for the media."

"No. You are helping to inspire children and bring fun, hope and joy to their lives. I know that. The media needs to see that side of you, so the world can know it, too. It's about building your brand. In this day and age, if an event is not recorded, then it didn't happen."

"The kids, their parents and doctors will know it happened. That's good enough for me."

"Then you focus on them and let me focus on the media. You already have a brand, Curtis. We are simply capitalizing on this to help build and solidify your brand in the *minds* of the populace. It's your brand that serves to help connect people to you and you to people. It's your brand that has opened up countless opportunities for you to speak and do exhibition runs across the country and half-way around the globe. It's your brand that presents what you do to the world in a cohesive package for their consideration. And it's your brand which draws people who want to invest in what you create."

"Well," Curtis muses, "when you put it like that..."

"Don't worry. There won't be a media frenzy at the children's hospital. You can focus on the children and their families. They get what they want. We get what we want. Everybody wins."

"I guess..."

"Trust me on this, Curtis. I've been handling public relations for a very long time."

"OK. We can do things your way."

"Excellent. As soon as you pick a date, let me know. In the meantime, I'll have Erica begin to put things in place for the event."

[]

New York. Westchester.

Jim Grabowski sits at his work desk. Sparks bounce off of his protective gloves, clothing and goggles as he grinds down a piece of metal. He stops for a moment, takes his gloves off, removes his goggles and wipes his face with a rag. After taking a gulp of water, he prepares to continue.

RING. RING.

Jim answers. "Hello Curtis. How are you today?"

"I'm good," Curtis hesitates. "How are you?"

"Well!" Jim exclaims. "Just working on a metal wind-chime project for my back yard."

"Okay. Sorry to bother you. I can call back."

"You are never a bother, Curtis. I was just taking a break. What's up?"

"First, I wanted to say… I'm sorry."

Jim smiles, "I appreciate your apology. I know relationships can be hard sometimes."

"And I did tell Kelly what happened."

"I'm proud of you. How did she respond?"

"We're kind of taking a break for a little while."

"I'm sorry to hear that."

"She said she couldn't compete with Erica. She said we both needed some time to determine what we really wanted. She said she loves me, but the real decision is on me."

"So, what are you going to do?"

"I don't know. I mean I love Kelly. But she's right. I have to be sure about what I want. But that's not why I called you."

"No? OK, what's up?"

"I wanted to talk about the letter from the Children's Hospital. Are you still willing to help pull that event together?"

"Of course I am! But we'll need to talk with your mother about it."

"OK. I'll call her. And then we can pick some potential dates."

[]

New York. Bronx. Powers Residence.

"Hello?" Miranda says while sweeping through the living room.

"Hey Mom!"

"Well if it's not my 'number two' Son."

"Do you have a minute?"

"Sure," Miranda replies while putting her broom down. "What's up?"

"I just spoke to Mr. G about the children's hospital. We need to set a date and work out the logistics."

"First, we need to discuss our last conversation."

"Yeah. Mom. I'm sorry for yelling at you. I was frustrated and scared. I did talk to Kelly. We are taking a break so we can figure things out."

"I am sorry to hear that, Son."

"Me, too."

"Even though it hurts, it is better to be honest. Then you can deal with the real issues instead of hiding from them."

"I guess."

"There's no guessing about it."

"So, can you tell me why you came down to Atlanta? What business were you on?"

CHAPTER TWELVE

AS A CHILD...

THE OCTOBER AIR IS CRISP ON this beautiful Saturday morning. Puffy white cumulus clouds punctuate the clear blue sky as the sunlight warmly bathes everything in its reach. Hundreds of children stare out of their hospital windows with eager smiles as the Team Speedsuit Powers RV pulls up in the circular driveway. The kids brim with growing anticipation as the back door of the vehicle opens and Jetstream steps onto the pavement. Loud cheers rumble through the facility as kids clap and scream with joy.

"He's here! He's here!" becomes the chant that fills the hallways as the children hurriedly make their way to the meeting hall. The media populates the outside area as well as the inner hallways, capturing every moment and expression of adoration.

"Do you hear that?" Jim says, as he, Omar and Miranda exit the vehicle. They stop to listen to the children's voices.

"You can even hear them from outside!" Curtis exclaims.

"Simply beautiful," Miranda replies.

"Too bad Gavin couldn't be here to see this," Jim says.

"Yeah," Curtis agrees. "He's still doing physical therapy."

The front doors to the hospital open as Erica leads a delegation of children and staff out to meet them. "Curtis!" Erica waves as the group approaches. Miranda, Jim and Omar look at each other and then at Curtis, who nervously responds to Erica's greeting. "Curtis," Erica continues, "I would like to introduce you to the president of the Children's Hospital."

"It's a pleasure to have you with us today, Mr. Powers," the president smiles as they both shake hands. "I am Dr. Reginald Kirkland."

"It's nice to meet you," Curtis replies.

"You have been such an inspiration to so many of the children here," the doctor continues. "I am glad you were able to come and address them."

"Thank you for the invitation!" Curtis replies. "Let me introduce you to the rest of the team."

After a moment of pleasantries, the president also introduces the children from the welcome committee. "Here we have five of our amazing and wonderful children to welcome you. This is Claire, Jonathan, Emily, Houston and Schuyler."

"Welcome!" they exclaim. "We've watched you on TV and Youtube!"

"Thank you," Curtis smiles warmly. "Today I get to watch *you*!"

"After our main event," the president continues, "we hope Team Speedsuit will be able to stay for lunch. Our Board of Trustees luncheon is today and we would love to have you as our guests."

"Sure thing," Curtis replies. "Thank you so much."

"You're welcome. Now, please," Dr. Kirkland motions as he and Erica lead the way into the hospital. "Follow us."

The children eagerly grab the hands of their visitors and escort them into the building. A moment later, they enter the massive meeting hall to the cheers of several hundred children, nurses, doctors, parents and staff. Curtis and the rest of the team wave heartily, as a plethora of pictures are taken by media and hospital personnel. Giant screens line the front of the room, each in sync with the other—displaying a variety of video footage of Curtis running in the Mach-1 Speedsuit.

"Jetstream! Jetstream! Jetstream! Jetstream!" crescendos as Curtis takes the stage with Dr. Kirkland. Dr. Kirkland raises his hands and the children almost instantly become silent. Miranda, Jim and Omar look at each other—surprised by the instant reaction of the children.

"Good morning children!" Dr. Kirkland booms in the microphone.

"Good morning Dr. Kirkland," the children scream back amidst laughs and giggles.

"As you can see," the doctor continues, "we have a real treat for you this morning."

Sporadic applause can be heard throughout the room.

"Many of you asked if we could get Curtis Powers to visit you. Now… today… here he is! I introduce to you—live and in person—Curtis Powers, aka Jetstream!!!"

The children erupt into thunderous applause again as Curtis shakes Dr. Kirkland's hand and stands in front of the microphone. He scans the room, trying to focus on every face as he takes his helmet off and wipes away tears. The applause continues for another moment before dying down.

"You're my hero!" one of the kids shouts—the declaration echoing confidently through the hall.

"Thank you," Curtis replies into the microphone, "but you all are the real heroes! Every child in this room. Everyday you are facing super-villains… viruses and other ailments attacking your own bodies. And everyday you—with an unwavering faith —summon the will to not give up. There have been times in my life when I have wanted to give up—for lesser reasons—but seeing you here this morning shows me that if you can keep going; if you can keep believing; if you can still laugh and giggle and have faith at the end of each day, then *you* are the heroes. I am honored to be here with you this morning. And I applaud you!"

Curtis begins to clap for each child as the video screens switch to display groups of children in the room. Miranda, Jim and Omar stand and clap as well. One by one, every adult in the room stands, turns towards the children and salutes them with applause. Finally, the children join in and clap as well.

"We applaud you!" Curtis declares. "You are the heroes who show us everyday what it means to believe and have hope!"

Dr. Kirkland comes back to the podium as the applause ends. "In a moment, Curtis will begin making his way to say hello to each of you. Our staff photographers will also be taking pictures so each of you will have your own photo to put in your room."

The children cheer.

"That's not all," Dr. Kirkland continues. "Team Speedsuit Powers has also donated copies of the book that was written about Curtis' life. So, each of you will receive your own signed copy!"

The children shout for joy again.

"And," Dr. Kirkland continues, "we have a presentation! I now turn the microphone over to Ms. Erica Cosway!"

"Hello children," Erica proclaims warmly as she stands at the podium. "It has been a wonderful experience to be here with you this morning. As some of you may or may not know, my boss, Chasm Montgomery, is a large supporter of this hospital and several other children's hospitals around the country. He is also one of Curtis' mentors. So, on behalf of Chasm Montgomery and Team Speedsuit Powers, I would like to present this hospital with a donation of $10 million dollars to help ensure that you not only get access to the latest medical technology and life-changing medications and procedures, but that you *also* have access to increasing levels of fun, inspirational and educational experiences!"

The children applaud as a large cardboard check is brought to the stage in full view of everyone.

"Did you know about this," Jim asks Miranda.

"No," Miranda replies with a chuckle, "I am just as surprised as the kids!"

For the next several hours, Curtis speaks, laughs and takes pictures with every child in the hospital. He also takes group photos with the parents, doctors, nurses and aids. Once the main event is over, Curtis changes out of the Mach-1 and attends the Board of Trustees luncheon.

[]

Atlanta. The Montgomery Group facilities.

"What did you discover about the Mach-2 issue," Chasm asks Erica.

"A faulty component in the receiver kept draining the power cells. Seemed to be a polarity issue. Once I replaced it, the power cells were able to hold a charge and the suit seemed to power up fine."

"Good. Schedule a demonstration the moment the engineers return from their vacation. How long did it take to determine the issue?"

"About twenty-five minutes."

"And a room full of engineers couldn't figure it out in the same amount of time. You truly are a prodigy."

"I do what I can," Erica grins.

"Speaking of that," I saw the broadcast of the children's hospital visit. You did a great job of helping to pull the media coverage together, as well as representing our company."

"Thank you," Erica replies. "It really was a great event. Curtis did a great job. And those children... They are so inspiring. I can't imagine what it's like to be in their shoes. My heart goes out to them."

"As does mine. They do teach us about having character in the midst of adversity; as well as what it means to be grateful for each moment we experience—whether good or bad. We plan for tomorrow, but tomorrow is not promised to any of us."

CHAPTER THIRTEEN

THE RIGHT STUFF!

NOVEMBER 2013. THE MONTGOMERY GROUP FACILITIES: Underground Level Two. An expansive indoor obstacle course is prepped—waiting for the first full test to begin. The 57,600 square foot course—the size of a football field—begins with a straight track, which transitions into a series of turns. The next phase of the course consists of numerous walls—all standing at various heights—the tallest being fifteen feet high. Following the walls is a series of warped ramps. Ending the course are four rising platforms, followed by a long runway leading to 500 cardboard boxes packed with high impact foam core—stacked as a precaution against an unexpected crash.

Chasm and Erica enter the arena and approach the starting block. Just off to the side, four engineers prepare to help the Mach-2 operator with the "suit up" procedure. Chasm and Erica watch as the operator zips up his black compression-undersuit and steps up to a raised platform that is surrounded by rectangular piping, spanning 6 feet wide and 12 feet high. The Mach-2 hangs—separated into its various components—on the platform, connected to the rectangular frame by restraints, hoses, and electrical cabling.

"Dr. Hitachi," Chasm calls, "I thought the Mach-2 was supposed to be designed as a single entry unit."

"It is," Dr. Hitachi replies. "Once we work out all of the deviations, the components will be connected into a single mass. Then the suit will open from the front, as designed, and the operator will be able to step into it."

"Acceptable," Chasm decides. "Continue with the process."

The boot-leg harness is the first part of the suit the operator steps into. It supports the weight of the rest of the suit. Once strapped in, the engineers lower the front and rear torso components into position. The modified Slipstream chest piece connects with the Vortex dual-nozzle thrust pack and encases the operator's abdomen and chest while attaching at several anchor points. The operator extends his arms as the engineers strap on the arm plating and connect them to the shoulder mounts. Finally, the helmet—with the faceplate open—lowers and attaches to the cowl.

The operator raises his arm and presses a button on his glove. Various indicator lights on the suit blink as a slight electrical hum is heard. The engineers open the metal framework.

"Go ahead," one of them says. "Come on down." The suit operator smiles as he hops down—a bit awkwardly. He walks around, while assuming different positions to get a feel for the suit's flexibility and range of motion.

"It's not as flexible as I remember," he says.

"We had to make some modifications since your last fitting," an engineer responds. "It needed more structural support."

With a press of a button on his glove, the electromagnetic leveraging system engages on the Kinetic Redistribution Boots. The operator jumps several times, each with increasing height. With two clicks of another button, the thrust pack fires up for three seconds and then shuts down.

"I'm ready."

"Good," Chasm smiles as he approaches. "The course is yours. Show us what the Mach-2 can do."

The operator takes his place at the starting block. The faceplate on his helmet descends and locks in place as the suit's diagnostics display on the visor. A green light at the front of the course flashes as a large horn blares. The operator launches down the track—bounding a greater distance with each step.

He quickly reaches 50 mph before engaging the Vortex thrust pack. It roars to life as he accelerates down the remainder of the long straightaway at over 75 mph. He banks through the left turn and then the right with ease—each thruster nozzle adjusting accordingly for increased maneuverability.

The engineers look at Chasm and Erica with glee. "He's doing great, Sir!" Dr. Hitachi shouts.

"Yes," Chasm smiles approvingly. "Yes, he is."

The Mach-2 leaps over each wall with ease and barrels into the warped walls—running almost perpendicular to the ground. He comes out of the warped walls, leaps across the four rising platforms and enters the final straightaway.

"Throttle it up!" Chasm bellows as the engineers relay the message.

The operator cranks up the thrusters, dials up the Electromagnetic Kinetic Redistribution Boots to seventy-five percent and accelerates down the runway at 125 mph! He crosses the finish line and engages the braking system, but the system does not respond! The group watches in horror as the Mach-2 operator screams before crashing into the impact blockade at the end of the runway!

"Unacceptable!" Chasm yells frustratedly. "Get the medics down here now!"

A siren sounds as Erica summons the medics. The group jumps into several vehicles and speeds across the track course. At the end of the runway, among mounds of high-impact foam core and cardboard boxes, they find the mangled operator pressed against the wall with the thruster still firing.

"Shut it down!" Dr. Hitachi yells, as another engineer leaps through the wreckage and tries to power the suit down.

"It won't stop!"

"Disconnect the power cables from the belt!"

After a bit of fumbling, the engineer pulls the cables causing the suit and thrusters to shut down. The medics arrive as the engineers assist in getting the operator out of the suit.

Chasm glares at his head engineer sternly. "I want a full report on the operator *and* the suit by the end of the day. Am I understood?"

"Yes Sir," Dr. Hitachi mutters nervously.

Chasm shakes his head as he and Erica walk back towards his private elevator. "We can build tanks, aircraft and strength-enhancing exosuits!" Chasm vents. "Why is this Speedsuit giving us such a headache?!"

"Maybe," Erica muses, "Curtis' ingenuity is more advanced than we realized. Maybe you should invite him in to work on this with the engineers."

"No. Even though he's been able to do so much with so little, I still want to wait. He needs to see the Mach-2 when it's completed and working properly so he can truly understand the benefits of working with us. He is not to see this suit before it is completed."

"Understood."

"I will examine the suit myself to determine where the problems are. I cannot afford to push my timetable back any further."

CHAPTER FOURTEEN

HAPPY THANKSGIVING

KELLY LOOKS OUT OF THE WINDOW at the rising sun as the airplane lands at LaGuardia Airport. She meanders through the concourse with her carryon bags and quietly descends the escalator to 'baggage claim.' She gazes at the ground, oblivious to the external world, as her burdening thoughts flash through her mind. I don't want to be here. I don't want to deal with this right now.

"Kelly!"

Kelly looks up in the direction of the call, while forcing a smile. "Hey Mom!"

Stacey runs over to greet her daughter. "How's my baby?" They both embrace before Stacey pulls away a bit. "Let me look at you."

Kelly glances away slightly.

"What's wrong, baby?"

John approaches with his two sons right behind him—carrying Kelly's bags. "My college girl is finally home!"

"Hey Sis," Kevin greets his sister. "Glad you made it."

"Hey," Kelvin adds. "Where's Curtis?"

"Yeah," Kevin continues, "You two usually come in together."

"He couldn't make it." Kelly tries to clear her throat. "He had some other things to do."

"Ok," John replies. "Well, let's go. The car's double-parked outside. I hope we don't get a ticket."

"You guys go ahead," Stacey suggests. "We're right behind you." The guys quickly head for the door as Stacey turns and looks intently at her daughter. Kelly does her best to stem the tide, but tears swell and burst down her cheeks. Stacey pulls her daughter into an embrace as she crumples into her mother's strong arms. No words are spoken. The sobbing says it all as a broken heart speaks its own language.

[]

Later that day...

Treyshawn stands on the sidewalk with luggage in his hands as the taxi pulls away from the curb and drives down the street. He smiles as he bounds up the stairs, takes out his keys and opens the front door.

"Ma! I'm home!" Treyshawn barely makes it into the living room before he's assaulted by hugs and kisses.

"My baby is home! My baby is home!" Shakira cheers. Treyshawn laughs heartily as he tries to resist her advances. "Oh, no," She retorts, "you've been on the west coast for three months! You ain't fighting me off that easily!" She grabs Treyshawn around his neck and throws him into a headlock.

"Ma!"

"Are you *supposed* to fight with your mother?" Shakira teases.

"No," Treyshawn laughs.

"I can't hear you!" Shakira smiles. "Are you *supposed* to push your mother away when she's trying to give you hugs and kisses?"

"No!" Treyshawn laughs again as he starts tickling her.

"That's cheating!" Shakira yelps as she loses her grip.

"Cheating?" Treyshawn quips. "You're the one who threw me into a headlock!" He and his mother tumble onto the couch.

"OK! OK!" Shakira roars in between gasps. "I'm sorry! I'm sorry!"

"Oh, you're *sorry* alright!" Treyshawn laughs. "No more headlocks?"

"Yes!" Shakira cries. "No more headlocks!"

"Good!" Treyshawn abruptly stops tickling his mother and plants a solid kiss on her cheek. "I'm glad you're happy to see me."

Shakira struggles to catch her breath. "Boy, you almost made me pee in my pants!"

"TMI, Ma!" Treyshawn squints his eyes and shakes his head. "I don't need to know that kind of information."

"I'm glad you're home. Happy Thanksgiving. I want to hear all about your college experience."

"Happy Thanksgiving, Ma," Treyshawn smiles. "It's good to be home. I can't wait to tell you about everything. But—"

"I know," Shakira interjects. "First you want to go see your father."

"Is that OK?"

"I'm sure he's eager to see you, too," Shakira smiles. "Eat first. Burger's in the oven."

"Did you make it?"

"Boy, you know I don't cook!" Shakira jumps up from the couch and heads to her room. Treyshawn smiles as he thinks about what just took place. *If this living room could talk... The last time my mother and I got into it, she slapped me across my face and told me I'd never be anything. Now, we can laugh and have a good time together.*

[]

Prison Visitors Center. That evening.

Treyshawn and his dad sit—engaged in a lively discussion. They are laughing so hard, both almost forget where they are.

"I'm proud of you, Trey," Treyshawn Sr. smiles. "You are really coming into your own out there in Cali. And the art exhibit sounds real nice."

"I wish you could see what I have planned," Treyshawn responds. "You know, Cali's so different from New York."

"Oh, I've seen California plenty of times."

"Really?"

"Yeah. I used to live there—twice."

"Wow..."

"Grew up in Compton. Left when I was 18 and came back a few years later to start my record label. Eventually, I moved everything here to New York. But that was so long ago. I'm sure a lot has changed."

"Did you meet my mom when you were living in California?"

"No. I met her when I was visiting South Carolina. Then I brought her to New York."

[]

July 1990. Harlem, New York. Club One.

Darkness greets Treyshawn Sr.and Shakira as they approach a building. An extremely long line of people eagerly wait to enter. The closer they get, the more prevalent the deep bass and music becomes. Shakira holds onto Treyshawn Sr.'s arm tightly while looking around with wide eyes. She's been in New York for several days and still everything is so foreign. Shakira does a double take as they walk right past everyone.

"Wait—don't we have to wait in line?"

"Nah, girl," Treyshawn Sr. responds smoothly. "I *never* wait in line. Besides, *I'm* the one throwing this launch party." All eyes are on Treyshawn Sr. and Shakira as they approach the three large men guarding the front gates. Their frowns turn upside down as they greet them with hearty handshakes and allow them entrance.

Inside, a constant barrage of meet-and-greets smother them. Treyshawn Sr. is bold with every interaction. Shakira, on the other hand, is rather bashful. They wade through the growing crowd and stop at the foot of the stage.

"I'm gonna get this party started," Treyshawn Sr. says to Shakira. "When I call your name, be ready to come up."

"C-come up?" Shakira stutters. "F-for what?"

"To sing of course," Treyshawn Sr. replies. "I want people to hear those pipes you got."

"But, I'm not ready..."

"Doesn't your 'good book' say to always be ready?"

"But—"

"No buts. Do the song you were singing in the car the other day. The one I told you to write."

"But it's not finished, Trey."

"Doesn't matter. Tonight is just an intro, girl. We just tryin' to whet people's appetite."

Treyshawn Sr. takes the stage. Shakira looks at him, from the dance floor, with terrified eyes. After a moment of banter, her new manager hypes the crowd and bellows his dreaded introduction.

"You all came here to see my new rap artist. And let me say his album is going to take New York and the world by storm! But before we bring him out, I want to introduce one of my new upcoming R&B artists. Her name is 'Kira. She's from down South and we just signed her last week. She'll hit the studio in a few days to work on her first single. But I wanted you to get a taste of the fire she's bringin'. So, make some noise for 'Kiiiiiirrrrrraaaaaa!"

The crowd roars as Shakira stands—frozen by fear. Treyshawn Sr. glares at her as his huge smile—momentarily—turns ominous. She—seeing his expression—takes a deep breath and makes her way up the stairs to the stage. Treyshawn

Sr. smiles broadly and claps for her as he throws his hands up several times before handing Shakira the microphone and taking a few steps back. The spotlight trains on her as she stands in front of the awaiting crowd.

A nervous smile dances across her lips. She closes her eyes and raises the microphone. As she exhales, a soothing, warm vocal flows—immediately capturing the attention of everyone in the club. Before they know it, two verses have come and gone as Shakira stops. The crowd stands speechless as she steps back, shrinking from the spotlight. A single clap rings out from the back of the club as a wave of applause join together—filling the room like thunder.

Shakira steps back into the spotlight, flaunts a bashful smile and waves her hand at the crowd as Treyshawn Sr. takes the microphone from her.

"What did I tell you?" He exclaims to the crowd.

"FIRE!!!" They yell back.

"That's right! Fire," he smiles. "Ya'll ain't ready!"

"'Kira, Kira, Kira, Kira," the crowd chants back.

[]

Present Day. Prison Visitors Center.

"Wow," Treyshawn utters to his father. "So, *that's* how things got started."

"Yeah," Treyshawn Sr. replies. "I already knew your mom had what it took to be a star. I saw it when we met down in South Carolina at that talent show. But the crowd's response confirmed it."

Treyshawn sits up and stares at his father. "Let me ask you something,"

"Shoot."

"Man-to-man."

Treyshawn Sr. straightens his posture and stares intently at his son.

"OK. Man-to-man."

Treyshawn looks at his father and takes a deep breath.

"I know you dropped her because she got pregnant with me."

"Yeah... I did."

"And I ain't mad at you for that no more."

Treyshawn Sr. nods his head.

"But, did you ever put your hands on her?"

"You mean, did I ever hit her?"

"Yeah."

Treyshawn Sr. takes a deep breath and looks away for a moment as he collects his thoughts. "You sure you want to know this, Trey?"

Treyshawn nods his head.

"The first time I put my hands on your mother was that same night after she finished singing."

[]

July 1990. Harlem, New York. Club One.

Shakira and Treyshawn Sr. enter the empty green room as his new rap artist performs on stage.

"That was insane!" Shakira laughs as she leans against the wall.

"It was, wasn't it?" Treyshawn Sr. smiles. He leans next to her and slowly rubs her shoulders as his hands make their way to her neck.

"Mmmm," Shakira closes her eyes, "that feels good, Trey. But a little *tight* on the grip, though. Ease up a bit, OK?"

His grip increases like a vice around her neck.

"Treyshawn," she coughs as she grabs his rock-hard hands. "You're hurting me!"

He keeps the pressure constant as she claws to get free. "I want you to remember what this *feels* like, 'Kira,'" he snarls as he glares into her eyes. "When I give orders, people don't question and they don't refuse. They DO. If I ASK, then they are free to speak their mind. But when I tell'em what to do they get to it! The next time I *tell* you to do something, you betta do it. You hesitate again—especially in front of a room full of people—and you won't like the repercussions."

He releases his grip as she slumps to the floor in a coughing heap. "Drink the bottled water on the table. Then pull yourself together. We goin' back out to see the show."

[]

Present Day. Prison Visitors Center.

Treyshawn Sr. looks at his son's clenched fists. "You *wanted* man-to-man."

"Yeah, I did," Treyshawn replies while relaxing his fingers.

"Look. There are many things in my life I'm not proud of. It's just the way things went down. And I can't change it."

"I know, Dad. But let me ask you... would you change things if you could?"

Treyshawn Sr. looks long and hard at his son. "Before you gave me that journal, I would have said, 'No.' But now... sitting here looking at you—thinking about our conversations over the last couple of months—if I could go back and change things... I think I would."

[]

The morning sunlight beams through the large window—bathing Miranda, Jim and Omar in its warmth. They squint as a private jet descends from the sky and lands on the runway.

"I didn't even know this airport had private terminals," Miranda admits while shaking her head.

"I did," Jim replies, "but I've never been in one until now."

"Lifestyles of the rich and famous," Omar adds.

"What time do you leave tomorrow?" Miranda asks Jim.

"My flight is at 8:00am. Looking forward to seeing my daughter and her family."

"I'm glad you can go see them," Omar adds, "but it won't be the same without you."

The trio watches as the jet taxis to their position and stops in front of the gate. The aircraft's engines power down as two crew members approach the tarmac. After a few hand signals to the pilots, the plane's main side door opens and the steps lower to the ground. A moment later Curtis steps to the plane's entrance and walks down the stairs.

The trio barely recognizes him. His usual jeans and t-shirt ensemble has been replaced with top-quality shoes, slacks, dress shirt with an open collar, sports jacket, and sunglasses.

"Is that *your* son?" Omar asks.

"I-I don't know," Miranda stutters—shocked as her son approaches the gate's entry door.

Curtis enters the private terminal with a huge smile, followed by a gentleman carrying his luggage.

"Mom! Omar! Mr.G!" Curtis shouts as he approaches and hugs each of them.

"Can you take your sunglasses off so I can make sure it's you?" Miranda asks.

"It's me, Mom," he laughs, while removing his sunglasses. "See?"

"Yeah, we see," Omar interjects. "We see you looking like a million bucks!"

"And what's up with the last minute change of flight?" Jim asks. "Two days ago you were coming in on Delta."

"Chasm—I mean Mr. Montgomery arranged for me to take one of his private jets to get me home quicker."

"One?" Miranda responds. "He has more than one?"

"Yeah. Crazy right? I just found out the other day! He's got three or four jets that he uses for different purposes. He and his mentor, Dr. Winters, also provided me with this wardrobe upgrade!"

"Nice," Omar responds. "But, I didn't think Mr. Montgomery had a mentor. What was that like?"

"He's amazing! Dr. Winters is 70-something years old and is a self-made multi-billionaire. I think he's the twelfth richest man in the world! Mr. Montgomery met him in college and he became his mentor. Much like how Mr. Montgomery has become mine!"

"I don't know," Miranda cautions. "That's great and all. But... it seems like they're trying to *buy* you with all of these fancy things."

"Mom," Curtis grins, "I'm still the same old me."

"Uh, huh," Miranda replies.

"Hey Omar, can you carry my bags?"

"Carry your bags?" Omar looks at his mom, Mr. Grabowski and then back at Curtis. "Still the *same* old you, huh?"

"Fine," Curtis smiles. "I can carry them myself."

"You don't have to do that," Omar replies. "We'll split them. Which one's the heaviest?"

"That one," Curtis smiles, while pointing at the larger suitcase.

"OK," Omar replies as he approaches both. "You take that one and I'll take the smaller one."

Curtis stares at his brother incredulously as he walks away with the smaller suitcase.

"You're serious?"

"How else are you going to get the 'big guns' like me?" Omar quips while flexing his biceps—which easily expand the wool-knit shirt he's wearing.

Jim, Miranda and Omar laugh as they walk away and Curtis struggles to carry his oversized piece of luggage.

□

Later that day...

Shakira slides a rolled up piece of paper across the kitchen table as she and Treyshawn sit eating lunch.

"Here."

"What's this?"

"Open it and see," she smiles.

Treyshawn puts his fork down and pulls the rubber band off of the paper as it unrolls. "Is this what I think it is?"

Shakira smiles, "What do you think it is?"

Treyshawn looks up at his mother. "You got your GED!"

"That's right, baby! I got my GED!"

Treyshawn jumps up from the table, comes around to the other side, pulls his mother up to her feet and gives her a huge bear hug.

"That's great, Ma! I am so proud of you!"

"Me?" Shakira laughs as she returns her son's hug. "I'm so proud of *you*! You are making something good out of your life!"

Treyshawn pulls back and stares at his mother. There's a twinkle in her eyes—something he hasn't seen since the day she kicked Melvin out of her house. "So, what are you going to do now, Ma?"

Shakira smiles as she gazes at her son, "Now? I'm going to apply to community college."

□

Thanksgiving Day.

The doorbell rings at the Powers' residence. Miranda strolls from the kitchen and opens the front door. To her surprise, two massive figures cast their shadows before her.

"Kevin! Kelvin! Happy Thanksgiving!"

"Happy Thanksgiving to you, Ms. Powers," the twins reply in unison.

"How are you both doing? How's the family?"

"We are all doing well. Thanks," Kevin replies.

"We just stopped by to talk to Curtis," Kelvin adds. "Is he around?"

"Sure. I'll get him. Feel free to come inside and have a seat."

"Thanks Ms. Powers, but we're good," Kevin responds. "Just a quick visit."

"OK," Miranda chuckles. "Be right back." She turns from the doorway and walks to the stairs. "Curtis! You've got company!"

"OK, Mom!" Curtis replies as he exits his bedroom and makes his way to the stairs.

Miranda heads back into the kitchen and tends to dinner as Curtis gets to the front door.

"Hey K and K!" Curtis shouts. "What's up? Nice workout outfits!"

"Uh, oh," Miranda mumbles as her memory snaps into gear. "This may *not* be good."

Kevin and Kelvin swiftly pull Curtis outside and press him up against the side of the house.

"Hey!" Curtis exclaims as he throws his hands up.

"Don't 'hey' us!" Kevin says.

"Do you know why we're here?" Kelvin asks.

"N-no," Curtis responds nervously as he cranes his neck back, attempting to see their towering faces.

"No?" Kelvin replies.

"You broke our sister's heart!" Kevin yells as he leans in closer—his colossal physique completely eclipsing Curtis'. "*That's* why we're here."

"Guys. W-wait a minute."

"Why?" Kelvin says as his hands clench into fists.

"It's not what you think!"

"You kissed another girl!" They both say in unison.

"Erica kissed me!" Curtis exclaims. "I didn't ask her to! She just did it! Right out the blue!"

Kevin and Kelvin hesitate as they look at each other and then back at Curtis.

"You guys are star athletes. You ever had a girl just come up and kiss you after your team won a game?" he asks.

Again, Kevin and Kelvin share a momentary glance. "Don't try to change the subject," Kevin replies. "This isn't about us. It's about you."

"But, for the record," Kelvin adds, "we know what it feels like when that happens. But even if this girl, Erica, kissed you out the blue, we heard you didn't stop her."

"No," Curtis whispers as he looks away, "not at first." He looks back up at the brothers. "I'll admit that I *did* like it, OK? Erica is attractive... and a *great* kisser."

Kevin pushes Curtis even harder into the wall.

"But..." Curtis stammers, "that's neither here or there."

The screen door springs open as Omar steps outside and faces the trio. His sports shirt barely contains his chiseled frame as he glares at the two giants holding his brother against the house.

"Is there a problem here?" Omar asks in a deep bass voice. Kevin and Kelvin look at Omar—sizing him up.

"Omar!" Curtis exclaims. "Thank God! I am SO glad you are here! Can you please help a brother out?"

"Like I said," Omar continues, "is there a *problem* here?"

"Nah," Kevin replies as his brother shakes his head. "There's no problem."

"Good," Omar replies. "Talk to him all you want. Make him see he's in danger of being a real jerk. But don't hit him—or you *will* have a problem."

"We got you," Kelvin grins.

"Good. Let me know when you're done. My mom's got some sweet potato pies for you guys."

"Omar?" Curtis whimpers as he looks at his brother—bewildered. Omar glances at his younger brother, raises his eyebrows and slightly shakes his head. He goes back inside, leaving Curtis to deal with the two giants.

"Listen," Kevin says as he lessens his grip on Curtis, "we like you. You're a decent guy and we don't want to have to rough you up."

"We know what it's like to get some fame and notoriety," Kelvin adds. "It can go to your head and mess your life up real bad if you're not careful."

"You *really* hurt Kelly," Kevin admits.

"I know," Curtis mumbles.

"We don't think you do," Kevin counters. "If you did, you'd have been to the house already trying to make things right."

"But she said she wanted some space."

"Too much space," Kelvin replies, "leaves room for other people to enter the equation."

"Wait. Is she talking to someone else?"

"Some guy named Carlos did call a couple of times," Kevin responds.

"If she's giving him the time of day, that's only because she's hurt. That relationship isn't real—at least not yet."

"You two have been through a lot together," Kelvin adds. "If you want her back, you need to let her know and you need to accept full responsibility for your actions."

"That's right," Kevin continues. "This girl, Erica wouldn't have tried to kiss you if she didn't think you *wanted* it to happen. So, you're not completely innocent in this."

"You're right," Curtis mumbles.

"We know," the brothers say in unison.

"If you don't want Kelly back," Kevin says, "then let her go. If you *do* want her back, then let her know."

"But if you hurt our sister again," Kelvin warns, "we won't have any problem going toe-to-toe with your brother."

[]

Later that night...

Curtis walks up the stoop and knocks on the front door, fidgeting with his hands in his pockets as he waits. His lips move repeatedly as he tries to get his words together. He takes several deep breaths and looks around as he hears steps slowly coming down stairs on the other side of the door. Three locks disengage as the door sluggishly opens. Kelly stands before him —motionless and silent.

"H-hey Kelly," Curtis stammers. She looks at him without uttering a word. Curtis clears his throat as he wipes sweat from his forehead. "Listen... I-I know I've hurt you and I've been a real jerk. I wanted to say… I'm sorry."

Again, Kelly stands silently.

Curtis continues, "Is there any way we can move forward from here?"

"Is that what you *really* want?" Kelly asks. "I mean, it *only* took my brothers having to almost beat you up to get you to come over here to talk to me."

"You said you wanted your space," Curtis answers, "and I was scared."

"You're so smart. You should have known that 'space' meant you should have come after me if you really wanted me."

"I do want you."

"Really? What about Erica?"

"I'll admit that part of me did like it when she kissed me. But not *all* of me."

Kelly silently examines Curtis' eyes for traces of the truth.

"Can I come in so we can talk about this?"

"Talking right here is fine." Kelly crosses her arms.

Curtis' sorrow gives way to a slight bit of anger. "Fine. If you're mad at me because some girl kissed me, then do I have a right to be mad cause you're talking to some new guy?"

Kelly sucks her teeth, "You are unbelievable." She closes the door in his face and runs back upstairs.

Curtis stands motionless for a moment before turning and making his way down the steps. Kelly watches from the living room window as he walks down the block. Her mother approaches.

"Well? How did it go?"

"He's not ready."

"I heard the conversation, honey. Are you sure it's him who's not ready?"

[]

The next day...

Curtis, Omar and Miranda sit at the kitchen table eating breakfast, as the doorbell rings. Miranda motions for Curtis to answer the door. When he opens it, he finds Kelly staring at him through the screen.

"Hey," Curtis says.

"Hey," Kelly whispers. "I'm sorry about last night. It's just that… I'm scared. You've had my heart for so long... and you crushed it."

"Kelly—"

"Let me finish, Curtis. Please."

"Okay."

"I know it wasn't completely your fault. I get that—really I do. But if *part* of you liked kissing Erica, then that's a part of you that no longer likes me. I don't want to be hurt again. I *can't* be hurt again. You asked if there was a way to move forward… Do you still want to move forward?"

A slight smile flashes across Curtis' face, "Yes. I do."

Kelly smiles as she looks at him, "Can I come in?"

Curtis quickly opens the screen door as Kelly walks in and heads into the living room. She waves to Omar and Miranda. They wave back as she sits on the couch. Curtis sits next to her.

"The way I see it," Kelly sighs, "the way forward is for us to have *no* secrets. However we honestly feel and think—we share it with each other—even if we're afraid the other won't like what we have to say. Can we do that?"

Curtis gazes into Kelly's eyes. "Yes. We can do that."

"So, any time Erica tries to come on to you, you've got to tell her to back off *and* you've got to tell me. I don't want you trying to handle her all by yourself."

"What will you do if I tell you?"

"*When* you tell me."

"Yes. *When* I tell you."

"Oh, I will just make it clear to Erica that she can't get between us," Kelly smiles slyly. "Woman-to-woman talk."

Curtis hugs Kelly warmly. "So, are we OK?"

Kelly smiles as she returns his hug. "Yes, we are."

Omar and Miranda smile at each other.

"So," Curtis asks, "who is this guy you've been talking to?"

"Oh, Carlos? He's a non-issue now."

"Okay," Curtis replies. "Just make sure *he* knows that."

CHAPTER FIFTEEN

BACK ON CAMPUS

DECEMBER 2013. CURTIS WALKS UP THE stairs to the third floor landing and swipes his ID card on the panel next to the big metal door. He pulls it open and walks down the carpeted hallway and stops in front of his dorm room. He fiddles with his keys as he tries to hold several bags in his hand and a book bag strung over his shoulder. A moment later he enters his room to an amazing sight.

"Gavin!" Curtis exclaims as he drops his bags.

Gavin limps across the room with his cane—just coming out of the bathroom, "Hey Curtis! Good to see you!"

"It's good to see *you*!"

"Yeah," Gavin smiles. "Just got clearance for a cane last week over Thanksgiving. Talk about having a reason to be thankful... Doctor said I should be walking just fine in another month or so. Should be able to run again in about three months."

"Bro, that is good news!"

"Who you tellin'?" Gavin laughs. "So, how was your Thanksgiving?"

"It was pretty eventful. Almost got beat up by Kelly's brothers..."

"Whoa!"

"Yeah, but I did say 'almost.' Kelly and I talked through everything, so we're cool now."

"Back together again?"

"Yep!"

"Great. Now, what are you going to do about Erica?"

"Stay away from her as long as possible."

"Dude, you work with her! That's gonna be hard!"

"Yeah. Seriously though, as long as she doesn't try anything, I should be good."

"And when she does? How you gonna put the fire out?"

"Stop, drop and roll," Curtis laughs. "Roll right out of the room!" Both boys laugh and joke around for several more minutes as Curtis unpacks his things. "So, how was your Thanksgiving?"

"Good. First time eating Thanksgiving dinner with my dad and his family. A bit weird, but we got through it. I also finished The Ant."

"Really? When can I see it?"

"Patience, young Padawan learner. You'll see it once I finish testing it out."

"Okay. So... what are you doing for Christmas break?" Curtis asks.

Gavin's eyes light up. "My mom is coming here! We're going to spend Christmas at the mansion with my dad's family!"

"Wow!" Curtis smiles. "That sounds great! But don't you think... *that* might be a little awkward?"

"You mean the fact that my mom hasn't met my dad's wife or his kids in person before? Yeah, it could be. But they talked everything out and think it will be good for *all* of us. What about you?"

"We'll all probably get together at Mr. G's house. It'll be great to see everyone."

"Yeah, well," Gavin says with a heavy dose of reality, "we won't see anyone if we don't pass these final exams!"

The two spend the rest of the evening discussing their class load. Classes end in two weeks and then a week of intensive final exams begin. If they can survive the tests, they will be free to enjoy a relaxing Christmas break. But if they fail any of their exams, their planned vacation will become more drudgery than anything else. Long days and late nights lie ahead.

[]

The next afternoon…

Curtis arrives at the Montgomery Group headquarters. "Thanks Ralph," he says as he exits the private car with his bookbag. With a nervous, but brisk walk, he enters through the massive double doors of the facility and approaches the first security check point.

"Mr. Powers," the security guard smiles, "good to see you. How was your Thanksgiving?"

Curtis swipes his ID badge pass the sensor as the security gate opens. "It was great Tommy! What about yours?"

"It was quiet," Tom smiles. "I was here, working."

"Sorry to hear that," Curtis frowns.

"No worries," Tom grins, "comes with the big paycheck."

Curtis laughs as he heads to the elevator, "Glad you're here to keep us safe!"

A few moments later, he exits the elevator on the 12th floor and cautiously makes his way to his lab. He quickly swipes his ID badge again as the lab door unlocks and he enters—shutting the door expeditiously behind him. "Whew," he sighs, while leaning against the door. "I made it." Curtis unloads his books on his desk and sits down.

"Man," he mumbles as he looks at a class syllabus, "I got a lot of studying to do for tomorrow. The final exam isn't going to be easy."

Several hours pass, as he reads through his notes from class and peruses several chapters from his text books. He stops to stretch. "I sure could use a snack." He picks up his desk phone and calls in an order to the café. That's when he notices the blinking light: a message waits on his voicemail.

"Hello Curtis. This is Chasm. I hope you had a wonderful Thanksgiving holiday. Please let me know when you are back in your lab. I need you to consult with Erica on an upcoming project. And yes, I know that you have finals in a couple of weeks. You're probably studying even now. I am out of state on business for the next ten days. See you when I return."

Curtis hangs up the phone, grabs his ID badge and walks to the door. He opens it to find Erica standing there—her hand positioned to knock.

"Ah!"

"Sorry!" Erica chuckles.

"Are you trying to give me a heart attack?"

"Just coming to see if you were here." Erica looks down the hall— both ways—and then pushes Curtis back into his lab, quickly shutting the door behind her. "I missed you," she smiles as she places her hands on his shoulders and leans in to kiss him.

Curtis turns his head away and takes a step back. "Erica, listen. This is *not* going to work."

"Why not? I thought you *liked* my kiss."

"You caught me off guard." Curtis pushes her hands away. "Look, you and I need to *remain* friends."

Erica frowns slightly, "So, you got back together with Kelly."

"Yes. Your little surprise kiss really messed things up for us. But we worked through it."

"Are you sure she's who you want?"

"Yes," Curtis says confidently. "I'm sure."

"Fine. I'll respect your decision. You don't have to worry about me making any more advances," she smiles slightly, "at least not for a while."

"Uh, huh. Kelly might want to *talk* with you about that if you do."

"Alright, I get the picture. She's ready to fight for her man. I like that. So, where are you going?"

"Upstairs for a snack—ordered an extra-thick strawberry shake and some french fries."

"Great. I'll go with you. That way we can talk about the project Chasm has tasked us with. He wants to create a brand new Powersuit tour for next summer—something that will knock people's socks off!"

"That sounds great! But listen. How about *I* go up alone and I'll meet you in the conference room after I'm done eating?"

"Look at you..." Erica smiles. "Acting all *grown*. I like that." She turns and exits the lab. "See you in an hour."

"Whew," Curtis whispers to himself, "*that* was close."

[]

Erica's Office...

"So, where do things stand?"

Erica swivels her chair away from the closed door and speaks into her phone in a slightly hushed tone. "He got back together with Kelly. I don't think my advances will work anymore."

"Do not underestimate yourself," Chasm replies. "We determined this would most likely happen. You got him to kiss you once, so we know he is attracted to you."

"But now Curtis is adamant about keeping his distance from me."

"Of course he is my dear," Chasm chuckles. "Of course he is. So, do what he wants. Keep things purely platonic. But every now and then, test his defenses to see if there are any weak spots we can exploit. I want to own him."

"He *already* thinks the world of you."

"True. But for things to work, I will need his absolute loyalty and allegiance. *That* is what we don't have yet. Did you begin with the next phase?"

"Yes. We will be meeting in an hour to discuss next year's tour."

"Excellent. The ideas he births and develops out of that conversation will serve our purposes well. Things are going well here in New York. The new facilities are just about complete. I will see you next week when I return."

Erica hangs up her cell phone and places it on her desk. She takes a deep breath and then unlocks one of her desk drawers. She pulls out a small metal bin, unlocks it and opens the lid. She reaches in and retrieves *another* phone and an earpiece. She turns it on, places the earpiece in place and hesitates as she pulls her hand away from the phone. Her eyes dart back and forth as she leans back in her chair and mumbles to herself. "Erica… *what* are you doing?"

She swivels her chair around towards the window—into the path of incoming sunlight. The warm rays bathe her face in a soft glow as she closes her eyes and arches her head back slightly. A moment passes before she slowly opens her eyes and gazes at a framed photo hanging on the wall: she and Chasm laughing as she holds up the large trophy at the national science competition. She was in 11th grade at the time.

"Maybe I should just tell him…" she whispers as she focuses on the second phone sitting on her desk. She breathes deeply and steels herself. "No. This is the only way." She picks up the phone and dials a series of numbers. A computerized voice rings in her ear.

"Encrypted line established."

In an undisclosed location, several computer screens illuminate a dark office. A phone on the desk begins to emit a blue glow around its perimeter as a shadowed man picks up a custom, glowing earpiece and places it in his ear.

Erica looks out of her window as the phone rings three times before it is answered on the other end.

"You are always so punctual," a digitized male voice declares.

"As you always say," Erica replies, "punctuality is the hallmark of excellence."

"Yes, my dear. A person's punctuality reveals how they view the world. So, tell me, where do things stand?"

"I've done everything possible to delay the completion. But now, Chasm has decided to comb through the suit himself. He is examining it in its entirety. I only hope that I've been able to adequately cover up my… involvement."

"Don't worry my dear," the man replies, "I have arranged a smoke screen to make sure your deeds are not detected."

"What *kind* of smoke screen?"

"You'll know it when it happens. It's a necessary measure. Chasm can be *very* detailed in his examinations. Does he suspect you?"

"I don't think so."

"Good. You *are* very thorough."

"Thank you. But, he wants to move up the timeline. I imagine the suit will be fully operational by the end of the month. A comprehensive testing phase will last about six to eight weeks. He wants Curtis to see it by March—April at the latest."

"Oh, the suit *will* be seen… And it will be glorious when it happens."

"You still haven't told me about that part of the plan."

"You still don't need to know. Leave the details to me."

Erica bites her lip as she looks out of her window, "Yes… Sir."

"Erica," the man says, "I can hear your frustration. My withholding information has nothing to do with *trust*. The less you *know*, the *less* you have to lie and the easier it is to keep up our facade."

"Understood, Sir."

"Good. And what of our young friend?"

"Curtis is oblivious to everything. Right now he's focused on his final exams. Although, today I will be talking to him about next year's tour."

"Keep up the good work. I look forward to your next report."

CHAPTER SIXTEEN

UNCOVERED

MIRANDA SITS IN HER ROOM, AT her desk—pouring over the documents Marge gave her. She combs through each line on each page, looking for any connections she may have missed. It's late in the evening and she's been at this for the last five hours.

"There has to be something I'm missing." She mumbles to herself. "Some kind of additional connection." She stops for a moment, rubs her eyes and takes a few deep breaths while massaging her neck. She looks at the four smiling faces in a picture on her night table. Malcolm, I wish you were here right now. I could really use your help. Our boys are growing up so fast. I wish you could see them again. She glances at the calendar —December 22nd. After another moment, she gets back to work.

"Ma!" A double knock rings at her door as Omar abruptly opens it.

"Omar!" Miranda huffs.

"Sorry," he replies as he approaches her desk with a large folder in his hands. "You gotta see this."

Miranda looks at him, while shaking her head. Then she dismisses her son's infraction due to his eagerness. "What is it?"

Omar plops the folder on her desk, "I called in a few favors and got an extensive background check done on Mr. Montgomery."

"Really?" Miranda says intrigued. She slowly drops her papers and picks up the folder. "How extensive?"

"Very," Omar states flatly. "It's *everything* there is to know about him. How he grew up, the schools he went to, his work history, business deals, media appearances, known associates in his inner circle—everything."

"Why did you do this?"

"Because of your story about how his adopted father had a *direct* connection to John Whaley."

"Yeah. That's a *big* coincidence," Miranda says. "But his explanation seemed solid. You know the world is an increasingly small place."

"True. But something kept nagging me about it, so I made some calls."

"And what did you discover?"

Omar sits next to his mother and stares directly into her eyes. "A whole lot of *coincidences*. Ma. When Curtis comes home tomorrow, we need to talk to him. He may be in trouble. We *all* might be."

[]

The next evening…

A private car pulls up to the Powers' residence. A driver pops open the trunk, exits the vehicle and opens the rear door. Curtis steps out and looks around with a smile. *It's good to be home. I am so glad finals are over!* The driver pulls his luggage from the trunk and sets it on the curb.

"Have a good evening Mr. Powers. And Happy Holidays."

"Thanks Tony. Merry Christmas to you. Drive safely."

The driver tips his hat at Curtis and smiles. He reenters his vehicle and drives off down the street. Curtis slings his bookbag over his shoulder, picks up his two travel cases and heads to the front door. He fiddles with his keys before getting the door open.

"I'm home," he yells with a smile as he closes the door with his feet and walks into the living room. Miranda, Omar and Jim sit on the couch—each with a solemn expression. "Hey," Curtis says, looking at them with a sudden reservation. "What's the matter? You guys look like somebody died."

"Curtis," Miranda says softly, "we need to talk."

"Someone *did* die," Curtis shouts as he drops his bags.

"*Nobody* died," Omar counters. "But this is very important. That's why Mr. G is here, too."

"What is it?" Curtis asks while sitting in the recliner chair. He looks down on the coffee table at a large folder filled with papers.

Miranda begins, "Let me first say that we love you very much and only want what's best for you. You know that right?"

Curtis smiles and looks at each of them, "Of course I know that."

"Good," she smiles, "because what I have to say may not sound like love when you hear it."

"Go on," Curtis replies. "Spit it out already. I'm an adult."

"Baby," Miranda continues, "remember how we lost your father's life insurance policy?"

"How could I forget," Curtis quips. "Our whole lives got turned upside down!"

"Well, due to a secret investigation, I discovered that the cancellation of the policy wasn't an accident."

"W-what?" Curtis' eyelids flutter as he tries to process her words. "Are you saying somebody canceled Dad's insurance on purpose?"

"That's what I'm saying," Miranda replies.

"But why would somebody do that?"

"We're still trying to figure that out," Jim interjects. "But everything we've discovered indicates there's something bigger going on here."

"So you all knew this and didn't tell me?"

"Son," Miranda replies, "you're in college—focused on your school work and on your Speedsuit. We didn't want to worry *or* distract you until we could determine what's going on."

"So, what *is* going on?" Curtis asks flatly. "Tell me what's so important that you all are here right now."

"John Whaley," Omar replies. "Somehow he's at the top of the list."

"John Whaley? The founder of the architect firm? But he was always so nice to us. Why would he do anything to harm us?"

"We can't share that information with you yet," Miranda replies.

"Why not?" Curtis huffs. "Why tell me there's trouble, but not give me specifics!"

"Because we don't want to put you at risk," Omar responds.

"Wait," Curtis stops, remembering something. "That picture in Chasm's office—the one with him and Mr. Whaley. The one I told you about, Mom. *That* has something to do with this, doesn't it?"

Miranda nods her head.

"More than you think," Omar says.

"Which brings us to our second issue," Miranda admits while taking a deep breath. "There's no easy way to say this..." she runs her hands through her hair and looks at Omar and Jim before continuing.

"What? You think Chasm is in on this?" Curtis says sarcastically.

"Yes," Miranda answers, "we do think he's involved."

"That's crazy!" Curtis sucks his teeth. "He's been helping us!"

"Yeah," Omar replies. "The question is *why* has he been so helpful?"

"He likes to develop the potential of students," Curtis answers. "You've *heard* him say that."

"Yes, but for what purpose?" Jim interjects. "Is he developing students out of the goodness of his heart or does he have an ulterior motive?"

"Why are you guys bringing this up?" Curtis asks defiantly. "Is it because he bought me a new wardrobe? Or because I'm working for him? Or are you guys jealous of the attention he gives me?"

"What?" Miranda yells. "We are *not* jealous! Up until now, we've been grateful for his involvement in all of our lives."

"So what changed?" Curtis asks.

"You need to lower your voice," Omar commands while standing to his feet. "Don't forget who you are talking to."

Curtis reigns in his emotions a bit, "...Sorry. It's just—"

"It's hard," Omar finishes his brother's thought. "I *know* it's hard to hear that your mentor may not be who you think he is."

"But what *proof* do you guys have?"

Omar picks up the thick folder from the coffee table. "This is an extensive background check on Mr. Montgomery. Goes all the way back to his childhood. Covers *every* major association he has had—both personally and professionally—all the way to three months ago. Do you know what's buried in here?"

"No. What?"

"Your mentor *knows* Mr. Whaley... like *very* well. Do you think that's a coincidence?"

"He told me about his adopted father and how they met," Curtis counters.

"That's *one* coincidence," Omar shrugs. "Nobody would think much about that. Everybody's connected to everyone else by six degrees. The world's a small place, right?"

"Right."

"Well, in *this* folder is a *series* of coincidences—a pattern of them... related to *us*."

"What do you mean?"

"Did you know that Mr. Montgomery was in London at the same time we were in London for your Olympic run?" Jim inquires.

"Yes," Curtis answers. "He told me about that. He was there on business and had a break to come watch me run since we were getting so much exposure from the world record we set. He was even sitting close to where we were in the stadium. So, what?"

"That's two coincidences," Omar says, matter-of-factly.

"Did you know," Miranda interjects, "that Mr. Montgomery serves on the Board of your university?"

"Well, he said he was very involved in the university, as an alumnus."

"And did you know," Miranda continues, "that he also has ties to several of the *other* schools which initially offered you full scholarships—but either withdrew them or reduced them to partial scholarships?"

"Are you saying he manipulated my admissions process?" Curtis asks.

"What if you being where you are is not a coincidence?" Omar queries. "What if he *wanted* you to go to your school—the one where he has the most influence and control?"

"So, now he's some kind of diabolical mastermind and I'm a pawn?"

"I'm not sure about the 'diabolical' part, but that's exactly what we are saying," Miranda states seriously. "And you *can't* let him know that we know this. So, that's why you need to switch schools."

"What?" Curtis yells as he jumps to his feet. "I like my school!"

"Son," Miranda continues, "something is going on here and we need to be careful! We don't have all the pieces yet, but whatever this is, it's big! And somehow, we seem to be caught up in the middle of it!"

"You guys are crazy!" Curtis counters. "I am *not* leaving school!"

"Curtis," Jim interjects, "you said after the Colorado shooting that you were wondering if you were supposed to leave school."

"Leave school to go *help* people," Curtis yells, "*this* is different!"

"Curtis, if you don't do this on your own," Miranda cautions, "then I will have to withdraw you, myself."

"You can't withdraw me! I'm an adult and I have a full scholarship!"

"Your life may be on the line! And I'm your mother!"

"If my life is on the line, then it's *my* life!" Curtis yells. "Why are you trying to hold me back?"

"Is that what you think this is? Curtis, we are not trying to hold you back. We are trying to save you!"

"I don't need saving!" Curtis retorts.

"Baby," Miranda replies, "I don't want to withdraw you. But your defiant response is not leaving me with any options."

"Is that an ultimatum?" Curtis scoffs. "Are you threatening me, Mom? Since when have you *ever* threatened me?

"Curtis," Jim interjects, "listen to your mother."

"Why? She's not making any sense!"

Jim looks at Curtis with an empathetic stare. "Son—"

"I'm *not* your son!"

"Curtis!" Miranda interjects, struggling to temper her alarm.

"Lil' Bro, you *just* crossed the line," Omar declares.

"No," Jim replies while holding up his hands, "he's right. I'm *not* his father." He faces Curtis squarely and looks him straight in his eyes. "*Forgive me* for caring for you *as if* you were my son. Forgive me, Curtis, for *sacrificing* my time, money and resources to help you with *your* adventures. Forgive me for opening up *my heart and soul* to you as a mentor to help you overcome the obstacles you faced so you could *pursue* your dreams. No, I am *not* your father. And you can disrespect me if you want. But you will *not* disrespect your mother, your brother or your *father's* legacy."

Curtis looks at his mother, his brother and his former physics teacher. Then he turns and runs out of the house.

"Curtis!" Miranda yells as the front door slams. "Come back here!"

"Let him go, Ma," Omar says as he holds her gently. "We did just unload a lot on him. Give him some time to think. He'll come around."

A moment of silence passes.

"Well," Jim chuckles, "that went well."

[]

An hour later…

Kelly opens her front door to find Curtis standing there. The street light is reflected in the tears rolling down his face.

"Curtis! What happened?"

"My family wants me to leave school."

"What? Why?"

"They—they think it's not safe for me there."

"Well, you did have that break in at your workstation on campus."

Curtis stops for a moment as he suddenly considers that fact, in light of the new information that was revealed to him. But, as quickly as he considers the possibility—he dismisses it from his mind.

"I know you love the school," Kelly continues, "and I don't know what this is all about. But I trust your mom and brother. If they're telling you to withdraw, then they must have a really good reason. Did they tell you why?"

"Yeah. But it didn't make any sense to me."

"What did they say?"

"I don't want to get into it right now. I just don't know what to do!"

"Why don't you sleep on it? Talk to them more tomorrow."

Curtis gazes at Kelly and kisses her. "Merry Christmas."

Surprised and perplexed—Kelly stares at Curtis as he walks away. "Merry Christmas, Curtis," she replies. He turns and smiles as he aims a single wave in her direction. Kelly watches him until he disappears into the distance. She closes her front door and runs upstairs to her room where she takes out her phone and texts Miranda and Omar. "Curtis was just here. I think he's heading back home. Can you let me know if he's okay? He didn't seem like himself."

[]

The next morning...

Miranda and Omar awake to find Curtis' bed undisturbed and his luggage gone. A note sits on the bed.

"I'm going back to school. DO NOT call me and DO NOT come down there."

Miranda crumbles into her eldest son's arms as she is unable to control a flood of tears.

CHAPTER SEVENTEEN

INTO THE FIRE...

CURTIS STANDS IN CHASM'S PRIVATE ELEVATOR as it rises to the penthouse suite. I don't need them. I can do this on my own. Besides... I've got Chasm and Erica to help me, he concludes. The elevator stops as the doors open. Classical music spills into the space as a female artificial intelligence voice says, "Welcome, Curtis Powers." Curtis exits the elevator and walks down the short hall to the open door which leads to Chasm's living area.

What if they're right? flashes through his mind like a blue spark between electrodes. But Curtis stuffs the thought down as quickly as it comes. *They can't be right,* he thinks, uncertainty creeping in as Chasm approaches from the far window. *They've got this all wrong. There's no way Chasm is involved.*

"Curtis," Chasm smiles. "I was surprised when you called to say you wanted to come back to campus for Christmas. Is everything okay at home?"

"Couldn't be better," Curtis replies coolly. "I just needed some space is all."

Chasm's eyebrows wrinkle. "Are you sure that is all?"

Curtis hesitates. "Actually... my mom and I aren't seeing eye to eye at the moment."

"I'm sorry to hear that. What happened?"

Curtis wants to blurt out everything about his conversation from the previous night. He rehearsed this very moment from the time he got on the plane to return. But there's a knot in his gut—tying up his insides. He's never had this feeling before, but it started to form the moment he stepped into Chasm's private elevator. And the feeling has grown in intensity with every passing second.

"I just feel like she's trying to hold me back. She sees the new wardrobe and all the extra help you've been giving me. I think she's afraid that my success is going to go to my head."

"I can understand her hesitation, but there comes a time in every child's life when they have to stand on their own two feet—despite what their parents may be feeling. You are at the precipice of a great achievement Curtis. As I said to you before, your mother, brother and friends have taken you as far as they can. Dr. Winters and I can take you far beyond what they think is possible. With our help, you will impact the world on a level that even exceeds *your* expectations."

"That's what I want. I want to make a difference."

"I know you do, Son," Chasm smiles warmly. "Would you like to have something to eat? I was just about to call down to the chef and place an order."

"No thanks. I'm actually not hungry. I'll just have some water. And thanks for the encouragement."

Chasm walks to his kitchen, retrieves a bottle of water from the refrigerator and hands it to Curtis.

"So, Erica informed you about the tour possibilities for the summer. What are your thoughts?"

"I'm all in."

"Really?"

"Yeah. I've been thinking about it since she mentioned it. I was a little hesitant at first, but hey, why not. You know what they say, 'either go big or go home.'"

Chasm smiles, "So, we will increase the number of cities to visit, as well as the size and scope of the presentation. The masses will be talking about this tour for decades."

"The only thing is, Erica didn't mention how many suits you want me to create."

"As many as you can imagine."

"Besides the three I've already built, I've got some ideas for suits that can manipulate fire, light, agility, strength, sound, climb walls, and protect from blunt-force trauma. I even have an idea for trying to solve the problem of personal human flight. If it works, maybe it could be tested with Law Enforcement and other first responders. But that's something we can look at after the tour is over."

"Your mind *has* been busy!" Chasm laughs.

"All the time," Curtis smirks.

"Well, I'm glad you agreed to my vision for your next Powersuit tour. With your ideas and my resources, the world will be amazed. And who knows what other opportunities will open up. Listen, why don't you let my driver take you back to the dorm, so you can get some rest."

"Do you have any plans for tomorrow?"

"Christmas… is always a quiet time for me."

"You and Erica don't plan an event?"

"No. I give Erica time off to go visit her family."

"Well, if you're not doing anything, maybe the two of us could hang out."

"Since you *are* going to be around, perhaps that would be a good idea. I'll check to see if Dr. Winters is available for a Christmas brunch."

"That sounds like a plan!"

[]

Curtis walks into his quiet dorm room, drops his bags and collapses onto his bed. He looks over at Gavin's empty area. *Man, he must be having a good time with his parents. Maybe I could stop by after Christmas.* He shakes his head. Not a good idea. They might ask some questions I'm not comfortable answering. His phone rings. He looks at the screen and answers it.

"Hey Treyshawn!"

"I heard you left. You didn't even wait to see me?"

"Sorry about that."

"What happened?" Treyshawn can hear the tension in Curtis' voice.

"Kelly said you had some kind of argument with your mom."

"Look, I don't want to talk about it."

"This isn't like you, Bro. Arguing with your mom—running away. I'm supposed to be the one with all the family drama."

"We *all* have drama," Curtis responds curtly.

"Yeah, but I could always count on you to hold *your drama* together. You always had a level head. Now," Treyshawn hesitates, "now it seems like you're getting the 'big head.'"

"What's that supposed to mean," Curtis quips.

"Bro, you've changed. It's been slow, but you're not the same cat you used to be."

"So now you're a counselor?" Curtis asks sarcastically while rolling his eyes. "You've been out in California! What do *you* know?"

Treyshawn doesn't reply for a moment. "See, that's what I'm talkin' about. The 'big head.' Ever since you got with that Chasm Montgomery dude and his assistant Erica you've been changin'."

"That's what people do when they *grow up*, Treyshawn... They change. And what do you know about Chasm? You've never even met him."

"I don't *need* to meet him to know the deal. Big rich guy taking you under his wing. I can see how that can change a person. But some things should remain the same. *Good* qualities shouldn't be replaced by bad ones."

"All of a sudden you got all this wisdom?" Curtis scoffs. "Don't forget who helped *you*."

"That's why I'm talking to you Curtis. Because you helped me. And this... how you actin'... it's *not* you. When I was bullying you, I got in your face every day and you always held it together. Now, you're taking *cheap* shots at me. What happened with your moms? What's going on?"

"*Nothing* is going on!"

"Yeah," Treyshawn states flatly, "I can see that. Why don't you *read* the journal you gave me. Maybe your dad's words will remind you of who you're supposed to be."

"Don't you talk to me about *my* dad. You didn't know him. And don't you tell me what to do!"

Silence greets Curtis' sharp remark.

"Merry Christmas, Curtis."

CLICK.

Curtis stares at the phone as the call abruptly ends. "Did he just hang up on me?" He throws his phone across the room! It crashes into the wall and splinters into pieces!

[]

Treyshawn sits on his bed—his eyes wide in disbelief. He can't imagine what could have happened that would cause Curtis to act this way. After a moment of quiet reflection, he jumps up, grabs his coat and walks out his room. "Ma! I'm heading over to Curtis' house for a bit!"

"Wait!" Shakira yells as Treyshawn bounds down the stairs. "I have a surprise for you!"

"Can it wait until I get back in a few hours?" Just as Treyshawn gets to the door—

KNOCK. KNOCK. KNOCK.

Treyshawn opens the door to find his grandmother standing in front of him, dressed in a thick coat, wearing a huge smile on her face and carrying several bags.

"Treyshawn!" she cries.

"Grandma?" Treyshawn asks as she steps forward and hugs him. He smiles as he returns her embrace. "What are you doing here?"

"Wherever you're going will have to wait," she laughs.

"Shakira approaches from the kitchen, a broad grin on her face.

"Grandma Lucille *is* the surprise."

"That's right, Grandson!" Lucille chirps. "I came here to see you. Merry Christmas!"

[]

Christmas morning. The Commerce Club. 49th floor.

Chasm and Dr. Winters sit quietly at their usual table. Traditional Christmas music fills the air as the two look at their watches. Only a handful of people are dining, yet that doesn't stop the restaurant from having a full brunch display available.

"He's late," Dr. Winters speaks with a slight tension in his voice.

"I know," Chasm concurs. "He is usually on time."

Just then, the double doors open and Curtis hurriedly enters, comes over to the table and plops into his seat.

"I am so sorry for being late!" He says. "My phone broke last night and I… overslept."

"Your phone broke?" Chasm asks.

"Yeah. I dropped it by accident," Curtis replies.

"Curtis," Dr. Winters interjects with an air of stern thoughtfulness, "punctuality is the hallmark of excellence. When you are late to meet someone you are saying you don't value their time nor do you truly value yourself."

"But my phone—"

"Even if your phone breaking is a good reason for why you didn't arrive here on time, ultimately it is merely an excuse. Rarely is there only *one* way to accomplish a goal. Why did you not take other measures to ensure you woke up on time? Do you not own a regular alarm clock? Or could you have asked the resident assistant on duty in your dormitory to come and wake you?"

"I... understand, Sir." Curtis utters, lowering his head.

"Dr. Winters is a stickler for punctuality," Chasm adds.

"I am," Dr. Winters confirms. "You must understand, Curtis. You waste time at your own peril. How a person uses his or her time determines what kind of life they will live. It determines the level of their accomplishments in life and the amount of failure they will encounter on a day-to-day basis. How you view time—and what you do with it— reveals your perspective on reality."

"Now," Chasm interjects with a smile, "since you have taken your scolding quietly, let us have brunch. It *is* Christmas after all."

"Yes," Dr. Winters smiles, "it is Christmas." He motions to their waiter and the special meal is served.

After brunch, Dr. Winters reaches into the breast pocket of his jacket and pulls out a small, white box with a red ribbon wrapped around it. "This is for you," he says as he lays the box on the table and pushes it towards Curtis.

"It's from both of us," Chasm smiles.

"Wow," Curtis says as he glances at both of them. "I didn't expect this. Thank you."

"You're welcome," both men reply as they motion for Curtis to proceed. Curtis unties the red ribbon and removes the lid to the white box.

"It's a watch," he says with a bit of surprise.

"Not just *any* watch," Chasm replies.

"That watch is a vintage Rolex Precision 'Campbell' model," Dr. Winters adds.

"That watch you are holding," Chasm informs, "is worth more than most people's lives."

Curtis suddenly holds the watch in shaky hands. His nervousness is obvious as Dr. Winters continues his commentary. "Rolex created 12 of these watches to honor Sir.

Malcolm Campbell. He was from Chislehurst, Kent, England, and had shattered the motorcar world land speed record in the 1930's."

"Dr. Winters and I decided that this was fitting for you," Chasm continues. "We thought this watch would serve as a notable present, given *your* accomplishments with your Mach-1 Speedsuit."

"And," Dr. Winters adds, "this will serve as a reminder to *always* be on time."

□

Three Years Earlier.

Erica Cosway sits across from Dr. Winters as he eats his evening meal. Separating them is an exquisite mahogany wood table, furnished with all the crystal culinary trappings of wealth. A cloth napkin embroidered with his initials is tucked neatly around his collar. Erica watches as he cuts through his food with his silverware and raises a forkful of lobster to his lips. She does the same with her food. Meanwhile, the butler and maid work with feverish elegance to ensure every need is provided for.

"I'm glad you were able to stop by my estate. The documents Chasm had you hand deliver are extremely important. And I'm glad you agreed to stay for dinner!"

"Thank you for the offer," Erica replies. "This is the best lobster I have ever had!"

"Yes, it is. I had it imported directly from the sea around a certain tropical island I frequently visit. Best seafood on the planet, as far as I'm concerned."

A few moments of silence pass before Dr. Winters finishes his final bite and dismisses the help from the large dining room. He removes his napkin from his collar and wipes his mouth a final time before folding the napkin and setting it beside his plate. Erica looks on with a bit of hesitancy—not sure what will come next.

"Punctuality is the hallmark of excellence. And you, my dear Ms. Cosway, are *always* on time. In fact, in practically every encounter we have had over the years, you have been early!"

"I don't like to be late," Erica concurs.

"Neither do I. This is why I'm glad you happen to be here today. I have a proposition for you."

"For me?"

"For you. I have been watching you since Chasm first introduced us back when you were a child. Your work ethic is unrivaled and your sense of loyalty is unquestionable. This is why I want you to work for me."

"In… what capacity?" Erica asks. "Honestly, with my classes and the responsibilities I have as Chasm's assistant, I don't have the *bandwidth* to take on another job."

"I anticipated your concerns," Dr. Winters remarks while crossing his legs and placing his hand confidently on his knee. "What I need you to do for me can be done with minimal effort while you continue to work for Chasm."

"Is this job something you could get someone else to do?"

"I could, but no one with your position, attention to detail and skill-set."

Erica sits quietly as she contemplates Dr. Winters' words.

"You will be handsomely compensated for your time and effort."

"What… would you need me to do?"

"As you know, I have been mentoring Chasm for quite some time now. Through our relationship, he has been able to achieve a level of success most people can't even imagine. Even so, there are times when his decisions are not… in the best interest of the larger picture. Sometimes, he can be too smart for his own good. So, I want you to keep watch over him and inform me of his endeavors. And when necessary, I need you to… *intervene* in his affairs per my instructions."

"You want me to be a spy?"

"That word choice is so dramatic," Dr. Winters chuckles. "I don't want you to be a spy. What I want is for you to help me help him see... the larger picture. Sometimes people need assistance and they don't even realize it."

Erica's eyes dart back and forth as she processes the information that's just been presented to her. "So, what would you require of me... specifically?"

"Straight to the point," Dr. Winters smiles broadly as he leans forward in his chair. "You will share the specifics of all projects Chasm and his company are working on. Whatever I want to know, down to the last iota, you will tell me. And whatever I want you to do to steer his efforts—from subterfuge to sabotage—you will do. In return, your efforts on my behalf, will be both protected and well compensated."

"Why are you doing this?"

"My agenda is just that... mine. However, at a fixed point in the future, everything will be made clear."

Erica sits motionless, weighing every word. *What happens if I don't agree to his terms?*

"By the way, how are your parents and siblings doing? I know they are so proud of you."

"Y-Yes," Erica hesitates, "they are."

Dr. Winters smiles broadly while silently staring at Erica. She breaks his gaze and begins to shift uncomfortably in her chair.

"So, will you do this for me?"

"Do I have a choice?"

"We all make decisions about the path our life will take. I will assume your silence means you are compliant." He looks at his watch. "It is getting late. I'm sure you have somewhere to be."

"Yes," Erica replies while abruptly standing to her feet. "Thank you for dinner."

"Thank you for staying," Dr. Winters responds with a broad smile while standing to his feet and extending his hand. Erica shakes his hand, but Dr. Winters doesn't release his firm grip.

"Your employer is to know nothing of our arrangement. When you arrive at your apartment, you will find a box on your kitchen table. An encrypted phone system is inside. I will be in touch."

Erica struggles as Dr. Winters releases her hand and calls for his butler to escort her to the front entrance. As the butler leads Erica out of the dining room Dr. Winters makes one final remark.

"I *always* want your family to be proud of you, Ms. Cosway. And may you *always* remain in good health!"

Once outside, Erica jumps in her car and speeds down the long driveway of the estate. As soon as she turns onto the main road, she burst into tears and suddenly swerves—barely missing an oncoming truck. She wipes the tears from her eyes in an effort to maintain control over her vehicle. That's when she notices her hands on the steering wheel... shaking.

Once home, she rushes into her kitchen… and finds everything arranged just as Dr. Winters had said. Fear overwhelms her as she slumps against the kitchen wall and slowly slides down to the floor. Her chest heaves as she tries to catch her breath. But she can't. All she can do is cry. In between sobs a single question rises to the forefront of her mind and makes its way to her lips.

"What have I gotten myself into?"

CHAPTER EIGHTEEN

WHAT'S SO MERRY ABOUT CHRISTMAS?

MIRANDA MAKES BREAKFAST FOR HER ELDEST son. Omar sits quietly and watches his mother move about the kitchen. Her body language clearly reflects the fractured state of her emotions as she sniffles to fight back her tears. She prepares her son's plate—heaping with scrambled eggs, bacon, sausage and grits—and places it on the table. She then grabs a glass of orange juice for him, a cup of hot tea for her and quietly sits down.

"You're not going to eat?" Omar queries.

Miranda shakes her head slowly, "You eat. You need your strength."

"So do you, Ma," Omar smiles softly. "You've been up all night."

Miranda forces a smile as she places her hand on his. "I've been up praying all night. Don't you worry about me."

"Too late."

Mother and son share a long, searching gaze before Miranda turns her face towards the window and quietly takes a sip of her Chamomile tea. Omar silently says his grace and begins to eat.

KNOCK. KNOCK. KNOCK.

Miranda rises from her chair and shuffles her way to the front door. Jim greets her as she opens it.

"Merry Christmas."

"What's so *merry* about it?" Miranda quips as she lets him in. "I—I'm sorry, Jim."

"No need to apologize, Miranda," Jim says soothingly. "The last forty-eight hours has been a bit rough."

"A bit?" Miranda chuckles as they both walk into the kitchen.

Jim acknowledges Omar with a light pat on the shoulder.

"Morning Mr. G."

"Do you want anything to eat?" Miranda asks.

"I could eat something," Jim answers, taking a seat next to Omar. Miranda makes Jim a plate and joins them at the table. "I thought having to do Christmas without Malcolm was tough. Now, I feel like I'm *losing* my son!"

"That's the most she's said all morning," Omar informs.

"Yes, it is tough for us all," Jim answers, "But at least Curtis is still alive—even if he's being defiant."

"True," Miranda agrees. "I guess I can't blame him. He came home for a break and we blindsided him with all of this information!"

"That is a lot to take in," Omar agrees.

"Maybe we should have handled it a different way," Miranda muses. "We should have eased him into it over the course of several days."

"We did what we thought was right," Jim counters. "Don't start second-guessing yourself."

"And even though he's mad," Omar adds, "he'll cool down and will hopefully trust us on this."

"I agree," Jim adds, "we all, including Malcolm, have poured a lot into Curtis over the years. He's a great kid, but like the rest of us, he's not perfect. We have to trust the process."

Miranda sits quietly before speaking. "But what happens to him in the meantime? What if his anger and defiance leads him into a situation he can't handle? Then what do we do?"

"What we do," Omar says with conviction in his voice, "is call in the cavalry and come to the rescue."

[]

Kelly sits in the midst of a flurry of activity. The gifts have been opened and now her family eats at the table in their small dining room. But even the laughter, chatter and chomping can't hide the truth.

"Kelly," her mother says, "you've been quiet all morning."

"What did Curtis do *this* time," Kevin jokes.

"Really?" Kelvin says as he jabs his brother in the ribs.

"What's going on," her father asks. "Are you okay?"

Kelly looks at her family for a moment. "I didn't tell you guys, but Curtis left yesterday and went back to school."

"Are you serious?" Kelvin replies.

"No, I'm *making* this up," Kelly quips, "Of course I'm serious!"

"Sorry…" Kelvin holds up his hands in surrender.

Stacy and Johnny catch each other's gaze.

"Does this have to do with that girl, Erica?" her father asks.

"No."

Her family lets out a collective, "Whew…"

"I'm glad it doesn't," Kevin declares, "because I didn't want to have to go down there and rough him up."

"So, do you know why he left?" her mother asks.

"He came by the other night—just after getting in some kind of argument with his mom, Omar and Mr. G."

"Wow," her mother says. "Have you ever known Curtis to get in an argument with them?"

"Never," Kelly says flatly.

"Then it must have been a pretty serious situation," her dad says.

"Yeah," Kelly replies. "But he was too broken up to explain."

"He's a good dude," Kevin says confidently.

"Yeah," Kelvin adds. "Whatever it is, I'm sure he'll come around."

[]

Treyshawn hears a lively conversation coming from the living room as he walks down the steps. His mother and grandmother are surprised to find him fully dressed, with his coat in his hand.

"Trey," his mother says, "it's Christmas. Where are you going?"

"I need to go to Curtis' house."

"Oh," Lucille exclaims, "I've heard so much about your friend! When do I get a chance to meet him? Is he coming over later?"

"That's a good idea," Shakira agrees. "Why don't you see if he can come over this afternoon. Or we could go over to his house."

"He's not here."

Shakira's surprise is obvious. "What you *mean* he's not here? He's at his mother's, right?"

"He was. But he left yesterday and went back to school."

"Why would he do that?" she inquires.

"That's what I'm tryin' to figure out."

"Well okay," Lucille replies. "You go check on your friend and make sure he's alright. We'll be here when you get back."

"Thanks Grandma," Treyshawn smiles as he gives his grandma and mom hugs and kisses. "I'll be back as soon as I can." With that, he leaves the house and treks across town.

[]

The Powers' residence…

KNOCK. KNOCK. KNOCK.

Omar opens the front door. "Hey Treyshawn."

"Hey Omar," Treyshawn says, while blowing into his cupped hands to keep them warm.

"Come on in out of the cold."

"Thanks. Treyshawn enters the house and finds Miranda and Jim in the living room. After a short round of pleasantries Treyshawn gets to the point.

"I came by to talk about Curtis."

"He's not here," Miranda replies.

"I know. He's back at school."

Miranda, Jim and Omar look at each other.

"So, you spoke to him?" Omar asks.

"Yeah. Last night."

"What did he say?" Miranda presses.

"Nothin' good. He actually blew me off. But it's what he *didn't* say that's botherin' me. That's why I came over here."

"So, what do you think is going on?" Jim asks.

"From what I figure, he got into some kind of argument with you guys over that Chasm Montgomery dude."

"How do you figure that?" Miranda asks—feigning ignorance.

"Cause I told him that ever since that guy took him under his wing, he's been changing—and not in a good way. But he doesn't see it like I see it."

"And he doesn't see it like we see it either," Miranda replies. "Well Treyshawn, we can't tell you specifics, but we think someone is trying to manipulate our family."

"And you think it's this Chasm dude?"

"We're not sure," Miranda continues, "but we definitely think he's connected somehow."

"So, what can we do?" Treyshawn asks.

"At this point," Miranda responds, "we wait and see what happens.

But you can't let Curtis know you spoke to us. It's for your own safety."

"Curtis is my friend—even though he may not be *acting* like it right now. If he's in trouble, I want to help."

"You can help," Omar interjects, "by not saying anything. As soon as we know what's going on and can figure out a way for you to help, we'll let you know. OK?"

"OK," Treyshawn agrees. "I trust you guys."

"See," Miranda responds, "why couldn't Curtis trust us like Treyshawn just did?"

"Wow," Treyshawn replies with a slight smile. "I never thought the day would come when someone would say Curtis needs to be more like *me*."

[]

Later that day at the Cosway residence. Indiana.

Erica sits with her family around the dining room table—eating an early dinner.

"It is *so* good to see you baby," her mother exclaims.

"Mom," Erica chuckles, "You're talking like I haven't been home for the last three days!"

"I know," her mother concedes with a huge grin. "It's just that we don't get to see you much. The last time you were home was Easter. You're so busy, you didn't even come home for Thanksgiving anymore. So, I'm happy whenever you do!"

"*Very* happy," her father adds.

They all laugh.

"And I'm sure your brother and sister are happy to have you home."

"It would be better if I didn't have to move back into my old room," her sister insists.

"Hey!" Erica shoots her the classic 'big sister' disapproval stare.

"What?" Her sister says, "you *always* had the best room! Now it's mine—except when you come back home."

"Well good thing I'm only home to visit," Erica declares.

"Well *I'm* happy you're here!" her brother adds.

"Thank you," Erica replies with an air of diplomacy.

"So," her dad asks, "how's Mr. Montgomery doing?"

"Good as usual," Erica answers. "Chasm has been spending a lot of time flying back and forth. He's busy getting the New York facilities ready for opening day."

"So, he's been leaving you in charge while he's gone?" her father asks.

"Yes. He says he's grooming me for another promotion."

"That's excellent!" her father grins. "You know, one day you may be CEO of his company—if he moves to bigger and better things, of course."

"Well, Dad, his company is pretty big and a pretty great place to work already. I don't know where he'd go from there."

"And how's that Curtis Powers?" her mother asks. "He seems like a bright young man."

"He's cool too!" her brother shouts.

"And he's so cute!" her sister smiles. "Can you introduce us?"

"He's great to work with," Erica confirms. "He has a good head on his shoulders."

"Could there be a potential *future* there?" her mother asks as her voice rises higher in pitch.

"Mom..." Erica drones, "he has a girlfriend."

"He does?" her mother feigns excitement. "Good for him. He's still a nice young man, even if he's not... available."

"Too bad you can't stay longer," her father laments. "Are you sure you can't talk Mr. Montgomery into letting you stay here for a full week?"

"Sorry Dad. There's too much to do. You have no idea how many projects I'm juggling all at once. In some ways I feel like I have the workload of *two* bosses."

"Well," her father says confidently, "you've always been able to handle a lot of pressure and make good decisions. That's why you'll have *two* masters degrees in science."

"Yeah, well sometimes the pressure really takes a toll on me. I wish I could take a break from the grind every now and then."

"Well, this is your break *now*," her mother insists, "and Easter will be your break *then*."

They all laugh.

"Mr. Montgomery has been good to you and to us," her father says.

"Here we go," Erica rolls her eyes in feigned annoyance.

"I know I sound like a broken record," her father concedes with a chuckle, "but he did come into our lives at the right time. And we've been better off because of him. "He values your work ethic, ingenuity and loyalty. I know you won't let him down. Keep up the good work."

"Yes, baby," her mother smiles, "we are *all* so proud of you."

Erica forces a grin and glances away as she eats a forkful of food.

[]

The Powers' Residence. Evening.

DING. DONG.

Miranda opens her front door to find a delivery truck driving away. She looks down at the huge box on her doorstep.

"Omar! I'm going to need your help with this!" Miranda clears off the dining room table as Omar places the large box on top of it.

"What do you think it is?" Jim asks.

"Judging by the size," Miranda muses, "It's probably a gift basket from Chasm Montgomery."

Jim frowns as Miranda cuts away the wrapping paper with her scissors. Inside, she finds the card and opens it.

"Yep, it's from Mr. Montgomery."

Miranda,

Please accept these hand-picked chocolates during this Holiday season. Each set has its origin in a different part of the world. And each delicacy is almost as sweet as you. Thank you for your friendship and for your continued trust in my mentorship of your son.

With warm regards...
Chasm Montgomery

Omar and Jim groan as Miranda puts the card down and opens the inner box.

"Well, he sure does know how to make an impression."

With Omar's help, she pulls out a Christmas-themed gift basket full of an assortment of high-quality chocolates and other exotic sweets.

Jim whistles at the sight. "You sure can't get those chocolates at your local store."

"Ma, do you think he knows?" Omar inquires.

"Honestly," Miranda replies, "I'm not sure. My gut says 'no.' But we can never be too sure about anything at this point. As long as Curtis hasn't told him… I think we are okay—for now."

[]

Curtis lays on his bed in his dorm room—staring at the ceiling. A question keeps flipping through his mind. *Should I confront Chasm about what my mom said?* But every time he considers doing so, the knotted feeling resurfaces in his stomach. It is that feeling which causes him to pause.

"But they can't be right," he mumbles to himself. "That makes absolutely no sense." He looks at his father's journal which sits on the far corner of his desk. He stares at it—for what seems like an hour—before slowly rising from his bed to pick it up. He flips the journal open to a random page. The title at the top catches his attention.

WHEN YOU DON'T KNOW WHAT TO DO

Boys.

Judgment can be a tricky thing. Often we have to make decisions armed with only half the facts. (And sometimes even less!) Someone who takes their decision-making seriously works hard to make their best judgments. In many cases this is interpreted to mean 'one's best educated guess.'

Most people tend to think that this is the best we can do. On a certain level, this is true. However, for a person of Faith there is a deeper… higher level to consider. And that is to submit our decision-making process to God.

Now, this doesn't mean we 'check our brains at the door.' On the contrary, God has given each of us a wonderful mind with which to understand this world. But the truth is our understanding is—in fact —limited. There are things we don't know. And, if we're honest—the more we learn, the more we realize how little we do know! There are often situations at play in our lives which are larger and greater than we are. So, when we submit our minds to God, we are in fact bringing to him everything we know about a situation and asking him to guide us. We are asking him to 'plug the holes' in our knowledge base and understanding. To reveal to us the things we've missed—the things we cannot see. We are asking God to act on our behalf, for our good and for his glory.

No doubt, in this life you will have trouble. No doubt, you will have to make some difficult decisions. You will have to try and distinguish between right and wrong, good and evil. You may be faced with such decisions even now as you read these words. 'With all of your heart you must trust the LORD and lean not solely on your own understanding'. - Proverbs 3:5

I love you.
Your Father,
Malcolm

Curtis slowly closes the journal as tears well up in his eyes. He holds the book tightly in his hands for several moments before lessening his grip. He looks at the cover once more and grimaces as he throws the journal across the room.

CHAPTER NINETEEN

DORMANT

MARGE SITS IN HER PLUSH, QUIET living room pouring a cup of hot tea. She picks up a pair of silver tongs, removes the porcelain lid from her sugar bowl and gently retrieves two cubes—dropping them into her cup. She places the lid back on the bowl, picks up a small cup of milk and pours the creamer into her tea. She then takes a slender silver spoon from the end table and swirls the sugar, creamer and tea together. A smile forms on her lips as she inhales the fresh aroma. She raises the cup to her mouth and sips the warm sweet liquid.

"Mmm, there's nothing like a good spot of tea," she whispers as she revels in the silence of the moment and closes her eyes. "Just what one needs to relieve some tension..."

Behind her, on her desk, sits an open file folder. Several sheets of paper are stacked beside it: the coveted secret files she and Malcolm had amassed. The phone rings. Marge puts her tea cup down, stands up and walks over to her desk.

"Hello?" She utters as she raises the receiver to her ear.

Heavy breathing greets her inquiry.

"Hello?" she repeats. "Is anyone there? I can hear you breathing."

The heavy breathing continues with no break in rhythm. Marge's voice grows stern.

"If you are the *same* person who has been calling here, know that you will not intimidate me. Even as I speak, this call is being traced. Any information it yields will be turned over to the authorities!"

The heavy breathing stops. A second after that, the line goes dead. The receiver noticeably shakes in her trembling hands as Marge returns it to its base. Her chest heaves as her heart races.

The phone rings again. She quickly picks the receiver back up. "You will not scare me! Do you hear?"

"Marge?" Miranda responds gently. "Are you alright?"

"Oh, it's you." Marge presses her hand against her chest and takes a deep breath in an effort to calm herself down. "I can't talk right now." She immediately hangs up the phone, reaches into her desk drawer and retrieves a cell phone. A moment later she's talking on it.

"I'm sorry for that, Miranda."

"No need to apologize Marge. What happened?"

"Someone has been calling here. The person says nothing, but only breathes heavily. At first I thought it was a wrong number, but this is the fifth time within the last four weeks. I don't think this is a coincidence."

"Do you think someone's found out about us?" Miranda replies.

"Perhaps. My landline may no longer be trustworthy. If this is happening on purpose, then the phone line may be tapped."

"That's why we bought these disposable cell phones," Miranda replies, "to make it difficult for people to track us or our conversation. But right now, I'm more worried about your safety."

"Oh, you don't have to worry about me, my dear," Marge assures. "I am perfectly fine here."

"That's not how it sounded a few minutes ago."

Marge sits at her desk in silence. "I will admit that this has… ruffled my feathers a bit. But I'm alright. Really."

"Maybe you should move down here until everything is cleared up," Miranda suggests. "Our house is a bit small, but we have a guest room."

"I truly appreciate your offer," Marge smiles, "but I am okay right where I am."

"OK," Miranda concedes. "But the offer still stands."

"Thank you."

"So, have there been anymore updates from Mr. Harte?"

"Yes. He found an additional money trail which confirms the information we have already gathered. He will be sending copies soon."

"Speaking of *copies*," Miranda interjects, "you haven't given us copies of your originals."

"You know how I feel about this," Marge replies.

"Yes, I know," Miranda agrees. "But with this heavy-breather person calling you… maybe it's not safe for you to be the only one with these files."

"These documents are perfectly safe with me," Marge insists. "I am—as they say—off the grid. I barely have a digital fingerprint and I want to *keep* it that way."

"But Marge," Miranda urges, "we all have our own pieces of the puzzle, but yours is by far the biggest piece. If something happens to you or to your documents, we'll be dead in the water."

Marge weighs the validity of Miranda's words against her own sense of insecurity. "Fine. After our next meeting with Mr. Harte, we can talk about creating a backup system for *all* of our files."

"Thank you," Miranda smiles. "I know you mean well."

"Yes. It's just that I don't want to risk anything falling into the wrong hands. All of this information, together, will prove that many of the Firm's accomplishments were built on a foundation of criminal practices. These practices have cost many tax paying citizens their homes and businesses over the years. And, I believe we can now prove that Malcolm's refusal to adhere to the Firm's unethical practices was the primary reason that his life insurance policy was canceled."

Miranda sits back in her chair and breathes a deep sigh of relief as her eyes well with tears. She shakes her head slightly as a smile forms on her lips.

"It's been so long... Thank you for all of your help Marge."

"Don't thank me yet. There's still a lot left to do. Even with all of this information, our case is not airtight. Right now, what we have shows that criminal practices took place. But we have nothing which reveals John Whaley or any other executive actually gave the orders. At best, that can be implied, but without proof they might not be found guilty.

"What else can we do?"

"I'm not sure. Attorney Phillips is putting a prosecution team together. Perhaps they will have some ideas. Even if they do, the judicial process will no doubt take some time."

"We are so close to figuring all of this out," Miranda groans. "What about Chasm Montgomery?"

"I'll admit, he wasn't even a consideration in my mind before you sent me the documents Omar had compiled. While I do see the same coincidences, I have yet to find a paper trail on this end to support your theory. Mr. Montgomery would periodically stop by the office from time-to-time. He even had lunch with your husband on two occasions. He was always pleasant. His adopted father and Mr. Whaley were as close as brothers. Yet, he's still a mystery. If there was any collusion, the record of it was purely verbal."

"Okay," Miranda huffs. "So, you are saying that this may be a dead end. I was hoping to find a connection here—one that could help me convince Curtis to see the truth."

As if by magic, Miranda' s words hit Marge like a jolt. Marge's eyes flutter as she recalls a long-dormant memory.

[]

Pierce-Sterling and Whaley Architect Firm. New York City. April 1997.

Fingers move over computer keys with the speed of a professional drummer. Marge's eyes focus on her screen as she listens, through her headphones, to every word flowing from her voice recorder. Malcolm's dictation is almost complete as a hand knocks on the top of the wall that faces her desk. She feels the vibration and looks up to find a charismatic, smiling face staring at her.

"Mr. Montgomery!" She smiles.

"Please call me Chasm," he smiles back. "How's my favorite lady doing today?"

Marge blushes slightly. "You always have a way of bringing a smile to my face."

After a few minutes of small talk, Marge calls to the executive offices. A moment later, John Whaley and Malcolm walk onto the floor to greet their visitor.

"Chasm!" John exclaims. "It's good to see you! Are you ready for lunch?"

"I am famished," Chasm chuckles. "I've been in meetings since 7 o'clock this morning!" Chasm looks down. "And who do we have here?" he smiles.

A small boy hides behind Malcolm—holding tightly onto his leg.

"This is my son, Curtis. Say hello, Son."

A bashful Curtis barely peeks out from behind his father. "Hello."

Chasm stoops to Curtis' height. "Hello there!" he beams. "It's nice to meet you, Curtis." Chasm extends his hand with a warm smile. "Can you give me a high-five?"

Curtis looks at his father, who smiles with approval. He then smiles, raises his hand and brings it down as fast as he can.

SMACK!!!

Chasm shakes his stinging hand as the group laughs.

"What's your name?" Curtis asks.

"My name is Chasm Montgomery. But you can call me Chasm."

"He," Malcolm interrupts with a smile, "can call you *Mr. Montgomery*."

"Hello Mr. Montgomery," Curtis replies.

"Hello to you, too. Now tell me… how old are you?"

Curtis smiles from ear to ear. "I'm four and three quarters."

"Really?" Chasm exclaims.

"Yep! I'll be five in three months!"

"That's wonderful! Well, may I say Happy Birthday to you!"

"But it's not my birthday yet."

"But it will be very soon," Chasm smiles warmly. "So tell me, what do you like to do?"

"I like to invent stuff," Curtis declares without hesitation.

"Really?" Chasm nods his head. "When I have more time, I would love to hear all about your inventions. Did you know that is what *I* do for a living?"

Curtis shakes his head—his eyes wide with astonishment.

"Maybe one day, when you are older, you could come and work for me."

"That sounds great!" Curtis yells excitedly.

"Malcolm," Chasm utters as he stands to his feet and rubs Curtis' head softly, "you have a wonderful son!"

"Thank you," Malcolm declares as only a proud father can. "He inherited my love of science. But I wasn't as young as *he* was when I developed it."

"Well, you make sure to feed that passion and he will go far in life. You know, I have never met a four year old who speaks with such clarity as he does."

"Yes," Malcolm agrees. "He's very intelligent and keeps his mother and me on our toes—that's for sure!"

Marge looks on from her desk, smiling as Malcolm brings Curtis over to her.

"We'll see you in a couple of hours."

"Ok. Dad."

Curtis sits on Marge's lap and watches as his father walks out of the front doors with the two gentlemen.

[]

The Present.

"Marge…" Miranda utters in a gasped whisper.

"I-I'm sorry I didn't remember this sooner…"

"You didn't have a reason to until now. Memories are funny like that sometimes."

"It seemed… so random," Marge replies, "…how they met."

"Maybe," Miranda muses, "maybe it was. Maybe that is where the coincidences began. What terrifies me is that when we all met Chasm on Curtis' first day of college, he acted as if that was the very first time they had met. Could it be he didn't realize that Curtis was *Curtis*?"

"I don't think so," Marge speaks as she continues to recall their encounter. "For as long as I have know Chasm, he has always been a person who pays close attention to details. I find it hard to believe he didn't realize the connection."

"Well, Curtis *definitely* doesn't remember," Miranda states flatly. "And I guess, the meeting was so random that Malcolm didn't have reason to tell me about it. But why would Chasm want to hide this?"

Miranda and Marge stare at one another in silence before Marge speaks.

"I was just wondering the same thing."

CHAPTER TWENTY

A DIFFERENT PERSPECTIVE

FEBRUARY 2014. A BALL OF FIRE erupts from the gauntlet of a newly developed gold-colored pyrotechnic suit. Once the five-foot plume dissipates, a loud buzz sounds as engineers descend to check the suit's functionality. They are impressed with its ability to keep the wearer cool inside, while protecting him from the heat on the outside.

Several meters away in another part of the lab, stands a wall of ballistic-grade-glass covered with six inch thick acoustic padding. The suit operator stands twenty feet from a large chunk of concrete sitting on a platform. Next to it sits three additional platforms—each with remnants of different materials: toppled foam on one, broken glass on another, and disintegrated wood on the last. The engineers move behind a blast shield and don their protective helmets and body gear. One of them gives the operator a "thumbs up" signal. She smiles, puts her helmet on and powers up her black padded suit. A faint hum can be heard as a pulsing vibration is felt by the engineers, through the floor.

A red light on the wall begins to shine—indicating to everyone around to take caution and keep their distance. She takes her position and aims her hands at the concrete. A second later, the slab of concrete begins to rattle on the platform. Then it begins to shake. Then—it explodes! Shards hit the blast shield as the engineers smile and clap. A loud buzz is heard as the red light turns off. The operator powers down her suit and removes her helmet as the engineers run over to her with their diagnostic equipment.

Several meters away in another part of the lab, Curtis makes some last minute tweaks to the backpack worn by the last suit operator.

"Hold your arms up," Curtis commands. "I need to adjust the electromagnetic coupling that runs from the backpack to your rib area."

The operator holds his arms up as Curtis switches out a component and re-attaches it.

"Are you sure this is going to work?" an engineer asks as he runs a diagnostic. "I've never seen a configuration like this before."

"The concept is sound," Curtis responds. "I was building this at home over the summer. I just didn't have all of the materials to complete it." Curtis closes the housing covers on the torso and lowers the backpack lid into place with a snap. He double taps the operator and gives a "thumbs up" signal. The engineers walk past a number of heavy objects and move behind the blast shield. Curtis is the last to join them.

"I don't think this will work," an engineer says. "Electromagnets can't be harnessed this way. The suit won't be able to take the load."

"O, you of little faith," Curtis replies.

"It's not about faith," the engineer responds. "It's about physics."

The operator puts on his helmet and powers up his suit. He walks over to some exercise weights. With the press of a button on his forearm control module, the suit's output level is set to 25 percent.

"That first one is 200 pounds," Curtis says, smiling.

The operator crouches slightly and grabs the bar with both hands. He then lifts it effortlessly above his head. The operator puts the weights down and walks over to the next object—a large crate with two poles sticking out of it.

"The contents of that crate is just over 400 pounds," Curtis says, a broad smile playing on his face.

The operator increases the output level to 50 percent, grabs the two poles and positions himself. With minimal effort, he tilts the crate up into the air and then lowers it back to the ground. He then walks over to a larger crate that is twice the size of the previous one.

"This one's just for dramatic effect," Curtis notes, as the operator increase the output level of the suit to its maximum setting. He bends down, grabs the crate at one corner and stands up quickly while flinging it almost twenty feet across the room.

A loud buzz sounds as the red light disengages. The engineers descend onto the suit operator with their diagnostic tools. Curtis walks over to them nonchalantly.

"So," he smiles proudly, "the suit worked—*without* hydraulic pistons. Can you imagine the looks on kids' faces when these three suits are unveiled at this summer's tour?"

[]

Erica walks into Chasm's office and closes the door.

"Can I talk to you?"

"You always have my attention," Chasm replies while typing at his computer.

"I don't get it."

"What is it that you do not understand?" Chasm answers.

"We've been working with Curtis for about a month. His suit designs are great, but these are nothing we couldn't have built on our own."

"True. We could have built suits similar to Curtis' designs. But we would have had to do so *without* Curtis."

"So, what are you *not* telling me?"

Chasm stops typing and looks up at Erica. He leans back in his chair and presses his fingers together in front of his chin.

"What Curtis brings to this process is his *perspective*. We have some of the greatest scientist and engineers that money can buy. However, most of them consistently approach projects from a 'mathematics first' perspective. They do the work 'on paper' before they ever build anything. This has its place and ultimately can be very effective in saving valuable resources. But, I believe there is something lost on this process."

"How so?"

"We've been at this for thirty-seven days and we already have three different working prototypes. Did you see how Curtis approached these suits? He asked for several tables of parts and materials. He knew what the suits were supposed to do and he immediately went to work with a 'hands on' approach. How many suits do you think we would have if we approached this with our standard process?"

Erica thinks for a moment. "One."

"If that," Chasm adds. "*Barely* one suit. Compared to our competition, our approach is fast. However, it is not fast enough. Curtis has spearheaded the successful development of his Mach-1, Conduit and Compressor suits with off-the-shelf parts and with the help of family and friends. Look at what he's doing with access to my resources. He is—what I call—a *Creative*. And he *sees* the world differently. *That* is one of his greatest strengths."

"So, you know his process. Why don't we just train our people to think like he does?"

"To break our people out of their "box" would take a tremendous expenditure of time, energy and resources. That's something I'm not willing to do at the moment. Some things can be taught. Other things are an *intrinsic* quality to be developed. By the way, did you notice that Curtis' strength-augmentation suit is about *half* the weight of our previous suit?"

Erica stares at Chasm without a word. "How do you know so much about him?"

Chasm smiles slightly. "You and I met when you were how old?"

"Twelve. I was in middle school."

"Well, it's my job to find prodigies. And I stumbled upon Curtis when he was just four years old."

"Four years old!"

"Four and three quarters to be exact. It was a chance meeting. But I knew then that Curtis was someone to watch. And even though he remained 'under the radar' until he set the world record in his Mach-1 prototype, I had been following all of his quiet developments: attended his first science camp when he was five. Attended several advanced science camps from ages six to nine. Took his first AP science course at ten. Passed biology and chemistry in middle school. The only 9th grade student to take physics. The rest, as you know, is history."

"So, you have had your eye on him all of these years? Why doesn't Curtis remember?"

"He doesn't remember because we only met once. I made a point to keep my distance to see how he would turn out. After all, his father—whom I had met on several occasions—was a brilliant architect. I simply waited for the appropriate time while determining where Curtis would best fit in my empire."

"And now that you know?"

"We will be in a position to increase our reach exponentially and achieve our goals."

[]

Gavin arrives back at his dorm room happy to have had an extended winter break.

"Glad I didn't schedule any classes for the intense January semester," he utters to himself while unpacking his bags. "One class, five days a week, for the entire month? No, thank you!"
He looks towards Curtis' side of the room and notices his personal belongings—but his bed looks like it hasn't been slept

in at all. "Curtis is not a neat freak. Looks like he hasn't been here in days. I wonder where he is."

Gavin notices a book awkwardly lying in a corner of the room. He walks over and picks up the slightly crumbled and ripped book.

"What happened to Curtis's journal? How did it end up over here?"

[]

Flurries fall steadily from the evening sky as Kelly and Curtis sit in a booth at a local diner—just off of Spelman's campus. Their winter coats are stuffed in the cramped space beside them. Both have a full plate of food which has barely been touched. Curtis sits silently, twirling the spaghetti on his plate with his fork. Kelly stares at him intently while sipping her hot chocolate. She then places it on the table with a sense of resoluteness.

"Curtis. I've been trying to give you some space to think things through," she says gently. "But you haven't spoken to your family in over a month. This isn't *you*."

Curtis continues to swirl the food on his plate.

"I know you're hurt by what they said."

"They want me to leave school," Curtis replies, curtly.

"No," Kelly counters. "They want you to *switch* schools. There's a difference."

"They think my life is in danger!"

"I know."

"Well, they're wrong."

"Maybe," Kelly takes his hand in hers. "But what if they're right?"

"They think Chasm is a threat." Curtis gazes into her eyes. "What do *you* think?"

"I like Mr. Montgomery just as much as you do," Kelly gazes into Curtis' eyes for a moment before continuing. "He's been a big help to all of us. I know he means so much to you as a mentor; especially since your dad… is no longer here. But who have you known longer? Your new mentor or your mom, Omar and Mr. G?"

"Length of time doesn't mean anything," Curtis scoffs. "Plenty of people mess up their lives because they listened to bad advice from people they've known for years."

"You're right," Kelly agrees. "But that's not always the case. You've only known Mr. Montgomery for what, a year and a half? But you've known your mom and brother all your life. And me, Mr. G and Treyshawn for the last six years. Look at the *track record* Curtis. In your whole life, has your mom or brother ever *intentionally* tried to mislead you?"

Curtis hesitates, not wanting to answer. "…No."

"Have they always had your best interest at heart?"

Again he hesitates. "…Yes."

"And have they made sacrifices to protect you and help you achieve your dreams?"

Curtis rolls his eyes while taking a deep breath. "…Yeah."

"Then why is it so hard for you to trust them with *this* situation?" Kelly presses. "Their track record speaks for itself."

Curtis pulls his hand away and slouches back as the reality of Kelly's words sink into his consciousness.

"Like I said," Kelly continues, "I like Mr. Montgomery. But if there's even a *small* chance that your mom is right and he's hiding something, then I'll stand with your mom. I *know* I can trust her."

Curtis stares out the window at the falling snow as their waitress approaches their table.

"You two have hardly touched your food," she declares in her southern drawl. "Is it okay?"

"Yes," Kelly assures her. "The food is fine."

"We're just talking," Curtis adds without turning his face from the window.

"Ah, young love," the waitress smiles. "I remember when I was in college. Relationships—while exciting—seemed so… complicated."

"Tell me about it," Curtis huffs.

The waitress cocks her eyebrow at his remark and looks at Kelly, who's shaking her head.

"OK," the waitress states, her voice rising. "I'm going to get you two a couple of doggy bags." As the waitress walks away, Kelly kicks Curtis' feet under the table.

"Ouch! What did you do that for?" Curtis exclaims.

"So, our relationship is complicated?"

"No. Sorry," Curtis replies. "*We're* good. It's all of my other relationships that seem to be complicated right now."

"Uh, huh," Kelly smirks. "Good save."

Curtis smiles as he takes hold of Kelly's hand—causing her to blush.

"So," Kelly inquires, "about the matter at hand. What does your heart tell you?"

Curtis looks Kelly in her eyes. This time she can see his hesitation.

"There *has* been this… knot in the pit of my stomach," he admits.

"What do you mean? What kind of knot?"

"Every time I've wanted to confront Chasm," Curtis continues, "I get this tightening in my stomach. It's like nervousness that grows more each time I attempt to open my mouth."

"So, what do you think it means?" Kelly asks.

"I think…" Curtis begins. "I think it means… in the back of my mind I've been wondering if my mom is right. But she can't be! Can she?"

Kelly breathes deeply. "The only way for you to know is if you do what she says… or at least talk things through with her. Maybe you guys can find another option besides you having to leave school."

[]

After Curtis walks Kelly back to her dorm, he heads back to his campus. Soon, he nears the old church where he met the little boy, Javier. The lights are on, indicating that a service might be in session. He stops on the sidewalk, at the walkway to the entrance, but decides to keep moving. He barely walks past the church before hearing a familiar voice calling his name.

"Hey Curtis!"

He turns around to see Javier running up the pathway in his direction.

"Javier?" Curtis answers in disbelief. "How did you know it was me?"

"I just happened to be looking out the window. Besides, I would know you anywhere! You want to come inside?"

"Uh, no. I have to get back to campus." Curtis looks at the boy, who is wearing sneakers, pants and a t-shirt. "Where's your coat?"

"It's inside," a shivering Javier replies. "I didn't want to miss you."

"Well you better go back inside before you catch a cold or worse."

"What's worse?"

"Before your mom finds out you left," Curtis smirks.

"Yikes!" Javier yells. "You're right! Can you please walk me back? It's dark out here and I don't want anyone to kidnap me."

"You're *good*," Curtis chuckles as he turns to walk Javier back to the church.

Both come to the front doors and stop.

"Here you are," Curtis smiles. "Safe and sound."

"Thanks! You sure you don't want to come in?"

"Maybe another time."

"OK," Javier replies in a low tone before becoming chipper again. "You remember what I said last time we met?"

"What?" Curtis tries to recollect the conversation. "About the new suits?"

"Which are pretty cool! But, that's not what I'm talking about."

"What then?"

"I told you I wanted to be like you! Do you remember?"

"Yeah," Curtis smiles at the memory. "I remember."

"Well I still do!" Javier declares confidently while giving Curtis a huge hug. "Bye!" Javier releases Curtis from his grip and rushes back into the church.

[]

Curtis walks into his dorm room and turns on the light. Gavin lies asleep in his bed—snoring like a tree cutter. Curtis notices his father's journal sitting on his desk. *Didn't I throw this in the corner? Gavin must have found it.* He grabs the book and sits on his bed.

"I miss you dad," he mumbles to himself. "I wish you were still alive." He looks at the journal's cover for a moment longer before sitting it next to him on the bed. He reaches into his bag and pulls out his new cell phone.

[]

At the Power's residence, Miranda, Omar and Jim sit in the living room pouring over mounds of documents. The phone rings. Miranda picks up the handset and looks at the caller ID. A smile beams across her face as she motions to Omar and Jim.

"Hello?" Miranda utters eagerly.

"Hey Mom," Curtis replies sheepishly.

"Curtis!" She exclaims. "It's good to hear your voice! Are you alright?"

"Yeah, Mom. I'm OK. I just wanted to talk. Are you busy?"

"Never too busy for you, baby. I'm here with your brother and Jim."

"Can you put me on speaker so everybody can hear?"

Miranda engages the speaker and places the phone on the table. "Go ahead. We can all hear you!"

"Hey Omar and Mr. G," Curtis utters. "How are you guys?"

"We're good," Jim and Omar declare in unison. "How are you?"

"Listen. I just wanted to apologize for leaving and for being a real jerk. Can you all forgive me?"

The trio smiles at each other as each nods their approval.

"We do Bro," Omar declares. "We forgive you."

"So, what brought about this change of heart?" Miranda asks.

"Just had time to think. Had a couple of conversations, too, which helped give me a different perspective on things. I still don't know if you guys are right about Chasm, but I do trust you enough for us to find out together."

"That's good to hear," Miranda says, relief clear on her face. "That's really good to hear. Speaking of Mr. Montgomery, you haven't shared any of this with him have you?"

"No. I wanted to, but I couldn't."

"Good. So, what have you been up to for the past month?"

"I've been working with Chasm, Erica and their team of engineers on some new suits! Mom, it's crazy what we've been able to do with access to so many resources. I'm like a kid in a candy store! We've already built three new prototypes for fire, sonics and strength-augmentation."

"What are you going to do with the suits once they're complete?" Jim inquires.

"We're going to use them for the new Powersuit Tour this summer. Guys, you have to see what Chasm and Erica have planned. This tour is going to be absolutely amazing! But we still have three more suits to design. It's going to be great! Chasm has given me access to whatever I need!"

"Kid in a candy store," Omar repeats.

"Baby, I need to ask you something."

"Sure thing, Mom."

"Do you remember the first time you met Mr. Montgomery?"

"Mom, you were there. We all met him on my first day of college. Why?"

"When you met him, did he seem *familiar* at all? Did you feel like you'd seen him before?"

"No, not really." Curtis tries to think back to that moment. "Gavin asked me if I knew who he was, but I didn't. What's this about?"

"Curtis," Miranda continues, "this might be hard to believe, but we discovered that you and Chasm did meet before you got to college."

"What?" Curtis exclaims. "That makes no sense! Are you kidding? I'd remember something like that!"

"Maybe not, baby. It was a long time ago. You were only four years old. You had gone to work with your father and Mr. Montgomery had come by to meet him and John Whaley for lunch. You and he even had a conversation. Does any of this ring a bell?"

"I don't remember much from that age." Curtis tries hard to think back. "Are you sure this really happened? I've got no memory of it."

"I'm sure."

"How do you know?"

"I can't tell you."

"If you can't trust me, then what's the use talking about this?"

"Ma," Omar interjects. "Maybe it's time."

"Time for what?" Curtis asks.

Miranda runs her hands through her hair while breathing deeply. "Curtis, we have a meeting this Saturday. I'm going to get you a plane ticket home so you can be there. There's someone you need to meet."

"Saturday? But that's—"

"I know."

"Well… Who is the person?"

"You said you wanted me to trust you more? Well, this is it. All of your questions will be answered on Saturday. Okay?"

"OK Mom. I'll talk with you guys later."

"Before you go," Jim interjects, "what will happen to the suits you're creating once the summer tour is over?"

"I dunno," Curtis muses in a surprised tone. "I mean, they're *my* designs. I just figured we could use them over and over as a part of our current collection."

"You might want to confirm that before you build anything else," Jim replies in a serious tone. "I know Mr. Montgomery is your mentor, but he's also a businessman."

"I gotta go," Curtis replies. "I'll see you guys on Saturday."

CHAPTER TWENTY-ONE

THE REVEAL

CURTIS AND OMAR WALK UP THE steps at the 125th street train station. The cold air immediately makes every breath visible on this sunny, winter day. They adjust their coats to retain as much of their body heat as possible, as they strut down the Harlem streets.

"That's a nice jacket," Omar says, admiringly. "Is it new?"

"Yep!" Curtis smiles. "Chasm bought it for me a few weeks ago."

The two brothers navigate through the neighborhoods of Harlem and eventually come to a stop in front of an immaculately kept brownstone home.

DING. DONG.

The door quickly opens as they are greeted by a lanky teenage boy with dreadlocks.

"Curtis Powers! It's actually you!" The boy smiles widely. "Wow. You're actually here at my house."

"Yep!" Curtis smiles awkwardly while stealing a glance at Omar.

"My name is Matthew Harte. I'm a huge fan of yours!" He and Curtis shake hands.

"Wow!" Curtis grimaces. "You got a grip like my brother!"

"Sorry," Matthew releases his grip. "So excited. Guess I don't know my own strength. Come on in!" He rushes the boys inside, quickly closes the door and engages several locks.

A short man with glasses stands at the foyer entrance. "Hello boys," he says with a slight Ghanaian accent. "I see you've met my son."

"Yes," Curtis and Omar say in unison.

"You must be Curtis," the man smiles as he motions for Matthew to leave. "My name is Emmanuel Harte."

"Nice to meet you," Curtis replies.

"I've heard quite a bit about you, both from the media and from your mother and brother. How are you, Omar?"

"I'm doing well, Mr. Harte," Omar remarks. "It's good to see you again."

"It is good to see you too." He shakes Omar's hand and extends his hand to his brother.

Curtis extends his hand and then pulls it back suddenly. "Wait. Do you shake hands like your son?"

"No," Mr. Harte chuckles. "Not at all."

Curtis breathes a sigh of relief as he shakes his hand. "It's nice to meet you."

"You know, my son Matthew is a big fan of yours. He even wrote you a letter about a year ago."

"He *seems* like a big fan," Curtis replies.

"Please. Let us not stand here in the foyer any longer. Come into the living room. The rest of the group is already here."

They exit the foyer and walk down a long hallway to the living room. Curtis notices the family portraits and African paintings on the walls. As he enters the living room, he is greeted by Miranda and Jim, who are sitting on the couch. Curtis stops mid-stride as he looks at an elderly, well-dressed woman sitting in one of the chairs near a lamp-stand.

"Hello Curtis," she declares in her British accent, as she peers at him over the rim of her glasses.

Curtis is shocked. "Mrs... Cunningham?"

She rises from her seat and extends her arms. "The one and only."

Curtis all-but-runs and embraces her with a strong hug. She chuckles loudly—surprised by the intensity of the hug.

"It's been a very long time since we last saw each other!"

"Yeah," Curtis agrees. "It was at my dad's funeral." He pulls away from her slightly. "Wait. What are you doing here? Are you the one my mom has been working with?"

"You are correct." She motions for him to sit as she and the rest of the group take their seats.

Curtis takes off his coat and sits down across from her. She stares at him lovingly and takes his hands in hers.

"So, how have you been?"

"I'm doing alright," Curtis replies, a hint of uncertainty lingering in his voice.

"I have been following your exploits with great interest. You are on an exciting road—yet one that has many harrowing twists and turns."

Curtis nods his head in quiet agreement.

"My dear young Curtis. It is time for you to know everything we know."

Curtis looks at everyone before fixing his gaze back on her. After a moments pause he responds. "And what's that?"

"The cancellation of your father's life insurance policy was not an accident."

"That's something I *already* know."

"Correct. But did you know that someone or a group of someones have targeted *your* family?"

"Because of my dad? What did he do that would cause someone to target us?"

"It's not what your father did. It's what your father *did not* do."

[]

May 1996. Pierce-Sterling and Whaley Architect Firm. New York City.

John Whaley stands in his corner office on the 32nd floor. With his hands in his pants pockets, he stares out the expansive window down to the Manhattan streets below. His suit jacket sits draped over his large leather chair behind his custom built wooden desk.

KNOCK. KNOCK.

He turns around to find Malcolm standing at the door.

"Hey John. You wanted to see me?"

"Yes, I do" John smiles as he walks over to his desk. "Please come in."

Malcolm and John sit on opposite sides of the desk.

"I'll get right to it, Malcolm. We want to make you a partner here at Pierce-Sterling and Whaley."

"Really?" Malcolm utters, trying to hold back his enthusiasm.

"You have done excellent work over the years. No other architect here has your level of expertise and attention to detail."

"Thank you, Sir."

"No," John smiles broadly, "thank you. Now, greater responsibility will come with this promotion. Your salary will triple as a result."

"Triple!" Malcolm exclaims. "I didn't realize the increase would be so much."

"We can reduce it if you'd like," John quips.

"No, thank you," Malcolm laughs. "Triple is just fine."

John stands and motions for Malcolm to join him at the window. They gaze at the buildings across from them and then down to the people and traffic below.

"I need to know that I can count on you," John says firmly.

"I thought that point was already proven," Malcolm replies with a hint of curious surprise.

"You have proven it to a certain level," John weighs his words. "What do you see down there on the street?"

"I… I see people."

"People." John nods his head in agreement. "People going about their lives—mostly oblivious to the way the larger world works. Do you know what *I* see?"

Malcolm stares at John silently.

"Ants. You know, it's amazing how much people are like ants. Now, don't get me wrong, ants are amazing creatures! In fact, I had several ant farms as a young boy growing up in the rural Midwest. However, as amazing as they are, ants are creatures nonetheless."

"Where are you going with this analogy?"

"Have you ever had to step on an anthill?"

"…Yes."

"The hill is destroyed and the ants scatter. Yet, when given enough time, the ants will… recalibrate and adjust to their new way of life. People are exactly the same way. And a company like this one, which has designed and built buildings across the planet, doesn't reach our level of influence without… stepping on a few anthills and making a few enemies."

"Are you saying that this company has done some things that you are not proud of?"

"Not at all," John chuckles. "I have been proud of *everything* we have done here at this company. We have worked the way the *larger* world works and we have helped to produce major change in countless lives. What I'm saying is that if you accept this position as partner, you will become privy to the inner workings of this Firm. You will have unparalleled access to our information, and you will see some things that may make you uncomfortable, if you only look at the world from the perspective of *those people* at street level."

Silence lingers in the air for several moments.

"I see," Malcolm finally responds.

"The founding partners and our shareholders need to know that we can trust you with this level of responsibility." John holds out his hand in Malcolm's direction. "Can we?"

"Yes," Malcolm says while shaking John's hand firmly. "You can trust me."

[]

The Present.

"So, what didn't my dad do?" Curtis interrupts.

"Patience," Marge replies, "I am getting to that. But you need to understand the foundation upon which *all* of his decisions were then to be made."

[]

July 1996. New Jersey.

Malcolm sits in his expansive private office, in his new dream home, going over pages and pages of company documents. His stomach grows increasingly unsettled as he reviews project after project. The projects themselves are not what bother him. These buildings his company has built have become tremendous beacons for innovation and have created jobs for thousands. Even more so, the company has worked tirelessly in a number of philanthropic endeavors to "give back" to the communities in which its buildings stand.

But what upsets him is what he discovers when he cross references these building projects with city, public and media records for timeframes before, during and after each project. After some heavy digging, for a handful of instances, these records highlight accidents that have happened in the vicinity of where these new buildings were determined to be built.

"Is it just a coincidence that people have lost their homes and businesses to floods and fires?" he asks himself. "And some of those who tried to lead the fight against zoning law changes inexplicably got sick, died or suddenly moved out of town due to family issues."

Malcolm puts the papers down on his desk, shuts down his computer and lowers his head into his hands. "What have I gotten myself into?"

KNOCK. KNOCK.

Malcolm looks up to see his door open and Miranda standing with a tray of food.

"How's it going?" she asks.

"Oh, you know," Malcolm declares while sitting up and taking a deep breath. "Just swamped. I didn't realize how big of a hand the Firm had in the community."

◘

The Present.

"I remember that!" Miranda exclaims. "I just thought he was stressed from his increased workload. Even now I still wonder why he didn't tell me about this."

"He was trying to protect you and the boys," Marge replies. "And he wasn't sure how deep all of this went."

◘

August 1997. Pierce-Sterling and Whaley Architect Firm. New York City.

John Whaley sits with the founding partners and the Board of Trustees chairman. Marge takes notes for the meeting.

"Malcolm has continued to do great work," a founding partner states, "but he is beginning to ask questions that I find… uncomfortable."

"Perhaps," the chairman replies, "he is not fit to be in this position."

"Gentlemen," John Whaley interjects, "let us not jump to conclusions just yet. Malcolm has been a tremendous help since he accepted our offer to make him partner just over a year ago. He has landed us several multi-million dollar projects within a very small window. He said we could trust him and so far, he has done nothing wrong."

"But his questions—"

"Are just that," John counters, "questions. Questions from a man who has come into unexpected knowledge. Some of *you* had questions when you came into the *same* body of information and realized how *interconnected* our kind of work really is. Yet you found a way to bring a sense of… balance to things. Malcolm Powers is no different."

"Some of us do not maintain your level of trust," a founding partner declares flatly.

"*My* trust is not solely in him—but it is in the process. The way I see it," John smiles as he leans back in his chair, "we have made life *very* enjoyable for Malcolm and his family: the wealth, the new home, the health insurance, the opportunity to travel, the tax breaks. What man, in his right frame of mind, would turn his back on what we have provided? If you do not fully trust *him*—trust our process of *securing* him."

[]

The Present.

Everyone sits quietly—hanging on Marge's every word. She continues to share her thoughts with Curtis.

"From the time your father realized the scope of the Firm's infraction, he had been working to figure out a way to secure justice for the people, while providing for you. Along the way, he and I grew… close. I had always been well compensated and treated with respect as the senior executive administrative assistant. Having been with the Firm since its inception, my allegiance was unquestionable. But your father treated me as more than a valuable asset. He treated me as a legitimate *person*. I thought the founding partners were already doing that, but I discovered there's a fine line of demarcation between the two.

"I was devastated when Malcolm was diagnosed with cancer. I expected him to be devastated as well—and he was—until he found God. Or as he liked to say, 'God found him.' Even though he was dying, he became so much more vibrant in a way I had never experienced!

"It was shortly after that when he disclosed his plans to me. And it was then that I found my allegiance shifting from a blind following of a company I had been with for decades—to the deliberate *partnership* with a man who had earned my trust in a way I could not deny."

[]

Hospital. April 3, 2005.

Margery Cunningham enters the hospital room, greeted by the beeps and hisses of machines. She approaches a sleeping Malcolm and watches quietly as he labors to breathe. She places her hand on his hand, feeling his bones practically protruding through his skin. His eyes slowly open.

"Sorry, I'm late," she whispers as she gives him a gentle kiss on his forehead.

"I thought you weren't coming," Malcolm smiles with a twinkle in his eyes. "How are you?"

"I should be asking how you are doing?" Marge counters.

"I'm doing," Malcolm chuckles. "God is not through with me just yet."

"I'm not sure what to say," Marge declares as a tear streams down her cheek. "The doctors say they are out of options."

"You've been good to me all these years," Malcolm chuckles.

"Hush," Marge counters, "*You've* been good to me. Treated me like a genuine human being."

"That's what you are," Malcolm agrees.

"So, we've been good to each other," Marge smiles.

Malcolm nods in agreement as his expression becomes serious again. "When I die, you have to promise me that you'll watch over my family."

"Quit talking like that. We're going to get a twentieth opinion. There has to be a doctor somewhere who can figure out a solution for your condition."

"Marge," Malcolm counters, "the reality is that no doctor on two continents has been able to help me. My time is coming to a close. For things to change, I would need a miracle. So, if the miraculous does not happen, I need you to watch over my family and be ready to introduce the documents we've collected if the firm doesn't treat them right. And even if they do, at some point, the truth needs to be revealed. John Whaley and the others have destroyed the lives of a lot of people."

[]

The present. Atlanta. The Montgomery Group headquarters.

Erica strolls into Chasm's office as he reads through some documents. "You wanted to see me?"

"I thought Curtis was coming in today."

"He was supposed to, but something came up. Not sure what it was and I don't know where he is. Did you need him for something?"

"Just curious." Chasm turns to his computer and clicks on several icons. According to his GPS locator, he's in Harlem, New York." Chasm picks up his phone and dials a number.

[]

Harlem, New York.

"Just before Malcolm's death, someone decided that you all needed to be dealt a tragic blow which would absorb all of your attention—in case he had shared his knowledge with you."

"The life insurance policy cancellation," Miranda states flatly.

"That's correct," Marge confirms.

"How is Chasm connected to all of this?" Curtis asks as his jacket suddenly vibrates. He scrambles to pull his phone from the inside pocket and looks at the screen. Surprise and trepidation mark his expression. "It's Chasm!"

Everyone stands motionless as the phone continues to ring.

"Should I answer it?"

"Yes!"

"No!"

"Did you tell him you were coming here?"

Curtis shakes his head as he answers the phone. "Hey Chasm," he says in a cool voice.

"Hello Curtis," Chasm responds. "How are you?"

"I'm good. Is everything alright?"

"Yes. I just thought you were scheduled to come into the lab today."

"Yeah. Sorry about that. I needed to come home. It was a last minute thing. Today's the anniversary of my dad's… passing. My mom really wanted us all to be together."

"I'm… sorry." Chasm hesitates—unsure of what to say. "Enjoy your time with your family. I will see you when you return."

"OK," Curtis replies. "Thanks for checking on me. See you on Monday."

Curtis hangs up his phone.

"Are you sure your phone is off?" Miranda asks.

Curtis double checks. "Yeah. It's off. That was crazy!"

"That couldn't have been a coincidence," Omar replies.

"Him calling?" Curtis asks. "Come on, you can't be serious."

"Where's the business card he gave you?" Jim inquires. "He did say that it has a tracking function."

"It does. But I left it back in my dorm room."

[]

Atlanta. The Montgomery Group headquarters.

"I forgot what today was," Chasm admits with slight frustration.

"I'm sorry," Erica frowns. "Had I reviewed his file, I could have reminded you." She looks at Chasm's noticeable change in demeanor.

"Are you okay?"

"I will be." Chasm closes his eyes and takes a deep breath. "This just reminds me of my adoptive parents. Death does not sit well with me."

Erica walks over to Chasm's refrigerator, retrieves a bottle of water and hands it to him. Chasm opens it and drinks his fill. He places the bottle on his desk, stands up and walks over to his window.

"Thank you, Erica. That will be all for now."

Erica smiles as she turns and exits Chasm's office—closing the door behind her. Chasm stares out of the window—fighting back mental images of the wreckage that took his adoptive parents' lives.

[]

Harlem, New York.

"Are you sure that memory actually happened?" Curtis exclaims.

"Absolutely," Marge confirms with her quiet authority.

"But, why would he act like we had never met before?" Curtis asks.

"That is what we don't know," Marge replies. "But what we do know is that Chasm Montgomery and John Whaley have known each other for years and share a unique bond due to Chasm's adoptive father. And we know Mr. Montgomery was also a board member at the Firm. Along with the other facts Omar's investigation turned up, there has to be some kind of connection, even if it's not a direct one."

"So, what do we do?" Curtis inquires.

"My suggestion is you return to Atlanta tomorrow evening and continue working with Mr. Montgomery and his assistant. Use your *proximity* to discover any information which could be of use to us."

"Okay," Curtis agrees. "To do that, I'll need to put some *distance* between me and the rest of the family."

CHAPTER TWENTY-TWO

INTRUDER!

MARGE SITS WITH HER SHOULDER LEANING against the vibrating window, the snowy scenery quickly changes as the train speeds along its tracks. She slowly opens her eyes as a sudden deceleration stirs her from slumber. The conductor's voice echoes through the cabin. Marge loosens her grip on her satchel bag which contains her secret documents. Nine hours have passed and the train now pulls into the station. Marge inhales deeply, stretches and gathers her things. According to her watch, it is 3:00pm. She is almost home.

A half an hour later she exits a taxicab which has arrived at her residence: a quaint two-story home with a white picket fence. It's good to be home, she muses, as the vehicle drives off down the street. Marge picks up her two bags and trudges through the snow, up the path to the front door. It's colder than I thought, she realizes as she fumbles with her keys. As she opens the door, her happiness turns to trepidation. She sees envelopes from the mail slot strewn flippantly on the floor—opened.

Undecipherable sounds echo from another part of the house. Marge slowly lowers her bags to the floor and leans them against the wall. She quietly closes the front door and tip toes towards the living room, while picking up a nearby broom. She slowly pokes her head around the doorway of the living room. Overturned furniture, opened drawers and papers scattered on the floor greet her. As she inches fully into the room, another detail catches her eye. Through the opposite doorway, which leads to the kitchen, she sees a masked man wearing all black— standing on the far side of her island counter. She stands motionless as the intruder rummages through her drawers.

He snaps his head in her direction; his steely eyes trained on her while clutching a fistful of documents. Marge gasps as she struggles to find her voice.

"W-what are y-you doing in my house?" she yells.

The intruder drops the papers, leaps over the counter and charges at her! Her heart races as she quickly raises her broom and swings it swiftly down upon him! The masked man catches the broom which his hand, snatches it from her grasp and hurls it across the room behind him. Marge screams as she stumbles backward into the hallway, the unknown man barreling down on her—grasping her wrists and forcing her to the floor.

"Help!" She screams as the assailant muffles her mouth with his gloved hand.

"Scream again and you'll regret it," he growls in a deep, guttural voice as he clenches her jaw in a vise-like grip.

A delivery truck arrives at the curb in front of Marge's house. The driver, a bearded man wearing a thick company coat and hat, glances at his checklist, grabs his scanner and exits the vehicle with a package in hand. His sizable boots make easy work of the snow as he whistles his way to the front door.

Marge quiets as the intruder slowly leans down towards her. Their faces only inches apart. Tears stream from her fearful eyes. His menacing eyes are devoid of any remorse.

"Where do you keep them?" he growls again as he removes his hand from her mouth.

"Keep what?" She whispers.

"The documents! Where are they?"

DING. DONG.

Marge and the intruder stare at the front door.

KNOCK. KNOCK. KNOCK.

The intruder smothers Marge's mouth again.

"Don't you make a sound." He looks back to the door, notices her bags leaning against the wall, and jumps up.

"No!" she yells as she scrambles slowly to her feet.

The delivery man walks curiously over to the window and stares through the curtains into the living room—seeing the shambles.

The intruder grabs the satchel bag, rips it open and sees his prize. A scream pierces the atmosphere as Marge slams a nearby vase on the back of the man's head, causing him to crash to the ground.

The delivery man, hearing the commotion, runs to the door.

"Are you OK in there?" he yells.

"Please help me," Marge cries as she runs to the intruder, grabs the bag from his hands and takes a step for the front door. But the man grabs her ankle, causing her to trip and fall.

"Hold on, Ma'am! I'm coming!" The delivery man kicks the door— but it doesn't budge. He kicks it again and it rattles. He kicks the door a third time and it bursts open!

The intruder jumps up, with the bag in his hands.

"Stop right there," the delivery man yells! "Drop that bag and step away from the woman!"

The intruder turns and takes off through the house, with the delivery man in hot pursuit. But he escapes through the back door in the kitchen. The delivery man whips out his cell phone and calls the police.

Marge struggles to her feet. Her hair is in disarray as she is visibly shaken by the event. She snaps her head around at the sound of the delivery man coming back through the living room.

"It's just me," he declares. "Are you alright?"

"Yes. Thank you," she exclaims while hugging him tightly. "You saved my life! Thank you!"

"I called the police," he declares gently while holding her warmly. "They're on their way."

[]

5 hours later… 9:00pm

"What do you mean you were attacked?" Miranda yells into her cell phone. "Are you okay?"

"I'm fine," Marge smiles—speaking directly into her phone.

"Did you call the police?"

"Yes. They've been here for the past few hours. I can't stay here until their investigation is over. That may take a few days."

"What are you going to do?"

"I've arranged to stay with a friend."

"OK. Great. Now what about the documents?"

"The thief took them."

Miranda lets out a frustrated cry! "What are we to do now?" She all-but-yells. "I told you we should have made those copies!"

"Miranda," Marge concedes, "I am sorry. Yes, we should have, but I didn't *plan* to be robbed in my own house."

"I'm sorry," Miranda whispers. "I shouldn't have snapped at you."

"You hush now."

"How can you be so calm?" Miranda presses. "We've lost everything!

We are dead in the water!"

"Miranda," Marge says confidently, "Your husband had a failsafe. He kept the originals of all the documents that were just stolen from me. He also compiled additional evidence to go with the documents."

"He did? How come you didn't tell me?" Miranda huffs.

"It didn't matter at the time," Marge replies. "My documents were sufficient."

"He never mentioned any of this to me. So, where is this… failsafe?"

"At a bank. In a safety deposit box."

"Which bank?"

"I don't know."

"You don't know!"

"There's no need to shout."

"I'm sorry… it's just—"

"No need to apologize either. Malcolm told me if we ever needed those documents, Curtis is the key."

[]

30 minutes later… Laguardia Airport.

Curtis hastily makes his way through a crowd with his carryon luggage. He then notices the long line of people standing at the departure gate and rolls his eyes at the sight.

"Flying on Chasm's jet is *so* much quicker," he mumbles to himself as he stops at the back of the line. His phone rings.

"Hey Mom. Don't worry. I'm at the airport."

"I'm glad," Miranda confirms, "but that's not why I called."

"OK, what's up?" Curtis asks as he takes a seat.

"Listen," Miranda hesitates, "do you remember your father ever mentioning having a safety deposit box at a bank?"

Curtis thinks for a moment. "No… Not that I can remember. Why?"

"Are you sure?" Miranda urges.

"Yeah. Why?"

"Marge said your father told you he had one," she exhales deeply.

"Sorry, Mom, but she must have gotten her facts mixed up."

"Maybe. But if you remember anything, let me know. Okay?"

"I will. And don't forget I'm going to call you when I get there."

"No worries. I'll be ready. You enjoy your flight. Love you."

"Love you too, Mom."

[]

2 hours later. New York City. Pierce-Sterling and Whaley Architect Firm.

Three packets are tossed onto the executive meeting table —causing their contents to splash all over half of the table. John Whaley, two other founding partners and the former chairman of the board of trustees linger over each document.

"Unbelievable!!!" The hefty, former chairman yells as he pounds the table with his burly fists. "I thought these documents were destroyed!"

"They were," John utters flatly as his face changes several shades of red, "but apparently she made copies."

"If this information gets out," the former chairman bellows, "we'll be ruined!"

"But now, *we* have the evidence," John counters.

"How do you know there isn't more?" the former chairman insists.

"Margerie is very old fashioned," John smirks. "She would not have risked having additional copies getting into the wrong hands. Still... she's a loose end which needs tying up. It's a good thing our lawyers noticed someone was digging around."

"Who is she working with?" One of the founding partners asks with a slight air of panic in his voice.

"An attorney, Noreen Phillips, has done a number of searches. Margerie has also met with Miranda Powers. We are not exactly sure who all the other players are."

"Malcolm's widow," the former chairman huffs. "Even from the *grave* he's still a problem. What about the man who came to Margerie's aid?"

"Some delivery guy who got lucky. He's a nobody."

"If we don't figure out a plan of attack, we'll all become nobodies."

[]

Atlanta. The Montgomery Group headquarters.

DING, "Welcome Curtis Powers," the female elevator voice declares. The private elevator doors open at Chasm's penthouse suite as Curtis steps out with a frown on his face and his phone to his ear. Chasm and Erica stand at the end of the hallway, waiting to greet him.

"Mom, you can't tell me what to do anymore," Curtis huffs. "I'm an adult."

Chasm and Erica glance at each other with raised eyebrows.

"Is that an ultimatum?" Curtis yells. "You can't cancel the summer tour! These are *my* suits!"

Erica glances at Chasm again. "I think I'll wait inside," she whispers while turning and quickly stepping away.

"Why do you keep trying to hold me back? No. I'm not being unreasonable. You are! Look! If you guys don't want to help me, then I'll do this on my own. I've got more than enough resources here to get it done. Maybe I shouldn't have come home after all. I gotta go."

Curtis hangs up his phone and stuffs it in his back pocket as Chasm places his hand on Curtis' shoulder.

"Is everything alright, Curtis?"

"No," Curtis scoffs while wiping a few tears from his eyes. "Everything is *not* alright. My mom thinks these suits are becoming a distraction! She said I'm spending too much time with you guys and not enough time on my classwork!"

"What do *you* think?" Chasm inquires.

"I told her I can handle building suits and doing my school work. Sure it's tough, but I'm holding things together."

"Well, maybe I can talk to her… see if she'll come around."

"That's... not a good idea. She's *not* liking you right now."

"You let me take care of that," Chasm chuckles while putting his arm around Curtis. He looks at his young protege while they slowly begin to walk down the hallway.

"You know I've brokered some very high profile and volatile mergers in my day."

"But have you ever had to deal with an angry black woman?"

"Point taken," Chasm chuckles a bit hesitantly. "You let me worry about your mother. What you need to do is relax before you head back to your dorm and get ready for your classes tomorrow. Erica ordered some food from the cafeteria. Leave everything else to me."

CHAPTER TWENTY-THREE

SETUP

COMPUTER SCREENS FLICKER WITH INFORMATION ALONG one wall of the dark room. Every available media detail of Curtis' Mach-1 Speedsuit is displayed before the man who sits in this undisclosed location. At the touch of a button, all screens fade to black. He now sits in almost total darkness, brooding over the thoughts in his mind. The only light in the room now emanates from his computer keyboard and his digital clock which reads: 2:56pm / 2.22. 2014. At the press of another button, a 3-D schematic of the Mach-2 Speedsuit appears on the screen, with all pertinent details available. The man smiles slyly as he touches his custom bluetooth earpiece and places an encrypted call.

"Initiate the next phase."

[]

The Montgomery Group headquarters. 4:25pm.

An elevator descends to Sub-Basement 3.

"I've finished my diagnostic of the Mach-2," Chasm declares.

"Really?" Erica replies. "What did you discover?"

"First, I was able to correct the problems. So, the suit is now one hundred percent operational."

"That's great!" Erica smiles.

"I was also able to determine that the problems with the suit were caused *on purpose*."

"Do you mean sabotage?" Erica replies, trying to hide her nervousness.

"That is *exactly* what I mean."

The elevator comes to a stop and the doors open. Chasm and Erica exit and proceed down the hallway towards the lab designated for Mach-2 development.

"Who's behind it?" Erica asks as her hands begin to sweat.

"You won't believe it when I tell you. Quite frankly, I didn't believe it. This is someone I trusted completely. The fact that they could betray me like this… I triple checked the data, but the numbers do not lie."

Erica readjusts her shirt collar as she tries to clear her throat. She and Chasm approach the lab doors as two guards move aside to allow entrance.

"So, what are you going to do?" Erica inquires.

"I will have this person arrested and placed under the *full* weight of the Law."

Chasm swipes his keycard. The double doors slide open as they both enter the dark room. A split second later the lights engage, revealing an empty holding case where the Mach-2 once stood.

"Where's my Mach-2?" Chasm asks curtly.

"I-I don't know," Erica responds. "It was here yesterday."

"Guards!!!" Chasm yells. The guards run into the lab. "Where is my Mach-2?" Chasm bellows.

"We don't know," one guard nervously responds.

"No one has entered during our shift," the other interjects.

"Don't give me excuses!" Chasm declares. "Find my suit! NOW!!!

Lock this wing down! Call the security chief! Review the video feeds for the last 48 hours!"

"Yes Sir!" both guards say as one of them runs to the elevator and the other gets on his radio.

Chasm turns and faces Erica squarely. "And you…"

"Yes?" Erica replies—her eyes wide with fear.

“Locate Dr. Hitachi,” Chasm orders with a deep disdain, “and bring him to me.”

[]

3 hours later… 7.30pm.

Curtis and Gavin laugh hard while trying to do their classwork in their dorm room.

“Dude,” Curtis laughs, “we are never going to get our work done if you keep making jokes!”

“I can’t help it!” Gavin chuckles as he wipes tears from his eyes. “Maybe I could stop if you didn’t laugh!”

“Oh, don’t try to blame this on me,” Curtis quips. “We both have big tests tomorrow. We won’t be laughing then if we don’t buckle down.”

“Ok, Ok,” Gavin concedes as he throws his hands up in surrender. “Time to focus.”

A few minutes of silence pass as both boys attend to the task at hand. But the silence is interrupted by the Dean’s voice over the intercom speaker system in the hallway.

“Curtis Powers. Please come down to the main lobby. You have a visitor.”

Curtis looks at Gavin, who responds with his own look of curiosity.

“Who do you think it is?” Gavin inquires.

“Don’t know,” Curtis responds as he puts his sneakers on.

“I wasn’t expecting anyone.”

“Maybe it’s Kelly,” Gavin suggests.

“No. She usually calls to say she’s coming by.” Curtis opens the door. “I’ll be back in a minute.”

“I think I’ll come with you,” Gavin says as he jumps up from his desk and puts his shoes on. “Just in case you need backup.”

Curtis smiles at Gavin as they exit the room. “Backup huh?”

Curtis and Gavin enter the main lobby of their dormitory. As they walk down the hallway, the Dean points to three gentlemen: one dressed in a suit, the other two dressed in police uniforms.

"Can I help you guys?" Curtis says warily.

"Yes," the man in the suit smiles as he extends his hand. "Are you Curtis Powers?"

"That's me," Curtis replies as he shakes the man's hand.

"It's great to meet you," the man says as his grip solidifies like stone. "I'm Detective Malone. We need you to come down to the station to answer some questions."

Curtis' hand aches from the pressure. "Are you arresting me?"

"Yes." Detective Malone retrieves a pair of handcuffs from his rear pocket and slaps them on Curtis' wrist. "You are under arrest."

"Hey!" Curtis yells. "I haven't done anything wrong!"

Gavin approaches, but one of the officers puts his hand out and steps in between them.

"You need to back up young man."

"But Curtis is my friend!" Gavin replies. "Why are you guys arresting him?"

"Yeah," Curtis adds. "You guys got the wrong guy!"

"We'll have to sort this all out at the precinct," the detective states.

"Do you know who I am?" Curtis asks.

"Of course I do," the detective replies. "That's why I'm wondering why you would commit theft."

"Theft?" Curtis exclaims. "I haven't stolen anything! I've never stolen anything in my entire life! You guys definitely got the wrong guy!"

The second officer begins to read Curtis his rights as they handcuff him fully and escort him out of the lobby.

"Curtis!" Gavin yells.

"Call my mother!" Curtis yells back. "Tell her what's happening! She'll know what to do!"

□

Bronx. Powers' residence.

Omar walks into the kitchen where Miranda is cooking dinner.

"Mom?"

"Yeah baby?"

"Are you alright?"

"Sure. Why do you ask?"

"The past few days, you've been acting... I don't know... different."

"Oh?" Miranda replies coolly. "How so?"

"I don't know," Omar searches for the words. "You've been… happy."

Miranda laughs. "You don't want me to be happy?"

Omar laughs. "Of course I want you to be happy Ma!" Omar shakes his head. "You've just been overly happy—like more than usual."

"Is that a crime?"

"No," Omar shakes his head. "Never mind. I know it sounds crazy. Forget I asked."

The phone rings. Omar picks it up. "Hello? Hey Gavin. Whoah! Wait! Slow down!"

Miranda stops stirring the pot and looks over curiously.

"Yeah, she's here. Hold on." Omar turns to Miranda. "Mom. Something happened to Curtis!"

Miranda snatches the phone from Omar. "Gavin, this is Curtis' mother. What? What do you mean Curtis was arrested!"

"Arrested!" Omar yells as Miranda holds up her hand to shush him.

"They said he stole something?" Miranda can't believe what she's hearing. "Ok. Thanks for calling me. Let me make some calls. Yes. We'll talk soon." Miranda hangs up the phone and dials someone.

"Who are you calling?" Omar presses.

"Chasm Montgomery," Miranda states flatly.

"Why? He's the enemy!"

"Yes, well, right now, he's the person with the most power who's in the closest proximity to Curtis!"

"But what if he's behind this?" Omar yells.

"This doesn't sound like his style," Miranda counters as the phone begins to ring. "Besides, you know what they say, 'Keep your friends close and your enemies closer.'"

[]

The Montgomery Group headquarters.

Dr. Hitachi sits, handcuffed to a chair, with four guards in the room. Erica stands in the rear of the room while Chasm continues with his interrogation.

"You would *still* submit to know nothing about this?" Chasm declares with growing frustration. "We have *emails* from you stating that you were in collusion with an unknown party."

"I told you," Dr. Hitachi insists, "I *did not* write those emails nor do I know how those emails got in my account!"

"And what about the suit's system failures?" Chasm presses. "Do you still claim to have nothing to do with that as well?"

"Mr. Montgomery," Dr. Hitachi pleads, "I am one of your most loyal employees! I would never do anything to go against your wishes!"

"That is what I thought as well," Chasm concedes, "however, the data does not lie."

Erica leans against the back wall, trying to hide her sadness and displeasure. She knew her efforts to sabotage the development of the Mach-2 suit would be covered up, but she did not realize at what cost.

"You disabled the tracking device. Tell me the location of the Mach-2!" Chasm orders. "How did you fool the cameras to get it out of the building?"

"Again," Dr. Hitachi replies tiredly, "I have no idea where it is. I did not take it, nor do I have anything to do with the person or persons who took it. I'm being set up!"

"That is highly unlikely," Chasm replies. "What *is* likely is that you will never work another day of your life on the outside of a jail cell."

"No! Please! I am innocent!"

Erica's phone vibrates with a message. She steps out of the room to answer it. A moment later, she sticks her head back into the room.

"You need to come out here right now."

"Call the authorities," Chasm tells his guards as he exits the room. "What is it Erica? Have you found the suit?"

Erica shakes her head as she hands him the phone. "This is urgent. It's Miranda."

[]

Atlanta Police precinct. Interrogation room.

Curtis sits in a hard chair at a cold, steel table. In front of him sits the detective—smiling slightly. His partner is pacing behind him with a slight frown on his face.

"I knew you were too good to be true," the detective accuses as he paces. "You get into *everyone's* good graces with your world record and talks across the country. And then the *real* you comes out."

"I told you, I didn't steal anything," Curtis cries.

"You're lying," the detective shouts as he leans toward Curtis, staring—menacingly—mere inches from his face. "And you are going to tell us everything we want to know."

"You still haven't shown me any proof," Curtis replies. "And besides, you said these robberies happened a few hours ago? I've been in class all day!"

"Are you sure?" the smiling detective asks. "Are you sure you didn't skip class for a bit? Or get someone to take your place? After all, you're pretty smart. Maybe you thought class was a little boring and you needed to *spice* things up a bit."

The door to the interrogation room opens as a lieutenant enters with Chasm and his lawyer.

"Chasm!" Curtis exclaims.

"Do not say another word," Chasm smiles as his lawyer places a hefty document on the table.

"Curtis Powers will be leaving with me," Chasm speaks sternly, "unless you have irrefutable proof that he was involved in these robberies."

"Show them the video," the lieutenant orders.

"What video?" Curtis asks.

"We were just waiting until everyone arrived," the smiling detective replies as he pulls a remote out of his pocket and motions to a television screen on the wall. A moment later security footage begins to play.

"These are the security feeds from several banks and jewelry stores," the lieutenant points out.

The first feed shows a bank full of people waiting in line. Suddenly, a body barrels through a window, shattering it! People scream and run for cover as the body rolls on the floor and stands to its feet for a split second— "Freeze it," The lieutenant orders. Everyone in the room stares at the masked thief on the screen who is wearing a suit which resembles the Mach-1 Speedsuit.

"Now, either that's you," the lieutenant declares while pointing at his prisoner, "or someone else has a suit like yours."

"That could be anybody," Curtis exclaims. "You can't even see the guy's face!"

"Not another word," Chasm insists.

The lieutenant gives the order to continue playing the video. The thief jumps behind the teller counter, strikes the tellers and leaps back over the counter with money in a bag. He lands on the main floor, waves at the terrified onlookers, and runs out through the shattered window with a burst of pressurized wind that knocks several nearby persons off their feet.

The second feed shows the thief running into a jewelry store, breaking several display cases and running out with hundreds of thousands of dollars worth of rings, watches and necklaces.

"Fast forward to the last one," the lieutenant orders as he turns and faces Curtis, Chasm and the lawyer. "This guy hit eight businesses all across town in less than an hour. By the time we got to each scene, he was gone. Last I checked, the only person *on the planet* with a Speedsuit is this young man sitting right here."

"Can we be even *more* specific?" Chasm asks. "The only person on the planet with a Mach-1 Speedsuit is this young, *black* man sitting right here. You can't see the face, or any *other* body part of the person in the video, due to the fact that he or she is completely covered from head to toe by the suit. For all we know, the person wearing that suit could be white or some other nationality."

The lieutenant stares at Chasm and nods his head in agreement. "You're right," he says as he glances at his two detectives. "You know he could be right."

"Yeah, he could be," the smiling detective agrees.

"But he's not," the angry detective counters.

"How so?" Chasm asks.

"Play the last clip," the lieutenant orders. "This final feed is from one of the city's traffic light cameras. Watch what happens."

All eyes are on the screen as cars drive through the light. Then the cars stop when the light turns red. A second later, the masked thief is seen running up the street at high speed and then stops suddenly at the light. The face plate rises up half way —just enough to see the thief smile as he waves at the camera and then takes off, never to be seen again.

"Here's that part again," the lieutenant says, "where he stops, raises his faceplate and smiles. This is after we had our experts zoom in and enhance the video for greater clarity. Tell me, what do you see?"

Right on the screen, as clear as day, is the partial face of a smiling black man.

"That's not Curtis," Chasm says conclusively.

"How do you know?" the lieutenant replies.

"One: Curtis was in classes all day. My lawyer has the verified attendance sheets in his documents here. Two: That Speedsuit looks different from Curtis's Mach-1. Three: Curtis has a better smile."

"This is serious," the lieutenant replies. "Your boy's looking at some serious jail time and you want to joke around?"

"Obviously," Chasm counters, "someone has built a suit that resembles Curtis' and is trying to defame him. What other reason is there for a person to commit these crimes and then stop to pose for the cameras? Curtis has *never* engaged in *any* criminal activity. He is almost a straight A student who gets to travel and speak to audiences all over the world. He is respected by children, parents, politicians and presidents. And he even put his life on the line to stop a school shooting. With everything he's done to help people, and quite frankly, with all of the resources he has at his fingertips, does it make sense that he would stoop to committing petty larceny?"

The lieutenant and two detectives mull over Chasm's words.

"You make a good argument," the lieutenant agrees. "Quite frankly, I'm a big fan of Curtis. So are my kids. But the data doesn't lie."

"Perhaps," Chasm counters, "you don't have *all* of the data."

"That's why we're here," the lieutenant replies. "We're trying to put all of the pieces together."

"You do that," Chasm agrees. "I will also launch *my own* investigation."

"It's a free country," the lieutenant quips. "Feel free."

"Thank you," Chasm responds with a hint of sarcasm. "If you have nothing left to show us, then I believe Curtis Powers is free to go." Chasm extends his hand.

"I guess so," the lieutenant agrees as he shakes Chasm's hand. "At this point, Curtis Powers here is just a *person of interest.* Make sure he doesn't leave the country."

"Also," Chasm continues, "the media is already starting to have a field day with this. To make sure that Curtis' image is not further slandered, I would like the police department to make a statement—in good faith—alluding to a potential defamation of character plot and that Curtis has agreed to work with the authorities to get to the truth."

[]

Chasm's vehicle stops in front of Curtis' dormitory.

"Listen," Chasm says calmly, "we will get to the bottom of this. I know it will be difficult, but you focus on your studies. Try not to answer anyone's questions—especially any reporters! I'll be in touch."

"Thank you Chasm," Curtis smiles as he steps out of the car. "I *really* appreciate you." Curtis closes the car door and walks back to his dorm room.

Chasm watches Curtis before giving the command for the driver to leave. As he rides back to his headquarters, Chasm thinks through every possible angle while figuring out his next plan of attack. Once back in his penthouse apartment, Erica meets him in his office.

"What happened?" Erica asked.

"Someone is trying to frame Curtis," Chasm responds angrily. "And they are using *my* Mach-2 Speedsuit to do it."

[]

Bronx. Powers' Residence.

Miranda, Omar and Jim sit in the living room, huddled around the phone—waiting for it to ring. The phone rings. Miranda snatches it from the table and smiles as she looks at the caller ID.

"Curtis!" she yells. "Is that you?"

"It's me, Mom," Curtis shouts back. "I'm back in my dorm room!"

The group cheers.

"So Chasm was able to get you out?" Miranda presses. "Baby. What happened?"

"Yes, Chasm came right away, with his lawyer too. Walked in and out of the police station like he owned the place."

"He probably does," Jim replies as Omar and Miranda chuckle.

"Someone is trying to set me up," Curtis continues. "Someone's created another Speedsuit."

"Are you serious?" Jim exclaims.

"Yeah," Curtis answers. "I can't believe it myself!"

"What was Chasm's response?" Omar asks.

"He seemed shocked, just like I was," Curtis replies. "He's determined to get to the bottom of this. And you should have seen him in the precinct. He *really* vouched for my reputation!"

"Curtis," Miranda asks, "I asked Chasm to help because he was the most high-powered person near you. And I'm glad he was able to be a big help. But, given what we already know, do you think that Chasm had something to do with this whole ordeal?"

"I honestly don't think so Mom. If he does, then he's a really good actor."

"OK, baby." Miranda agrees. "We have to be even more vigilant if there's another unknown player in this scenario."

"Yeah. I wonder who this guy is?"

"You know," Jim interjects while looking at his calendar. "We may get a chance to find out."

"How's that?" Curtis asks.

"Because, according to our calendar, you've got an expedition run in Atlanta in a few weeks. Perhaps our Speedsuit Doppelgänger will make an appearance."

[]

Later that night.

Miranda sits in her room, on the phone, with the door closed. "I just wanted to say thank you for coming to the rescue."

"I'm glad you felt comfortable enough to call me for help," Chasm responds.

"I know when something happens that's *bigger* than me. Without your intervention, Curtis' situation may have been *very* different."

"We have to do what we can to ensure that our young men are given every opportunity to succeed. Even more so when we know they are being wrongly accused of something."

"You got that right," Miranda agrees. "Any idea who this *other* Speedsuit guy is and where he got his suit?"

"I started my own investigation to try and discern the answer to those very questions."

"You know," Miranda adds, "on the news… when I saw the footage of the guy in the other suit, it made me think of you. I know your company has its hands in a lot of things—including military contracts."

"My company is involved with many different sectors of public, private and government innovation. But if you are implying that I or my company had something to do with this man who is trying to destroy your son's reputation, rest assured this is *not* the case. I am as irritated over this as you are."

"That's good to know. I was hoping this wasn't part of some elaborate scheme to win my son over to your way of thinking."

Chasm laughs. "Your mind is constantly imagining scenarios —even if they are unfounded."

"In this day and age, Mr. Montgomery, you can never be too careful with anyone," Miranda chuckles while rubbing her tired eyes.

"So true, Miranda," Chasm agrees. "So true."

"Well, it's been a long day. Thank you again for all of your help. I truly appreciate it."

"Glad to be of service," Chasm replies. "But can I ask you one thing before you go?"

"Sure."

"Curtis told me that I'm not your favorite person due to all of the time he's been spending here at my facilities. Is that true?"

"Yes, it is," Miranda confirms. "Do you remember the promise you made when we first met? That my son's grades would come first?"

"Of course."

"Can you honestly say that you are upholding that promise?" Chasm sits in his office chair, contemplating Miranda's words as she continues. "The primary reason Curtis is in college is to master his studies. I assume, by your silence, that you would agree."

"There are very few times when I am at a loss for words," Chasm says, chuckling.

"So, I have just become a part of a very elite group of individuals," Miranda replies.

"It would appear so," Chasm concedes. "To your pointed question about me keeping my promise… there is always room for improvement."

"And I *expect* you to improve," Miranda insists.

"I will do just that," Chasm agrees. "By the way, I know you all have a demonstration run here in Atlanta in a couple of weeks. Is it alright if I send Erica to assist you? She, Curtis and I have been planning for the summer tour. It would be nice to get an up close look at how you all are currently executing these events."

"As you know," Miranda replies, "I'm not very excited about you and Erica planning a summer tour without us being included."

"My apologies, Miranda. Curtis had given the impression that you both didn't see eye to eye on this issue."

"We don't seem to be on the same page about a lot of things lately. But this event was already planned."

"I see. But, it was never my intention to place a wedge between you and your son. Why don't we combine our efforts? I am sure that together we can create a tour that will inspire people for decades to come."

"Since you have agreed to uphold your end of the bargain, I see no reason why we can't work together in that capacity," Miranda replies.

"Great! So, I will send Erica to assist you all."

"We'd be happy to have her. And, on behalf of the team here, we look forward to working with you to create a wonderful summer tour experience. Have a good night, Mr. Montgomery."

"You as well," Chasm responds. "Have a wonderful evening." As he slowly hangs up his phone, he ponders… *she is truly a remarkable woman.*

CHAPTER TWENTY-FOUR

DOPPELGÄNGER

TELEVISION NEWSCASTS AND RADIO TALK SHOWS are full of banter surrounding the possibility that Curtis Powers has indeed pulled 'a fast one' on society. Thousands have tuned in to these programs over the past few days. A growing number of supporters stagger on both sides of the issue. Some who hailed Curtis a hero in the past, now declare him a liar and a thief. Others who were unsure what to make of him cry that something seems amiss with the story. And those who supported Curtis from the very beginning, still voice their support.

"He's polarized the country!" a talk show host claims.

"No, he hasn't," another host counters, "this *situation* has. The police have already stated someone else may be purposefully trying to slander his reputation."

"You believe that?" the first host snorts.

"And you don't?" the second host huffs. "What's more likely? Curtis Powers—who's done a whole lot of good suddenly becomes a thief? Or there's someone out there trying to destroy his reputation?"

Some in the studio audience cheer in agreement.

"I think the simplest answer is often the right one."

"Really? Just last year, you hailed Curtis a hero for stopping the school shooting! How easily you have switched sides."

"How many people, just within the past ten years, have done a whole lot of good only to later betray the public's trust? We'd take up the rest of the show just listing the names!"

Many audience members nod their heads in agreement.

"You're right, but—"

"I know I'm right!" the talk show host exclaims rather bullishly.

Many in the audience laugh.

"But that doesn't mean because others had moral failings or were deliberately trying to deceive the public that Curtis is the same as they are!"

"There's a higher likelihood that he *is* like them."

"I know what your problem is…"

"Really? What is it?"

"And it's not just your problem. It's all of our problem. We've seen so many people fall in the past that we just sit around waiting for other people to fall. We've experienced so much betrayal that we can barely trust anyone anymore! But let me go on record: I believe that Curtis Powers is innocent. Someone is trying to destroy his reputation. And those of us who believed in what he's done in the past to inspire people, should *still* believe in him today—at least until there is definitive evidence to prove otherwise. And right now, it is my professional opinion as a reporter that there is not."

"Well, we are all entitled to our opinions, aren't we? Whether they be professional or otherwise. And why don't you go and ask people who went to the hospital to be operated on by professionals—only to discover that the 'professional' amputated the wrong leg!"

"Now you know that's not—"

"And that's our time for tonight!" the talk show host declares in grand fashion. "Tune in tomorrow. We will be talking about the latest entertainment craze that's sweeping the nation! Have a great night!"

Rikers Island.

Treyshawn Sr. and a host of other inmates turn away from the television as the talk show goes off. Even in prison, this story is big news.

"What you think T-Rock?" Tyrone shouts from across the table. "That Curtis Powers boy guilty?"

"Why you so concerned," Treyshawn Sr. replies. "We locked in here. Doesn't matter what I think about that."

"But don't yo' boy know him?" Tyrone quips. "I thought they was friends."

"What do you care?"

Tyrone gets up from his bench, walks around to the other side of the table and sits next to Treyshawn Sr. "Way I see it, if everybody talkin' about this, and we keep talkin' it up, then nobody will pay attention to us talkin' about what we need to talk about. We just six months out."

[]

Two weeks later. March. Atlanta stadium.

It's 52 degrees on this sunny day. Fans have almost packed out the Georgia Dome, waiting to see Curtis Powers and the Powersuit Team give their latest Mach-1 Speedsuit demonstration. This event will serve as an opportunity to both inspire the audience and to whet their appetites for the major summer tour that is to come. Outside, some people picket the event with signs stating that Curtis Powers is a thief and should be arrested. Yet, the cheers of the fans far outweigh the cries of a handful of detractors. Several media outlets have sent camera crews to cover both aspects of this event.

Miranda, Omar, Jim, Kelly, Gavin and Erica prepare to enter the stadium, ready to begin their first death-defying feat. A team of technicians triple check every aspect of the event.

"I don't know why she has to be here," Kelly scoffs.

"Kelly…" Miranda tries to soothe her, "Chasm asked for Erica to be present. She's already been a help to us."

"Uh, huh," Kelly frowns. "She also tried to help *herself* to Curtis."

"Look," Erica concedes as she walks over to Kelly, "I understand why you don't like me. But Curtis chose you and I respect his decision. So, you don't have to worry about me trying to steal him again."

"Well if you do try something crazy like that again," Kelly replies curtly, "you and I will have *more* than words. Are we clear?"

"Absolutely," Erica responds.

"Welcome ladies and gentlemen, boys and girls," an announcer proclaims. "We are very excited to have you here with us today to witness something truly astounding! May I present to you Team Speedsuit Powers!"

The team exits the stadium tunnel, being driven on the back of a flatbed truck wrapped in Team Speedsuit Powers artwork. The sizable audience claps and cheers as the team takes their place on an elevated platform placed at the edge of the field.

"Now," the announcer shouts, "put your hands together for Curtis Powers - a.k.a. JETSTREAM!!!!"

The fans leap to their feet in thunderous applause as Curtis powers up his Mach-1 and runs out to the platform. The crowd cheers for a few minutes as Curtis and the team wave and smile. Many people hold up signs which read, "We Believe in Curtis Powers!"

"We all need to focus on the task at hand," Miranda says as they wave to the crowd. "I still think we could have used a bit more practice."

"It's a little late to be bringing that up now, isn't it?" Jim laughs.

After the applause dies down, Curtis takes his position at the starting line. In front of him is a long stretch of pavement leading to a ramp. At the end of the ramp are cars parked end to end, followed by another ramp, a short runway and a large swath of cardboard boxes.

"For his first demonstration," the announcer bellows, "Jetstream will use his Mach-1 Speedsuit to hopefully run fast enough to leap over eight cars and land safely!"

The crowd settles down as all eyes and camera phones are on Curtis.

"Alright Bro," Omar speaks through their communications array, "your vitals and suit diagnostics look good."

"Great," Curtis replies. "How's the A/V capturing?"

"We've got sharp HD video and sound coming from the suit's built in cameras," Gavin answers. " And the technicians are set with five other cameras to capture every frame of the jump."

"Are you ready?" Kelly asks.

"Yeah. Let's do this." As is his custom, Curtis looks up to the sky. "God, it's now or never."

The announcer receives the green light from the team and begins the countdown. Two large video screens light up with the number ten and count down to the number one as the word LAUNCH blasts across the screens.

Curtis takes off down the track—his Kinetic Redistribution Boots fully functioning! Two seconds later, he engages the Vortex Pack and accelerates to 70 miles per hour in three seconds! Curtis bounds up the ramp and leaps into the air! He hurls over the eight cars with maximum clearance.

"Mommy?" a boy watches from the stands, "how is he going to land safely?"

Before the mother can respond, Curtis throws the Vortex turbine in reverse. The turbine motor powers down—causing the fan blade assembly to quickly slow to a halt. The motor roars back to life as the fan blades spin in the opposite direction —causing the massive airflow it generates to blow forward through the Slipstream Vest—reducing Curtis' speed and trajectory. Curtis lands firmly on the ramp, and descends without incident, stopping just before the cardboard boxes.

The crowd erupts into thunderous applause as Curtis makes his way back to the front of the field. As the applause quiets, the announcer hands Curtis a microphone to address the crowd.

"Thank you so much for coming out today to show your support for us and the work we do."

People shout, "We love you Curtis!" from the stands.

"Thank you!" Curtis responds with a wide grin. "We love you guys too!"

A roar suddenly echoes through one of the side tunnels. The sound grows louder as everyone's attention is drawn to the mouth of the tunnel. Suddenly, someone exits the tunnel at tremendous speed and stops right in front of Curtis and the team just long enough to wave to them and the crowd, before taking off out of the opposite exit.

"It's the doppelgänger!" Miranda yells.

"Go after him!" Omar orders.

"Yes!" Jim agrees. "We're right behind you!"

The crowd watches in astonishment as Curtis turns and blasts out of the stadium in hot pursuit. Outside the stadium, Curtis runs through the main parking lot, follows the unknown speedster to the top of the parking garage and comes to a screeching halt. Standing in front of him is the doppelgänger; wearing a Speedsuit that is remarkably similar to the Mach-1, but with some obvious style differences and design upgrades.

"Guys are you getting this?" Curtis asks as he stares at the unknown person in front of him. "This guy is at least six inches taller than me."

"We're getting it," Jim yells back through the communicator. "Try and get him talking!"

Curtis and the unknown individual notice that multiple helicopters are beginning to encircle their position.

"Jetstream!" the doppelgänger chuckles in a digitized voice. "Glad you could catch up! I'm a really big fan."

"So you know my name."

"Who doesn't know the famous Curtis Powers?"

"Nice paint job," Curtis remarks. "I think I've *seen* it before."

"Well, the goal is for *my* Speedsuit to closely resemble yours. As you can see, my suit comes with some... enhancements."

"Enhancements are just another way to cover up your insecurities," Curtis quips. "And by the way... Who are you?"

"Me?" The lower part of his visor opens to reveal his grinning mouth. "I'm your replacement."

"That's funny," Curtis smirks. "I didn't know I needed a stunt double."

"Technology doubles every three to six months, Curtis. You've been wearing that suit for what—about a year now? Mine is brand-spanking new! So, you know what that makes me?"

"Inexperienced?"

The doppelgänger laughs. "You *are* quick-witted! But compared to my suit that's all you are. I was going to say that I am the next level!"

"You know," Curtis replies, "you really have an 'Iron Man' thing going on with that hard armor exoskeleton. I can see how that can be a little intimidating."

"I'm glad you noticed. And you can call me... *Turbulence*. Now, would you like to know my nefarious plan?"

"Sure thing Flatulence. I've got a few minutes."

The doppelgänger's smile diminishes. "The name is *Turbulence*! And everything you've built with *that* suit... *I* will tear down."

"But people have seen you now," Curtis counters as he points to the flying helicopters. "In an hour, everyone will know that we are *not* the same person and that we're *not* on the same team."

"All a part of the plan!" Turbulence chuckles. "I know you're recording this conversation. So, feel free to share my message! Just know that where you have used your suit to inspire wonder, I will use my suit to instill fear. And people will loathe you because you're the reason this is happening."

"You know Ambulance, I think you're crazy."

"The name... is *Turbulence*!! And I'm certifiable!" the doppelgänger hisses. "But the crazy thing about 'crazy' is that you can still walk the streets! If I was insane, then I'd have to be locked up!"

"Oh, you *will* be locked up, because the police will stop you!"

"The cops?" Turbulence laughs. "They can't even catch me!"

"Then I will stop you."

"I hope you'll try." The doppelgänger's visor closes as a digitized voice yells, "Catch me if you can, Jetstream!"

He turns and launches across the parking garage and descends each level to the main entrance. Curtis gives chase and is soon right behind him! They both run through the stadium's parking lot and out onto the street, dodging traffic—making moving cars seem like they are standing still. Street after street and turn after turn they run—neck and neck.

"Give it up!" Curtis yells. "You can't get away!"

Turbulence glares at Jetstream through his visor. "I can get away *whenever* I want!"

Air flaps deploy as the thrust from his backpack reverses, bringing him to a sudden stop as Curtis overshoots and has to make an emergency deceleration to try and catch up. Once again Curtis is in hot pursuit, but this time, the doppelgänger easily weaves in and out of traffic at a pace Curtis' suit and reflexes can't match.

"Can your suit do *this*?" Turbulence yells as he proceeds to run up the side of a building. Curtis comes to a halt in wide-eyed disbelief.

"Whoah..." He utters as his neck cranes to track his rival's trajectory. "That's impossible..." He watches as Turbulence leaps from the building and lands a block away.

"Giving up already?" he laughs.

Curtis' awe gives way to anger as he blasts down the street. The doppelgänger turns and takes off, but once again they are neck-and-neck as they take an on-ramp to the I-285 highway.

"Thanks for playing!" the unknown assailant shouts as he grabs Curtis' arm. A jolt of 50,000 volts shoot from his glove through Curtis' suit. Curtis yells out in pain, loses control and takes a bad tumble. Cars screech to a halt as his enemy jets off into the distance with increased acceleration, leaving a bruised and battered Curtis lying in the middle of the highway.

[]

Atlanta Hospital.

Curtis lays bandaged up in a hospital bed surrounded by his family and friends; his banged up Mach-1 Speedsuit stands in the corner of the room. The doctor has just finished examining his patient.

"Thankfully, Curtis doesn't have any broken bones," the doctor announces to the group.

"Thank God!" Miranda shouts as the group expresses their relief.

"However," the doctor continues, "he does have a mild concussion and some deep bruising on his arms, torso and legs. We'll keep him here over night for observation. When he gets home, he needs bed rest for the next two weeks. Minimal walking and definitely *no* running."

"Thank you doctor." Miranda shakes his hand.

"Your welcome," he replies. "I noticed from his records that this isn't his *first* time in the hospital with similar injuries."

"It's the price I pay for wearing the Mach-1," Curtis replies.

"Yes. Well, good thing you all built that Speedsuit to be as sturdy as it is. Without it, a crash at the speed you were traveling could very well have killed you." The doctor leaves the room as the group continues their conversation.

"I'm glad you made it through lil Bro," Omar says. "That was a pretty bad crash. Worse than the first crash when your boot broke."

"Felt about the same," Curtis says, smiling.

"Well," Jim adds, "you banged up the suit really good. Not sure if I'll be able to fix it."

"Mr. G," Curtis smirks, "you and Omar can fix anything."

"Dude," Gavin interjects, "your doppelgänger—I hate to say it, but he ran rings around you!"

"I know," Curtis' tone becomes serious. "He was just playing with me. That Speedsuit is definitely out of my league! I don't know how we can catch him!"

"I looked at the footage," Jim replies. "He's able to alternate nozzle usage on his thrust pack. And he has air flaps which work in concert with the nozzles. I think that allows him to make tighter turns and increases his overall maneuverability."

"And did you see his boots?" Curtis asks. "They looked similar to my new design—the one I haven't gotten to work yet."

"Your electromagnetic Kinetic distribution system?"

"Yeah. Whoever built that suit had access to the plans I kept in my lab on campus."

"Like the officer said after the break in," Gavin adds, "someone could have easily taken pics of what they wanted to steal, without having to physically steal it."

"That's *just* what someone did," Curtis frowns.

"I'm just happy you're alive," Kelly interjects, "and that you're going to get better." She hugs Curtis as he yells out in response to the pain.

"Sorry!"

Everyone laughs.

"Not to change the subject," Curtis says as he looks around the room, "but has anyone seen Erica?"

"She said she had to leave for a meeting," Miranda replies.

"Well, I'm glad she's gone," Kelly smiles as she rubs Curtis' hand.

A newscast on the television catches everyone's attention as Omar turns up the volume.

"Now to late breaking news," the newscaster declares, "Curtis Powers has been admitted to the hospital after experiencing a crash while apparently chasing another individual wearing a Speedsuit. We now go live to a reporter at the scene of the crash."

"Thank you, Chuck. I'm here on the side of I-285 where the crash happened not too long ago. From what we have learned, Curtis Powers *has in fact* been targeted by an unknown assailant who is using an advanced version of Curtis' Mach-1 Speedsuit to wreak havoc across the city and to try and malign Curtis' reputation. After an altercation, which resulted in a crash, Curtis Powers was taken to an area hospital where he is being treated as we speak. However, the authorities are still here on the scene cleaning up the collateral damage from the chase.

Drivers are stranded on the highway for several miles while cleanup crews attend to twenty-three damaged cars. While people may be happy to know that Mr. Powers has now been cleared of accusations of theft from last week's robberies, many individuals on I-285 are not happy about their extended stay during rush hour. Back to you in the studio."

"Thank you Tim. As mentioned, the police have obtained a recording of the entire altercation which occurred between Curtis Powers and the unknown assailant. This evidence exonerated Mr. Powers. However, the aftermath of this chase raises new questions as an invention which has been used to inspire so many people across the country and the world has now caused so much damage on this local highway. Who is to blame? Will this encounter be categorized and shunned as a type of vigilante justice? And who will cover the cost of repairing what has been damaged? More on this during our nightly news broadcast."

The group look at the television in stunned silence.

"Are they serious?" Curtis asks.

"Bro," Omar replies, "things just got *real*."

[]

Undisclosed location.

Turbulence stands in a dark elevator as it descends several stories to a dark subterranean dwelling. The muffled sound of trains passing nearby echo in the distance. He exits the elevator and makes his way across the room to a large computer screen. With the press of a button, the computer screen comes to life, revealing a flashing icon.

"Initiate encrypted transmission."

A second passes before a heavily pixelated image of a woman fills the screen.

"What do you think?" he asks as he removes his helmet. "Things worked out pretty much according to plan."

"They did," a digitized female voice replies. "You did well. My employer will be pleased."

"So, when do I get to look under the hood and meet you and your employer?"

"You don't. It's better this way. The less you know, the less you have to lie."

"I don't mind lying."

"Just make sure you leave the suit in its charging station. I will run a diagnostic from here and determine if there are any issues which need to be addressed."

"What if I wanted to *take* the suit and run—literally?"

"You wouldn't get very far."

An electrical surge passes through the suit as Turbulence falls to the ground.

"I… can hardly… move!" he yells.

"That's because I engaged the emergency shut down protocols. And even if I didn't, once the suit runs out of power, it can only be charged through a unique process. Otherwise it's just dead weight."

"Can you turn me back on now?"

The suit powers back up as Turbulence slowly stands to his feet.

"My employer has gone through tremendous amounts of discretion to secure and train you Mr. Kind. I do not need to remind you about the extensive files we have compiled."

"Don't worry. Don't worry. No need to bring that up. You can count on me to fulfill the mission."

"Is that what you told your commanding officer before you were dishonorably discharged from the military?"

"Now that's a low blow," Mr. Kind laughs. "Just keep the money coming in and I will do *whatever* your employer needs me to do. Besides, I'm having fun playing with Curtis Powers. I don't know why people think he's hot stuff."

"Curtis Powers is not to be underestimated. If you do, that will be *your* downfall. At some point he will no doubt try to draw you out. When he does… be ready."

CHAPTER TWENTY-FIVE

BAGGAGE

IT'S BEEN THREE WEEKS AND CHASM is no closer to discovering the whereabouts of his Mach-2 Speedsuit nor the identity of Turbulence. Security is set to high alert as all TMG employees are on edge, especially when Chasm is on site. Erica prepares for his arrival as his helicopter lands on the roof's helipad. The engine powers down as the blades come to a halt. One of the doors opens as Chasm disembarks.

"Hello Boss," Erica says as she approaches. "How was the flight from New York?"

"Skip the pleasantries Erica," Chasm says as they walk quickly to the elevator. "Where do we stand with the Mach-2?"

"Still no luck."

"I do not rely on luck. You already *know* that." They enter the elevator and descend to the main level. "Have you reviewed the data from our satellites?"

"Inconclusive. They weren't in geosynchronous orbit at the time of the altercation."

"What about accessing the city's camera feeds?"

"We have video from the chase until the highway. Camera coverage is limited there."

The elevator reaches the main lobby and opens its doors. Chasm and Erica head to the front of the building.

"We know the general direction he took and the time things took place," Chasm continues. "Did you analyze camera footage near *all* the highway exit ramps?"

"No... I didn't think of that."

Chasm stops mid-stride and stares at Erica. "You're slipping."

"Sorry. With this whole issue and my studies… my bandwidth is a bit low at the moment."

"You know I am not a fan of excuses. If you can't handle this, I will find someone who can."

"No, I can do it," Erica asserts. "I'll get right on that."

"You do that. And expand the radius of the search to at least fifty miles."

"Understood," Erica responds while typing notes into her digital tablet. She looks up curiously at Chasm as he approaches his driver, who stands at the ready next to his car.

"Where are you going?" she asks. "You are scheduled to have a meeting on the 5th floor with a potential new partner."

"I canceled it on the way here from the airport," Chasm replies matter-of-factly as he enters the rear of the car. "Didn't have time to let you know."

"So, where are you going now?"

The driver starts the car and prepares to drive away as Chasm rolls down his window.

"I need to meet with Dr. Winters. I'll call when I'm on my way back."

The car speeds away, leaving Erica at the curbside. *I've never seen him like this,* she considers, her eyebrows wrinkling. *This situation is really bothering him.*

[]

Chasm sits, brooding in the back of his limo. The drive across town has taken a restless 45 minutes. But he is able to calm his nerves a bit as he approaches the secured gates to Dr. Winters' sizable estate.

There's a reason he's the 12th richest man on the planet, Chasm muses as the security guards acknowledge him and buzz him in. Even with the wealth and material possessions Chasm has amassed, he is always stunned by the opulence which surrounds Dr. Winters. It takes several minutes to ascend the driveway to the main house. Every visit, without fail, workers are seen engaged in landscaping or making some kind of addition to various monuments which are strategically positioned on the property.

Soon, the vehicle arrives in front of the mansion. Chasm exits the car and is accosted by soothing classical music, flowing freely from unseen speakers. He stands in front of two massive front doors, but doesn't bother to ring the bell. He knows the staff which maintains the dwelling have already been notified by security of his presence. A second later, one door opens revealing the butler standing with perfect posture, as a warm smile graces his expression. He speaks with impeccable English.

"Good afternoon, Mr. Montgomery."

"Good afternoon, Sebastian," Chasm smiles, enjoying the pleasantries.

Sebastian bows slightly. "It is so good to see you again, Sir. Please come in. Dr. Winters is expecting you."

"Thank you very much," Chasm replies as he enters through the doors and waits for Sebastian to lock them. Even though he knows his way around, he knows it would be rude to walk *without* an escort.

"Dr. Winters is sitting in the library. Please... this way." The butler leads the way across marble floors, past ancient relics and beneath mammoth chandeliers hanging thirty feet above their heads. Maids greet Chasm as he passes by—happy to see his familiar face. He makes his way from the mansion's main hub to its east wing as he and Sebastian finally arrive at two wood-lined glass doors. The butler knocks twice.

"Enter," echoes from the other side of the doors.

Both doors open towards the hallway as the butler announces the guest. Chasm enters the room as the doors close behind him. Although Chasm has been in this room before, he is always impressed with the sight: four levels of books—thousands of books—surround the perimeter of the large room; stretching from the floor to the 30 foot high ceiling. Five exquisite rolling ladders are stationed at various points in the room. The sun floods the room with warm, natural light through a skylight and several windows. Two chairs sit at the center of the room facing each other. Dr. Winters, holding a book while wearing white gloves, rests in the larger of the two. Surrounding them are a number of other chairs and small reading desks.

Dr. Winters puts the book down and removes his gloves. He rises from the center chair with a broad smile and holds his arms out towards Chasm who is approaching him.

"It is good to see you again," he remarks as he and Chasm share a hearty handshake. "Please, sit down."

Both men sit, facing each other. Chasm inhales deeply, taking in the calming aroma of countless pieces of parchment once created on continents down through the ages. He notices the Latin words on the aged cover of the book his mentor is currently reading.

"Wisdom written in books can be an unparalleled resource," Dr. Winters asserts. "You know, many years ago, I met a gentleman with an extensive library—not as massive as this one—but expansive none-the-less. He made an impression on me because he had read all ten thousand books in his library during his adult life. At the time of our meeting, I had a number of books that were still crisp from non-usage. I knew then that *my* level of excellence needed to rise. Today, I have almost reached my goal of reading all of the books housed in this library."

"Really?" Chasm asks astounded, "You've never told me this story."

"You know the old saying," Dr. Winters smiles, 'you learn something new every day.'"

"What you are doing takes a serious commitment."

"Warren Buffett reads several hours every morning before he attacks the rest of his day. I have used a similar protocol over the years and now only one hundred and twenty six books stand between me and my goal. And to think that as a very young man I did not *value* reading. Now, when I make decisions, it's based on the cumulative knowledge of over 20,000 books."

Chasm nods as he contemplates the thought.

"So what brings you here today? Our usual monthly meeting isn't until next week."

"Yes. I am dealing with a strenuous situation and I need your… perspective."

"That's what mentors are for," Dr. Winters' notes, "to provide perspective." He motions for his mentee to continue.

"As you know, the Mach-2 Speedsuit I was developing was stolen."

"I am aware. Do you have any leads?"

"I only have dead ends," Chasm replies. "That is what's stressing me."

"I thought your lead engineer had been detained for questioning."

"Yes, I interrogated Dr. Hitachi myself. While the evidence points to him, he maintains he is innocent and denies *any* involvement."

"That's what thieves and liars do, Chasm. They deny the truth that is right in front of you."

"Yes, that is true. But whoever committed this theft had to have an intimate knowledge of my facilities and security systems. Dr. Hitachi has never struck me as the type of person who cares about such matters. His focus has always been on the projects themselves—almost to the point of obsession."

"Obsession can lead a person to extreme action."

"True. But I believe he lacks the level of coordination to pull off such a feat. If he is involved, he definitely had help."

"What are you thinking?"

"I don't want to believe this, but I think we have more than a traitor here… we may have a mole."

"A spy? With all of the vetting and background checks that are done on your employees?"

"I know. But even the best of employees can be tempted if the price is right." Chasm replies.

"One of your competitors is involved," Dr. Winters states with certainty. "Someone is trying to dismantle your life's work.

"I agree," Chasm nods. "But why?"

Dr. Winters dons his white gloves and picks up the weathered book he was reading. "This book was written in the 1700's. It's amazing how its truth is relevant to us today." He opens to a particular page. "Before you arrived, I had just read this quote: 'Enemies are often made, not because you have directly clashed with them, but because they see in you, something they either desire, despise or fear.'" He places the book back on the table. "Do you have a list of possibilities?"

"We are involved in so many industries. It could be any number of entities."

"You need to narrow down the list."

"And why would they use my Speedsuit to target Curtis?"

"I know the assailant said he targeted Curtis because of his ability to inspire others," Dr. Winters muses. "However, I think that is a secondary reason. In my estimation, if this person is working with the competitor who *actually* stole the suit, then the primary reason he is targeting Curtis is because Curtis is connected to you. So, it's imperative that you track down the suit as soon as possible. Now, back to your original issue: if you don't think Dr. Hitachi is your mole, then who do you believe it to be?"

"I can barely bring myself to say this," Chasm struggles, "but... do you think Erica could be the mole?"

Dr. Winters stares at Chasm before blurting out a laugh. "I am sorry for the unexpected outburst, but Erica Cosway *is* your most loyal employee. Quite honestly, I would trust her with my life."

"Yes, but she has the level of knowledge and expertise necessary to commit this type of crime."

"You are correct. But tell me... what would be her motive?" Dr. Winters leans forward in his chair. "Chasm," he utters intently, "you have been her benefactor since she was a child. She has proven herself time and again over the years and you have rewarded her handsomely with promotions and financial compensation. She is the closest thing you have to a daughter. You and I are pretty good judges of character. And everything I know about Erica Cosway says that she is loyal to our cause."

"You're right," Chasm agrees, a deep breath punctuating his response. "I guess I just needed to at least consider the possibility since the question *did* arise within my mind. But her track record does speak for itself. If it's not her, then I am back where I was when I first arrived here: no leads. Just questions."

Dr. Winters studies his mentee for several moments before speaking. "You are further along than you realize, Chasm. This conversation has allowed you to rule out certain things while focusing on others. Your key to solving this riddle will be patience. And judging by the video footage, the man in your Speedsuit seems to be arrogant. Pride always comes before a fall. I am sure, if you give things enough time, the truth will become clear."

[]

The Montgomery Group headquarters.

Chasm arrives back at his office where Erica is eagerly waiting for him.

"You were right," she says smiling. "The cameras near the I-285 exit ramps. We enlarged the search radius and found where he got off. He possibly took route 400 and could be located somewhere in Dunwoody, GA."

“Excellent work,” Chasm responds in a lighter tone than before. “For right now, let’s use our satellites to survey the area.”

“Understood.” She looks directly at her boss. “You seem to be in a better mood.”

Chasm nods. “Sometimes all you need to be in a better mood is a change in perspective.”

CHAPTER TWENTY-SIX

KEYS TO THE KINGDOM

CURTIS SITS AT HIS DESK WORKING on homework. He's been sitting in the same position for a number of hours and can feel the strain on his neck, back and in his fingers. He grimaces as a slight pain shoots through his neck. Placing the pen down on his desk, he reaches to the ceiling and stretches. His phone vibrates as it registers a new text message. He looks down at it and joins the conversation:

Big Brother: Hey Bro. You busy? How are you? You still following doctor's orders?

Me: Yep! Gavin dropped off my classwork before going out with his dad. Doing it now.

Big Brother: Glad you're staying in bed.

Me: Can't wait till Monday. Need to get out of here. What's up?

Big Brother: Was reading through dad's journal... Thought of you when I got to page 123.

Me: I still haven't read the entire journal. It's too painful.

Big Brother: Yeah. Me too. Just take it a couple of journal entries at a time.

Me: Ok. I'll take a look at it now.

Curtis reaches into his drawer, retrieves his journal and opens up to page 123.

M.A.K.E. IT HAPPEN

To my glorious boys,

People will try to label you as victims. They will say that you are prisoners to the trauma of your past. And you may be tempted to believe them and claim a victim mentality. Perhaps you may think it will get you pity that will open doors or will allow you to make excuses when you fail.

By the time you read these words, you will have lived several years without me. My absence will be traumatic and will no doubt forge dark caverns through the course of your lives, taking you in directions you don't want to go. But when the raging waters calm and you have a solid moment to think things through, know that you are not victims.

Even when you try to rise and for whatever reason you may fall —you are not victims. When the world looks at you and claims you are inferior, don't you claim that mentality. Instead you must be determined to take responsibility for the life you want to live and MAKE IT HAPPEN!

Your life is yours to live. Though indelibly connected to those around you, no one can perform the actions that are yours alone to produce. Whatever challenges you face in life, whatever goals and dreams you desire to reach, whatever obstacles stand in front of you to be overcome, you both take the necessary steps to MAKE it happen. And here are the steps.

M *is for Mindset. What you believe is how you will act and react. Your focus determines your reality.*

A *is for Ability. What you can do is determined by the skills you acquire and develop throughout your life.*

K *is for Knowledge. Learn from each and every situation and circumstance.*

***E** is for Execution. All the talk in the world means nothing if you can't back up your words with action.*

Wherever you find yourselves when you read these words... know that you are not victims. God created you to be victorious! You are overcomers! You have brilliant minds and together, you can M.A.K.E. anything happen. Be there for one another. Help to guide and encourage each other. And be there for your mother.

I love you both very much.

Your Father...
Malcolm

Curtis sets his journal down as he wipes his eyes. Then he notices the rip on the inside of the thick cover of the journal has spread. Curiously, he flips the pages away from the cover to examine the tear. His eyebrows wrinkle as he purses his lips. *What is that?* he thinks, as he sees what appears to be paper protruding from the tear. He takes his scissors and makes an incision to lengthen the opening. With precision, he retrieves a 3 by 5 inch rectangular piece of folded paper.

"Who put this in here?" he mumbles to himself. As he opens it, a small bronze key falls with a thud on his desk. He slowly picks up the key and examines it. On one side are the initials UNB. On the other, the number 845. Curtis puts the key on the desk and looks at the writing on the paper.

"It's a letter from Dad!" he exclaims as he reads the first line.

Curtis and Omar...

Curtis picks up his phone and calls his brother.

"Hello?"

"Omar!"

"Did you read the entry?"

"Yes, but there's something else! I found a letter from dad hidden *inside* the front cover of the journal!"

"Are you serious?" Omar yells.

"Yes!" Curtis replies. "He wrote it to both of us!"

"Well read it to me!"

Curtis and Omar,

The cancellation of my life insurance policy was not an accident. It was done deliberately by John Whaley, with the full knowledge of the other founding partners and the chairman of the board of directors.

After I was promoted to Partner, I discovered that many of my architect firm's major early projects were completed using criminal practices. Thanks to loopholes in zoning laws, many people were "legally" dispossessed of their homes and businesses. In other instances, obstinate home owners and tenants were forced from their residences. Some, by questionable circumstances—like arson—were never to be seen again. When John Whaley and the others determined that I would not go along with their coverup, they began to slowly ostracize me as they tried to determine what course of action they wanted to pursue. They knew they couldn't fire me because I would sue the pants off of them. A short time later, I was diagnosed with this bone cancer.

Below, you will see a partial list of the actual file names and case numbers. Boys, please show this letter to your mother and tell her to find my executive assistant, Margerie Cunningham. She has copies of all of the listed files. Once you have done this, go to United National Bank in Madison New Jersey and use your keys to open safety deposit box #845. Inside you will find the original documents as well as audio/video recordings of key conversations. Only you two and your mother are authorized to open the box. It will take both keys to do so.

Know that if John Whaley discovers that you are privy to this knowledge, your lives will be in considerable danger. Not only will these documents ensure that you receive the money that is due you, this evidence will absolutely ruin their careers and help to ensure reparations are granted to all home and business owners who were swindled out of their properties.

I am sorry you must carry this burden. I just pray you both possess the courage to do what is right... even if you are afraid.

Take care and know that I love you both very much!

Your Father,
Malcolm

Curtis looks at the list of names and case numbers.

"So, you have *both* keys?" Omar asks.

"No. There was only one."

"One?" Omar yells. "Where's the other one?"

"Wait. What about *your* journal? Maybe that's why dad gave us the same exact one!"

Omar opens his leather journal's front cover, quickly takes a cutting blade from the kitchen and slices through it. He reaches into the space in between the layers and feels something. A second later, he pulls out a folded rectangular piece of paper. A key falls out onto the kitchen counter. The same initials and numbers are inscribed on it.

"I have it!" Omar says with an obvious excitement. "We've got to tell mom."

"But I'm all the way down here," Curtis yelps. "We need to be *together* to open the safety deposit box!"

"Don't worry. Let me talk to mom and see what she says. In the meantime, tell no one. Not even Gavin. And put that letter and key in the most secure place you've got."

CHAPTER TWENTY-SEVEN

ART EXHIBIT

TREYSHAWN EAGERLY TREKS ACROSS CAMPUS ON this crisp April afternoon with his arms full of artwork and supplies. His pace quickens every few seconds as he tries to look at his wristwatch without dropping his possessions. He huffs his way through labored breathing and increasingly aching arms. Finally, after several minutes of stuttered sprints, he enters the school's massive Fine Arts building and makes his way through the halls to the gallery. As he stumbles through the gallery doors, the contents held by his failing arms, spew all over the nearest table.

"Whew!" he breathes heavily, bent over from exhaustion. "That was close."

His fellow classmates stop and stare at him with a mix of emotions.

"Look who finally decided to show up," one of them declares as others laugh or shake their heads. "I mean, it's not like this is anything *important*; only a chance to introduce our artwork to the world."

"I'm glad you help to keep me on my toes, Angel," Treyshawn replies sarcastically as he wipes sweat from his forehead. "I'm not sure how I would make it without your *daily* commentary. You know, if you paid more attention to your artwork than to me, maybe you'd be a better artist than I am."

"Oooooh," The other students laugh as Treyshawn approaches the other student.

"Seriously though," he says, while holding out his hand in truce-like fashion, "This last piece was harder than I thought. But I'm here now. Sorry I'm late."

"I'm just glad you're here," Angel admits as he shakes Treyshawn's hand. "You need any help setting up? We only got twenty minutes left."

"Thanks, but I'm good," Treyshawn responds. "I don't want you to have any reasons to blame me for not having *your* stuff ready."

Angel laughs hard. "Y'all New Yorkers sure do have a way with words."

"Says the guy who talks constantly," Treyshawn chuckles.

Treyshawn and Angel break away as everyone gets back to work. They've had a friendly rivalry since the first week of classes. Ask any other student and they will say Angel and Treyshawn are two of the best artists in the class. But Angel and Treyshawn will never admit their admiration for each other's work nor their insecurity about their own.

Treyshawn carries his things over to his assigned station and begins to remove his artwork from their protective sleeves. He sets up 3 easels and places each piece on them. He then attaches the descriptions to the side of each easel and makes minor adjustments to their placement and height.

Ten minutes remain as the art professor enters with glee. The waiting area of the gallery is full and a line stretches halfway around the building.

"We are just minutes away from our 21st annual gallery exhibition. This may be *your* first, but you are part of a long-standing tradition within the art department of this educational Institution. The attendees are from all over California and range from the average spectator to curators of professional art galleries. Each year, a handful of students are selected to have their artwork displayed in other exhibits. So, cross your fingers, be ready to explain your art to anyone who inquires and make sure you enjoy the moment."

Treyshawn, Angel and others watch from the second floor level as people flow into the gallery as soon as the doors officially open. In a matter of minutes, the sea of people rises to fill every level of the exhibition. Soon, Treyshawn is engaged in lively conversation with several people at once as queries keep coming. Growing crowds center on his pieces as word begins to spread throughout the gallery.

"I did this first piece with charcoal. And I used a particular kind of canvas to help to release the grittiness of the charcoal. The rough aspects of the texture represents the kind of life I was living—trapped…"

"My second piece was done with mixed media: charcoal and acrylic paint. The piece is mostly charcoal, layered with acrylic in certain places to represent the changes that were beginning to take place in my life. At this point, I wanted *more* than what I was experiencing, but I was unsure of the path I needed to take to get there, and whether or not I had what it took to be successful."

"I mainly used watercolors for my third piece—with a hint of charcoal to show that I had indeed encountered life transformation, even though it was still incomplete. But, I was *way* further along in the process than before it began."

By the end of this Friday night, Treyshawn barely has a voice. He also has a slew of business cards and several verbal invitations to display his work elsewhere in the state. As the last person leaves, Treyshawn slumps into a nearby chair, so exhausted he can barely sigh. He rubs his aching legs and knees. Yet, a grin grows on his face. His expectations—though low—have been fully exceeded! And all he can do is smile and be content. *Even if nothing else happens from this, this was a great night*, he muses. *Although, I hope something does come of this.*

Monday morning, when Treyshawn enters his art class, Professor Melody immediately hands him a sealed envelop. She motions for him to open it. He carefully rips through the paper and removes the folded document. It's a letter from a prominent art gallery curator in the city. He looks back up at his professor with a type of scared wonder.

"Go on," she urges with a smile, "read it!"

Treyshawn looks back down at the letter in his trembling hands and begins to read it out loud.

Mr. Treyshawn Jinkins,

It was a true pleasure to meet you this past Friday night at the university's art exhibit. I was extremely moved by your work and your explanation. After conferring with Professor Melody, I would like to offer you the opportunity to display your own exhibit here in my gallery. It is my expert opinion that people need to experience your story. Will you expand your work on the 'Life-Change' theme to 15-20 pieces and agree to display them here? The work you do will be counted as college credit. You will also receive a stipend. Please confer with your professor and let me know as soon as possible.

Sincerely,

Christopher P. Underwood, II
Curator, California Art Gallery, USA

Treyshawn looks up at his professor as she lets out a chuckle. "Who would have thought," she smiles. "You are *really* shining. So, what do you say?"

"I-I'm speechless," he barely utters.

"Well then, just nod if you agree to take this opportunity."

Treyshawn nods eagerly then gives Professor Melody an unexpected hug. She announces the good news to the class. All of Treyshawn's fellow students—including Angel, applaud and cheer at this accomplishment. *She's right*, Treyshawn ponders, *who would have thought this would ever happen? Definitely not me.*

[]

Later that evening.

Treyshawn paces his dorm room floor, barely able to contain his excitement as he talks on his cell phone.

"So, that's it," he smiles. "I'm going to have my own gallery exhibit!"

"That's great Trey," his father says, smiling as he sits at a payphone in his cell block. He is so focused on the conversation that the surrounding noise from the inmates barely distracts him. "What did your mom say?"

"I haven't spoken to her yet," Treyshawn replies, "I wanted to tell you first."

Treyshawn Sr. pulls the receiver away from his ear, slightly, as he looks away—trying to hide his expression. His eyes well with tears and he takes a few deep breaths in an attempt to gain control.

"Dad?" Treyshawn inquires as the pause becomes increasingly noticeable, "Are you still there?"

Treyshawn Sr. laughs as he clears his throat and wipes his eyes. "Yeah Trey," he smiles, "I'm still here. So... I'm the first person you told?"

"This is a special moment for me... You and I don't have many special moments."

Treyshawn Sr. tries to clear his throat again. "Thank you Trey. For telling me *first*. I appreciate that."

Treyshawn finally sits on the edge of his bed. "I don't think you've *ever* thanked me for anything before."

"Well, I'm *thanking you* now." An inmate walks by and quickly taps Treyshawn Sr. on the shoulder. "Listen Trey, I gotta to get going."

"Oh, OK," Treyshawn replies sadly. "Guess we'll talk next week?"

"You got it," his father assures him.

"Hey Dad, when I come home for the summer, I... just want you to know that I'm going to visit you every week. OK?"

"Trey," his father replies, "I really appreciate that. And I'm looking forward to seeing you. But believe it or not, sometimes there's a lot going on here in prison. We got license plates to make you know."

They both laugh.

"So, July is cool. But maybe we should take a break for August. Things might be a bit hectic. OK?"

"Oh, OK."

"But know that I'm *proud* of you, Son. Keep up the great work."

With that, the line goes dead, leaving Treyshawn staring at his phone. He throws himself back onto his bed. Laughter bubbles up from his gut and he lets it tumble out. After a few minutes he grows still and silent, staring at the ceiling.

"My dad is proud of *me*..."

[]

Treyshawn Sr. walks out of the recreation area in his cell block and heads down the hall, past the showers to a meeting room. Two guards stand watch at the door as he approaches. They nod at him and open the door. Treyshawn Sr. enters as the door closes behind him. Eight of his fellow inmates look up at him from their huddle.

"Bout time you got here," Tyrone scoffs. "Where you been?"

"I'm here *now*," Treyshawn Sr. states flatly. "Keep going. I'll jump in when necessary."

The inmates go back to their conversation as Treyshawn Sr. slowly approaches. He watches quietly as Tyrone discusses their prison break plans. Time is winding down as The Day fast approaches. While each man revels in the thought of freedom at any cost, Treyshawn Sr. wrestles with his *own* dilemma: *is stolen freedom worth the loss of his son's trust and admiration?*

CHAPTER TWENTY-EIGHT

BAIT AND SWITCH

ONLY TWO WEEKS LEFT UNTIL THE end of the semester. Then comes a whirlwind of activity as Curtis and team will jump into high gear to finalize all of the components for the summer tour. Curtis has been studying hard in his room for most of the day, in preparation for a two-part final exam which begins tomorrow morning at 8am sharp.

Gavin enters with an armful of textbooks, having just come from a class study group which met in the library for the past four hours. Gavin drops his books on his desk and crumbles to his bed.

"Ugh…" he moans loudly. "My brain hurts!"

"Who you tellin?" Curtis huffs. "These exams are going to be crazy!"

"Final paper is due at the end of the week!" Gavin cries. "I still have twenty more pages to write!"

"You knew about that paper since the beginning of the semester," Curtis says, laughing as he looks up at his bewildered friend. "Why'd you wait until *today* to start?"

"Procrastination is a silent killer!" Gavin bellows as his body goes limp on his bed.

"We might as well take a break for a few minutes," Curtis says as he rubs his eyes and stands to his feet to stretch. "Maybe I'll go for a run."

Gavin jumps up from his bed. "I was so tired, I almost forgot!"

"Forgot what?"

"Running! I've been thinking about a way to stop Turbulence from running! I'll explain once we call everybody."

[]

Jim Grabowski's home.

"That's great!" Jim shouts as he looks at Miranda and Omar. "I don't know why *I* didn't think of that idea."

"That's why they pay me the big bucks," Gavin laughs as his voice is heard over Jim's speaker phone in the living room.

"What do you think?" Curtis' voice booms from the same speaker.

"I think it sounds good," Omar chuckles. "Can't wait to see Turbulence's face when he gets a taste of his own medicine."

"Talk with Chasm," Miranda adds. "I'm sure very few people know Atlanta like he does. There's no way we can pull this off without him."

"For this to work," Jim adds, "we need to modify the Mach-1. I'm sure we don't want a repeat of what happened last time."

[]

Two and a half weeks later. The streets of downtown Atlanta.

People scream and dive for cover as three cars careen out of control—the first slamming into a fire hydrant, the second smashing through a bus stop, and the third ramming through a storefront.

Turbulence comes to a halt long enough to admire his handiwork. He grips his black duffel bag and slings it over his shoulder before taking off down the street as two police cars give chase.

"Are they serious?" Turbulence says, laughing hysterically as his visor's heads up display superimposes current data over a rearview image of the approaching cars. He easily weaves through traffic before disengaging his boosters and deploying his airbrakes. His sudden deceleration puts him right between the two cars, as officers struggle to get their guns out of their holsters.

The airbrakes close as he reengages boosters to keep pace with the cars and then reaches out and touches both of them. A surge of over 50 thousand volts short-circuits the vehicles, causing the officers to swerve out of control and crash into surrounding automobiles. Turbulence cackles loudly as he zooms down the street towards the highway.

"Bank robbery—check! Car accidents—check! Making the police look *stupid*—check!" His suit's proximity sensor beeps, alerting him to a fast approaching object from his left side. But the warning is too late!

WHAM!!!!

A quick bodycheck sends Turbulence stumbling out of control at over 60 miles per hour. Curtis skids to a halt and smiles as his nemesis crashes into a parked car. But he is amazed by what he sees—the phenomenon which takes place in a fraction of a second. Just before impact, eight airbags deploy from the Mach-2 Speedsuit—absorbing much of the blunt-force trauma. Turbulence stumbles to his feet, barely fazed by the impact, as the airbags retract.

"Never thought about airbags before," Curtis admits.

"When you're going as fast as I do," Turbulence replies, "better to have them and not need them… well, you know the rest."

"You need to give yourself up and return the money you stole."

"Only if you catch me!" Turbulence turns to run away.

"Wait!" Curtis yells. "What if you can't catch *me*? Then you turn yourself in."

"You can't outrun me!"

"Sure I can!"

Curtis takes off down the street in a burst of pressurized air. Turbulence removes the duffel bag from his shoulder, drops it to the ground and leaps into action.

"There's always another bank!" He laughs as he engages his boosters. Within moments, he closes in on Curtis.

"Here he comes," Chasm relays to Curtis through the communications system. "Just stick to the plan."

"Right!" Curtis replies while moving at top speed.

Turbulence speeds right beside Curtis and grabs his arm.

"You're it!" he yells as he discharges 50,000 volts!

Curtis laughs as he shakes his arm free. "Is that *all* you got?"

"I-I don't understand," Turbulence yells.

Curtis quickly grabs an object from a pouch on his belt and throws it at Turbulence's legs. The object separates and spins—revealing two weighted balls connected by a cord. In an instant, Turbulence slams head-over-heels to the ground and skids to a stop.

"The bolas worked!" Omar yells as he watches the screen.

"I don't fall for the same trick twice," Curtis declares with a smile as he approaches his nemesis. "More insulation this time!"

"Quick Curtis!" Jim yells, "Hit him with phase two!"

As Turbulence struggles to get his legs untangled, Curtis raises his right arm, aims and slams his left hand on a pressure-sensitive forearm button. A nozzle on the side of his wrist sprays a sheet of oil, which covers the Mach-2 suit. Curtis switches arms and fires more oil from his left gauntlet—this time specifically spraying Turbulence's boots and the ground around him.

"You're done!" Curtis shouts as police sirens blare in the distance.

Turbulence cuts through the bola with a retractable blade and stands to his feet, but quickly falls again due to a lack of traction on his boots.

"I can't believe it worked!" Gavin cheers.

"Curtis, security teams are en route," Chasm declares. "They'll be to your position in less than two minutes. Police are right behind them."

"Tell them to take their time," Curtis says, while laughing unreservedly, "Flatulence isn't going anywhere." Curtis watches as his adversary struggles to stand to his feet. Each time, he fails and falls to the ground. "Just give up already," Curtis quips. "That oil puddle you're in is specially formulated to render surface friction down to zero. There's *no* way you can stand up without help."

Security and police vehicles arrive on the scene as personnel surround their target. Turbulence laughs as he lightly rests on his hands and knees.

"What's so funny?" Curtis asks.

"I forgot to tell you," Turbulence exclaims as he raises his head towards Curtis, "I don't need to stand to go fast."

His boosters engage as he raises his torso perpendicular to the ground. A second later, he rises into the air as the police, security team and Curtis himself stumble back from the powerful exhaust blast! Everyone gapes in disbelief as Turbulence flies off past a nearby building.

"He can fly!" Curtis yells. "Why didn't anyone *tell* us he can fly?"

Gavin, Jim and Omar stare at Chasm while he shakes his head. "Apparently, someone gave that suit a serious upgrade."

[]

Dr. Winters walks through the east wing of his mansion and descends a flight of stairs, which brings him to a huge steel door. He enters a code into the keypad and waits as the door opens. He proceeds down the dark hallway and enters a room illuminated by television screens. He sits in his large, plush leather chair and makes an encrypted phone call.

"Initiate the next phase. Release the coordinates."

[]

Erica bursts into the security room where Chasm, Omar, Jim and Gavin are stationed. "I found him!" She shouts while holding up her digital tablet. "He must have gotten sloppy. I'm tracking him with one of our satellites!"

"Get a security detail together," Chasm replies. "It's time to end these shenanigans."

[]

Chasm's security team rappel down a dark elevator shaft and blow the doors to the underground lair! Twenty men in tactical gear storm the area with guns and flashlights. A computer—emanating wafts of smoke—sits on a solitary desk, while a human-like silhouette stands in the distant shadows.

"Freeze!" the security personnel yell as they surround Turbulence. "Sir," an operative relays through his earpiece, "we have him."

A moment later, Chasm, Erica, Curtis, Omar, Jim and Gavin enter the lair just in time to see twenty guards with their guns and flashlights trained on a motionless foe.

"He's not in the suit," Chasm declares as he quickly walks over.

"How do you know that, Sir?" asks the team leader.

"Because," Chasm states as he walks through the guards, "he's not moving." Chasm pushes the front of the suit, with both hands, causing the figure to fall backward to the ground with a loud, resounding clang! "Search the rest of the premises! He has to be here somewhere!"

Chasm squats next to the suit as the guards spread out. The rest of the group approaches as Chasm finds the release lever. To their astonishment, with the press of a button, the front of the suit opens up to reveal an empty internal housing.

"I don't get it," Curtis mumbles, "how did you know how to do that?"

"Because," Chasm sighs as he turns and faces Curtis, "I designed it."

The security team leader returns. "Sir, there's no sign of the suit's operator. We think he may have exited through one of several tunnels we found on the far side of the structure. They connect to the MARTA train tunnels."

"Then he could be anywhere by now," Chasm interjects.

"I'm afraid so, Sir. Also his computer hard drive was destroyed. The housing is still warm; probably happened just before we arrived."

[]

The security convoy drives back to The Montgomery Group headquarters. Chasm and Erica sit quietly in the truck with Curtis and the rest of the group.

"You have to believe me," Chasm says. "I did create the suit, but I had nothing to do with it being stolen and used in this manner."

"How are we supposed to believe you," Curtis presses.

"The same way you believe me about everything else," Chasm replies. "Curtis, I give you *my word*… I had nothing to do with this."

"So why did you create the suit?" Jim asks.

"It was supposed to be a surprise for Curtis."

"For me?"

"Yes. You've done much with your Mach-1—inspired many people—but you all built that suit from off-the-shelf parts. I wanted to surprise you with a custom-made suit, created from the resources at my disposal. The Mach-2 is a revolutionary leap forward in every way. But someone—one of my competitors—figured out a way to steal it and use it for criminal intent. Whoever is behind this, is still at large. But now that we have the suit back, I'm sure there may be some clues we can use to determine their identity."

"How so?" Omar asks.

"I can analyze the operating system. Unless you completely power the suit down, it *always* records operational data, even when it's in standby mode. I'm hoping whoever used it, didn't know that." Chasm smiles at Curtis, "Once we get the suit back up to spec, you can take it out for a test run if you like."

"I'll *think* about it," Curtis replies.

"Again, thank you for helping to locate the suit. That was pretty impressive using 'old school' technology to take down a hi-tech villain. Please accept my offer of gratitude. Jim and Omar… why don't you move down here temporarily and stay at my facilities to help us develop a few new suits for our summer tour?"

Jim and Omar gaze from Chasm to each other to Curtis.

"His facilities *are* really nice," Curtis adds, chuckling.

"Of course, I will cover all of your costs," Chasm continues his appeal. "Consider it a working vacation."

"Are you kidding?" Omar replies while confirming with Jim, "we'd be like kids in a candy store!"

"A *really big* candy store," Chasm smiles.

CHAPTER TWENTY-NINE

GRADUATION

EXCITEMENT AND ANTICIPATION FILL THE AIR as students, faculty, administration, families, friends and media arrive at 10th Street N.W. to enter the McCamish Pavilion. Friday May 2, 2014. Georgia Tech Spring Masters and Ph.D Graduation. Thousands fill the arena for the Commencement Ceremony. Graduates line up in their black caps and gowns, wearing tassels signifying their GPA levels and departmental designations. Among them stands Erica Cosway, her eyes beaming with promise and her smile brilliant as the sun. After so many years of excruciating hard work, her big day is here.

Music fills the pavilion as the ceremony begins. Thanks to Chasm's generosity and influence, Curtis, Omar, Miranda, Jim, Kelly and Gavin sit in a special VIP section with Erica's family. They all cheer incessantly as they watch Erica enter the main floor in the graduate procession. Moments later, she passes near their section and takes a seat—well within ear shot. She smiles at them as they take countless photos with their camera phones.

After a rousing commencement speech, the conferring of the degrees begins. Erica's mother and father hold each other tightly, with tears in their eyes as they watch their eldest daughter traverse the main stage and receive her double degrees—presented by a very proud Chasm Montgomery who is garbed in his own educational alum cap and robe.

After the conferring of the final degree to the university's last 2014 Spring graduate, they all cheer as they celebrate the completion of a major life milestone. The commencement ceremony ends, but the multitude of family celebrations continue well into the evening.

[]

Erica sits with her family and friends high above the city at the 191 Club. A quartet bathes the atmosphere in classical music as waiters prepare to serve the special group. Dr. Winters looks on with great interest as Chasm rises to make a toast. With a glass of champaign in hand, he smiles as he makes his declaration.

"I still remember when we met all those years ago. You were so young, and so filled with promise. But you are not a little girl any longer. This evening we celebrate an amazing individual... A young woman who, so far in life, has defied all of the odds that were stacked against her. With great tenacity she has begun to make her mark on the world. And she has made her mark on *me*. I know her family has served as a solid support system—for no one rises in life without assistance. And if I may say, she is like a *daughter* to me."

Erica blushes at her mentor's words.

"Erica Cosway," Chasm continues, "you have worked hard to master not only your studies, but also *yourself*. And you strive daily to make an indelible mark on the world. For this, you are to be celebrated. Congratulations on your graduation! And beginning Monday, we at The Montgomery Group look forward to having you with us officially as our full-time Director of Operations."

The group cheers as they raise their glasses in the air.

"To Erica!" Chasm beams.

"To Erica!" Everyone responds.

Dr. Winters takes a sip of his champaign and rests the glass back on the dinner table. He gazes at Erica, who sits a few tables away. As she laughs and makes small talk with the others, her eyes catch his for an instant. She quickly smiles and glances in another direction. Dr. Winters smiles as well as he turns his gaze towards the larger group. *So jovial*, he muses. *And so... unsuspecting. Soon, my plan will be complete. And everything Chasm holds dear... will be mine for the taking.*

Chasm walks over to Dr. Winters as they share a hearty handshake.

"I'm so glad you were able to come today," Chasm declares warmly. "It means a lot to Erica and to me."

"Erica's accomplishments are worthy of the utmost recognition," Dr. Winters replies. "She is a fine testament to the quality leadership *you* provide. I would not miss this day for the world."

The waiters arrive with the entrées and the jovial celebration continues well into the night.

CHAPTER THIRTY

HEROES AND VILLAINS

THE WORLD IS FULL OF HEROES and villains. The decisions we *make* determine which one we will become and affects those around us. This will be the theme of the upcoming Powersuit Tour. With seven suits already created and Curtis and team working feverishly to complete the last three, the tour should capture the heart and mind of every person in attendance.

Erica's first order of business is to give the tour's development process her full-time attention. Although she and Chasm have already been working on this project for months, she is now working closely with Curtis, Miranda, Omar, Jim and Gavin—as well as her own team of engineers, marketing, finance, computer technicians and others to ensure that *every* facet works like clockwork and goes according to Chasm's plan and vision.

Twelve cities have been selected for the tour: New York City, Philadelphia, Washington D.C., Charlotte, Atlanta, Chicago, Houston, San Antonio, Dallas, Phoenix, Los Angeles, and San Diego. The tour will arrive at each city two days prior to the event night and will take a day and a half to break down in preparation for the next leg of the journey.

A number of teams work around the clock to ensure everything is in place for the July 4th launch. An audacious plan to be sure—launching on Independence Day—but this is all about making a statement to the United States and to the world. For this year's tour, no expense has been spared as the best directors, theatrical and stunt crews, musical composers, musicians, and actors have been secured. Almost two thousand individuals are working diligently to ensure success. Heroes and Villains will have a production value on par with Disney, Hollywood, Broadway and Cirque du Soleil.

Curtis, Gavin, Omar and Jim have been living in one of Chasm's labs for the past couple of weeks. With ready access to almost every resource imaginable, they have been able to work four to five times faster than if they were doing this on their own. Three new suits stand in support cases. The first increases agility. The second generates multi-wavelength light. The third enables its wearer to climb walls.

Chasm and Erica descend in an elevator to one of their underground indoor testing ranges for a demonstration. They watch as Curtis, Omar and Jim help Gavin get into the first suit.

"This is amazing," Erica whispers.

"How so?" Chasm asks.

"They've been at this for less than a month and look at the progress they've made! Our own engineers don't work this efficiently!"

"We had a *similar* discussion before," Chasm smiles.

"About Curtis," Erica agrees. "I remember."

"Curtis, fueled by his inquisitiveness, sees connections where others do not. He is a prodigy working with a physics teacher, an aircraft mechanic, and a self-proclaimed robotics expert. Don't forget about the three initial Powersuits they created on their own. They have this process down to a science and that is impressive."

"That's why you brought them all together," Erica states.

"Yes. Everything is going according to plan."

"OK," Curtis declares with a clap as he approaches them both, "we are ready."

Erica and Chasm watch as Gavin demonstrates the first Powersuit. The suit's designation, Acrobat-1, looks quite similar to a human skeleton—but made out of carbon fiber with suit extension points at each joint, connecting to cables. He launches himself down the testing range, executing a series of impressive somersaults, before leaping over five obstacles ranging six to ten feet high. All of his movements are done with great ease as he finally lands right in front of the group.

"Very nice," Chasm says, clapping as he and Erica approach for a closer look.

"So, how does it work?" Erica inquires.

"You're basically a human spring in this suit," Gavin replies.

"Right," Curtis agrees as he turns Gavin around so everyone can see the back of the suit. "The backpack houses a spring-pulley system which connects, by cables, to various anchor points across the suit."

"It's the same concept used in Curtis's Kinetic Redistribution Boots," Omar adds.

"Except in *this* case," Jim interjects, "the suit *itself* acts like the boots. Meaning, the wearer can cover more ground in this suit, than if they were wearing the boots alone. And not only can the suit operator go further faster, they can survive jumps from greater heights because the suit absorbs the bulk of the impact and redistributes the stress load *away* from the person inside."

"It's a low-tech suit," Curtis smiles, "with no power source and *no* batteries. It's all mechanical and harnesses the wearer's weight to generate kinetic energy and momentum."

Twenty minutes later, the group is ready to test the second suit designated—Illuminator. They are standing in another section of the testing facility that has been retrofitted with various climate environment set pieces and painted in a variety of solid and combined colors.

"You know the engineers hit a dead end with this concept," Chasm admits, "But Curtis figured it out."

"Ok," Curtis says, "we're ready. Can either of you find Gavin?"

Chasm and Erica gaze around the room, looking at all of the different simulated environments.

"I don't see him," Erica huffs. "Do you?"

"No," Chasm shakes his head and smiles, "And that's the point."

Curtis, Omar and Jim smirk at each other.

"Mr. G," Omar says, "can you do the honors?"

"Gavin," Jim Grabowski shouts, "where are you?"

"Right here," a voice booms on their right-hand side.

The group turns to the right and barely makes out a silhouette standing among the foliage. With the click of a switch, Gavin seems to materialize out of thin air—wearing an all-white Powersuit that covers his entire body.

"Camouflage!" Erica shouts. "Chasm, they figured out a way to bend light around a person?"

"Not exactly," Chasm replies. "Curtis, would you care to explain?"

"This suit manipulates light, but it doesn't bend it like the alien from the Predator movies. Almost every inch is covered with extremely small LED lights—similar to the ones found in the latest flat screen televisions. Those lights are tied into several computer processors which are connected to tiny cameras positioned on the suit. Those cameras capture images of the surrounding environment and feed that data to the computers, which then output an approximate image of the environments' color and exposure, which the LED lights project."

"Where did you get this idea from?" Erica asks.

"My intention for this suit was for it to generate bursts of light."

FLASH!!!

The entire group shields their eyes as Gavin produces a blast of white light with the intensity of a flare.

"Wow," Erica gasps.

"I love it!" Chasm says, applauding.

"The suit can emit light at multiple wavelengths and intensities." Gavin's suit suddenly flashes through every color of the rainbow at high and low luminance.

"But Chasm mentioned that his engineers were having a problem trying to produce a suit that can camouflage like a chameleon. That got me thinking about a video I saw awhile back on cephalopods."

"Octopus?" Erica asks.

"Octopus," Chasm declares.

"We studied them in one of my biomimetics classes," Erica replies as she shudders, "*not* a fan."

"Many octopus squirt ink to get away from predators," Omar divulges, "but certain ones can change their appearance in order to blend in with their environment. And not just the color of their skin, but also the *perceived* texture as well."

"So," Curtis continues, "the more I thought about those octopus and studied what scientists already know about how their skin could change like that, the more the idea seemed feasible. We just needed to figure out a *similar* way to do it."

"The suit isn't perfect," Jim adds. "You can see it more distinctly depending on the angle you view it from."

"But it's a great first step!" Chasm replies. "Excellent job! Now what about the last suit?"

Thirty minutes later, the team is ready to unveil their last creation designated—Wall Climber. Erica and Chasm arrive at another section of the training facility where Curtis, Omar and Jim are standing.

"OK," Erica says, while rolling her eyes, "where's Gavin now?"

The three men smile and point upward. Erica and Chasm look up and see a figure clinging to the top of a thirty foot wall.

"You've *got* to be kidding," Erica quips as Chasm laughs.

Gavin climbs down the wall in true 'wall-crawler' fashion—the only thing heard as he gets closer, is a faint hissing sound.

"The wearer of this suit may not have been bitten by a radioactive spider," Curtis chuckles, "but he or she will be able to climb almost as well as Spiderman."

Gavin turns around so everyone can see the backpack.

"A micro-turbine runs the compressor fan blade assembly," Omar explains. "It sucks air out of the hoses connected to it. Those hoses run to the gloves, boots and several anchor pads on the suit."

Gavin holds up his gloves for a better look.

"As you can see," Omar continues, "the gloves are a bit oversized and have suction nozzles at the end of each finger and on the palm. When the compressor is activated, this creates a vacuum which allows the wearer to stick to relatively smooth surfaces. The same system is built into the boots and anchor pads."

"What about his weight?" Erica inquires. "His arms and legs must get tired having to climb and hang like that."

"Good point," Jim replies. "As you notice, the suit also has an exoskeletal framework. It actually *supports* the weight. So, when the wearer is strapped in, he's just... hanging around."

"And for a bit of stealth," Curtis adds, "we sheathed the compressor in a special foam and plastic honeycomb housing to increase noise suppression. Think of it like the muffler on a car. Without it, this suit would be *very* loud."

"Curtis," Chasm replies, "You all have *exceeded* my expectations."

"Thanks," Curtis answers. "All that's left is for us to do some fine-tuning. By next week, we should be able to integrate these into rotation."

"Good," Erica interjects. "The practice rotation has helped the stunt personnel master the use of the other suits."

"Then we are on schedule," Chasm concludes as he prepares to leave. "Time waits for no one, but I am confident we will be ready and this tour will be spectacular!"

[]

POWERSUIT TOUR: Live at Madison Square Garden. N.Y.C. July 4, 2014.

Thousands fill the arena for a chance to witness this awe-inspiring one night event. Media coverage is pervasive. Expectations are high. Smiles abound as the energy in the arena is palpable. Curtis, Treyshawn and Kelly sit with Omar, Miranda, Jim, Shakira, Gavin, Johnny, Clamille, Kevin, Kelvin and their parents in the VIP section.

"Dude," Treyshawn says, laughing, "I can't believe you guys pulled this off! This is SO MUCH bigger than last year!"

"I know, right!" Curtis agrees. "This is crazy! We helped create this, but I'm glad we can just sit back and watch it!"

"Yeah!" Treyshawn concurs. "Glad I was able to fly in for this. Been working hard on these pieces for my exhibit."

"Bro," Curtis replies, "that is so exciting! Can't wait to come out to California and see your artwork with my own eyes!"

"November will be here before you know it," Treyshawn assuringly answers, smiling at his friend.

"Whatever you need," Kelly interjects, "you just let us know. I'm so proud of you Treyshawn!"

"And I knew you had it in you to be a great artist," Curtis chuckles while jabbing Treyshawn in his ribs. "How are you and your dad doing?"

"We're good," Treyshawn responds. "We talk every week now. It's amazing you know… to finally have this… relationship that I've wanted for so long I can't even remember. But lately, he keeps pushing me away."

"What do you mean?"

"He keeps saying he's going to be busy in August. Some big prison project. So he doesn't want me to come around to visit until September."

"What could they be doing in prison that's so busy?" Curtis asks with wrinkled eyebrows.

"I dunno," Treyshawn replies. "He keeps joking about making license plates and stuff. But you know what?"

"What?"

"I'm gonna surprise him and just show up."

Both friends laugh.

"I'm sure he'll be glad to see you."

The house lights dim as Heroes and Villains is about to begin. Slow, dramatic music begins to play as the arena goes dark and spotlights illuminate the center stage revealing a walled lab of some kind. A young man, wearing a white lab coat and carrying a digital tablet enters. At the press of a button, a loud buzz emanates from a section of the floor which begins to open. Out of the darkness, a ring of ten containment cases rise on a round platform. Each case seems large enough to carry a single human inside.

With a mechanical thud—the platform stops and slowly rotates on its axis. The protective cases open to reveal within each a different Powersuit. The scientist quickly inspects them before going over to his desk and sitting in front of his computer. As he types, his voice is heard.

"We all create. And sometimes what we create comes from a single question: Is it possible? But what do we *do* with our creations? Do we use them to help others or to help ourselves? Do we become the heroes we *could* be? Or do we choose to morph into the villains?"

BOOM!!!

The lab walls suddenly explode in a ball of fire and thick smoke as thieves enter to steal as many suits as they can get their hands on! Alarms sound as guards enter and attempt to stop the intruders. Blasts and smoke fill the room as the scientist takes cover! In the commotion, the scientist hits the containment suit lockdown button which closes the cases and retracts them underneath the floor. When the smoke clears, the thieves are gone. Several of the guards are in distress. But the scientist is unharmed.

"Secure the perimeter and call the authorities!"

He disables the security protocols, causing the floor to open and the containment cases to ascend. When they re-open… only three suits remain. "I must determine who took my suits! And I have to get them back!"

The room goes black and lights up again.

A week has passed as the scientist is helping three other persons test the remaining Powersuits. Just then, a news report displays on the large computer monitors housed in the wall. A reporter speaks on location. Behind her, a battle seems to be raging.

"Today, the city has been hit by a rash of criminal acts carried out by individuals calling themselves the Villainous Seven Crime Syndicate. Law Enforcement Officers have been unable to stop this group, who are wearing some kind of hi-tech armor."

Explosions are heard as the reporter turns to see one of the criminals picking up a police car and tossing it towards nearby officers, while another criminal shoots an arc of fire across the street, setting a nearby bus on fire.

"We need help down here!" the reporter yells. "Where is the Army or the National Guard? Who's going to stop these villains?"

The screen goes black as the scientist looks at the three others who have agreed to help him.

"It's up to us to stop them." He gives each of them a case. "For this to work, you have to attach one of these surge devices to their suits."

A schematic appears on the screen.

"It doesn't matter where you place it. Just make sure it's armed before you do. Once attached, it will emit an electromagnetic pulse calibrated for each Powersuit's specific energy signature frequency. That pulse will deactivate the suit and allow you and the authorities to restrain them."

The lab goes black as the entire stage shifts. Flames fill portions of the stage as the spotlights once again brighten. A battle has just ended on the streets of the city and the Villainous Seven Crime Syndicate stand victorious as citizens and police retreat.

"No one can stop us!"

"We are invincible!"

But suddenly, the three heroes appear on the scene.

"Those suits don't belong to you!" the leader bellows. "Give up now and turn yourselves in!"

The Villains laugh rebelliously as they attack! A new battle rages as Heroes and Villains face off. Pyro throws the first blow —shooting a stream of flames right at the trio of Heroes. But one of them—Windstorm—steps forward and raises his hands. His Powersuit activates and the sound of a mighty rushing wind is heard as air blasts from his hands! The air meets the flames and both create a wall of resistance that swells back and forth!

While the Villains are focused on the fantastic display, the third Hero—Lightwave—takes two surge devices in his hands and activates his Powersuit. He camouflages into the environment and quickly makes his way around the debris to the rear of the Villains. In one fluid motion, he attaches a device on Pyro and on Hull. In a burst of electricity, both of their suits power down as they fall to the ground.

The flames dissipate as Windstorm closes in and blasts pressurized air at the remaining group, causing a couple of them to lose their balance and fall to the ground. One of the Villains picks up a large barrel and hurls it at Windstorm, but the barrel is deflected by the fast moving air.

Lightwave reappears and engages his supernova blast, which temporarily blinds the Villains. This allows Acrobat to move quickly through the debris and attach the surge devices to a few more Villains. The rest of the syndicate retreat, thanks to a thrust-vectoring aircraft that descends and drops cables for them to grab. Four Villains have been captured. The Heroes watch as three remaining Villains fly away to fight another day.

An hour passes and the audience is enthralled with the show. When it finally ends, the Villains have been thwarted, the Heroes have been victorious and the city has been saved—all while an emotionally moving soundtrack plays in the background. Thunderous applause erupts throughout the entire arena as the house lights are turned on. Minutes of cheering passes as the key characters come back on stage and take a bow. Chasm, Erica, Curtis and the rest of the team take the stage after them and share inspiring words about their life journey, the purpose of this tour and the importance of S.T.E.A.M.: science, technology, engineering, arts and math.

[]

The Powersuit Tour successfully travels to all twelve cities and the reception is the same: excitement, awe-inspiring, educational, moving. The weeks fly by like a whirlwind as word spreads by mouth and media across the country and around the world. Towards the end of August, Chasm unveils a surprise in the city of Atlanta: plans that are already well underway for the building of a museum dedicated to house the Heroes and Villains tour, making it possible for people to travel from all around the world to see Powersuit replicas, stage sets, audio/visual presentations about Curtis, the team, S.T.E.A.M. and more.

CHAPTER THIRTY-ONE

PRISON BREAK

THE DAY HAS COME. TREYSHAWN SR. lays on his bed—in his cell. His orange jumper pulled down to his waist; the sleeves tied in a knot. His massive physique, even while lying still, would intimidate the walls—if that were possible. His eyes are wide open. His hands are crossed behind his head. He stares, motionless, at the ceiling.

Though he has decided *not* to take part in what's about to happen, his mind races as thoughts of his son battle against thoughts of his freedom. Somewhere in the back of his head, he thinks he should warn the guards and the warden. *But I'm no one's snitch.* And a number of the guards are corrupt anyway. So, those who are ignorant will get what's coming to them. He, on the other hand, will stay in his cell in relative safety and ride out the chaos that's about to be unleashed. Only minutes remain, so he closes his eyes and tries to rest.

CLANG! CLANG! A guard raps his flashlight against the cell bars.

"Wake up! You got a visitor."

"Take a message," Treyshawn Sr. mumbles without opening his eyes. "I ain't seein' anybody today."

"It's your son."

Treyshawn Sr.—startled by the news—jumps up in his bed and stares at the guard.

BUZZZZ... the gates open as a guard escorts Treyshawn Sr. into the visitors meeting area. He quickly scans the packed room, spots his son and moves towards him expeditiously.

"Surprise!" Treyshawn shouts as he stands with his arms wide open.

His dad scowls as he grabs his son by the shirt and forces him down on the bench.

"What are you doing here?" Treyshawn Sr. asks in an urgent tone while trying to disguise his worry.

"I wanted to surprise you," his son replies. "Dad? What's wrong?"

"I told you not to come here. Especially *today*!" Treyshawn Sr. glances at the clock and stares at his son. "Trey, you have to leave. Right now!"

"But Dad, I just got here! I don't understand—"

"There's about to be a—"

ALARMS BLARE OUTSIDE!!!

"Oh, no!" Treyshawn Sr. shouts. "They're *early*!"

Visitors, prisoners and guards look around in confusion as shouts can be heard in the distance.

"There's a fire outside in the quad!" a guard yells.

A blast rocks the prison followed by gunshots!

"Lock this place down!" another guard shouts. "Nobody leaves this room!"

"Dad!" Treyshawn shrieks. "What's happening?"

"It's a prison break!" Treyshawn Sr. bellows as he stands and grabs his son. "We gotta get outta here!"

"But the guard said to stay here!" Treyshawn counters. "We're safe in here, right?"

"No! Stay close to me!" Father and son get up and run over to the guard.

"Stay back!" the guard yells while reaching for his club."

"Listen," Treyshawn Sr. shouts as he grabs the guard's hand. "You gotta get these people outta here!"

"I can't," the guard replies. "We're on lockdown!"

"*Everybody dies* if they stay in here!"

Suddenly, several inmates approach with homemade bombs in their hands. Another breaks into the control booth, incapacitates the guard, and hits the override button to open the gate. The inmates hurl their bombs into the visitors center and run off. People scream as the shockwaves from the blasts knock some of them to the ground. The flames begin to quickly spread as the guards try to put them out.

"Come with me!" Treyshawn Sr. yells as he grabs his son and runs through the open gate.

"Dad!" Treyshawn yells. "Why are we running *into* the prison!"

"Just keep your head down and stay with me!"

Smoke, shouts, hideous laughter and gunshots fill the corridors as guards in riot gear try to fight off swarms of inmates. Treyshawn and his dad duck and dodge their way through the chaos—coming across the warden and two guards huddled behind a control desk. The guards shoot the approaching inmates while the warden tries to radio for help. They are clearly outnumbered. Treyshawn Sr. grabs his son and begins to head for a stairway. As they run, Treyshawn sees the warden huddled behind a large desk as two guards fire shots into the growing crowd of irate inmates trying to overrun the area.

"Dad! Wait!" Treyshawn halts. "That's the warden!"

"So!"

"We gotta help him!"

"If we do, we die!"

"I don't care! If it wasn't for him, we wouldn't be talking right now! We gotta help him!"

They both watch as the guards run out of ammunition.

Treyshawn Sr. growls. "Wait here!" He runs over, fights his way through the inmates, and puts himself between them and the warden—quickly getting everyone's attention.

"The warden and his goons are mine!" he roars as he grabs the warden by the throat. "Get outta here!"

The inmates disperse and soon Treyshawn Sr. lets the warden go. "Sorry Warden, but you gotta come with me if you wanna live!"

"Why should I believe you?" the warden says, coughing.

"Dad!" Treyshawn shouts as he runs over to their location. "Warden are you alright?"

"I thought I told you to stay put!"

The warden looks at the both of them.

"I'm just trying to keep my son alive. And *he* wants us to help *you*."

"Warden," the guard yells, "we need to move!"

"Let's get to my office!"

The group runs up the stairs, down the halls, through back doors and secret passages—all the while fighting off scores of inmates. They reach his office and dive through the large metal door, slamming it shut and bolting the locks.

"Quick!" the warden motions as the two guards open a panel on the wall, revealing a stockpile of weapons and ammunition. They reload their guns as the warden picks up his phone. "I've got to call for backup!"

"Your phones won't work!" Treyshawn Sr. counters.

"I have a *private* line," the warden replies as he begins dialing—but there's no signal. He taps his phone. "*None* of my lines are working!"

"I *told* you," Treyshawn Sr. huffs. "The plan was *very* thorough. Like three years in the making thorough."

"Take what you need and guard the door," the warden commands. "No one gets in!"

"Yes Sir," the guards reply while taking the weapons and exiting the room.

The warden locks the door as Treyshawn and his dad build a barricade from nearby bookshelves.

"How do you *know* so much, inmate?" the warden asks in an accusatory tone.

"Because I was part of the group that put the plan together."

The warden glares at the convict with a stone-wall expression.

Treyshawn Sr. stares at the warden and then at his son. "But then, *you* let my son break me… and as we built a relationship, I started to rethink my involvement with this plan. Treyshawn believed in me. And I was starting to believe in myself. Was freedom at any cost worth destroying what we were building?"

"I'm not sure I believe you," the warden replies. "But if I *did*, why didn't you tell us about the plan?"

"If I said some of your guards were in on this you wouldn't have believed me." Treyshawn Sr. replies flatly. "I told my guys I was out and that I wouldn't snitch. If I did, they'd know it was me and I'd be dead."

"So, instead, you kept your mouth shut and a whole lot of good people will have died because of you."

"What choice did I have?"

"There's *always* a choice."

BLAM! BLAM! BLAM!

"Hold it right there!" a guard yells from the other side of the door. "Don't you guys come any closer!"

A volley of gunshots and yells are heard… and then… silence.

KNOCK… KNOCK… KNOCK!

The three men turn and stare at the reinforced metal door.

"Hey Warden. Come on out!" a voice shouts from the other side of the entrance. "We know you're in there all alone. We just wanna talk! *Maybe* if you listen you can walk out of here alive!"

Treyshawn Sr. turns from the door and faces his son. Seeing his fear, he then faces the warden.

"Come on warden!" the voice shouts. "If you don't come out, we'll huff and puff and blow your door down!" The hysterical laughter of other inmates punctuates the command.

BANG! BANG!! BANG!!! The door shudders as the inmates crash the butts of their riffles into it.

"That door won't hold long," Treyshawn Sr. utters as he slowly walks over to the warden.

BLAM! BLAM!! BLAM!!! Shots ring out as bullets riddle the door's exterior—their impact causes small dents on the interior side inside the warden's office.

"No," the warden agrees. "It won't."

"I never liked you," Treyshawn Sr. admits, "but us inmates always knew where we stood with you. If you gave your word—it was as good as gold. I can respect that. At the end of the day, a man is only as good as his word."

Treyshawn Sr. extends his hand to the warden. The warden looks down at his hand and slowly raises his own. The two men shake hands and don't let go.

BANG! BANG!! BLAM!!! More dents form in the door.

"I'm going to go out there—"

"Dad!" Treyshawn shouts. "What are you talking about?"

"Shut up Trey!" He briefly glares at his son with a stern-but-compassionate glance before addressing the warden again. "I will do *everything* in my power to make sure those inmates don't get in here."

"Dad!" Treyshawn cries.

"I said, be quiet!" his father counters without taking his eyes off the warden. He breathes deeply. "If I fail… Warden I want you to give me *your word*—man-to-man. If I fail, you will do everything within your power to make sure my son has a future."

The warden studies the eyes of the man standing before him and increases the pressure of his grip. "You have my word."

Both men break their handshake as Treyshawn rushes to his father.

"Dad! Don't do this. There's gotta be another way!"

"There's always a choice," Treyshawn Sr. utters, "and *this* is mine. There's no other way."

"But what if you don't make it?"

Father and son stare into each others eyes—both full of tears.

"Then I'll die a man—protecting my son."

BLAM! BLAM!! BLAM!!! The door shudders again under the piercing weight of each blast.

"Treyshawn, you've given me the greatest gift a father could ever want. You showed me that change is possible. That growth is possible. And deep down, every father wants his seed to do better than him. And you are *doing* that!" He takes his son by the shoulders. "I may have helped conceive you, but your love and belief in me... *You* gave me life!"

BANG! BANG!! BANG!!!

"Are you comin' out warden?" the voice shouts. "Or are we comin' in to get you?"

"I gotta go." Treyshawn Sr. smiles as he lets go of his son. "That door ain't gonna hold forever."

"Wait," the warden says, "I have something that might help even the playing field."

The inmates stand outside the door—growing increasingly restless.

"Ok," the warden shouts from inside his office. "Don't shoot! I'm coming out!"

The convicts shout and laugh as they hear the locks disengage from the door.

"Here we go!" the leader whispers as the door opens and an unexpected sight reveals itself.

"T-Rock?" the inmate yells in astonishment as the door slams shut. "W-what you doin' in there?"

"You can't go in there Tyrone," Treyshawn Sr. replies. "And he's *not* coming out."

"But you know the plan!" Tyrone roars. "We need him to get what we want!"

"Plans change," Treyshawn Sr. answers. "And my son is in there."

"I knew your son was a problem!" Tyrone yells. "But listen, we don't care! Take him with you and just give us the warden!"

"I can't do that."

"You really messin' up everything T!"

"You guys can still leave while you got a chance. Take the tunnels like we planned—"

"Dead or alive, we *ain't* leaving without the warden!"

"Then you'll have to go through me."

The inmates stare at each other… "I-I didn't sign up for this," one of them sputters. "T-Rock will kill us with his bare hands!"

"Shut up!" the inmate leader yells back. "We've got guns! He's got nothin'! It's twelve of us! He's just one guy!" He turns towards his former cohort. "Really wish it didn't have to be this way, T."

"Yeah," Treyshawn Sr. agrees. "Me too."

Tyrone swings his shotgun into position and fires two rounds. BLAM! BLAM!! They find their marks—center mass—right in Treyshawn Sr.'s chest. He stumbles back, slams against the door and slowly begins to slide down to the floor.

"You just shot T-Rock!" an inmate shouts as others laugh. But just before Treyshawn Sr. hits the floor, he reaches down with his hands and stops his descent. While gritting his teeth, he pushes himself back up into a standing position.

"No way…" they whisper.

The upper part of his jumpsuit is ripped to shreds from the blast—revealing the bullet proof vest beneath it. Before they can react, Treyshawn Sr. charges full speed at them, dodging left and right as bullets fly! One by one, he engages them in fierce combat, landing blow after blow while taking punches and hits to his body.

Behind the dented metal door, Treyshawn and the warden huddle against a make-shift barricade as they listen to the yelling, shouting, gunshots and crashes in the hallway.

"I'm getting into *that* room!" Tyrone yells as he swings an ax at his assailant's head!

"You will *not* get my son or the warden!" Treyshawn Sr. roars as he deflects the blow and kicks two other inmates off of him!

"Come on dad…" Treyshawn whispers as he prays his hardest.

"You can do it…" the warden echoes.

A moment later the commotion dies down… and then… silence.

A light, rasping thump repeats on the door. Knock… Knock…

"Trey…" a labored voice is heard. "It's me."

Treyshawn and the warden jump up, push the barricade out of the way and open the door. Treyshawn Sr. stumbles in, his protective vest riddled with holes and his tattered orange jumpsuit barely hanging on his wounded and bruised body. He collapses to the floor with a mammoth thud.

"Dad!" Treyshawn rushes to his side, drops to his knees and cradles him in his arms. "Dad!"

The warden runs over with a medical kit and proceeds to treat Treyshawn Sr's wounds.

"It's okay Trey…" his father whispers.

"But you're hurt!"

"Didn't I tell you to shut up, boy?" he grins.

"Dad…" Treyshawn cries profusely—his tears wetting his father's bruised face.

"Just lie still," the warden speaks softly. "I'll do what I can."

"What you can do," Treyshawn Sr. says while taking hold of both of their hands, "is take care of my Son." He places their hands together on top of his chest. "You be strong, Trey."

"Dad," Treyshawn shakes his head as mucus runs freely from his nose. "I love you."

Treyshawn Sr. smiles slightly. "I love you too, Son. Thank you… for teaching me how to be a father.

Treyshawn nods his head.

With these words… Treyshawn Sr. closes his eyes as his hands slowly release their grip and slide down his chest to the floor.

"No…" Treyshawn mumbles.

"I'm sorry," the warden whispers as he places his hand on Treyshawn's shoulder.

Minutes pass as the distant noise of fighting fades away—replaced by the sound of arriving police teams sweeping their way through the prison and regaining control over the inmates. Officers finally make their way to the warden's office and see him and Treyshawn sitting on the floor.

"Sir! Are you alright? Are you injured?"

"No," the warden utters, "I'm fine."

"What about the boy?"

"He's fine. We *both* are unharmed. It is good to see all of you."

The officers look down at Treyshawn Sr.'s body, still being held in his son's arms.

"What do you want us to do with this *dead meat*?"

"He's not dead meat!" Treyshawn yells. "He's *my father*!"

"Officer," the warden replies sternly as he stands to his feet. "*This man* you are referring to is the *only* reason we are alive. He sacrificed himself to save us. He may have come to this prison as a criminal, but he gave his last ounce of strength as a *hero*. And his *body* will be treated as such! Do I make myself clear?"

"Y-Yes Sir," the officer stutters. "Sorry Sir." The officer motions for assistance as several others approach to help move Treyshawn Sr.'s body.

"Please… step back."

Treyshawn lowers his father's body and slowly releases him as he stands up and backs away. As the officers surround the body, Treyshawn moves across the room as the warden attempts to console him.

"Are you alright?"

"I-I can't believe he's gone," Treyshawn mutters as he looks off into the distance through his tears. "We were *just* starting to make things work."

"It may have been short-lived, but you and your father *did* get a second chance. Some sons and fathers *never* get that."

"Yeah… I know. I just wish we had more time."

"Wait!" one of the officers yells as he supports Treyshawn Sr.'s arm at the wrist. "This guy's got a pulse!"

"What?" the warden replies, as he spins around.

"Are you sure?" Treyshawn shouts, as he runs over to his father's body.

"Yeah! The pulse is faint… but it's there. He's alive… barely."

[]

Two weeks later… Queens College. Department of Corrections. Clemency Ceremony.

Treyshawn Amar Jinkins Sr. rests in a wheelchair on the stage in front of a large police detail standing at the ready, dressed in their official garb, wearing white gloves. Camera flashes punctuate this important moment as the warden, mayor, governor and a host of other dignitaries stand on a nearby podium. All have spoken as the media—stationed throughout the crowd—records this singular story which has gripped the nation: A Governors' Pardon for an inmate who made the ultimate sacrifice.

The governor holds up a framed declaration, which carries his signature. Just minutes ago, he read its words for all the world to hear. Now, he gives one of the highest honors from his office to this former inmate. Treyshawn Sr. looks at the words which declare his freedom—made possible by a full pardon from his crimes. The governor extends his hand. Treyshawn Sr. does the same.

As the governor steps back, the warden approaches with a bag in his hands. Treyshawn gazes at him with curiosity as he displays a soft grin. He stands before Treyshawn and reaches into the bag. To his amazement, the warden retrieves the journal Treyshawn had given to his father. All take notice as Treyshawn rises to his feet and firmly holds the journal in his hands.

"Thank you for this…" Treyshawn smiles as the crowd looks on, "…for everything."

"This was the least I could do to honor your father and to honor you," the warden replies. "You not only taught your father something, but you have taught *me* as well. And perhaps the world is listening. If the love of a son could cause a father to be rehabilitated, then perhaps anything is possible for those held within our country's prisons. Both you and your father have received what many fathers and sons with broken relationships never get… a *second chance*. Make it count! Be well, Treyshawn."

Two nearby officers fold the American Flag as the mayor descends from the podium to retrieve it. Treyshawn watches with pride as the flag is brought back on stage and given to his father. His mother and grandmother sit close by his side. Curtis, Kelly, and the others sit behind him. The unexpected dream of a father and son has finally come to fruition. *They are free.*

CHAPTER THIRTY-TWO

THE REAL DEAL

TUESDAY SEPTEMBER 2, 2014. GAVIN AND CURTIS walk through the halls at the Montgomery Group's headquarters. Their third year of college has just begun and they are excited by the possibilities before them.

"That is one of the most *amazing* stories I've ever heard in my entire life," Gavin exclaims.

"Yeah," Curtis agrees wholeheartedly. "I remember when I used to tell Treyshawn he should be grateful his dad is still alive. Because that meant there was always a chance for things to change. And now, after all these years, it's finally happened!"

The boys arrive at an elevator which leads to the underground testing ranges. They enter and begin the long descent.

"I told you my dad and I had a similar experience. Being forced to face the truth can really help a relationship. I'm happy for Treyshawn."

"Me too," Curtis utters. "You know, his gallery exhibit is only a couple of months away. His art professor gave him an independent study so he could produce the artwork. He even has time to finish some extra pieces he added to honor his dad."

"Nice," Gavin agrees. "You should publish your dad's journal. If it could help Treyshawn and his dad, think of what it could do for others!"

"Huh. I never thought of that!"

"Underground level three," the voice chimes as the doors open. Curtis and Gavin step out and head to the end of the hallway where two guards are stationed in front of two sizable double doors.

"Hey guys," Curtis greets them, waving.

"I'm sorry," the guard replies, "but access is restricted."

"Oh, no. It's okay," Curtis smiles, "Gavin's with me."

"I'm sorry for not making myself clear," the guard answers, "access is restricted for *everyone*. Even you, Curtis."

"But why? We were just here a couple of weeks ago when we got back from the Powersuit Tour."

"We're just following orders," the other guard interjects. "Apparently, when all of the equipment from the tour came back, there was some damage done to the structural supports inside. Access is restricted until further notice, while repair crews fix the damage."

"I don't *hear* any repairs," Gavin interjects.

The first guard stares at him. "The crew just went to lunch."

"Well can we just take a peek?" Curtis presses.

"What you *can* do is take your requests to Ms. Cosway or Mr. Montgomery," the second guard replies.

"What about all of the equipment and the Powersuits that were in there?" Gavin inquires.

"As far as we know, everything was moved to a storage unit."

"OK." Curtis smiles as he and Gavin back away. "Thanks guys!"

The guards barely smile as Curtis and Gavin walk down the corridor and get back on the elevator.

"What do you think?" Curtis asks as the elevator doors close.

"I think someone's hiding something," Gavin replies.

They arrive at the executive level floor just in time to catch Chasm and Erica leaving the boardroom with briefcases in hand.

"Hello gentlemen," Chasm acknowledges them with a smile as he slows his pace. "What brings you two here today?"

"Just wanted to get away from campus," Curtis replies. "We were going to take a look at the Powersuits down on level three."

"I'm afraid the level three range is restricted while repair crews fix some damaged structural supports," Erica replies.

"That's what the guard said... *verbatim*," Gavin quips.

The group arrives at an elevator which leads to the roof's helipad.

"Chasm, can you give us access just to take a look inside at the repair work?" Curtis inquires. "It'll be cool to see what it looks like in there."

The elevator doors open as Chasm and Erica step inside.

"I'm afraid not," Chasm answers. "Safety first. Sorry we can't stay, but we have meetings in New York."

"See you in a few days." Erica waves at them as the doors close.

The boys look at each other inquisitively.

"You know," Gavin suggests, "we could go back to the dorm and get my Dragonfly robot."

"Dragonfly?" Curtis asks. "I thought you called it the Ant."

"I changed it. You'll see why."

Curtis smiles as he looks at his roommate.

[]

Two hours later... Curtis's work lab at the Montgomery Group.

Curtis and Gavin are huddled at the desk. A grate in the upper corner of his office has been removed—revealing a rather large entry point into the air conditioning ducts. Curtis peers at facility schematics on his computer screen while Gavin manipulates his hand-held remote control unit while wearing an audio/video headset, which receives images and sound from the

Dragonfly's onboard cameras. The headset is also linked to the computer, which allows Curtis to see and hear everything Gavin does.

"I've never seen so many ventilator shafts in my life!" Curtis huffs. "We've been at this for almost an hour."

"Patience," Gavin says while trying to control his robot. "Patience. We're almost there, right?"

Curtis reviews the schematics again. "Yes. Another few minutes or so until we're there."

The Dragonfly rolls along the interior of the ventilator shaft system; turning right and left at various intersections. When the shaft goes vertical, Gavin causes the robotic vehicle to augment its shape to shift its center of gravity. A lever extends from the bottom to lift it as special suction cups, attached to the wheels, engage the vertical surface—making it possible for the vehicle to traverse almost any terrain in any direction. The ventilator shaft widens as it approaches a large junction with a huge gap in the floor.

"Uh, oh," Curtis mumbles as he looks at the schematic. "Watch out. There's a fan blade assembly for one of the environmental control units down there. If the Dragonfly falls in, it'll be ripped to bits!"

"No problem," Gavin grins. "Sit back and watch the robot work its magic."

At the touch of a button, folded rotor blades on top of the vehicle unlock and rotate into position. With the rise of a toggle switch, the blades spin and gently lift the Dragonfly into the air.

"You can't be serious!" Curtis exclaims as Gavin laughs.

"Yep! New upgrade I installed over the summer. See why I call it the Dragonfly? I'm telling you, robots are going to rule the world."

The robotic vehicle flies over the gap, with Gavin making minor adjustments to compensate for the downdraft.

"How do you keep it stable?" Curtis asks. "I don't see a tail rotor."

"Gyroscopes," Gavin smiles. "Better than duct tape."

A few minutes later, the vehicle finally reaches its target: a ventilator grate which overlooks the Level three testing range. Gavin and Curtis pay special attention as the robot rolls up to the grate and aims its cameras at the small open spaces. Gavin zooms in on the range and manually focuses on the movement below. To their unbelief, they discover that the testing range is not under repair after all! The room appears to be full of Powersuits.

"No way," Gavin gasps.

Curtis is speechless as he sees replicas of his Powersuits being assembled and organized below.

"He lied to me," Curtis whispers as he looks intently at the screen. "Chasm lied to me."

"Looks like he's building an army…" Gavin utters.

"Can you boost the sound?"

"This is as good as it gets from this height," Gavin replies. "The noise from all of the machinery is making it difficult."

"Then let's move the robot to another shaft near the ground level."

A few minutes pass as Gavin repositions the Dragonfly at a new ventilation grate. This one happens to be next to several men talking.

"We're a third of the way through the first order," the first man says to the others. "Mr. Montgomery wants everything ready to be shipped by the end of the month."

"These are a lot of Powersuits," the second man replies.

"We received a lot of orders," the first man answers.

"The tour this summer turned out to be a great way to *advertise*," the third man says as the three of them laugh.

"At $200,000.00 a suit, Mr. Montgomery is going to make a killing."

"I'm just glad he's selling these things to our *allies* and not to our enemies."

"Yeah. Let's just hope he gives us bonuses *this* Christmas!"

The three men laugh again.

Curtis' fist slams down on the desk as he listens to the conversation.

"I can't believe he used me!" he yells. "I told him I did not want my suits used like this!" Curtis picks up his phone and begins dialing.

Gavin turns on the remote's homing beacon and engages the robot's autonomous mode. He removes his headset and stares at Curtis.

[]

Chasm and Erica relax on the private jet as it prepares to make its descent into LaGuardia Airport. His phone rings.

"Curtis. Now's not a good time—"

"How could you lie to me?" Curtis yells.

"Calm down," Chasm replies. "What are you talking about?"

"My suits, Chasm! I told you I *didn't* want them weaponized for the military and you went behind my back!"

"Curtis. I don't know what you know—"

"I know everything! Level three isn't under repair! You're building Powersuits! You lied to me and you *used* me!"

Chasm covers his phone and motions to Erica. "Somehow Curtis found out about level three. Call security. I want to know who let him in there."

"So, what do you have to say for yourself?" Curtis presses. "I trusted you!"

"And you can *still* trust me to do what I think is necessary for the benefit of you, my company and the world."

"Do you even hear yourself? You deceive me and say you're doing me and everyone else a favor?"

"Curtis," Chasm moans, "you are too narrow minded and naive about this. What you have created will help save lives all around the world. I could not sit back and not act on this truth. The enemies of America—both international and domestic—are growing and we need to be ready to do something about it before our way of life is placed in disrepair. The United States Military has tanks. Imagine what will happen when we give a single solider the wearable ability *of* a tank. We will have changed the very nature of warfare and greatly tipped the scales in favor of truth, justice and the American way."

"And you will have also "tipped" a boatload of money into your pockets."

"Freedom has a price tag. Nothing you get for 'free' is *actually* free. Someone, somewhere has to pay for it."

"Chasm, these are *my* suits. I designed them."

"You did design them Curtis, but they don't belong to you. You've been working for me for the last year and some months. Your ideas, while employed at my company are the intellectual property *of* the company. Not to mention you used *my* resources to build the suits."

"I'm calling the cops."

"You are free to do that, but I guarantee it will get you absolutely nowhere. Everything I've done is perfectly legal and will hold up in *any* court of law. However, if you *do* call the authorities and make this situation a nuisance, then I will be forced to make things… complicated."

"What does that mean?"

"I hope you never have to find out. But, for starters, your scholarship would be nullified and you would have to pay back *every* cent which was already granted to you. So far, that's over $60,000.00."

Curtis stands quietly listening as Chasm's plane touches down.

"I know you are upset," Chasm soothes, "that's why I didn't plan to tell you about this until a more opportune time. But let's talk when I return in a few days. This will give you some time to cool down so we can have a *rational* discussion. Try to have a good evening."

Chasm hangs up his phone and notices that Erica is staring at him. "What?"

"I didn't say anything."

"Everything I'm doing is *mostly* legal."

"You better hope Curtis doesn't figure that out."

"This may become a problem. For right now, place Curtis under observation and if he tries to do anything unusual, restrict his facility access."

"You don't want to just restrict his access *now*?"

"No. That will send the wrong message," Chasm replies. "*I* would be upset right now if I were him. He is not the enemy. Hopefully, this unexpected turn of events can still work in our favor. One way or another, he will come to see things my way."

[]

Back in Curtis' work lab…

"What are you going to do?" Gavin stutters as Curtis repeatedly paces across the room and back.

"I don't know."

"Well, we can't let him get away with this," Gavin adds.

"I know!" Curtis huffs. "We just… need a plan of attack."

Just then, the Dragonfly appears at the open ventilator shaft. As Gavin retrieves it, a plan begins to form in Curtis' mind.

"Hey Gavin?"

"Yeah?"

"How customizable is your robot?"

[]

Later that night…

Curtis, Gavin, Kelly, Miranda, Omar and Jim video conference to discuss the situation. The rest of the group is just as upset as Curtis.

"Unbelievable..." Jim declares.

"I'm just as mad as everyone else," Omar admits, "but what's the plan? Those Powersuits will be shipped out at the end of the month."

"Omar's right," Jim concurs. "We have to do something. What are your thoughts Curtis?"

"We take back our suits, destroy the replicas he's built, and erase the plans from his hard drives."

"Oh, yeah, *that* sounds easy!" Miranda quips.

"Yeah," Kelly adds, "and he probably has the plans all over the place!"

"Not really," Curtis replies. "Chasm is not a big fan of 'the cloud.' He stores most of his work on a dedicated server. Everything else is on the company servers which are located on the premises."

"So if we can hack his servers," Gavin suggests, "then we can delete the information from all of his computers."

"That's right," Curtis confirms. "We may not be able to stop him completely, but we can definitely slow him down."

"Wait," Miranda cautions. "Let's stop for a minute. Curtis, what you are proposing is illegal. We'd be breaking the law. I think we should just go to the police."

"Mom," Curtis replies, "When Chasm rescued me from the kidnappers he had police and federal agents with him."

"And," Gavin insists, "when Curtis told him he was going to call the cops, Chasm told him to go ahead!"

"So," Jim surmises, "you're saying we don't know *who* he's got in his back pocket?"

"Exactly," Curtis responds. "He's involved with local police in Atlanta and New York. And he works with the military. I don't know who we can trust besides us."

"Okay," Miranda concedes. "You're right. But this still sounds dangerous. You know Chasm Montgomery is not going down without a fight."

"We'll need some kind of leverage," Omar adds.

"If he *does* come after us," Curtis muses, "then he'll be coming for the suits. We may have to fight him off."

"I think I can offer some assistance in that area," Jim replies. "If Chasm does send his forces after us, we'll need someplace *we* can control in order to have the upper hand. A friend of mine owns a few warehouses near LaGuardia and JFK airports. They're pretty secure. We could store the Powersuits there, and if Chasm decides to attack, he'd be fighting on *our* turf."

"All of this sounds crazy," Kelly admits. "What about the suits? How do we get them from Atlanta to New York?"

Gavin smiles. "I think I know a guy who can help us with that."

[]

The next day… 9:00am.

Gavin and Curtis have been up the entire night talking through logistics. Both are mentally and emotionally exhausted, but it's time for class. As they rush to get ready, Curtis makes a quick phone call.

"Hello?" a voice answers.

"Hi, Eric? This is Curtis Powers."

"Curtis! How are you?"

"I'm good! Sorry to call you so early…"

"Not a problem. I was just about to walk out the door. What's up? Been a long time since we were being chased on a motorcycle and held hostage at gunpoint."

"Yeah," Curtis laughs. "About that. Remember when you said if I ever needed your help I should let you know? Well, I need your help."

[]

The Powers residence. 11:00am.

The phone rings as Miranda prepares to head to the diner for her 12 o'clock shift.

"Hello?"

"Good morning Miranda. This is Emmanuel."

"Hello Emmanuel! How are you doing?"

"I am well. Thank you. I am sorry to call you out of the blue, but I was informed by our mutual acquaintance that you and your sons are about to embark on an adventure."

"Uh, yes we are…"

"Well, based on what was told to me about the nature and scope of the adventure, I believe you may require assistance during the festivities here in New York."

"We can *always* use good help. What do you have in mind?"

"My son, Matthew. Hey may be a bit lanky, but he is a very good athlete, with impeccable hand-eye coordination. He is also very strong for his size. I am sure he could be helpful to you."

[]

11:00am (California time).

Treyshawn walks across his school's sprawling campus towards his art class while engaged in deep conversation with Curtis.

"Dude, you have always been there for me! I'll just tell my advisor I have a family emergency. After all, you *are* family. Count me in."

"But with everything that happened with your father," Curtis replies.

"My father demonstrated what real sacrifice means. So, if we can figure out how to get me to New York, I *want* to be there."

[]

Atlanta. 3:00pm. Spelman College.

Curtis arrives on campus where Kelly is waiting for him.

"Hey," Curtis says as he hugs her. "Is everything alright?"

They both begin walking to the quad.

"I just wanted to see you," Kelly smiles. "Thanks for coming."

"My next class doesn't start until 5pm. You sounded a bit anxious on the phone."

"I wanted to tell you in person," Kelly grins. "I spoke to my brothers. They'll be free at the end of the month and are willing to come help."

"That is awesome!" Curtis exclaims. "Let's bring them up to speed. Treyshawn's coming too. Just spoke to my mom and somehow she's going to cover his plane ticket. Our team is slowly coming together."

[]

Atlanta. 8:00pm. Curtis and Gavin's dorm room.

"My dad said he'd do it," Gavin says, rushing into the room.

"Great!" Curtis replies while drawing some new schematics.

"Please tell me that's not another suit," Gavin laughs as he looks at the design.

"It's an idea I got when I saw Turbulence deploy the Mach-2's airbags," Curtis grins. "This suit will definitely help to even the playing field a bit. I have to send it to Omar and Mr. G tomorrow. Hopefully they can get it built in time."

CHAPTER THIRTY-THREE

LET'S ROLL!

FRIDAY SEPTEMBER 5, 2014. CURTIS AND Erica ride the main building's elevator to Chasm's penthouse. Curtis says nothing as Erica tries to make small talk. As the elevator doors open, Erica leads Curtis down the hall to Chasm's private office. A moment later, they enter and sit as Chasm finishes up an email at his desk. Once done, he turns and faces them.

"Curtis," Chasm smiles, "thank you for coming to meet with me. Honestly, given the situation I was not sure if you would agree to it."

"I am still mad about what you did," Curtis replies, "but I don't have $60,000.00 lying around… so here I am."

"I appreciate your level-headed response."

"It's not like I have many options."

"Let me tell you why you are here. Whether you believe it or not, I am *fully* committed to your success, Curtis. And I believe we can still work together to impact the world."

Curtis stares out the window as he contemplates his mentor's words.

"Sometimes," Chasm continues, "we have to be pushed beyond our comfort zones in order to truly shine."

"And that's what you're doing?" Curtis inquires. "All of this… you're *pushing* me?"

"Yes. In the end, you will see that I am right."

Curtis inhales deeply as he looks away again. Erica notices his knee beginning to shake. "Who's buying the Powersuits?" Curtis looks back at Chasm intently.

“Personnel in military and law enforcement; friends and allies of this country. People who want to maintain freedom and justice.”

“So, no under-the-table sales to our enemies?”

“Absolutely not.”

Curtis studies Chasm’s eyes for any signs of hesitation.

“I have your word?”

“Yes. You have my word.”

Curtis stares out the window again. “OK… let’s see what happens.”

“Excellent,” Chasm says, clapping triumphantly.

“But I want to see the suits on Level three. Right now.”

[]

Underground Testing Range: Level Three.

Chasm proudly leads the way as he, Curtis and Erica pass the security checkpoint and enter through the doors of Level Three. They immediately find themselves in a White Room, where workers help them don protective lab coats, gloves and head gear. They exit at the rear of the room and walk through a clear hallway, which gives them a birds-eye view of the entire range. Even though he’s still unhappy, Curtis is amazed at the massiveness and complexity of the operation as men and women below work with machines and robots in several sections.

The process begins on the left side of the range, near where the original suits stand prominently for all to see. One group assembles each component and places them in their designated holding crates. Robotic vehicles move each crate from the assembly stage to the build line. There, conveyor belts slowly move each Powersuit down the line as a group of workers attach each component to the Powersuits.

At the end of the build line, the suits are hung up on a rack, which is transported, again by robots, to the testing stage. Here, technicians handle each suit, testing its capabilities and making sure every component works. From there, the suits are hung on another rack where robots move them to the storage line, where they will hang in preparation for packaging and shipping. Each suit is specially packed in its own case, which is then stacked against the wall under designations for function and end user.

Chasm, Curtis and Erica descend the steps leading from the hallway to the ground floor and take a close look at the process. Chasm smiles as he watches his mentee's excitement momentarily overtake him.

"These parts are *way better* quality than what we were using" Curtis exclaims.

"Yes," Chasm chuckles. "I told you your ideas *with* my resources would yield impressive results. These are the next iteration of what you've already created."

As they inspect the actual suits, Curtis makes additional observations.

"I see you've added additional padding, insulation and exterior paneling to most of the suits."

"Comfortability and protection are important for soldiers on the field of combat," Chasm smiles. "We've recently developed new padding that better absorbs impact forces. It should make the suits more comfortable to wear. The increased insulation will help shield the operator from the higher electrical output of the suits' new batteries. And the new external paneling is made of a proprietary ballistic alloy which makes Kevlar look like tissue paper."

"Wow..." Curtis admits. "But I'm still mad at you."

Both Chasm and Erica laugh heartily at the remark. Curtis does too.

"When are these being shipped?"

"First shipment leaves at the end of the month," Erica answers. "Just about three weeks from now."

"So, what do you think of all this?" Chasm asks while extending his hands.

"I'm not going to lie," Curtis replies with a smile. "This is really impressive!"

"Well, none of this would have been possible without you."

"Thank you for showing me all of this," Curtis says while shaking Chasm's hand. "This has been really helpful in giving me a better understanding of things."

[]

Later that night...

Gavin excitedly downloads the high definition video footage from the special camera-glasses Curtis wore while with Chasm and Erica. As they watch it, they firm up their plan of attack and send updates to the rest of the group.

[]

Two weeks later...

Omar rents a car, drives down to Atlanta and checks into a local hotel. The first night he's there, Curtis and Gavin drop by for a visit.

"So, I made some calls and got us some help," Omar says as the toilet flushes in the bathroom. A minute later, the door opens and a guy walks out while wiping his hands with a towel. He's a white male, mid twenties, with short brown hair, about 5 foot nine inches tall, medium build, wearing blue jeans, a gray shirt and a black leather motorcycle jacket.

"Who's he?" Gavin asks.

"This is ET and he comes highly recommended," Omar replies.

"Have you phoned home yet?" Gavin laughs.

"That's *all* you got?" ET chuckles with a slight country drawl. "Been dealing with the whole 'ET phone home' thing for years. Try again."

"Sorry," Gavin surrenders. "I couldn't resist."

"ET is one of the *best* analysts I know," Omar says.

"Analyst?" Curtis repeats. "What's that?"

"Currently, companies and organizations pay me to find holes in their computer systems."

"So, you're a hacker," Gavin says.

"To put it crassly, yes," ET responds. "I prefer Digital Analog Transmission Analyst. Omar said you guys needed help. I'm your guy."

"But how do we get him into Chasm's headquarters?" Curtis asks.

"You don't," ET responds while grabbing a black box from one of his bags. "This is about the size of an external hard drive. You take it in with you and plug it to any computer connected to their network. Every computer system has back doors. You just need to know where and how to look. Once you connect this and power it up, I'll be able to use my computer *here* to go anywhere in their network: servers, master files, hidden drives, security systems, the Cloud, you name it. If it's connected, I can get to it. When we're done, just bring it back. And if you can't retrieve it, it's programmed to self-destruct."

"Wow!" Gavin laughs. "Where'd you get the black box from?"

"You can't buy this from anywhere," ET smiles. "I made it."

[]

Monday, September 29, 2014. 10:29pm. The Montgomery Group headquarters.

Security guards watch a wall of camera monitors as they banter back and forth about the latest sports game. At 10:30pm all of the screens flicker for less than a second—barely visible to those actually paying attention. At 10:57pm an elevator begins to descend to Level Three. Then at 11:00pm it arrives at the underground testing range.

"Underground Level Three," a voice chimes as the doors open.

The two guards at the end of the corridor watch as the Dragonfly vehicle drives out of the elevator and heads towards them. Caution turns to curiosity as they see their company's logo—TMG—highly visible on the robot.

"Huh," the first guard says as he kneels down to look at it. "Robotics must be working on a new prototype."

"Yeah," the second guard agrees as he looks over at is as well.

Suddenly, the robot ejects a plume of gas, causing the guards to cough profusely before passing out and collapsing onto the floor. Curtis and Gavin stick their heads out of the elevator to make sure the guards are down.

"OK," ET's voice relays through their earpieces, "I've looped all of the video feeds for Level Three's security cameras. The guards in the control room will see empty hallways. You've got twenty-eight minutes."

Curtis and Gavin run down the hall to the security doors. Gavin lifts his visor and swings the remote control to his side, while picking up the Dragonfly and magnetically attaching it to a metal plate he's wearing on his back. ET unlocks the doors to give the guys entrance to the range.

"Everyone left for the night," ET updates, "so this is all you!"

Curtis and Gavin run through the White Room, down the hallway and descend the stairs to the main floor.

"Phase two!" Curtis yells as he starts removing his original Powersuits from their containment cases. Gavin grabs Dragonfly from his back and disengages the magnetic seal. He drops it to the floor and retrieves two canisters from a bag that's hanging over his shoulder.

"Hey Curtis! You want to take some of these new composite alloy paneling Chasm was talking about? They would give our suits added protection."

"No. We're only here for what's ours."

"Okay. Don't really have time to grab extra stuff anyway." Gavin quickly kneels down and connects the canisters to his robot and pulls the visor down over his eyes. As he stands, he grabs the remote and begins flipping switches. A second later, the Dragonfly zooms down rows of hanging Powersuits while spraying flammable liquid on them. Curtis puts each of *his* suits in one of the nearby crates and wheels them over to a large entry doorway.

"Come on guys!" ET shouts, "You've got fifteen minutes!"

Once the Powersuits are thoroughly drenched, Gavin douses the Assembly Station, Building Line, Testing Stage and the storage wall where a large number of crates are waiting to be shipped.

"Eight minutes!" ET yells.

"OK, we're ready!" Curtis shouts.

The large entry bay door begins to rise as Curtis and Gavin eagerly stand by. A moment later, it's completely open, revealing Omar standing with a black van. He swings open the back doors and helps Curtis and Gavin put the Powersuits inside.

"OK!" Omar yells. "We're done!"

"Great!" ET responds. "Gavin! Light it up!"

Gavin presses a red button on the remote. Dragonfly shoots out a stream of flame, which sets the flammable liquid on fire! He drives the Dragonfly back to him as the replica suits and all of the equipment begin to burn. Omar starts the van and throws the gear into 'drive.' Gavin grabs his robot, pulls it inside and closes the door. ET drops the entry door as the van drives away, keeping the fire contained inside the range.

"I've accessed and disabled the fire suppression system to allow for the maximum burn time. Then I'll re-enable the system to stop the fire before it can burn the whole place down."

"What about the guard gate?" Omar asks as he rapidly approaches the perimeter checkpoint.

"I got it." ET smiles. "Just keep driving."

"But the gate—"

"Don't stop! I got it!"

A guard, seeing the approaching headlights, steps out of the guard shack and quickly dives back in, as the van speeds past it —the gate already up. Omar, Curtis and Gavin give a victory shout at the top of their lungs as they speed off down the street!

"ET," Curtis shouts, "can you extend the video loop for a few extra minutes?"

"I can do that, but the guards are going to be waking up about now."

"And what about the files," Curtis replies.

"Already taken care of," ET chuckles. "That will be the *last hurrah* as I log out of the system."

The two guards stir as they regain consciousness and sit up.

"What happened?"

"I don't know… How did we end up on the floor?"

"...The robot."

The guards stumble to their feet and look around. The double doors are secure. Nothing seems out of place.

"You good?"

"Yeah. You?"

"Should we call this in?"

At 11:38pm the computer and black box in Curtis' work lab short out in a flash of flame and smoke. The security video screens flicker as the loop ceases and all of the computers immediately shut down—causing every screen to go dark. The guards in the control room jump to their feet in a panic as they try and reboot the system. As the system comes back online and the video feeds reinitialize, the guards go into pandemonium as they see a raging inferno in the Underground Level Three Testing Area. The alarms sound and emergency lights flash as the fire suppression system engages.

[]

Thirty minutes later, Chasm and Erica arrive at Level Three and wade through security and fire personnel. A look of disgust is clearly evident on Chasm's face as all others nervously stand at attention as Chasm speaks to Erica.

"We need to find out why every computer in this company shut down at the same time."

"I-I'm s-sorry Sir," one of his chief engineers stutters. "I'm afraid it's all ruined."

"Ruined?" Chasm yells.

"Y-yes," the engineer cowers. "I-I'm afraid all of the Powersuits... have been destroyed."

"Are you sure they were *all* destroyed?" Chasm growls.

"Y-yes. All of the replicas."

"Replicas?" Erica repeats. "What about the *original* suits?"

"Their cases are empty," the engineer answers. "We just assumed..."

At that moment, the security chief gets a call on his radio.

"Sir. I was just informed that a dark van sped off of the premises just over thirty minutes ago."

"Erica," Chasm shouts, "check all of the hard drives for the Powersuit schematics!"

Erica searches her digital tablet and immediately becomes alarmed. "They're gone! Every copy... They're *all* gone!"

Chasm lets out a blood curdling, anger-filled cry as he clenches his fists in the air.

"Curtis!!!"

[]

A private jet takes off from Atlanta International airport, heading for New York. Gavin sits in the cockpit with his father at the controls. Curtis, Omar and ET sit in the passenger area. The Powersuits are safely stored below in the baggage compartment.

"I can't believe we pulled it off," Curtis mumbles to his brother.

"We pulled *this* part off," Omar replies. "Now comes the really *hard* part. Chasm is probably looking for us right now."

[]

The Montgomery Group Headquarters. Security Control Room.

The control room is buzzing with movement as all security personnel are on high alert. Chasm and Erica stand in front of a wall of screens as the radio channels are full of chatter. Chasm presses a communication button on the console.

"Report!"

"Sir, this is Security Team One."

"Have you found them?"

"We tracked the signal and found your business card in his dorm room. But he's not here. Doesn't look like he's been here for a while."

"Keep looking. Search the entire campus—every lab, every classroom, every closet. Everywhere."

"Understood Sir."

"Unbelievable," Chasm growls as he rubs his tired eyes. "Almost a hundred million dollars in product—gone... Where are you hiding?"

"What if he's not in Atlanta?" Erica suggests.

Chasm turns towards his Director of Operations.

"What if he's headed somewhere else? Maybe... back to New York."

"He's not taking eight to ten Powersuits on a commercial flight," Chasm replies. "And that's a 16 hour drive…"

"Seems highly improbable that they would be driving all that distance," Erica answers. "What about a private jet?"

"Get the flight logs for all of the area airports and see if any private planes have left for New York within the past four hours."

Twenty minutes later, Erica comes back with a list.

"Okay. Ten private planes left for New York within the past four hours. Based on the number of Powersuits Curtis would be carrying, I've ruled out four of the planes. But six are large enough."

Chasm extends his hand as Erica gives him her digital tablet. He studies it meticulously.

"These four aren't it," Chasm quickly determines. "What about this one? It's owned by a Gavin Pierce Sr. What's the chance that *this* Gavin is related to Curtis' roommate?"

"But Gavin's last name is Ortiz."

"Get into the registrar's system at the school and pull up his personal information. See if they have his father's name on file."

A few minutes later, Erica has the information displayed on the screen, confirming Chasm's hunch.

"That's him!"

"They've been in the air for an hour," Erica notes. "That's quite a head start."

"Just find out where his plane is landing!"

"I could call the authorities in New York and have them detain the plane…"

"No. That will raise too many questions. Call one of our contacts and have them follow Curtis after he lands." Chasm turns to his Security Chief. "I want you to pull a detail of our best men and women. Put them on two cargo planes with whatever equipment and weapons you need. Arrive just before dark. Our contact will give you Curtis' location and your team will then take back those suits! Erica and I will stay here and monitor the progress."

"Understood Sir," the chief says as he heads out the door.

"What about Curtis and whoever he's working with?" Erica asks.

"Bring him back as well. As for everyone else, I am fine with injuries. But there are to be no deaths. Only non-lethal force is authorized."

CHAPTER THIRTY-FOUR

WORLDS COLLIDE

TUESDAY NIGHT, SEPTEMBER 30, 2014. 8:00PM. Under the cover of darkness, a host of unmarked trucks and vans arrive at an abandoned strip near several waterfront warehouses. The rear doors open as security operatives quickly and silently disembark with their weapons drawn. They surround one of the warehouses and prepare to enter. Curtis and several others are inside, however the windows are blocked, so it's impossible to determine what is happening within the structure.

"I've got movement outside," ET whispers from his makeshift control room at the top level of the building. "They're here." Curtis and the others receive his transmission loud and clear.

"What can you tell me?" the Security Chief asks his 2nd-in-command.

"All the windows are masked and the doors are locked."

"Scan the building."

"Whoa," ET grunts, "my systems are going all crazy! We're being scanned!"

"We knew they'd probably do that," Omar relays back. "That's why we shielded those sections."

"Sir," the security officer says, "the entire building has been wired with surveillance, including thermal and night vision. No doubt, they know we are here."

"And what do *we* know?"

"There's one person standing on the ground floor, in the middle of the warehouse—most likely Curtis Powers. It's like he's waiting for us."

"I'm sure."

"We can see the stairs and other structures, but can't make out anything else. There seems to be some shielding in a number of areas."

"To keep us guessing," the Security Chief replies. "No doubt, there's *more* than one person inside. Doesn't matter. This will be like taking candy from a baby. Okay! All teams, we will stagger our approach to force our targets to reveal their plan! Let's bag and tag! Teams one and two storm the gates! Teams three and four wait for my signal! Team five be ready with the big guns!"

The front and rear doors to the warehouse explode off of their hinges as teams one and two enter with their weapons drawn and surround Curtis.

"Hey guys," Curtis waves with a smile. "What took you so long?"

"You're surrounded! Are you going to surrender the Powersuits?"

"No. Will you *all* surrender before somebody gets hurt?"

One of the ten operatives fires their net gun, but Curtis dives out of the way and engages his Speedsuit for some added distance. All ten operatives open fire with a hail of rubber bullets and stun shells as Curtis runs rings around them. One of them hurls a Smother Bomb, which explodes in his path, covering him in sticky goo which almost instantly immobilizes him. Curtis tumbles to the ground as the operatives approach.

"Chief," one of them radios, "target is down."

"Uh, guys," Curtis relays, "I could use a little help."

"Turn off your ears!" Gavin relays back as he fires sonic pulses in their direction.

The operatives yell as they stagger to the ground—grabbing their ears—their weapons sprawled around them.

"Chief! Teams one and two are down!"

"Unbelievable! Team three... engage! Team one and two—gas!"

Multiple small canisters roll into the warehouse, spewing thick smoke. Team three rushes in, wearing gas masks. A coughing Curtis struggles to his feet and stumbles into the shadows as a sudden gust of wind blows through the warehouse, dissipating the gas. Treyshawn approaches with his arms outstretched—wearing the Compressor-X.

"I forgot how much I *love* this suit!"

The operatives turn in his direction as one of them throws a Smother Bomb, but Treyshawn activates his air gauntlets—diverting the bomb away from him.

"You'll have to do better than that!"

While they're distracted, Gavin and Eric—both wearing their own Powersuit—drop from ropes into the center of the fifteen operatives. Moving like lightning, they disarm each one with punches, kicks, joint locks and body throws while discharging lightning blasts and ultrasonic bursts. One-by-one the assailants fall as Gavin and Eric work in tandem, playing off each other's strengths and covering each other's weaknesses.

"OK Treyshawn!" ET relays, "pull back and help Curtis!"

Curtis and Treyshawn make their way to a shielded side room where his mother awaits them.

"Mom! We need your help cleaning this gunk off!"

Outside, the Security Chief's second in command runs over to his position.

"Chief! Teams one, two and three are down!"

"Come on!" the Chief yells. "Team four! Get in there!"

A team of ten operatives rush in and find their fallen teammates alone, in the middle of the warehouse floor, groaning and struggling to get to their feet.

"Who are *these guys?*" one of them utters while trying to gain his bearings.

"We're getting our butts handed to us!" another mumbles.

"This is working out better than I thought," ET says.

"Kelly," Jim inquires, "how do things look from where you are?"

Kelly, wearing the wall-crawling suit, is perched three stories above the intruders. "The bulk of the guards are right in the bullseye. I say drop it now."

"Consider it done," Jim replies while pressing a button. A massive, weighted net falls from the ceiling, completely trapping the twenty-five operatives under its thick and heavy webbing.

Outside, Chasm video conferences his Chief of Security. "It appears you *do not* have everything under control."

"I-I'm sorry Sir. They've proven to be a bit harder to trap than we anticipated."

"You and I will discuss strategy if and when you return. Send in team five. If they want to hide in the shadows, then we need to open things up a bit."

"Yes Sir. Understood." The Chief wipes the sweat from his brow and orders team five to engage. The rear of two sizable trucks Open. Five juggernauts drop from the carriage with a noticeable thud on the ground which can be felt from several feet away. The W.A.R. suits' mechanized feet retract, as gyroscopically controlled wheels extend in their place. They begin to quickly roll towards the warehouse.

"Team Five, you are to free the others and stop everyone wearing a Powersuit. Let's show these hotshots what the *real* war suits can do!"

"Guys…" ET moans. "You don't want to know what's about to walk in the front door!"

"You've got five rolling battle suits heading your way!" Jim yells into the microphone.

"No problem," Gavin relays back. "Eric and I will bring the sight and sound. If that doesn't work, send in the Flame and our *own* heavy metal."

"You're having *too much* fun with this," Eric replies as they both take their positions on the ground level.

"I have to," Gavin admits, "otherwise I'd be shaking in my boots!"

The five juggernauts roll into the warehouse and come to a halt forty feet from their targets. Their suits' wheels retract as the mechanized feet extend into place. The leader blasts his demands over his suit's loudspeakers—which are modulated for intense psychological warfare.

"Stand down now," a deep guttural voice blares through the structure, "or face the consequences."

"Let's see what you got!" Gavin yells as he runs closer and lets loose with an intense sonic barrage!

The W.A.R. suits shake, but do not fall as the team leader approaches him.

"Have it your way," the deep voice blares with each crushing step.

Eric runs next to Gavin and fires several lighting blasts at the W.A.R. suit. Again, the juggernaut slows momentarily, but then increases speed.

"Uh, guys, we need some help here!" Eric yells as the juggernaut knocks them to the ground.

The other four metal men quickly tear through the net, allowing those who are injured to retreat while the others rejoin the fight.

An arc of flame creates a barrier, allowing Gavin and Eric to regroup. Kevin steps into the fray—his suit's flamethrower blazing as he blasts flames at the lead juggernaut.

A deep sinister laugh blares from the W.A.R. suit as it is engulfed in the flames.

"Are you serious?" the leader asks. "You don't think this suit is able to *withstand* fire?"

Kevin extinguishes his pyrotechnic display.

"He's right," Curtis relays, "don't waste your flames on those W.A.R. suits. Use them to intimidate the others into submission."

"You can't hit what you can't see!" Kelvin yells as he jumps into the fray and activates his Powersuit. "Supernova blast!" The intense light from his suit temporarily blinds almost everyone, except the war suit operators.

"Thanks for the warning," the W.A.R. suit operator laughs. "Our visors automatically tint to compensate for differences in light intensity."

"Way to go Kelvin!" ET groans. "You just knocked the team out of commission!"

"Sorry!" Kelvin replies.

"Matt! Omar!" Curtis relays, "You guys got to get in there! We've almost got my suit cleaned off."

"This is your last chance to surrender," the team leader yells as he raises his arms and prepares to strike.

"But you haven't met me yet," Matthew shouts as he jumps in front of the juggernaut, wearing the Strength Augmentation Exo-suit.

The juggernaut brings his arms down swiftly as Matthew catches them in his armored hands. Hydraulic mechanisms strain against the electromagnetic repulsion of the Strength Augmentation Exo-suit.

"How are you so *strong*?" the leader yells as he presses in even harder, shifting his grip and spinning Matthew off to the side. Matthew skids on the ground as he regains his stance and comes in for another round. The juggernaut swings and misses as Matthew dodges it, while throwing several punches of his own with his armored gloves. Visible dents rivet the W.A.R. suit as it stumbles back under the onslaught. The team leader tries to go on the offensive.

As the two continue their battle, remaining operatives prepare to fight Gavin, Eric, Kevin and Kelvin when Omar causally walks up wearing his own Powersuit.

"Hang back a minute guys," he smiles. "I want to see what this suit can do."

As the operatives surround Omar, he activates his suit. A micro-turbine, built into the housing of the reinforced spinal column, revs to life during a five second charging cycle and then stops. Compressed gas courses through the suit, as multiple translucent bubbles expand from disc-shaped pores—encasIng him in a flexible tactile 'force field'.

"My brother calls this a Kinetic Expansion Suit."

The operatives fire their rubber bullets and stun shells, but it all bounces off Omar's suit. Angry, several of them grab their night sticks and attack, while others throw punches and kicks. Omar laughs as each blow is diffused by the bubble field.

"It's like they're hitting me with pillows!" Now he goes on the offensive as the force of his blows are magnified by the extended surface area the suit provides. He easily clears a path, but his glee is short-lived as the remaining four juggernauts use their offensive weaponry to start demolishing the building.

"This is *not* good!" ET yells as he feels the building shudder. "Kelly! Get off those walls!"

Before Kelly can come down, a blast rocks the wall that she's suctioned to. The entire section falls to the ground—with her barely having time to jump off. Omar moves to intercept, trying to catch her, but they both fall to the ground. She bounces off him and lands a few feet away with a thud. She's alive… but injured. One of the operatives picks her up and pulls her helmet off.

"It's the girl!" He takes Kelly at knife point and ushers her out of the warehouse as one of the juggernauts steps up and throws down a volley of suppressive fire.

"Sir, we have the girl." The Chief relays to Chasm.

"You have Kelly? Excellent! This will clear things up. Pull your people back, put her on the plane and bring her to me."

"But Sir, the Powersuits—"

"This battle is getting us nowhere. It seems we have underestimated Curtis Powers yet again. But if we have the girl, *he* will come and he will readily give me what I want. Do it now, while we still can!"

"Yes Sir!"

Several minutes later…

"Has anybody seen Kelly?" Curtis shouts.

"One of the guards took her outside!" Omar yells as dodges a juggernaut's blow which punches a huge hole in the wall. "I tried to get to her… but this W.A.R. suit guy's been holding me back!" No sooner do the words leave his lips than the juggernaut slams him into a wall—knocking the wind out of him. "Ouch!…" he gasps as he falls to his knees. "I… *felt* that!"

"If you weren't wearing that suit," ET adds, "you'd *feel* dead!"

"Curtis," Eric relays, "it looks like they're all retreating!"

"That's cause they know they can't beat us!" Gavin interjects.

"And they have Kelly!" Curtis answers. "They'll use her to get to me!"

"Is the Mach-1 operational?" Jim inquires.

"Yes!"

"Then go after her!" Jim insists. "If they put her on that plane it's game over. We'll be right behind you!"

Two SUV's speed off from the warehouse while the other operatives try to keep their challengers at bay. Curtis manages to slip through the fight and takes off after them. The two trucks drive towards LaGuardia airport, tearing down the highway at over ninety miles per hour. Curtis can barely keep up—pushing his Mach-1 Speedsuit to its structural limit.

He arrives at the airstrip—out of breath, but just in time to see Chasm's security forces climb onboard one of their cargo jets—with Kelly in tow—unsuccessfully trying to fight off her captors.

"I don't know if you guys can hear me. They just put Kelly on the plane and I can't stop them! But I'm going to try and hide in the landing gear! Get to Atlanta as soon as you can!"

The plane's engines rev up as it begins to taxi into position for takeoff. Curtis looks at the digital display on his arm gauntlet. Power levels are almost depleted. He grits his teeth and takes off down the runway as the plane begins to accelerate.

"I only have one chance!"

With mere seconds to spare, Curtis catches up to the plane and grabs onto the landing gear with all of his might, just before the plane's acceleration exceeds the maximum velocity of his Mach-1 Speedsuit. Moments later, the plane is airborne, headed back to Atlanta. The landing gear retracts into the belly of the aircraft, finally allowing an exhausted Curtis to fall off the support strut onto the floor of the compartment. It's pitch black, loud and increasingly cold as the plane ascends into the clouds.

The Mach-1's power cells are now depleted. Curtis has 1.5 hours to figure out his next move or else he and Kelly could be gone for good.

CHAPTER THIRTY-FIVE

CHECKMATE

THE CARGO PLANE SPEEDS THROUGH THE night sky. Estimated time of arrival to Atlanta: 1:00am—one hour, thirty minutes from now. Red lights illuminate the interior. Most of the security operatives are strapped into their seats. Kelly is strapped down and handcuffed to her chair. The sound of the aircraft's engines permeate the cargo hold.

"You'll never get away with this!" she shrieks.

"Can we *please* stop with the broken record?" the Security Chief yells. "You've said that already… *repeatedly*."

"And it's *still* true!"

"And who's going to stop us?" he walks over to her—his gun in his holster. "You're in a plane at 30,000 feet. All of your people are back in Queens! When we land, you're going straight to Chasm Montgomery. We've *already* won!"

Kelly relaxes in her chair, biting her lip.

"Nothing smart to say to that, huh? Let's keep it that way." The Security Chief walks back to his station as Chasm calls.

"Report."

"We are about 1.5 hours out. Everything's calm."

"Good. When you arrive, bring the girl to the top of 191 downtown."

"You don't want us to take her back to headquarters?

"No. The plans have changed."

"Understood."

Underneath the plane, Curtis sits in quiet frustration: unsure of himself and what he should do. He finally stands to his feet and checks his power cells. The inactivity has caused them to build up a slight reserve, just enough to operate the lights on his suit. Fortunately they are LEDs and use very little energy. The lights illuminate his surroundings as he cautiously makes his way through the underbelly of the plane. He comes to the storage compartment, climbs in and looks around. To his amazement, he sees a familiar containment crate strapped to the wall. As he draws near to it and looks closer, he can't believe his eyes.

"Thank you, God!"

[]

An hour and twenty minutes later, the plane lands on a private runway at Hartsfield-Jackson Atlanta International Airport. It taxis to four black SUVs waiting nearby. The rear door of the aircraft opens as the plane's engines power down. Curtis quietly lowers himself from the landing gear to the runway, wearing the Mach-2. He watches as Chasm's security personnel disembark—one of them hauling their prisoner by the arm. All of the operatives jump into the four vehicles—Kelly being thrown into the last one. The four vehicles speed off towards the exits.

"Here we go..." Curtis utters, as he powers up the Mach-2 and takes off after them.

"This takes some getting used to," he says to himself as he tries to adjust to all of the information projected on the visor's heads up display.

Ten minutes later, the trucks speed down the highway as one of the operatives sitting in the passenger seat of the last vehicle checks his side mirror.

"What the..." he says as he squints his eyes at the sight. "We've got a problem."

"You've got to be kidding me," the driver shouts as he looks in his rearview mirror.

The operative radios Chasm.

"What is it?"

"Sir, we've got a problem. It's that Curtis kid. He's behind us!"

"What?" Chasm yells into the radio.

Kelly turns in her seat and looks out the back window, smiling as she sees Curtis fast approaching.

"And it looks like he's wearing the Mach-2!"

"He took it from the plane," Chasm groans. "Lose him. Now!"

"Understood." The operative puts the radio down while looking at the driver. "Punch it!"

The four SUVs suddenly speed up to almost one hundred miles per hour—pulling away from Curtis—swerving in and out of traffic.

"Let's see what this thing can do," Curtis declares as he increases power to the vortex thrusters and the electromagnetic redistribution boots. In a sudden burst of speed, and with a sharp yell, he accelerates down the highway—covering greater distances with every leap and bound— quickly catching up to the vehicles.

"I don't care what he says," the operative yells, "take him out! Take him out!"

Windows roll down as guards extend their weapons in Curtis' direction and open fire!

"Whoa!" Curtis yells as he dodges a barrage of bullets.

"Curtis!" Kelly shouts as she starts fighting against her captors!

Two trucks drop back and create a moving barrier to restrict Curtis' approach. He barely runs around one and leapfrogs over the other. In all of the commotion, the back door accidentally opens as Kelly shoves one of the operatives out. The driver zigzags causing Kelly to lose her balance as she falls halfway out of the vehicle.

"Kelly!" Curtis shouts as he makes his way over to her.

"Nooooo!" She shrieks while holding on to the door with all of her strength!

Kelly looks directly at Curtis—filled with trepidation—as he reaches for her, but the SUV fishtails away as the driver oversteers, causing the vehicle to skid perpendicularly while hitting a dip in the road, catapulting it into the air! Kelly wails as the force of the barrel roll ejects her!

"No!" Curtis shouts as Kelly hurls through the air like a rag doll. Curtis maneuvers his body with laser-like focus—leaps into the air, matches her rotational spin and catches her!

"I got you!" He yells while deploying the Mach-2's air flaps and activating the vortex thruster to stabilize their descent.

The SUV bursts into flames as it flips to a stop! Curtis and Kelly land and skid to a halt.

"I got you," he declares warmly while retracting his visor. Kelly looks at him through her tears—her chest heaving from the terror.

"Curtis!" she cries as she hugs him tightly. "You *caught* me!"

"I did." He smiles as she gazes intently into his eyes. "Are you okay?"

"I am now."

"Good. We have to get out of here before—"

Bright spotlights suddenly pierce the night sky; shining on them as two stealth helicopters quietly hover above. Eight operatives descend on ropes and surround them.

"Don't move!" they command as one of the helicopters land.

Kelly and Curtis catch each other's gaze as Curtis grabs her around her waist and slowly moves his thumb to engage the vortex thrusters.

"Whoa there," an operative yells as he trains his gun on Curtis. "You may be the fastest man alive, but you are *not* the Flash. You best get out of that suit. Right now!"

Curtis moves his thumb *away* from the button while Kelly raise her hands and he exits the suit.

"We got two minutes before the cops arrive," an operative shouts. "Let's get them in the chopper, pack up the suit and get this mess cleaned up!"

Curtis and Kelly are forced into the helicopter. To their surprise, Erica is sitting across from them.

"You know Curtis, you are really making things difficult."

Kelly jumps up and smacks Erica across the face before she's restrained by the guards.

Erica winces as she rubs her stinging cheek. "Guess I had that coming."

[]

After landing on the helipad at the Montgomery Group's "A" building, Erica, Curtis and Kelly transfer to a black, armored limousine and drive towards downtown Atlanta.

"You know Chasm is not a happy camper," Erica chuckles as she looks at her captives in their restraints. "I've never seen him this mad before. Your *Mission Impossible* scheme has really stressed him out."

[]

Twenty minutes later, the limousine arrives at the 191 Tower. The driver opens the door and Erica steps out, followed by a guard, Curtis, Kelly and another two guards. As they enter the main lobby, Kelly spots a restroom.

"I need to go to the bathroom… really badly."

"You've got to be kidding," Erica huffs.

"Been holding it since they brought me from New York."

Erica takes Kelly by the arm and motions to the guards. "Watch Curtis while I take her to the bathroom. If I'm not out in five minutes, come and check on us."

Five minutes later, Erica drags Kelly back out and is startled to find Chasm standing directly in front of her with the guards.

"You two take Curtis and Kelly to the roof," Chasm commands without taking his eyes off of Erica. "*We'll* be up in a minute."

Erica watches as the three guards put Curtis and Kelly in an elevator. Chasm presses the call button for another elevator. When it arrives, he motions for Erica to enter. Once the doors close, he speaks.

"Is there something you want to tell me?"

"Uh, no... What are you referring to?"

"I am referring to the Mach-2. Did you know about its ability to record data unless it was *completely* powered down?"

"No... I didn't."

Chasm presses the 'emergency stop' button.

"I installed that feature after the repeated suit failures. So, what are you *not* telling me? Or should I make you aware of what I know?"

"What do you know?"

"It was you, Erica. The suit recorded it all. The last few sabotages, the theft. Turbulence. *You* were responsible."

Erica tries to hold back her tears. "I never meant to—"

"Who are you working for?"

"Chasm, you have to believe me. I would never do—"

"I will *believe* you when you tell me the truth!" Chasm snaps. His anger and insistence is met by her silence. He breathes deeply while releasing the 'emergency stop' button.

"Have it your way. I would fire you right now and have you arrested if I didn't *need* you to get through tonight. But tomorrow, you are done. And if you don't carry out the full extent of your duties tonight... you know what happens to people who cross me."

Erica says nothing as she looks down at the elevator floor. Chasm's cold expression eases slightly as he looks at her.

"Erica," he says softly, "This is your *last* chance... Who are you working for?"

Before she can answer, the elevator dings to a stop, and the doors open revealing Dr. Winters waiting a bit impatiently in his gray slacks, blue dress shirt and navy sports jacket.

"What took you two so long?" he asks as they exit the elevator.

"We're here *now*," Chasm replies. "Now, what's so urgent that you wanted to meet here instead of my headquarters?"

"We'll be going to your headquarters shortly," Dr. Winters answers, "but it was imperative that we meet here first."

"Why?"

"Because your young mentee needs to be taught a serious lesson," Dr. Winters answers as he and Chasm approach Curtis and Kelly, who are handcuffed to a metal guardrail. "Guards, please wait for us by the elevator."

The guards look at Dr. Winters and then at Chasm—who nods in confirmation of the command. They walk away, leaving Curtis and Kelly behind.

"Chasm… This is what I want you to do," Dr. Winters says as he unlocks Kelly's handcuffs. "I want you to throw this young lady *off* this roof."

"No!" Curtis yells as he tries to fight against his handcuffs.

"Please no!" Kelly shrieks in a futile attempt to pull away from Dr. Winters.

Erica stands at a distance, barely able to watch what is transpiring.

"I may be a manipulator," Chasm utters as he raises his hands in protest, "but I'm *not* a murderer."

"Of course you are!" Dr. Winters retorts. "Every weapon you build for the military is used to kill! You've just been a *few steps removed* from the death. But it's time for you to make the hard choices and get your hands dirty!"

"No, please!" Kelly shouts as she pleads for her life.

"Dr. Winters!" Curtis yells. "You don't have to do this!"

"Shut up!" Dr. Winters yells as he faces Chasm. "Do it! Throw her off of the roof!"

"Chasm!" Curtis shouts."Don't do it!"

Dr. Winters shoves Kelly into Chasm's arms."Do it… now!"

Chasm tightly grasps Kelly's arm as they both stand at the rooftop edge. He looks down at the city below them and then at Kelly's tear-stained face.

"Please," she whimpers,"please don't do this. You don't have to do this…"

Chasm gazes back at her as Dr. Winters growls again.

"Do it!"

"I'm sorry…" Chasm utters while Kelly shakes her head profusely.

"No… please!"

Chasm turns from her gaze and stares at his mentor. Waves of conflicting emotions stir within him. *He's my mentor. This is wrong. But he helped make me who I am. This is not who I am.*

"What are you waiting for?" Dr. Winters yells again as words spew from his lips."Do it! Right now!"

"I…I can't." Chasm pulls Kelly back from the edge and turns her over to his mentor. Kelly falls to the ground—heaving—as Curtis breathes a huge sigh of relief.

"Curtis stole from us!" Dr. Winters snarls at Chasm. "His actions have cost us almost one hundred million dollars in lost revenue and who knows how many hundreds of thousands of dollars in property damage! He needs to know there are equal and opposite consequences for every action!" Dr. Winters grabs Kelly and stands her to her feet.

"Erica!" he barks."Get *rid* of this girl!"

Erica takes a step.

"No!" Chasm yells.

She pulls out a gun and aims it at her boss.

"Erica!" Curtis yells."*What* are you doing?" Chasm raises his hands and takes a step back as Erica slowly saunters over, grabs Kelly and approaches the edge of the roof. Dr. Winters watches with a sinister grin on his face—his eyes wide with expectation. "Do it! Do it now!"

"I-I'm sorry!" Erica cries as she looks at Curtis and then pushes Kelly over the edge.

Kelly screams as she reaches for thin air, her body plummeting under gravity's pull.

"NOOOOOooooo!!!!" Curtis yells as Kelly disappears from view, her screams quickly fade into the night. He crumbles to his knees and wails at the top of his lungs.

"*Why* did you do that?" Chasm yells, glaring at Erica and Dr. Winters.

A helicopter approaches and hovers overhead. The downwash blows everything around as the passenger cabin floor lowers on four high tensile steel cables. Dr. Winters uncuffs a distraught Curtis and drags him to the lowered platform. He motions to Chasm and Erica. Chasm steps onto the platform as Dr. Winters gives Erica one last instruction.

"Clean up here and meet us back at headquarters!"

Erica nods, backing away as the cabin floor rises into the air and reconnects with the underbelly of the helicopter. With an extra burst of wind, the helicopter quickly rises into the air and flies away.

"How could you do that?" Chasm asks numbly as he gazes out of the window.

Curtis cries in the corner of his chair, his chest heaving and heart overcome with sadness.

"With all of your success," Dr. Winters answers, "you *still* have a problem making the hard choices."

"I-I don't understand why you had to kill her. There had to be *another* way to teach Curtis a lesson."

"This was the most definitive way. Don't worry. Soon, everything will be made clear."

[]

The Montgomery Group Headquarters. 3:00am.

The helicopter lands and powers down on the 'A' building's helipad as Dr. Winters, Chasm and Curtis descend in an elevator all the way to Underground Level Three.

"Curtis," Dr. Winters growls as Chasm drags his mentee down the corridor, "I want you to see the immense damage you caused."

Four guards stand at the ready with their weapons drawn.

"Open the doors!" Dr. Winters commands.

Three guards quickly stand to one side as a fourth swipes his card key. The double doors open and a gust of smoke-filled air blows into the corridor. The trio enters, makes their way down to the main floor and walks through the charred remains. Almost the entire testing range has been severely damaged.

"You know," Dr. Winters says as they stop by a group of pillars, "Chasm has been very fond of you, at least up until this point. And the things he's *fond* of... he manipulates for his own agenda. This was one of the great lessons I taught him over the years. I have taken pleasure in watching him manipulate your life. Quite frankly, in his own way, he loves you like a son. And in some ways, I look at him like the brother I never had."

"Why are you telling me all of this?" Curtis asks.

"I'm *telling* you this because sometimes things are not what they seem. Take Chasm's adoptive parents for example. James and Wilma Montgomery were wealthy beyond measure... but they could not have children. After several failed attempts at pregnancy, they were determined to adopt a son. The first time they were going to adopt, Wilma got pregnant. The doctors called it a miracle of modern science! They canceled that adoption and she gave birth to a beautiful bouncing baby boy: *William Wallace Montgomery*. All they wanted was a son to carry on their legacy.

"But as the years passed, it became painfully apparent that with all of their wealth and affluence, they were helpless in getting their son to take life seriously. William thought he was *entitled* to his opulent lifestyle and sought to use every possible moment to satisfy his longings at the *expense* of everyone else. He was a painful chore to be around…"

"But William died," Chasm interjects. "He was killed in a skiing accident."

"Yes," Dr. Winters agrees, "apparently on the Swiss Alps. A number of years before Chasm was adopted."

"But how did you know that he was a painful chore to be around?" Curtis asks. "Chasm never knew him."

"True," Dr. Winters purses his lips, "Chasm never knew young William, but *I* did."

"How could you have known him?" Chasm asks as he looks at his mentor.

"Because, my dear Chasm, I knew your parents for many years," Dr. Winters reveals.

"You never told me that," Chasm replies.

"We all have our secrets. It was a dark time for your parents, dealing with the apparent death of their son. But then, some years later, they adopted a young black boy who had grown up with nothing. This boy understood what it meant to have nothing because he was seen as *being* nothing. But, somehow, James and Wilma saw something in this boy and began to pour everything they had into him. *You*, Chasm, became their life's work. They sent you to all the right schools and put you in all the right social circles… They built you up beyond your wildest dreams. And soon, Chasm Montgomery became a shining beacon of his adoptive parents' legacy. But then—sadly—tragedy struck."

[]

May 13, 1977. Massachusetts.

The sun beams brightly on this Spring day as James and Wilma Montgomery wind their way down a wooded mountainside in their crystal blue Jaguar. The engine purrs with power. The ride is smooth. The windows are down and the sunroof is open. The wind blows through, causing Wilma's long brownish-gray hair to spiral around like cotton candy being spun. Both of them smile as they look at each other longingly, with a newfound love and purpose. After so many years of turmoil, they've finally found peace.

Wilma takes her husband's right hand. He presses down harder on the gas pedal and the car accelerates out of the final turn at the bottom of mountain. With a gasp, he slams on the brakes to avoid a stalled car—but the brakes don't engage. In an instant they're gone. The sound of the crash could be heard for miles.

[]

The present. Underground Level Three Testing Range.

"Why are you telling us all of this?" Chasm asks, as his heart races and a knot develops in the pit of his stomach. "I don't want to relive their deaths."

"But the boy needs to understand," Dr. Winters replies. "You *both* need to understand what's about to come."

"But I know about death," Curtis replies.

"Right!" Dr. Winters concurs. "You lost your father to cancer, which is one reason why Chasm has endeared himself to you. But did you know that you and Chasm had met back when you were younger?"

Curtis looks at Chasm cautiously.

"You were four years old. You probably don't remember."

"Is that true?" Curtis presses.

"Yes…" Chasm hesitates. "Dr. Winters, why are you saying all of this?"

"Because we *all* keep secrets, Chasm! You never told Curtis about that meeting so many years ago! Curtis never told *you* about his plan to ruin your agenda!"

"And what secrets are you keeping?" Curtis asks.

"My, he *is* intelligent," Dr. Winters chuckles. "You see, my dear boy, there is something that needs to happen next, but in order for it to take place, this story must finish. You see, Chasm was informed of his adoptive parents' deaths while he was away in Europe, preparing to graduate from Oxford. His future seemed bright, but this tragic blight threatened to destroy everything they had worked for… it threatened to destroy *him*. Then he met me and I was able to help him find his purpose. But there is something about his adoptive parents' death which he does not know."

[]

May 13, 1977. Massachusetts.

Twisted metal and shattered glass litter the pavement as the smell of smoke and gasoline fill the air. Pockets of fire punctuate the nearby landscape as a young man approaches from among the trees. He slowly makes his way through the mashed up wreckage of two automobiles set aflame and comes across the only victims, still strapped into their vehicle. Neither are alive. Their broken, mangled bodies rest awkwardly in their seats... sandwiched up against the dashboard.

The young man smiles at the destruction then walks away quietly, still holding a segment of the Jaguar's brake line in his hand.

[]

The present. Underground Level Three.

"What are you saying?" Chasm yells as he grabs hold of Dr. Winters' sports jacket. "Are you saying that someone *killed* my parents?"

Curtis watches as the drama plays out in front of him.

"Not just *someone*," Dr. Winters reveals, "but the brother you *thought* was dead. James and Wilma *lied* to you. William wasn't killed in a skiing accident. That's the lie they told everyone else to cover up the *truth*. They had *excommunicated* their son! Cut him off from the family name and inheritance. Do you understand? You have an adopted brother! And I know where he is."

"But why bring this up now?" Chasm yells. "For what purpose?"

Dr. Winters reaches into the inside pocket of his sports jacket, retrieves a folded black plastic bag and hands it to Chasm. Chasm looks at it intently as he unfolds the bag and reaches inside—pulling out an old rolled up section of tubing.

"*This* serves my purpose," Dr. Winters declares.

Chasm's eyebrows wrinkle as he tries to make sense of things.

"*I*... am William Wallace Montgomery."

"No way!" Curtis whispers with wide eyes as Chasm stumbles back in shock.

"But you—" Chasm stumbles over his words. "How? Why?" His confusion gives way to anger as he clenches his fists and prepares to attack.

"Don't move!" a female voice shouts from behind them. Curtis and Chasm turn to find Erica quickly approaching with her gun firmly aimed at Chasm.

"Ah, Erica," Dr. Winters smiles, "you arrived *just* in time."

"As you like to say," Erica grins as she takes her place beside him, "punctuality is the hallmark of excellence."

"Indeed it is!" Dr. Winters concurs.

Curtis and Chasm stand side-by-side—Curtis in a state of shock and Chasm in a growing fit of rage.

"Is it *really* you?" Chasm growls. "Are you really *William?*"

"Oh it's *me*, alright!" Dr. Winters laughs.

"All these years… I *trusted* you!"

"And that was the beauty of it all!" Dr. Winters replies, clapping gleefully. "You trusted me. Curtis trusted you! What a wonderful cycle of deception! Gaining your trust. Guiding you. Building you up, all the while waiting for just the right moment to tear you down. I may have taken pleasure in watching you manipulate Curtis, but I took *great pleasure* in *manipulating* you."

Chasm growls as he takes two steps forward.

"I wouldn't do that!" Dr. Winters retorts with a sly smile as Erica cocks her gun. "She *will* shoot."

"And you," Chasm says, his voice dripping with scorn, "after *everything* I did for you… how could you be working for him?"

"Oh, don't blame her," Dr. Winters quips. "Everybody has their asking price. When I propositioned Erica three years ago, I made sure to *exceed* hers."

"Now's not the time for cynicism, Chasm" Erica adds, "Why don't you just hear the rest of the story. I'm dying to know how it ends, myself."

"Yes," Dr. Winters continues, "back to *my* story. You know, you always thought this was all about you, Chasm. When in reality, it was all about *me*!"

"But Dr. Winters," Curtis interrupts.

"No more *Dr. Winters*… please call me William. You know it's amazing what faking one's death and getting plastic surgery will do. I guess, in a way, I should say *thank you*, Chasm."

"For what?"

"When I found out that my parents had chosen *you* instead of their own flesh and blood, I was a bit incensed. But my newfound anger gave me a sense of purpose. It caused me to study and become a connoisseur of learning. The anger caused me to become a strategist and to use my growing knowledge base to gain wealth, status and influence. You, Chasm, caused me to become a *better* me… and now I am in a position to reap the ultimate prize!"

"To kill me?" Chasm presses.

"Again," William sucks his teeth as he shakes his head, "here you go thinking everything is about you! You are where you are, not only because of your hard work and cunning ability, but more so because of the foundation you stand on—*my* parent's inheritance. And not only do I want back what's rightfully mine, but I will also strip your fantastic empire from your cold, stiff fingers and add it to my own!" William laughs heartily at the top of his lungs as he inhales deeply. "Oh, how I have waited for this moment! To revel in this outcome, which has been meticulously carried out over the course of *decades*! Wherever my parents may be, this is how I say, *no declare*, that they do not get to win! *I* am the winner!!!"

"So, what happens now?" Curtis asks.

"Well," William postulates, "if there is a winner, then there *must* be a loser. Or in your case, 'losers.' Erica, *kill* them."

Curtis and Chasm throw up their hands as Erica aims her gun at them. "I wish things could have been different," she admits, "but I am sorry." She quickly does an *about-face* and points her gun firmly at William.

"W-What are you doing?" William scoffs.

"I am doing what I always *planned* on doing," Erica declares confidently. Chasm and Curtis look on—unsure of what to make of the amazing turn of events. "You may have made me an offer I couldn't refuse," Erica continues, "but I *don't* work for you."

"But what about Kelly?" William shouts. "We were all there on the roof! You killed her!"

"Did *I*?" She asks. "Curtis, what do *you* think?"

"I don't think you did," he smiles.

"She didn't?" Chasm asks shockingly.

"No," a familiar voice echoes throughout the testing range as footsteps are heard approaching. "She didn't." The three of them turn to see Kelly walk out of the shadows.

"But how?" William exclaims. "I saw Erica *push* you *off* the roof!"

"Oh, she *did* push me off the roof," Kelly confirms, "but what you *didn't* see was what happened before that."

[]

Earlier that night…

The limousine arrives at the 191 Tower. The driver opens the door as Erica steps out, followed by a guard, Curtis, Kelly and two additional guards. As they enter the main lobby, Erica silently gestures to Kelly. At first Kelly is confused, but Erica again, silently gestures with her eyes and a slight nod of her head. This time Kelly understands as she spots a restroom in Erica's line of sight.

"I need to go to the bathroom… really badly."

"You've got to be kidding?" Erica huffs.

"Been holding it since they brought me from New York."

Erica grabs Kelly by the arm and motions to the guards. "Watch Curtis while I take her to the bathroom. If I'm not out in five minutes, come and check on us."

Erica shoves Kelly through the bathroom door and shuts it behind them. She quickly walks through the bathroom to make sure they're alone.

"So, what's the deal?" Kelly whispers, confused. "Why are we in here?"

“The *deal* is if you don’t listen to me, they will kill you when we get to the roof.”

Kelly stares at Erica in shock as Erica takes off her jacket, opens a hidden panel in the lining and retrieves carefully folded strips of fabric.

“So, what? I'm supposed to trust you now?"

“Yes. You are."

"Well, I *don't*. Give me one reason why I should."

"If you don't trust me, you die. Besides, who do you think helped Curtis get here in one piece?"

"So," Kelly mumbles while looking at Erica, "what do I do?”

“Take your shirt off and put this on underneath.”

“What is it?” Kelly asks while obeying Erica’s command.

“It’s a very powerful electromagnetic harness we developed. It has a strong pull that extends out from the wearer about seven feet.”

“What am I supposed to do with this?” Kelly asks while Erica helps her put it on.

“You *will* be pushed off the roof.”

“What?” Kelly says in a hushed, but startled tone.

“You're supposed to be made an example for Curtis to understand the consequences of his actions tonight. Dr. Winters will want either Chasm or me to push you off the building to your death. When you get pushed, press the belt buckle to activate the harness. It will pull you to the building and stop your fall. Then all you have to do is hang around for me to come get you.”

“*That’s* the best plan you got?” Kelly yells as Erica shushes her.

“Yes,” Erica confirms, “actually, this *is* the best plan I got. There’s so much going on you know nothing about. I need you to trust me. Okay?”

[]

The present. Underground Level Three.

"And here I am," Kelly smiles as Erica throws the keys to Chasm to unlock Curtis' handcuffs.

"You've been playing both sides," Chasm smiles as he releases Curtis.

"I had to," Erica admits. "That was the only way I could discover what was really going on. If Dr. Winters—William wanted to deceive you—with all of the power and influence he already had, I couldn't turn down his offer, or else I'd probably be dead already and he'd have found a way to move forward with his plans *without* your knowledge."

"I knew you were a genius," Chasm laughs, "I am sorry I ever doubted you."

'No need to apologize. I *did* give you reasons to doubt me."

"And Curtis," Chasm continues, "Erica helped you, too?"

[]

Earlier that night...

The lights on Curtis' suit illuminate his surroundings as he cautiously makes his way through the underbelly of the plane. He comes to the storage compartment, climbs in and looks around. To his amazement, he sees a familiar containment crate strapped to the wall. As he draws near to it and looks closer, he can't believe his eyes.

"Thank you, God!"

He quickly releases the safety clamps and pulls open the heavy door. The Mach-2 stands before him. The power indicators on the containment panel indicate the suit has a full charge.

"Now, *how* do you open this thing?"

Suddenly, the front of the suit opens—from helmet all the way down to boots, causing Curtis to stumble backwards in surprise.

"Wow. Voice commands?" he exclaims.

"Actually," a digitized female voice speaks through the suit's communication system, "I opened it. Before you can use this suit, you must first put on the accompanying under-armor."

Curtis takes off his Mach-1 Speedsuit and puts on the under-armor bodysuit stored in a compartment within the containment crate. He then slowly turns around and steps backwards into the Mach-2. The front of the suit encloses around him as internal pressure gauges recalibrate.

"Please wait," the digitized female voice utters, "while the suit adjusts to your size and dimensions." Curtis can feel internal bladders pressurizing around him, creating a tight-but-comfortable feel.

"So," Curtis says into the darkness. "Am I talking to the operating system for the Mach-2? Like an artificial intelligence program?"

"No," the voice replies as Erica appears on the screen within the visor heads up display, "you are talking to *me*."

"Erica!" Curtis shouts as he struggles in the immobilized suit. "Get me out of here!"

"Relax, Curtis. This is not a trap. The containment crate sent a signal to my tablet when you opened it."

"What do you want?" Curtis asks while trying to calm down.

"I want to help you! That's what I've *always* wanted."

"Uh, huh. Why should I trust you or Chasm?"

"Because Chasm is *not* the one in charge."

"What? What do you mean?"

"I'm already risking a lot by helping you. I don't have much time. But Chasm doesn't know he's being manipulated by someone else."

"Who?"

"I can't tell you. It's too dangerous. Listen, you have to trust me. If you want to save Kelly and get out of this ordeal alive... I'm your only hope."

"I guess I don't have much of a choice."

"Good. Stand by to power up."

"Great. It's getting hot in here. Please tell me this suit has internal climate control."

A moment later, the Mach-2 begins its 10 second startup procedure. The inside of the visor lights up with information, air ventilation begins to flow throughout the suit, power is supplied to the joint motors, and the limbs are unlocked and articulated —allowing Curtis to move about freely.

"Now, let me give you a crash course on how to use the suit."

[]

The present. Underground Level Three.

"Erica is a *true* secret agent," Curtis laughs.

"Do you think you've won?" William shouts.

"You have a gun pointed at you," Chasm remarks, "and you are outnumbered." Chasm pulls back his jacket and retrieves his phone from his belt holder. "And with your admission about killing our parents having been *recorded*, I'd say, once the authorities hear this, you will in fact be the ultimate *loser*."

"Seriously," Curtis agrees. "You had a chance to do something amazing with your life, and you chose to be guided by envy, jealousy, anger and revenge."

"And those endearing qualities will win out in the end." William snarls as he yells at the top of his lungs. "Turbulence!!!"

The sound of a roaring wind echoes through the chamber as Turbulence leaps from the second floor observatory and—with help from his thrusters—lands right next to his employer.

"Surprise, surprise!" William laughs as the group takes notice of Turbulence's new black and red color scheme. "I had a *second* suit built!"

Chasm runs to Erica and takes her gun, opening fire, but Turbulence steps in front of William to shield him—the bullets ricochet off his armor. He quickly raises his hand and releases an electrical jolt which knocks Chasm to the ground as Erica, Kelly and Curtis dive for cover.

"Stand down!" Turbulence orders. "You *barely* beat me with your Powersuit. Now you've got no chance!"

"You see," William muses as he smiles with glee, "I told you I would win in the end. You don't get to the level that I've reached without planning several moves *ahead* of your enemy."

A war cry echoes behind them. William and Turbulence turn to see a figure hurtling down through the air—casting a blow which catches them by surprise. William dives for cover as the flying punch shatters Turbulence's helmet and knocks him out cold. His armored body crashes to the floor with a loud, clanging thud!

"Sorry we're late," Matthew says as he stands tall in the Strength Augmentation Exo-suit.

"You're on time in my book!" Curtis cheers as he sees the rest of his group entering the range through the large entrance from the driveway.

"Did you see this coming?" Kelly asks, as William is now thoroughly surrounded by thirteen people—six of whom are wearing Powersuits.

"Give it up, William," Chasm commands. "You're finished. If mom and dad were alive, I'm sure this would be their most shameful day."

William charges at Chasm with all of his might, grabbing him by the throat. "I will destroy you!" he shouts as they struggle.

Everyone watches as the two brothers trade blow after blow, the scuffle taking them half way across the testing range.

"Let's help him!" Curtis yells as he and Omar step forward.

"No!" Chasm orders in between blows. "Stay where you are! This is *my* fight!" Chasm knocks William to the ground. "Stay down! It's *over* William."

"If I can't have your empire, then you won't either!" William screams as he scrambles to his feet and tackles Chasm, causing them to tumble down a nearby industrial incinerator shaft.

"No!" Curtis and Erica yell as Chasm and William are swallowed up by the darkness—echoes of screams heard fading into the distance.

Everyone runs over to the open doorway.

"We've got to get down there!" Curtis yells. As they peer over the edge, they can see Chasm desperately holding onto a broken rung about thirty feet below. "Chasm!" Curtis yells. "We're going to get you out!"

"Just hang on!" Omar shouts as he looks back at the group. "We need some rope! Something long enough to reach him!"

"It's no good," Chasm says, struggling to retain his grip on the metal rung as it shifts from the weight. "I'm too far down and I don't know how long this rung is going to hold."

A buzzer blares as a red light on the side of the incinerator shaft starts flashing.

"What's going on?" Jim and Miranda ask.

"The incinerator is about to fire up," Erica yells. We've got less than a minute!"

"Well turn it off!" Miranda orders.

Erica stands to her feet and runs over to a nearby control panel. Seconds speed by as the group struggles to figure out a way to save Chasm.

"It's not working!" Erica shouts.

"There's gotta be something we can do!" Gavin yells.

The buzzer blares again as the blast door begins to close on them. Matthew activates his power suit and jumps in front of the door to restrain it.

"Don't worry about me," Chasm yells as one of the rung's bolts dislodges from the wall. "Let the blast door close or else you'll all be in danger from the flames!"

"We're *not* leaving you!" Curtis shouts.

"You have to," Chasm says, resolutely.

The buzzer blares again as the incinerator comes to life. Flames ignite three hundred feet below as hot air howls through the shaft and rushes out of the open doorway. The force of the rushing hot air violently pushes Chasm into the wall and almost knocks the group to the floor.

"Let the door close now!" Chasm cries as the flames race up the tunnel corridor. "Do it now or you all will *die*!"

Omar pulls Curtis away from the opening and yells for Matthew to release the blast door. Everyone scrambles for cover as the door closes just as the flames reach it. Hot air and flames leap through the edges as the door seals shut. The entire shaft rumbles, shaking the ground. Everyone stands frozen in disbelief. The room grows silent. Erica, grieved, drops to her knees and sobs uncontrollably.

"I-I can't believe he's gone." Curtis stutters as he looks at the closed door. "We could have *saved* him… we just needed more time."

"Hey," Omar tries to soothe Curtis—putting his hands on his brother's shoulder, "we did what we could. Sometimes… our best is just not enough. We couldn't have known that their fight was going to end this way."

Kelly and Miranda weep as Jim and Gavin try to quietly assess everyone's condition. Curtis sees Chasm's phone near the incinerator and picks it up. Erica wipes her eyes and forces herself to her feet as Curtis walks over to her and extends his hand.

"I'm sorry," he says, trying to hold back the tears that already fill his eyes. Erica slowly removes Chasm's phone from his hand.

"You don't have to be sorry, Curtis," Erica replies. "We all watched it happen. We all did what we could do."

Curtis wipes the tears from his eyes as Kelly walks to his side and takes his hand.

"Now," Miranda says, "we need to call the police."

"*I'll* handle it," Erica replies, wiping tears from her eyes as she forces herself into 'work Mode.' She picks up her phone and dials a number. Within minutes, security personnel swarm throughout the room. Erica escorts Curtis and his team up to a private waiting room in the lobby. Everyone sits motionless. Silence fills the air, punctuated by sporadic moments of sobbing. Erica's phone vibrates as a text appears, indicating the authorities have arrived. She quietly exits the room.

"I didn't want things to end this way," Curtis mumbles to no one in particular. "Not like this."

□

Several hours pass without Erica returning.

"She's been out there a long time," Miranda says.

"Yeah," Jim agrees.

"What do you think she's telling the authorities?" Miranda asks.

"I don't know," Omar replies.

After a few minutes, the door slowly opens. Erica reenters the room as the group stands to their feet in anxious expectation. Erica looks at everyone and gently smiles.

"The authorities have left. You are all free to go."

"What did you tell them?" Miranda asks, astonished at the news.

"I told them what needed to be said," Erica replies. "I told them the truth."

"And what was that?" Curtis presses.

"It doesn't matter," Erica responds while rubbing her tired eyes. "Just be happy this whole ordeal is over—at least for you."

"Erica," Kelly says, walking towards her, "*thank you* for everything."

Erica gazes at Kelly and Curtis for a moment and then looks at everyone else. "I'm glad I could help."

Miranda, Omar and the rest of the team rally around them. "It looks like we did it." Miranda smiles somberly.

"Yeah," Curtis agrees. "It looks that way. Although, I wish we hadn't lost Chasm in the process." Curtis' sentiments speak for everyone, as their victory is tempered by an unnecessary loss of life.

"So," Gavin asks, "what do we do now?"

"Now," Curtis answers, "now we go home."

CHAPTER THIRTY-SIX

GOING HOME

WEDNESDAY OCTOBER 1, 2014. CURTIS AND the entire Powersuit team stand next to a hangar and private jet which belong to Gavin's father. The weather is beautiful on this breezy, sunny day. The group watches a jumbo jet speed down a nearby runway and rise into the air, before turning their attention back to each other.

"Before we all leave, I just want to say thank you to everyone!" Curtis declares with great gratitude. "You put your life on the line last night for me. For some of you, this endeavor was last minute. But you all came through and I am eternally in your debt. If I can be of help to you, anytime, anywhere, all you have to do is say the word."

Everyone hugs each other and shakes hands as they climb up the stairs and enters the jet. Curtis approaches Gavin, who remains on the tarmac.

"Surprised you're not coming along for the ride."

"Not like me to miss a free ride, but I need to play catch up for the classes we missed over the past week."

"Yeah," Curtis agrees. "I'll have to do that when I come back in a few days. With everything that's happened, I just need to get home for a bit. Glad my professors were understanding."

"No problem. I'll get the notes for you."

"Thanks Gavin. You've been a big help."

"I know." Gavin flashes a huge smile. "You couldn't have done all of this without me."

"Nope!" Curtis laughs. "See you in a few days!"

[]

Powers residence. Two days later… 9:00am.

A sleepy Curtis comes to the front door after hearing a knock. He opens it and finds Erica, dressed in her best business attire, standing with a well dressed gentleman holding a briefcase.

"Erica!" Curtis smiles. "This is an unexpected surprise!"

"Hello Curtis!" Erica beams. "How are you?"

"I'm well! Do you want to come in?"

"No, thank you," Erica says. She raises her empty right hand as the gentleman opens his briefcase and retrieves a thick envelope. "Not that I don't want to, but this is a quick stop. We're here for meetings at the new office downtown." He hands her the envelope. "This is The Montgomery Group's Chief Legal Counsel, Mr. Rinaldi."

"How do you do, Mr. Powers?"

"Hello Mr. Rinaldi," Curtis replies. "Nice to meet you."

"When Chasm died," Erica continues, "he left some significant alterations in his will. First, he named me his replacement as CEO."

"Wow!" Curtis yells. "That's great!"

"It is," Erica agrees, "although given the circumstances, I would rather have Chasm still *alive* and in charge. Nevertheless, the mantle has fallen on me to run his company."

"I can think of no one better than you to do it," Curtis replies without hesitation.

"Thank you," Erica smiles—blushing a bit as she hands Curtis the envelope. "The second thing Chasm did was to grant you a sizable number of company shares. Basically, once you sign the enclosed documents, you will become *very* wealthy. You know, even with all of his faults and secret agendas, Chasm *did* view you as a son."

“I’m not sure I want what he’s offering…”

“That’s your decision to make,” Erica replies, a bit curtly before softening her expression. “Why don’t you talk it over with your mom and brother before making your final decision.”

Erica and Mr. Rinaldi turn and walk back to their vehicle.

“Wait!” Curtis yells. “That’s it?”

Erica stops at the car as the driver opens the rear door. “We can discuss the particulars and any questions you may have after you return to Atlanta. Have a great day Curtis.”

With that, Erica and Mr. Rinaldi step into their car, as the driver closes the door. Curtis watches as they drive away into the distance. He then looks down at the sizable envelope and closes the door.

“Mom! Omar! We *have* to talk!”

CHAPTER THIRTY-SEVEN

INSURANCE POLICY

IT'S AN OVERCAST MORNING AS CURTIS, Omar, Miranda and Marge arrive in the parking lot at United National Bank in Madison, New Jersey. The three of them exit their vehicle. Marge stays in the car to finish up preparations for the latter part of the day. They enter the bank and speak with a manager, who then guides them downstairs to the secured room which houses several walls of safety deposit boxes.

The manager stands at the doorway, motioning for them to enter. Curtis and Omar lead the way, with Miranda closely behind them. The boys find box #845 and remove the keys which hang on a chain around their necks. They place the keys in the keyholes at both ends of the rectangle box and gaze at each other as Miranda stands in silence. The boys nod as they count, 1... 2... 3 and turn their keys clockwise at the same time.

The box unlocks as Miranda approaches and opens the door. She grasps the large, closed brass colored container, which spans about a foot and a half in length and pulls it out of the sleeve. Curtis, and Omar watch as their mother walks the container over to a nearby table. They stand by her curiously as she opens it. Inside, they find all of the incriminating documents which had been stolen. They also find copies of actual case files, as well as numerous audio and video tapes of critical conversations.

"With this," Miranda declares as she draws her sons to her, "we get back what is rightfully ours and help those who were also abused by the Firm."

The three of them quickly exit the bank and approach their car. Marge watches from the back seat as they approach—looking for any indication of success. Miranda smiles broadly with a thumbs-up signal as they get into their car.

"We have everything!" Miranda says, while Omar starts the car and drives away.

"Excellent!" Marge exclaims, retrieving her cell phone from her purse. "I will call the rest of the group."

[]

Five hours later…

John Whaley sits behind closed doors with the other founding partners and the former chairman of the board of trustees. The Firm is about to take on its largest building project to date and all employees are actively working through every detail. The afternoon sun shines brightly into the board room as intense conversation continues. Little do they know this project is about to become the least of their problems.

A large number of police officers enter through the Firm's main doors, led by several federal agents, detectives and representatives from other law enforcement agencies. The Firm's employees stare cautiously at the sheer number of enforcement agents. The executive administrative assistants, sitting at The Island, nervously stare as the lead agent stands in front of them with an arrest warrant and a warrant to search the premises.

"L-Let me call one of the founding partners," an assistant suggests.

"No need to do that, ma'am," the agent replies, "we know where to go."

The agents and officers swarm through every office as they converge on the board room. The doors burst open and the occupants spin around in their chairs to face the disturbance. John Whaley, the founding partners and the former chairman of the board all are forcibly taken into custody and escorted down to the lobby in handcuffs. As they exit the building, amid a myriad of onlookers and news reporters, they freeze as if they have seen a ghost.

"Miranda? Marge?" John Whaley exclaims as the other men stare in astonishment. "Is that you?"

Miranda stands silently with Curtis, Omar, Marge, Emmanuel and Attorney Noreen Phillips as the police parade their captives to the awaiting vehicles.

"You're *all* behind this?" John yells as he and his cohorts are placed in the nearest police car.

"I'm sorry John," Miranda replies, "but you left us with no other choice."

"You think this is over?" John shouts as he's forced into a police car. "This is not over!"

"Now the *fun* part begins," Attorney Phillips says sarcastically. "I'm not necessarily looking forward to that."

"They will fight us all of the way," Emanuel Harte adds, "but the evidence we have amassed is inexorable."

"We got the ball rolling," Miranda suggests, "and it's rolling down a *very large* hill. With enough momentum, the ball will roll right over whoever or whatever gets in its way. No matter what the future holds… we have done the right thing. And I thank you all for that."

CHAPTER THIRTY-EIGHT

LIFE TRANSFORMATION

NOVEMBER HAS FINALLY COME AND TREYSHAWN finds himself standing at a podium on a small platform about to address almost two hundred people. His artwork adorns the bright gallery walls which form the large room. His art professor and the gallery owner sit next to him, proudly displaying their smiles for those who are present. Treyshawn looks out at the crowd of California residents, a host of other visitors from across the country and members of local and national media.

He sees his roommate, Johnny and many of his fellow classmates. Curtis and his family. His mother, grandmother and relatives. He sees Mr. Andre, Mrs. Fuller and Haakim. Mr. Grabowski with his daughter, son-in-law and granddaughter. He sees Kelly and her family. Gavin Ortiz and his parents. Eric Peterson, Matthew and Emmanuel Harte, and Erica Cosway. Even Clarance, the corporate lawyer he met on the plane when he first came to California stands among the crowd. Lastly, but certainly not least, Treyshawn's father stands proudly at the forefront of the entire audience, with a broad grin on his face.

Treyshawn smiles as he hears his heart beating in his ears, feels the increasing perspiration on his hands and feet, and notices the decreasing moisture in his mouth. He takes a sip of water from the cup placed beside him and breathes deeply. Then... he speaks.

"I don't think... Outside of Curtis' Speedsuit tour... I've ever spoken to a crowd this big before."

A slight chuckle reverberates through the sea of people.

"First, I want to say *thank you*, to everyone, for coming out tonight and showing your support. Tonight is a dream that I *never knew* existed.

"It's a... *hope* that I didn't think would ever be possible. I mean it's crazy, right? The thought that a kid could come from the 'hood, who was headed in the wrong direction in life and somehow find himself here is amazing. And I know I didn't get here by myself. Most of my life the people closest to me thought I'd never amount to anything. And because they thought that, then that's the way I chose to act. That's what I came to believe about myself. But, looking back, I don't blame them 'cause they were broken and hurting just like I was. And as you know, 'hurt people hurt people.'

"So, there I was... a hurt individual hurting *other* people. And even those who believed I could be somebody great gave up on me because I was *ferocious* with my hurt. I mean, I wore it like a badge of honor. It was my strength and shield. And there was no way I was going to let anyone see the real me—that hurt *little kid* inside who was so afraid of life that he didn't know the way out of his own personal darkness. So, who could blame them for giving up on someone who didn't even believe in himself?

"But both groups of people I just mentioned are in this room right now... believing in me. You know why? Because by the grace of God, there came a point in my life where I was so low that the only way out was up. There was a point in my life where I was so beaten and so tired of being beaten that I no longer had the strength to keep up the walls of hurt that I used to keep people out. And it was at *that moment*—I'll never forget it as long as I live—when I ran into Curtis Powers, the very kid I had been bullying relentlessly for the whole school year. And when I was at my lowest point and couldn't fight anymore, he did something I never expected him to do. Instead of crushing my heart with his bare hands... instead of kicking me when I was down… he *listened* to me. And he not only listened, but he spoke truth. And that was the first day of the rest of my life.

"Now I ain't gonna lie to you. The road was tough enough when I was busy being the bully and when people acted like they didn't care about me. But once I changed direction and started trying to get my life together—man did things get harder! Some people didn't believe I had changed. Others didn't believe that I *could* change. And yet, day-by-day, step-by-step, second-by-second I *was* changing. And I'm *still* changing. But what *change* did for me, was that it showed me a larger world beyond what I knew. And it forced others in my life who needed to change, to wrestle with their own issues in order to decide whether or not they *would* change. And I'm happy to say that my mother changed and my father changed! And I'm grateful for that!

"Now, I know you all didn't come here to hear me talk all night, but—I dunno—I just felt like in order for you to really understand and appreciate my paintings, you have to get a sense of who I am and my journey in life.

"As most of you know, my father was locked up in prison all of my life, up until a few months ago. We had *never* had a relationship. He wanted nothing to do with me. But eventually, the power of change in my life began to affect *his* life. And just over a year ago, we started building a relationship. Now, if I was 'hood, then my father was gangsta! Nobody messed with him, if they wanted to live. But as we got to know each other and slowly became vulnerable with each other, we began to impact each other. And when the attempted prison break happened back in August, it happened to be the same day when I surprised him for a visit. And he had to choose between freedom at any cost or protecting *me* at any cost. And his choice to fight for me, caused him to fight for the things I cared about, which is why he also saved the warden, who had taken a chance on both of us.

"As you know, my father was pardoned. And I'm honored to say that he is standing right here with us tonight!"

The crowd applauds as father and son share a long gaze.

"He has become a great example to me," Treyshawn thankfully admits. "I just hope that fathers everywhere will see the need to fight for their sons and daughters so that we can *all* be free. Free to love each other. Free to believe in each other. Free to dream for each other. Free to support each other. Free to speak truth to one another—even if it hurts—knowing that only the truth can set us free to live the kind of life that inspires others to change. Again, thank you for coming out tonight. And I hope you thoroughly enjoy my artwork."

The crowd of two hundred people erupt into genuine applause as a Hip hop-infused-melody, created for this very event, begins to play through the gallery's audio speakers. Its tone and scope of contrasting beats and orchestral elements is as varied and unique as Treyshawn's life. Treyshawn gulps down the rest of his water as he shakes hands with the gallery owner and his art professor. He descends the podium as family, friends and strangers greet him.

Everyone spends the rest of the night appreciating his artwork, which chronicles his journey through life… from darkness into marvelous light.

CHAPTER THIRTY-NINE

INTO THE FUTURE

FRIDAY DECEMBER 5, 2014. THOUSANDS FILL the stadium at the first ever Compressor-X games. Excitement is at an all-time high as this brand new sport is about to be launched to the world. Major television and internet outlets cover this inaugural event, complete with pre-game commentary and on-location game announcers. Famous personalities from sports, entertainment, fashion and technology pepper the stands. Music blasts through the stadium speakers as digital posters of team players and the game area project on the jumbo screens stationed throughout the arena.

Curtis, Treyshawn, and Kelly sit court-side with their family and friends, eager to watch the game. People cheer as a picture of Curtis appears on the giant screens—naming him creator of the Compressor-X suits that will be used in the game. The cheering increases as a second picture displays the entire Speedsuit Powers Team. Suddenly, a live shot displays on the screens, as Curtis and company wave to everyone around them.

Suddenly, the lights dim and spotlights shine on two entry tunnels as both teams make their way from their locker rooms—running onto the court carrying a compressor ball in their hand. The arena erupts with applause as each red and green team member engages their Powersuits and hovers a ball above their heads—manipulating them solely with the pressurized air shooting from their palm gloves.

The referees blow their whistles and the game begins. The red team takes their position on the uneven, multilevel court.

The game clock counts down as the green team quickly attempts to make their way across the court! The red team hurls their compressor balls as their green opponents fire pressurized gusts of wind from their hands and project walls of air, as shields, to redirect the balls to prevent being hit.

Players run and dodge, and jump and roll in pursuit of their goal as the audience cheers. But Curtis is oblivious as thoughts envelop his mind. Curtis gazes from the players to the cheering crowd and then to his family and friends seated next to him. He looks down the row at each person—Treyshawn Jr. and Sr., Kelly, Omar, his mother, Mr. Grabowski, Shakira, Kevin, Kelvin, Gavin, Eric, and Erica.

He reaches into his book-bag and pulls out his journal. "It's been a while since I've written in this," he mumbles to himself with a hint of shame. "I was so caught up in pride… I didn't see the need to write in here anymore." As he opens the book and turns to the end of his last entry, he recounts the ways in which each person seated next to him has affected his life.

Journal Entry: 8,925. Friday December 5, 2014.

I have always written in my journals for me. A grief counselor suggested I do so, weeks after my dad died. That was a long time ago and I was in a very different place then. Through the years, writing has helped me to deal with my thoughts and emotions. And then I discovered that writing helped my dad to deal with his struggles, but the words he wrote weren't mainly for him, but for me and Omar.

I don't know if anyone else will ever read these words. Maybe some day I will share them. So, what I write now isn't just for me. If you are reading this... I am writing for you as well.

All I've ever wanted to do in life was run. Even in my dreams, over and over I've heard the sounds of sneakers hitting the pavement—rhythmic steps like mini explosions propelling me forward. For a long time, I looked at my problems and thought some dreams aren't meant to come true. Maybe some aren't, but this one actually did!

My mother was right. God has plans for us which exceed our wildest expectations. And my father was right when he would tell me to do my best so the miraculous can happen. Even so, I've learned just because our lives have purpose, that doesn't mean we won't encounter opposition along the way... In fact, it's the obstacles that help shape who we are meant to become. They work like sandpaper —creating friction to help cut away the fears and insecurities we would rather leave entrenched in our hearts. The resistance acts like a bully in some ways, but it provokes us to change. And if we approach each situation right, then the opposition can reveal the path we must take to grow bigger and better instead of bitter and badder.

I look back at all the times I wanted to give up on my life... And then I look down the row at my friends and family who are sitting right next to me. They have helped me get through each moment. Anything good I have built is because of them. And no matter what the future holds—finishing college, starting a company, changing the world—we will run into it together.

Even when others say it's impossible... when you run the dreams God has placed within your heart, he makes the impossible—possible! So... if you are reading these words, know that your success is not always determined by how fast you start, but by how well you choose to finish.

In life you will encounter bullies. Some people will stand in your way and try to stop you from moving forward. But the greatest bully you will encounter is not the person standing in your way. The greatest bully you face will be your own negative self talk. If you can conquer THAT bully, then nothing will be impossible for you. So, keep pressing forward and...

Run Your Dreams!

FROM AUTHOR TO READER...

THANK YOU FOR COMING ALONG WITH me on this epic urban adventure story! It's hard to believe that Book One released back in 2009. And now, almost 7 years later, Book Three is complete. I hope you have enjoyed the journey! I will admit, when I wrote the first book, there was no plan for a third. Only for the possibility of a second book.

This story almost didn't happen. I had the basic concept for almost a decade before a friend challenged me to take the concept and "do something with it!" That was in 2008. A year and a half later, the finished copy of Speedsuit Powers: Book I The Powersuit was in my hands and being released to the world. The feedback from readers was tremendous. That is when it became obvious that the story needed to continue with a second and third book.

Then writing Book Two halted when I decided to produce the independent film, Speedsuit, which is based on the first book. When I resumed writing, I knew since so much time had passed, books 2 & 3 needed to be written within close proximity of each other.

One Speedsuit Powers super-fan declared that the trilogy coming to an end was bitter-sweet. She was excited to see how the story concludes, but she was sad that the trilogy would be over. Though this trilogy has come to an end, the *world* of Speedsuit Powers is just opening up! New characters and storylines will be introduced in the near future. Stories that are separate, but take place in the same world as Curtis. In these stories, there may be some crossovers... At the very least, there will be some reference to the trilogy. After all, Curtis' future is just getting started. So stay tuned! The next few years look quite promising.

Sincerely,

Allen Paul Weaver III
Author of the Speedsuit Powers Trilogy.

READER'S GUIDE

SELECTED THEMES

This entire Trilogy deals with the following themes: Creative Problem Solving, Conflict Resolution, Decision Making, Fatherlessness & Mentoring, Forgiveness, Identity Formation, Overcoming Obstacles, Power of Believing, Relationship Building, School Bullying Solutions, Skill-set Discovery & Development, Trauma Recovery Skills and S.T.E.A.M. (Science, Technology, Engineering, Arts and Math). What themes did *you* notice in this book? Here are a few to get you started.

Theme 1:
Relationship Building

What ingredients are needed to build a strong relationship with someone else? Having common interests, being friendly, and listening to each other are important. One "key ingredient" is TRUST. How do the characters in this book deal with the issue of Trust in their relationships? How does lying affect their interaction? How do you deal with Trust in your life? Is Trust something given or is it earned? And can Trust be repaired when it is broken?

Theme 2:
Forgiveness

The ability to Forgive is one of the greatest abilities we posses. How we use it (or don't use it) will affect the trajectory of our lives. How does each character utilize Forgiveness? Who does not Forgive? Why not? What are the results of them choosing not to Forgive? How do you deal with Forgiveness in your life? Is Forgiveness quick or does it take time? When someone Forgives, do they have to "forget?" How does Forgiveness help us grow?

Theme 3:
Creative Problem Solving

Chasm calls Curtis a "Creative." What do you think that means? How does Curtis approach his problems? What is his perspective (mindset)? Which other characters uses their creativity to solve problems? In what ways are *you* creative? How can you find creative solutions to the problems you encounter in life?

Theme 4:
Skill-set Discovery & Development

Treyshawn makes several discoveries about his talents and ability to learn throughout the Trilogy. What are they? How does his unexpected discovery change the trajectory of his life? What does he do to develop his skills? Who helps him along the way? What is the end result? What are you good at? What can you do to develop your skills? How can you discover talents you may not know you have? What is the benefit of developing your skills and talents?

Theme 5:
Trauma Recovery Skills

Each character has experienced some kind of trauma in this story. How does each deal with their experience? What choices do they make that either keeps them "stuck" or helps them be resilient and "bounce back" from the trauma? The most important aspect to recovering from trauma is your mental perspective towards life. What skills can you use to help develop your resilience?

Theme 6:
S.T.E.A.M.

How does Science, Technology, Engineering, Arts and Math impact this story? Which characters use STEAM to solve their problems? How can you use STEAM principles in your life? Are all students capable of learning STEAM? Why or Why not?

A VISUAL LOOK

ALLEN'S BOOK 3 SKETCHES

Here are select sketches of Book 3 elements.
Sketches are drawn by Allen Paul Weaver III

The unknown wearer of the Mach-2 Speedsuit: "Turbulence"

NOTE: The Mach-2 is created using the latest technology (not released in the public sector) & advanced materials fabrication.

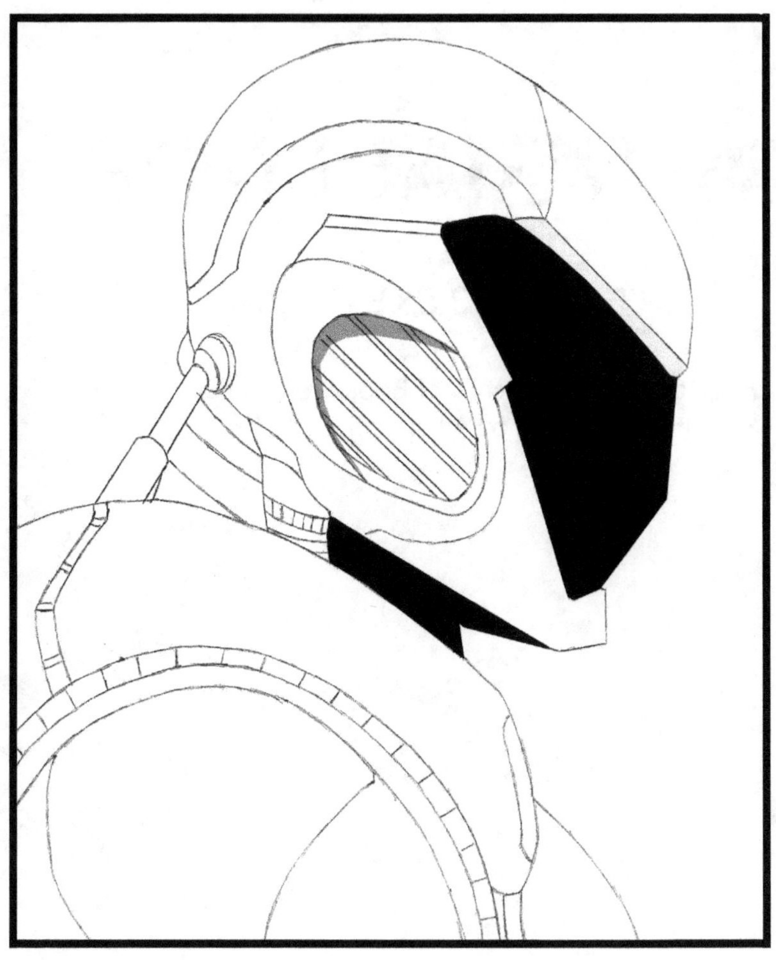

When Curtis Powers is in his Mach-1 Speedsuit he is known as: "Jetstream." Now, he encounters "Turbulence" for the first time.

NOTE: While having several upgrades since its inception, the Mach-1 is still created using optimized "off-the-shelf" parts.

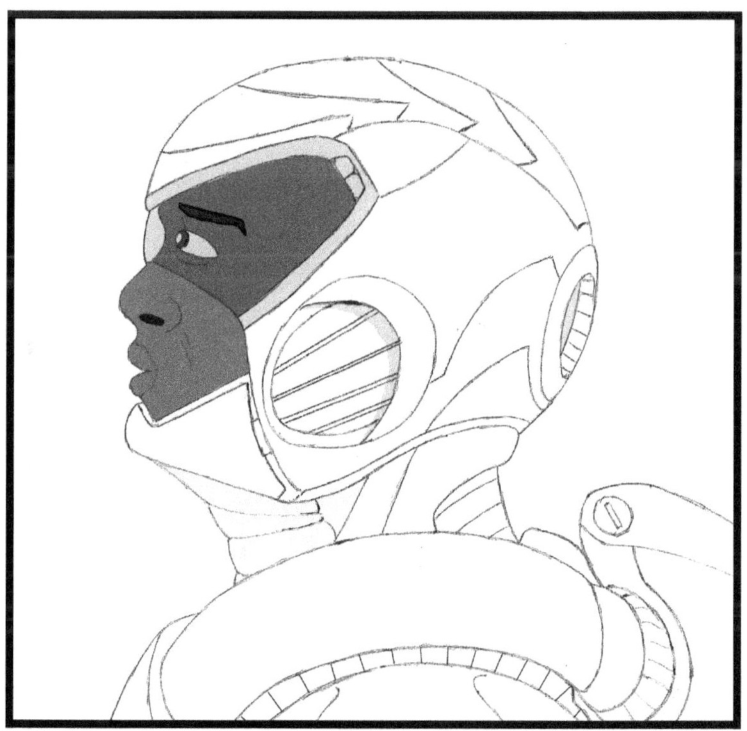

The Mach-2 Speedsuit: Rear

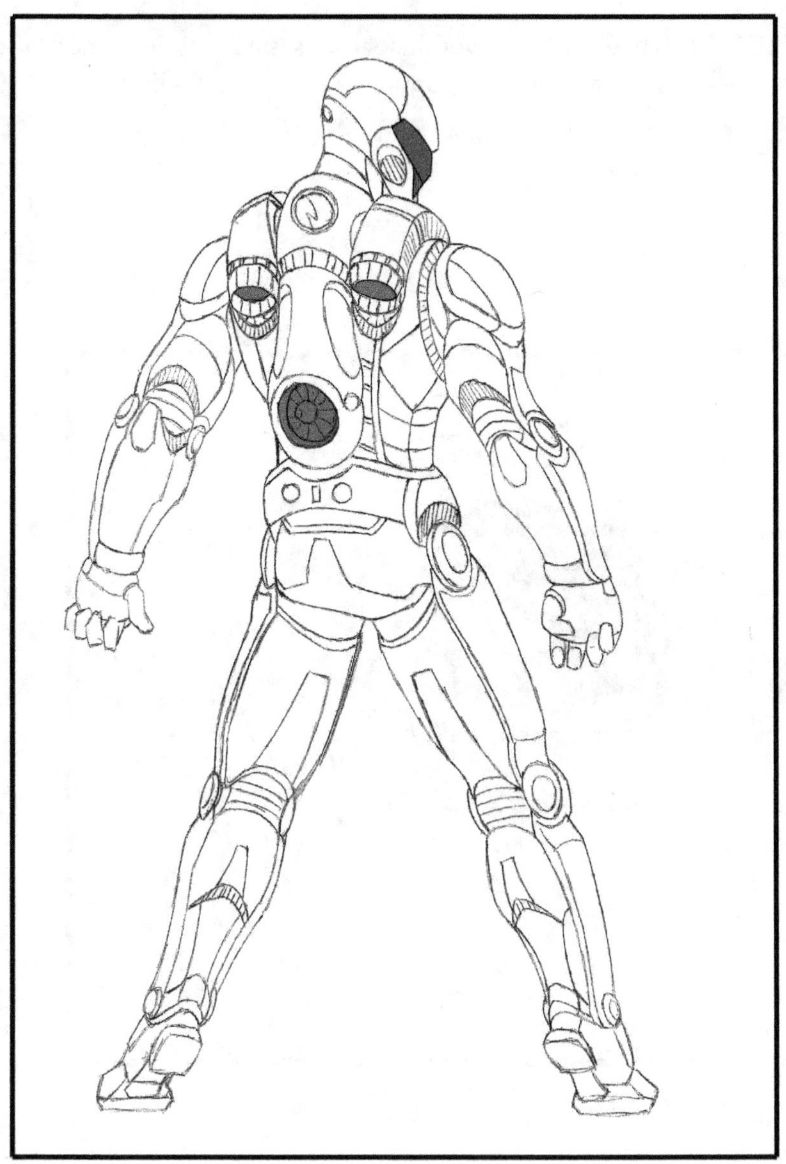

The Mach-2 Speedsuit: Front

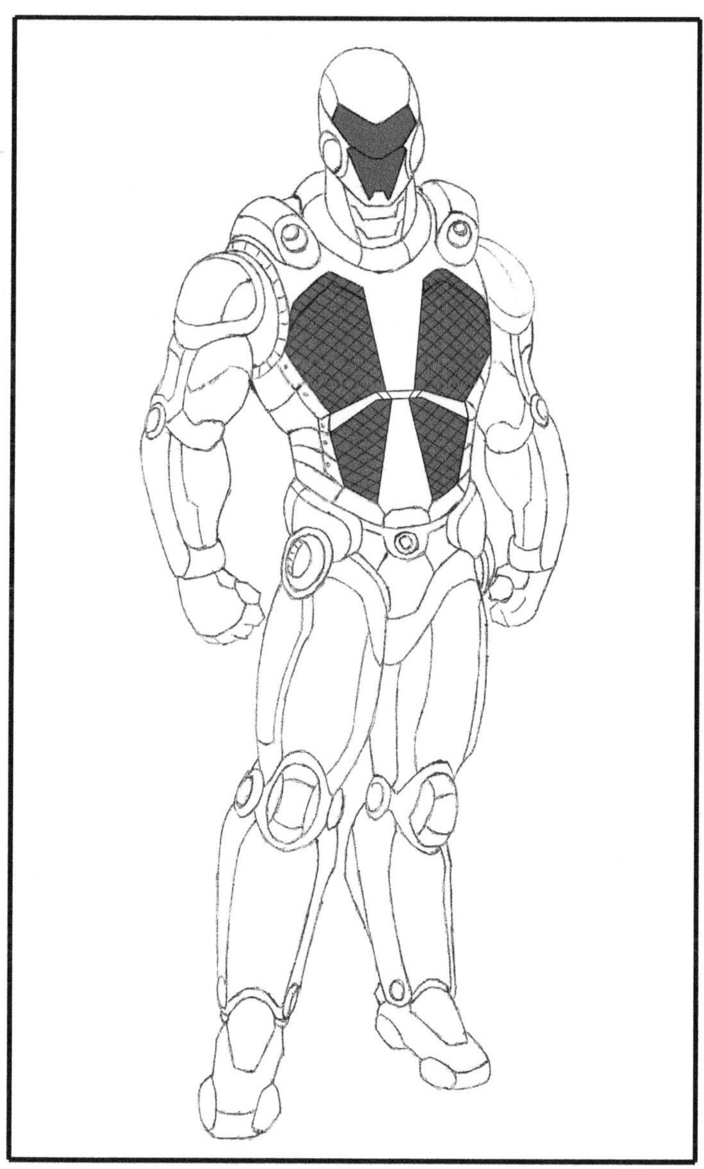

The Compressor-X Windsuit.
To be used in the "Compressor-X Games."

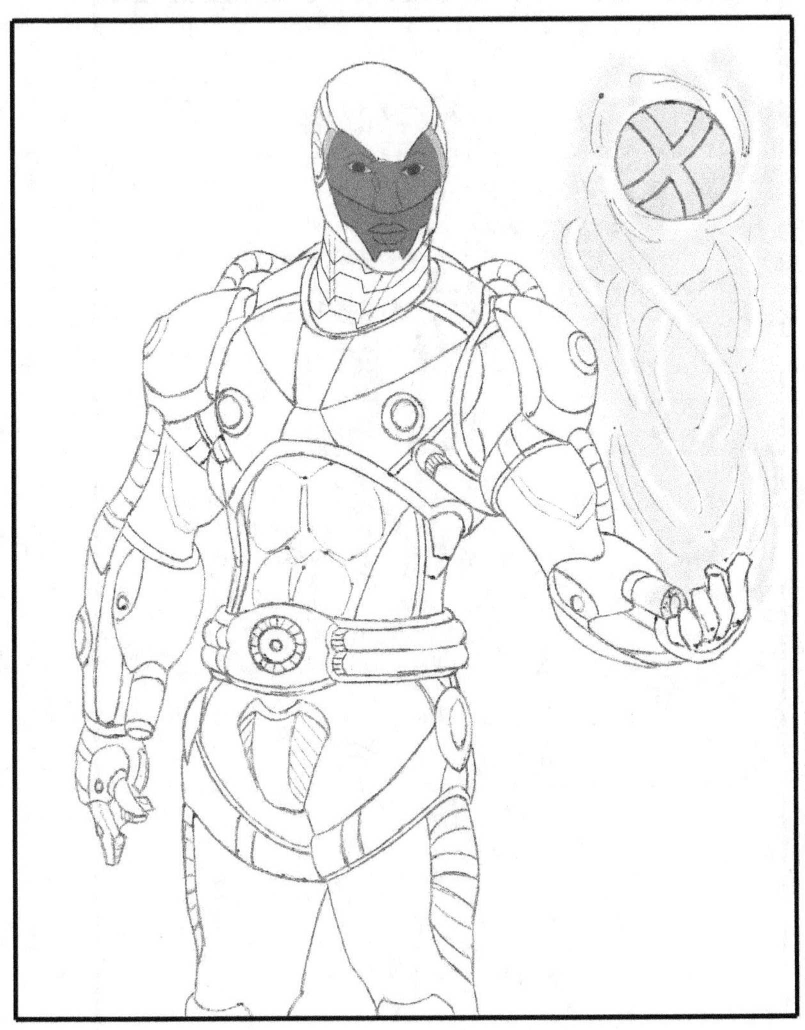

Multi-layered padded foam suit capable of producing powerful sonic blasts at various frequencies and intensities. (The special padding isolates the wearer from the sonic vibrations.)

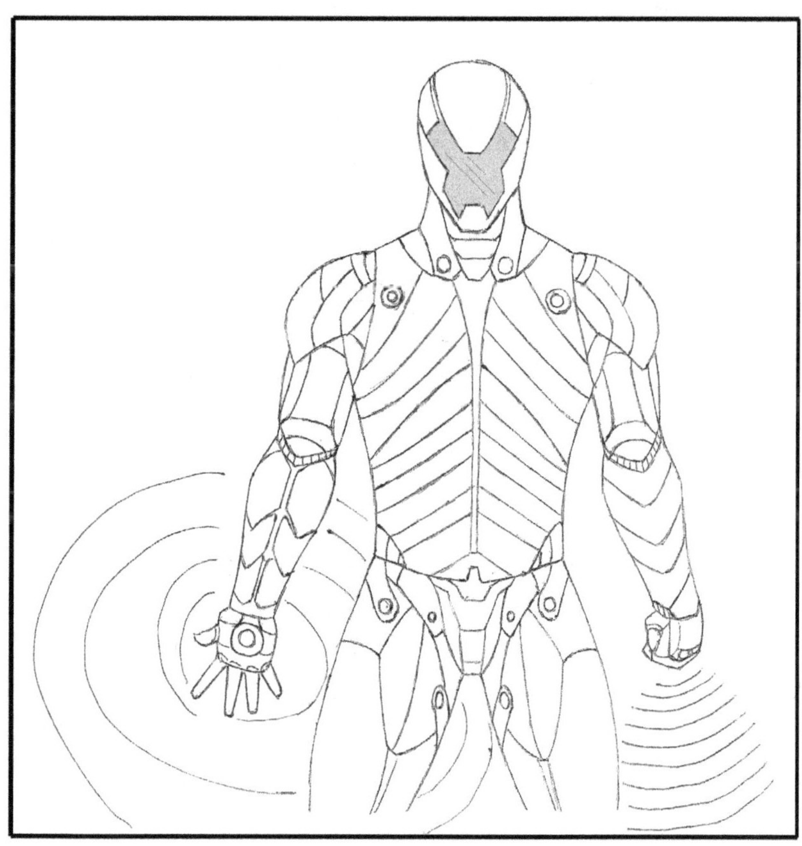

Below: Gavin with remote control & goggles for his Dragonfly robot. The goggles allow him to see what the robot sees.

Right: Dragonfly robot. Can reconfigure into several positions and heights to adapt to terrain. (Not shown)

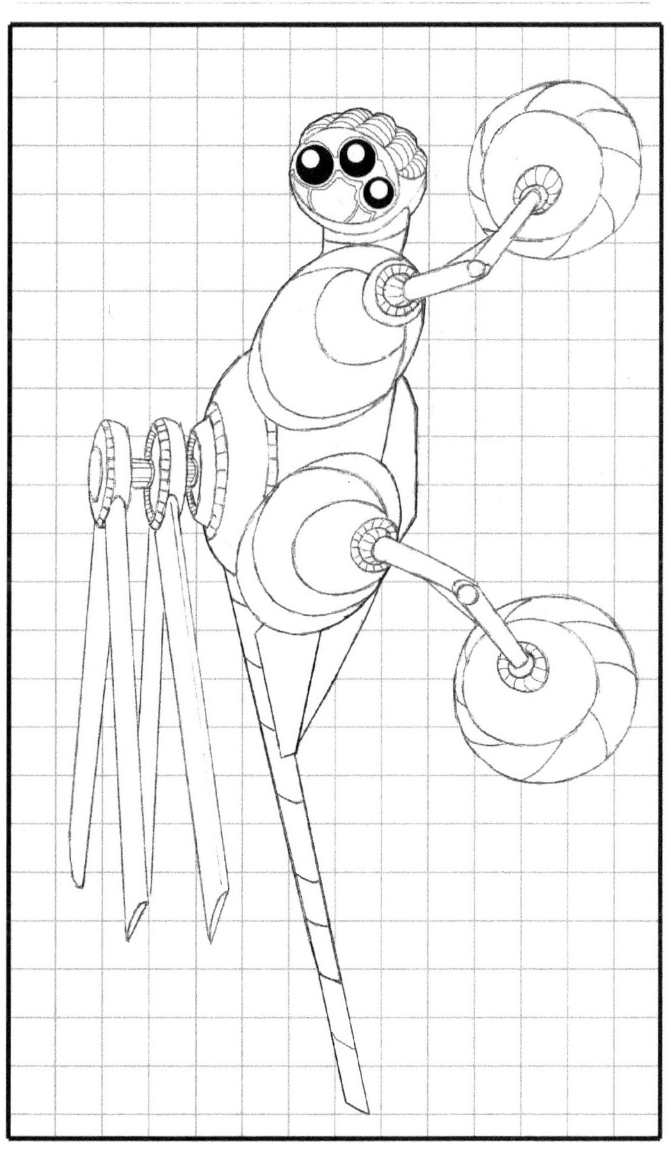

Treyshawn Jinkins Sr. standing outside of the warden's office.

Strength Augmentation Suit in action!

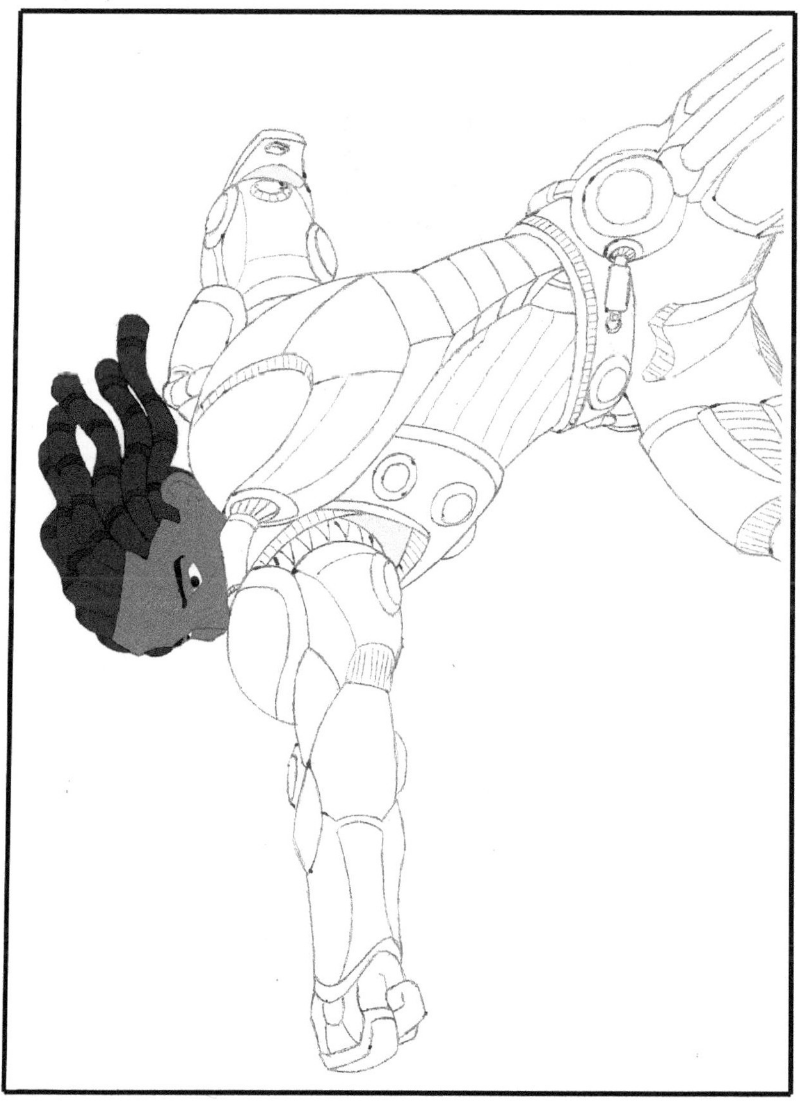

W.A.R. Suit: Front

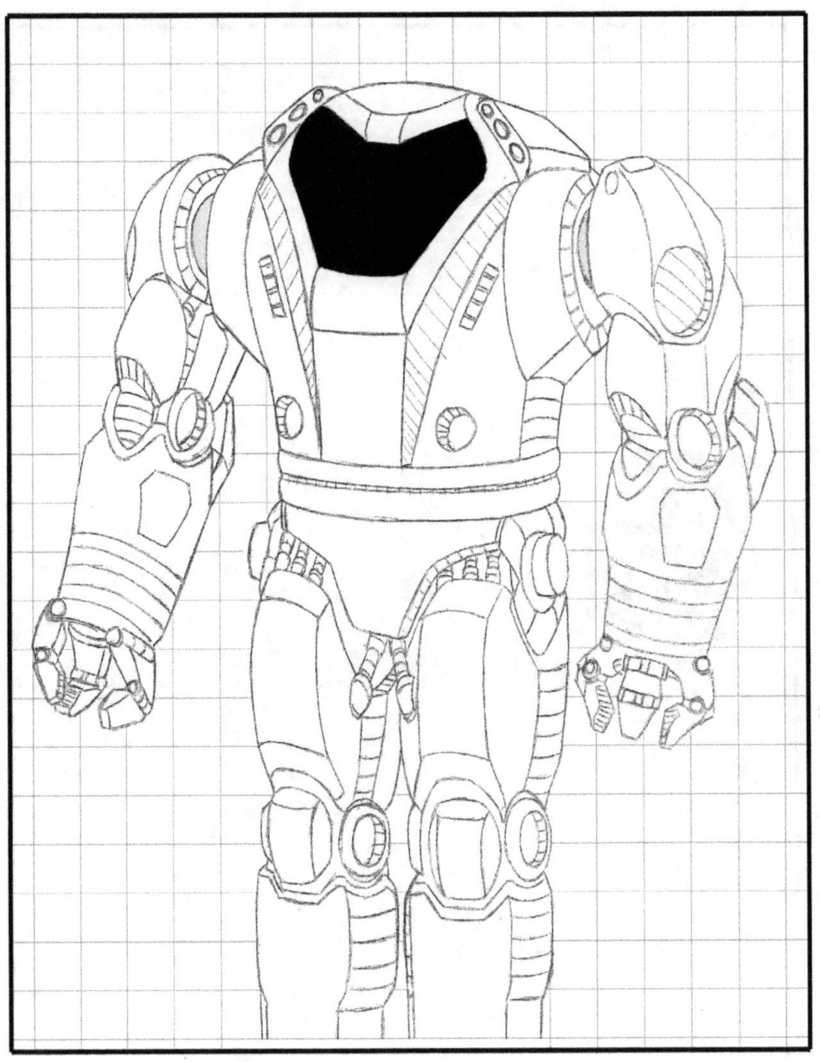

W.A.R. Suit: Rear

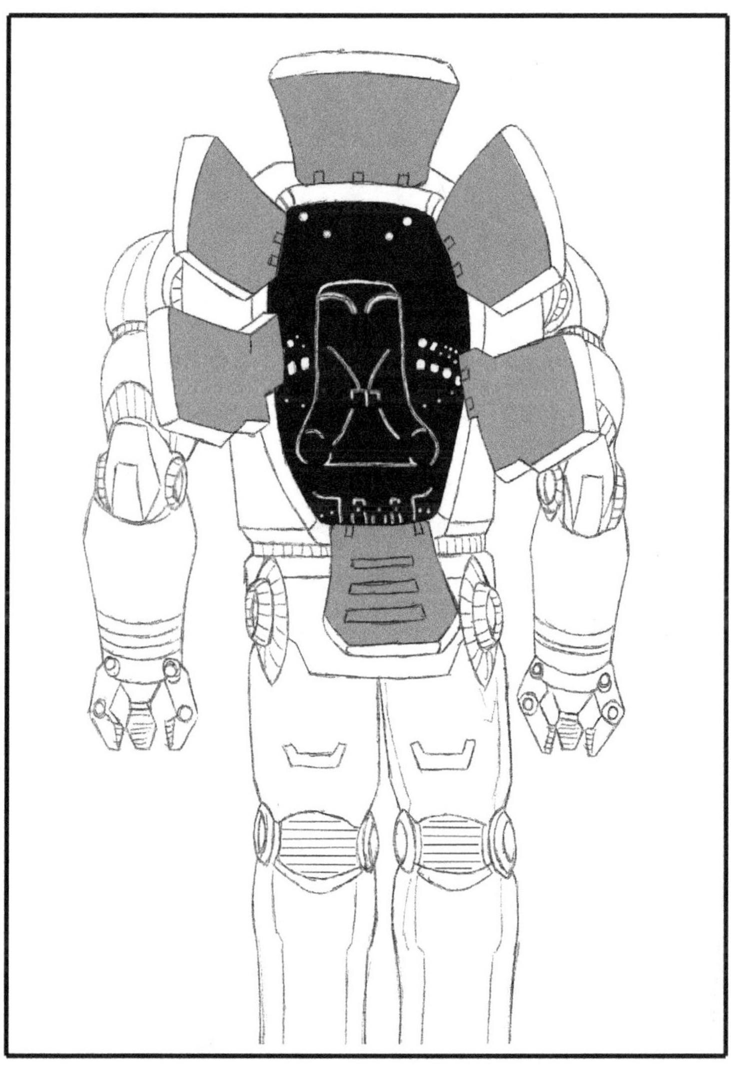

NOTE: *As a published author of a story that tackles the issue of school bullying, I seek to provide answers for how our communities can counteract this disturbing trend and help young people discover and pursue their purpose. Below is an article I wrote to help provide solutions-based-thinking for the school bullying epidemic in our country.*

MOVING BEYOND BULLYING:

LAYING THE GROUNDWORK FOR DISCOVERING SCHOOL BULLYING SOLUTIONS THAT WORK FOR EVERYONE

By: Allen Paul Weaver III (copyright 2012)

WE HAVE A PROBLEM...

Media reports - including Anderson Cooper 360, Oprah, Dr. Phil - and perhaps our own experiences have made us aware of tragic school bullying stories where deaths are often the result. According to the US Department of Justice bullying report, the situation is so dire, that 160, 000 youth create excuses to skip school every day for fear of torment from bullies. Sadly, many young people are too disillusioned to expect solutions from adult leaders and adults are often too shocked to see beyond the problem. Is there any way for our communities to move beyond bullying? By saying "beyond" I do not mean we ignore the problem and try to get on with our lives. Rather, we must begin to imagine a reality where the value of each individual is affirmed – thereby nullifying bullying. Then we must implement solutions to move us to that reality.

Let me say, there is no simple solution to this issue. Bullying is a very complex, growing epidemic in our culture; and due to Internet social media, it is mutating – much like a flu virus. No matter how fearful we may feel, we cannot allow the problem to 'frame' the solutions, but rather the solutions must systematically challenge and dismantle this epidemic at every known level. However, if youth and adults unite in meaningful discourse, we can create solutions.

DEFINING THE TERM

Every generation has a tendency to redefine terms used by previous generations. The problem reveals itself when different groups use the same term, but in reality consider the term to mean different things. For genuine discussion and discourse to occur, all parties involved must first agree to the meaning of key terms. The word 'bullying' is one such term.

To some groups of people bullying is seen as teasing and occasional harassment between peers. ("Occasional" because in the past, the harassment usually stopped once the victim came home from school). It is an unfortunate "part of growing up" and a "rite of passage" into adulthood – something you endure and go through. However, to this current technology-driven generation (with access to information and the ability to communicate with one another instantly and constantly), bullying goes beyond teasing and occasional harassment. Bullying, through cell phone and Internet technology, has been elevated to include new forms of mental and emotional torture that happens at school, at home and in almost all locations in between. The result is that many of our youth consider, attempt and succeed at taking their own lives in order to relieve the pain they experience on a daily basis.

Few would deny that the world is an increasingly complex place. Part of that complexity is seen in the following ways: 1) Internet and cell phone technology have enabled youth to make vicious statements with detached anonymity. 2) Youth have an increased lack of anger management, problem solving and coping skills, which leads to an escalation of violence. 3) There is an increasing disregard for the value and sanctity of life among young people and adults. 4) Adults seem unable to stop the bullying - especially in situations where the parents of the bully encourage or support the negative behavior.

CREATING NEW ENVIRONMENTS

We need new environments where bullying is not the norm, but seen by all as a correctable abnormality. One way we create such an environment and move beyond bullying is by striving for authentic relationships. A genuine relationship is one of mutual dealings between two (or more) people; anything else is manipulation. We must learn to establish relationships with identified bullied individuals as well as the bullies themselves. In reality, both the bully and the bullied are victims - just of a different sort. While the bullied is tormented by external factors (the bully); the bully is often tormented by internal issues which may also be a result of their own external factors (home life, self-image, etc...) Both need people they can trust, relationships that promote character development, and visions of a better-alternate reality to the one they are currently experiencing.

Once authentic relationships are established, they can be strengthened through mentor programs focused on the development of the talents of the youth involved -in relation to one another. Within the framework of honest relationships, character building and interpersonal talent development, a new community environment can be fostered where conflict is mediated, differences are celebrated, and common ground is discovered. By implementing positive relationship building through peer-to-peer and adult-to-teen mentoring, this new environment can be created.

Our main obstruction to this new reality is not our youth, but rather the repeated examples of adults (in almost every sphere of life) who no longer value civility as a key ingredient for relating to one another. Our current culture continues to lose sight of what genuine positive relationships look like and how to develop them. As people mistreat one another and don't care to solve conflicts, the result becomes selfishness that causes disparate communities. Society focuses on self-advancement and gratification at the expense of others.

3 KEY CONSIDERATIONS

First, bullying is a symptom of a deeper issue. Every bully has a context for their bullying: family trauma, internal turmoil, inferiority or superiority complex, desire to climb the social ladder of their peers, etc… Context plays a major factor in triggering bullying outbursts. To miss this is to make a grave error.

Beneath context, lies a root issue common to all persons who bully: a lack of value for life. If we are at war with ourselves – we will be at war with others. But if we have a healthy view of ourselves, we will have no reason to cause chaos in the lives of others. We must find a way to help bullies deal with this foundational reality – while taking responsibility for the pain and damage they cause. To understand why they lash out is to open up an entirely new realm of possibilities for positively changing their behavior!

Second, we cannot merely react to bullying. Reacting will always put us behind the problem, because a person cannot react until acted upon by an internal or external force. We need to act – meaning: make decisions based on the facts of the situation; foresee possible outcomes; take preventive measures to structure a bully-free environment; and have appropriate measures in place for when bullying takes place. In short, a proactive approach is necessary.

Rash "knee-jerk" actions often cause more harm than good because they are uninformed actions. The more time we take to examine bullying and walk through practical steps for a variety of scenarios, the more likely we will take appropriate actions when the time comes. The less time we spend seriously considering the reality and outcomes of this bullying epidemic, the more we put ourselves and the lives of our youth at risk. Everyone has his or her own opinion (whether informed or not) about what constitutes "appropriate" action. What standards of determination should we use? The question I propose - regardless of the bully prevention program being used or ignored -is this: "Is this action a "win-win" situation for both the bullied and the bully?" If not, then we must seek additional alternatives.

Third, we must help the bullied AND the bully. If we try to help the bullied, while only removing the bully from the equation, we ultimately participate in a win-lose situation. The bully will be left to his or her own devices, often carrying that negative behavior into adulthood, which puts others at risk, including themselves.

This approach is different from an anti-bullying/zero-tolerance perspective. While anti-bullying/zero-tolerance can be helpful and necessary in many circumstances: removing a bully from the immediate situation – its inherent failure is in its "one size fits all" stance. Zero tolerance says "no bullying will be tolerated under ANY circumstances." The result is a punishment that often doesn't fit the crime. So a first-time bully is given the same punishment as a person who constantly bullies others. And the person who has been a victim of bullying who lashes out because they have no other recourse, is punished just as if they were the bully themselves (often resulting in the actual bully being perceived as the victim!)

In almost every sphere of life, we regard the circumstances of others in an effort to discover context and motivations for actions and best practices for navigating through society. Take parenting as an example: a child's motivation behind an action will greatly influence the type of reaction presented by the parent. If a parent discovers that their car -which they lent to their child the night before - now has major damage, knowing the circumstances behind the damage is crucial! Was their child intoxicated? Or did someone else run a red light and crash into them?

Yet, Zero tolerance disregards circumstances and leaves the bully and/or bullied without a resolution for their present and future. Zero tolerance, as a win-lose approach, may work on some level; but it does not work on all levels. To work on all levels, we need a win-win approach incorporated into this "bullying equation." We need an environment that inspires winning for all instead of winning only for a few.

WHERE IS THE BYSTANDER'S POWER?

Bullying has a negative affect on the bystander community that witnesses such adverse behavior. It creates an atmosphere of fear where well-meaning youth and adults are paralyzed by a sense of powerlessness. A sort of "tunnel vision" takes place, which causes bystanders to feel isolated. Fear often triggers their self-preservation instincts (Fight or Flight) as thoughts play out in their mind, "What if the bully targets me?" The result is that many bystanders will either quietly retreat from conflict or -in an effort to keep themselves from being targeted - will join the negative behavior. What is lost is the fact that bystanders may often outnumber the bullies - providing them a greater advantage for positively changing the situation. "There is strength in numbers."

So, does the bystander have power? Yes. The power comes from the strength of their moral character and their ability to empathize with the person who is being bullied. Bystanders can use their power to influence the outcome of a bullying situation by directly getting involved, indirectly calling for help or providing some type of distraction that helps the bullied child to escape.

The bullied, bully and bystander each have their own power to influence, however, the greatest share of that power is realized by bystanders who unite. If one person musters the courage to intervene, then others will most likely do the same.

When I was a freshman in college, a fellow student had an extremely bad asthma attack in the lobby of my dormitory. When I arrived on the scene, the entire room full of students seemed paralyzed and helpless. To make the situation worse, the student's inhaler was nowhere to be found! We all just watched as the student wallowed on the floor, until one student had the courage to try and help him. As this upperclassman tried to calm our asthmatic classmate down until the ambulance arrived, she yelled out, "Don't just stand there! Somebody help me!" Immediately, I felt compelled to act and jumped to her side. As we tried to calm our fellow classmate, some other students ran outside to try and look for the ambulance.

While this was not a case of "bullying," it does illuminate a point about the nature of group dynamics. Almost all of us were bullied that day -internally coerced by fear and externally restrained by everyone else's lack of action. We felt powerless, but this was a false sense of powerlessness, which was exposed the moment the first student took action and called us to do the same. Bystanders must no longer see themselves as non-participants, as if their inaction has no bearing on the outcome of events.

Sometimes circumstance requires involvement. Instead of "By-standing," those youth and adults who witness bullying must begin to see themselves as being on "Stand-by" - ready to give their assistance when needed. Often bystanders do nothing because they are unsure of the actions they can take. We can help change this reality by clearly presenting ways that they can help.

CAN EVERYBODY WIN?

Our society thrives off of winners and losers. Sports empires and the fans who support them illustrate this fact. Big Business and the consumers who are cheated by them also illustrate this fact. Criminal enterprises are motivated by this fact as well. Somehow, deep down in the back of our psyches it has been ingrained that someone has to lose in order for someone else to be successful.

The perception is that there are not enough resources for everyone to be successful. It is "survival of the fittest" and those who are strong enough simply take what they want regardless of the effect it has on others. But what if we began to ask ourselves, "How can everybody win?" What possibilities would we discover as we looked at the situation from a completely new perspective? What if we were solutions-oriented instead of problem-focused?

Can everybody win? Is there a way for everyone to get what they truly need and not just what they have been coerced into believing was their lot in life? Our young people are dying and if we fail to answer this question correctly and envision a new future that they can see for themselves, then we will all be lost. The task seems insurmountable, but if enough people - youth and adults - can work together– then the dream of a new day will no longer be some future fairytale possibility, but will become a bright new present reality.

Can everybody win? Yes. Everyone CAN win if we are all willing to work together to make the impossible possible.

ACKNOWLEDGMENTS

I would like to thank my wife, Ijnanya. You constantly push and inspire me to be the best I can be in life and in my creative pursuits. Thank you for making time to listen to me read scenes and talk through this process. This trilogy is finally complete! Without you, I could not have made it.

I would like to thank my editor, Davina McDonald. You continually challenge every scene I write—as a good editor does—so I could make this story as compelling as possible. I value your time, talent and professional opinion. Thank you for strongly suggesting the rewrites and for sharing how the story has impacted you!

Also, thank you to Frank Gomez! Your review of this story and your great input has proven to be—as always—invaluable! Onward and upward!

ABOUT THE AUTHOR

Allen Paul Weaver III is an author, speaker and filmmaker. He holds a BA in Speech Communication from Bethune-Cookman University. He also holds a Master of Divinity degree in Theology from Colgate Rochester Crozer Divinity School.

Allen is an avid writer and lover of books - especially comic books. As a teen, he didn't like reading (although he could read well.) One thing he noticed as he devoured comics and science fiction books was the thin representation of key characters who looked like him and shared elements of his life experience.

During the early 2000's, while working as a youth director in the South Bronx, Allen saw the need to create a story which could inspire, motivate and educate entire communities to break through the opposition they faced in order to "Run their Dreams."

Shortly thereafter, the concept for Speedsuit Powers was born. Six years later, in December 2009, Book One of the Trilogy was released. During 2011-2012 Allen adapted Book One into the independent film, **Speedsuit**. He then finished writing Book Two and released it in June 2015. Now, seven years after Book One's release, the final book in the Trilogy is here!

What's next? Allen wants to make his Speedsuit Powers Trilogy a household name; especially in communities of Color. He is also pitching the Trilogy in an effort to have it produced as a television series or a major motion picture franchise. And he has continued the story through the creation of the Speedsuit Powers Expanded Universe! Follow along with new characters impacted by Team Speedsuit.

Allen enjoys drawing, producing films, indoor skydiving, and traveling with his wife and son. To date, he has traveled to seven African countries, Europe and China.

Find out more about SPT at:
www.SpeedsuitPowers.com / www.AllenPaulWeaver3.com

THE TRILOGY IS COMPLETE...
...BUT THE STORY CONTINUES!

BOOK 4: FLIGHT

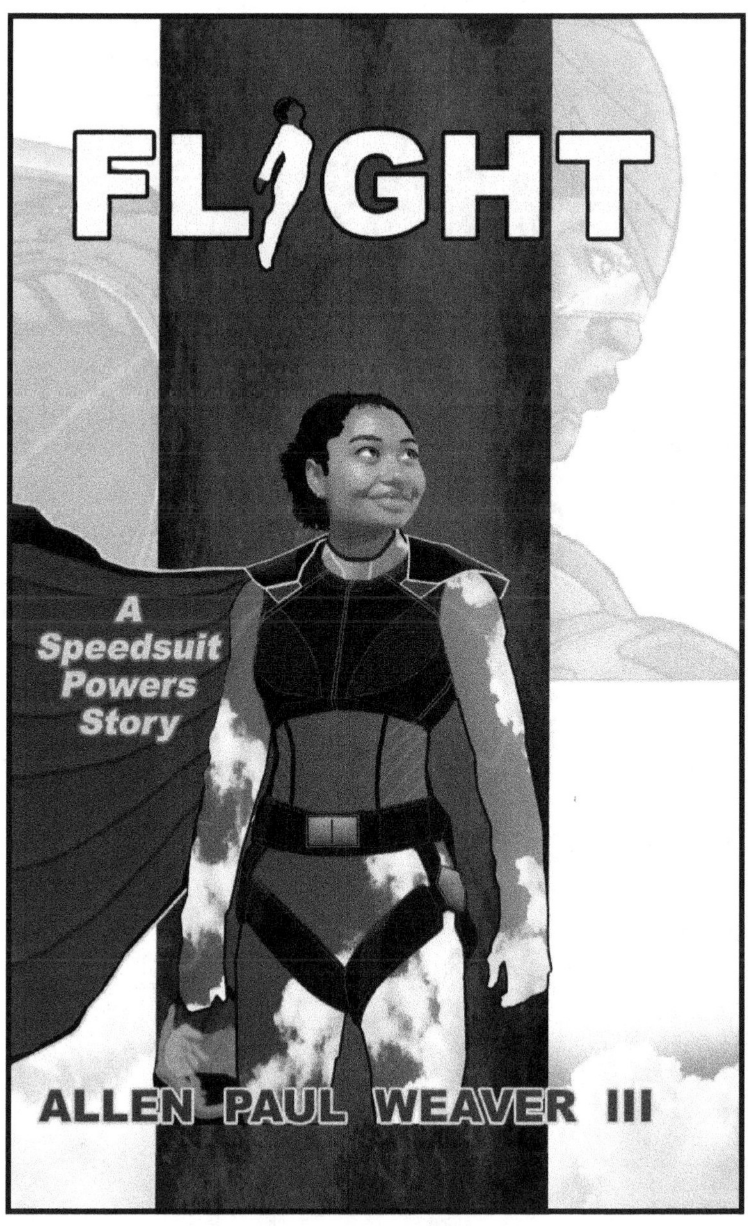

BOOK 5: DISCOURSE

WATCH THE MOVIE BASED ON BOOK 1 ON THE SPEEDSUIT POWERS YOUTUBE CHANNEL

LISTEN TO THE BOOK 1 AUDIOBOOK! AVAILABLE ON AUDIBLE, AMAZON AND ITUNES.

www.ingramcontent.com/pod-product-compliance
Lightning Source LLC
LaVergne TN
LVHW020652110826
845149LV00012B/1971

* 9 7 8 0 9 9 6 1 0 4 5 5 5 *